Other Novels and Novellas

*Many of these titles are also available as abridged and unabridged audiobooks.
Order the full range of Horus Heresy novels and audiobooks from*
blacklibrary.com

Also available

Audio Dramas

*Download the full range of Horus Heresy
audio dramas from
blacklibrary.com*

THE HORUS HERESY®

THE HORUS HERESY®

Chris Wraight

THE PATH OF HEAVEN

Riding out from the storm

BLACK LIBRARY

For Hannah, with love.

A BLACK LIBRARY PUBLICATION

Hardback edition first published in 2016.
This edition published in 2017 by
Black Library,
Games Workshop Ltd.,
Willow Road,
Nottingham, NG7 2WS, UK.

10 9 8 7 6 5 4 3 2 1

Produced by Games Workshop in Nottingham.
Cover illustration by Neil Roberts.

A CIP record for this book is available from the British Library.

ISBN 13: 978 1 78496 501 3

See Black Library on the internet at

blacklibrary.com

Find out more about Games Workshop
and the world of Warhammer 40,000 at

games-workshop.com

Printed and bound by CPI Group (UK) Ltd, Croydon, CR0 4YY

THE HORUS HERESY®

It is a time of legend.

The galaxy is in flames. The Emperor's glorious vision for humanity is in ruins. His favoured son, Horus, has turned from his father's light and embraced Chaos.

His armies, the mighty and redoubtable Space Marines, are locked in a brutal civil war. Once, these ultimate warriors fought side by side as brothers, protecting the galaxy and bringing mankind back into the Emperor's light.
Now they are divided.

Some remain loyal to the Emperor, whilst others have sided with the Warmaster. Pre-eminent amongst them, the leaders of their thousands-strong Legions are the primarchs. Magnificent, superhuman beings, they are the crowning achievement of the Emperor's genetic science. Thrust into battle against one another, victory is uncertain for either side.

Worlds are burning. At Isstvan V, Horus dealt a vicious blow and three loyal Legions were all but destroyed. War was begun, a conflict that will engulf all mankind in fire. Treachery and betrayal have usurped honour and nobility. Assassins lurk in every shadow. Armies are gathering. All must choose a side or die.

Horus musters his armada, Terra itself the object of his wrath. Seated upon the Golden Throne, the Emperor waits for his wayward son to return. But his true enemy is Chaos, a primordial force that seeks to enslave mankind to its capricious whims.

The screams of the innocent, the pleas of the righteous resound to the cruel laughter of Dark Gods. Suffering and damnation await all should the Emperor fail and the war be lost.

The age of knowledge and enlightenment has ended. The Age of Darkness has begun.

~ DRAMATIS PERSONAE ~

The V Legion 'White Scars'

JAGHATAI KHAN	The Khagan, the Warhawk, primarch of the V Legion
QIN XA	Master of the *keshig* guard
NAMAHI	Qin Xa's second
GANZORIG NOYAN-KHAN	Lord commander
QIN FAI NOYAN-KHAN	Lord commander
TARGUTAI YESUGEI	*Zadyin arga*, Stormseer
NARANBAATAR	
OSKH	
JUBAL KHAN	The Lord of Summer Lightning
KHULAN KHAN	Brotherhood of the Golden Path
AINBATAAR KHAN	Brotherhood of the Night's Star
ALGU KHAN	Brotherhood of the Pennant Spear
SHIBAN KHAN	Known as 'Tachseer', Brotherhood of the Storm
JOCHI	
YIMAN	
TORGHUN KHAN	*Sagyar mazan* kill-squad leader

SANYASA	*Sagyar mazan*
AHM	*Sagyar mazan*
GERG	*Sagyar mazan*
HOLIAN	*Sagyar mazan*
INCHIG	*Sagyar mazan*
OZAD	*Sagyar mazan*
WAI-LONG	*Sagyar mazan*
JAIJAN	*Emchi* Apothecary
TABAN	Sensorium master, *Swordstorm*
AVELINA HJELVOS	Master of Navigators, *Swordstorm*
TAMAZ	Sensorium master, *Kaljian*
IDDA	Master of the watch, *Melak Karta*
ERYA	Mistress of sub-warp navigation, *Melak Karta*

The XV Legion 'Thousand Sons'

| REVUEL ARVIDA | Errant sorcerer, and friend to the V Legion |

The III Legion 'Emperor's Children'

| EIDOLON | 'The Soul-Severed', Lord Commander Primus |
| VON KALDA | Apothecary, equerry to Lord Commander Eidolon |

AZAEL KONENOS	Legion consul and orchestrator
GALIAN ERATO	Vexillary
RAVASCH CARIO	Prefector of the Palatine Blades
AVANAROLA	Sub-prefector of the Palatine Blades
HAIMAN	
VORAINN	
URELIAS	
RAFFEL	
HARKIAN	Shipmaster of the *Suzerain*
ELEANORA KULBA	Shipmaster of the *Terce Falion*
FAEL ALOBUS	Deck-officer, *Terce Falion*
CAVELLI	Navigator, *Terce Falion*

The XIV Legion 'Death Guard'

MORTARION	The Death Lord, primarch of the XIV Legion
GREMUS KALGARO	Marshal, siegemaster
ULFAR	Shipmaster of the *Endurance*
LAGAAHN	Gunnery master, *Endurance*

TRANGH	Master of the watch, *Endurance*

Imperial personae

ILYA RAVALLION	General, Departmento Munitorum
PIETER HELIAN ACHELIEUX	Novator, Navis Nobilite
VEIL	Magister
KHALID HASSAN	Chosen of Malcador

Non-Imperial personae

MANUSHYA-RAKSHSASI

'The noblest kind of retribution is not to become like your enemy.'

– Markusa Relius, circa M1

PART I

ONE

A THOUSAND YEARS might pass and it would never lose its fascination.

He ran his eyes down the edge of the blade, watching the light glint from the metal. This sword had drunk deeply of blood, both xenos and human, yet now it was pristine, unmarked, as clear as when it had left the forge-fire. For two hundred years he had tended it as a mother tends a child, restoring it, respecting it, returning it to the ebony-ringed scabbard with a benediction to the weapon's soul that had never failed him.

Now he turned it again, watching the lumen-glow run down the pressed steel. The shallow curve held no flaw, not even so much as a notch to mark the years of service.

He held it loosely, relying on its weight to keep it balanced in his hands. He had once fought the eldar xenos on a world where the stones sang and the sky screamed, and he had remembered ever afterwards how those warriors had fought. The creatures' speed and precision had outmatched that of his brothers, and that had rankled ever since, for his Legion was one that valued such things. So he had learned, and studied, and honed the craft, and every hour in the practice cages brought a scintilla of improvement, though he knew it would never be enough.

In any case, the days of fighting xenos were gone. The war had changed, and he was expected to test his sword's edge against those he had once called kin. In the beginning that had been difficult; now it was second nature. The blade still cut as deeply and as well, and he had learned to find the hard beauty in killing his own.

His thoughts were interrupted as the lumen above his metal bunk pulsed softly, and he lifted his head from study. He knew without having to check the ident-rune where the communication came from – only the ship's commander would dare make contact during designated meditation hours.

'Yes?' he asked, sliding the blade back into its scabbard.

'*Lord, your pardon,*' came the voice of Harkian, shipmaster of the *Suzerain*. '*The scryer has detected incoming warp-wakes. Your activation is requested.*'

Before the man had finished speaking, Ravasch Cario, prefector of the III Legion's Palatine Blades, had reached for his helm. His ceramite faceguard was lacquered violet and blue, streaked with inlaid gold and blazoned with platinum, but not defiled in the way many of his brothers had defiled theirs. The time for that would come, perhaps, but not yet – not while he was yet to become the fastest he could be, the most precise he could be.

'What does he predict?' Cario asked, making for the meditation chamber's door.

'*Unknown,*' replied Harkian. '*Though in all probability–*'

'The Warhawk,' said Cario, striding out into the corridor even as he twisted his helm's atmosphere-seal into place. 'Good. Then let it begin anew.'

BATTLE-GROUP JEWEL SHARD re-entered real space, carving a trail of glittering molecular interference across the void. The fleet formation's escorts shot ahead like thrown spears, twisting as their plasma drives keyed into full power. The core of the battle-line slipped into the physical realm behind them, void shields sliding across flanks lined with heavy ordnance.

Every ship in that flotilla was in a state of transition: some war vessels looked much as they had done at the outset of the Great Crusade; others were unrecognisable. On the most affected, gunwales were crested with writhing golden gargoyles, vent housings were engraved with a filigree of platinum shaped into unsettling formations, and collated effigies of carnal excruciation had been scored across the panels of the ploughshare prows. The command spires had seen the greatest augmentation, with crystal bridges spanning the pinnacles and arcane energies snaking amongst the comms vanes.

On the bridge of the lead cruiser, an Avenger-class veteran named the *Ravisher,* Legion consul and orchestrator Azael Konenos adjusted his position in the command throne and studied the incoming position runes. Around him, the clamour of the bridge-space passed in a fog of muffled murmurs. His auditory organs were fused and melted and warped together, bulging out from his neck and swelling across his upper back, capable of appreciating a far greater range of sound than ever before – but the price of accessing this enhanced spectrum was impoverishment within normal frequencies.

'Confirm this,' Konenos said. His voice was metal-edged, filtered through the coiled tubes that had punctured his throat since Isstvan III.

'Rich hunting,' came the reply of his vexillary Galian Erato, standing a few feet from the throne and gazing intently at banks of bronze-rimmed data screens.

Erato was beautiful, even amongst a Legion that had ever been beautiful. He was tall and slender, with golden skin and bone-white hair. Since the scouring of the Halliadh Togaht he had taken to stitching patterns into his exposed flesh with black agony-wire. Sutures now criss-crossed his cheeks and forehead, every so often flaring dull red as random pain-pulses fired.

Every other soul on the bridge, whether of the Legion or one of the hundreds of mortal serfs and servitors who attended to it, had been improved. Skin was puckered and ruptured, pulled tight or pinned back, rouged, roughened, plucked clean and studded with blood-washed jewels. The low thrum of the main drives was punctuated by ritual screams from the decks below, marking the ship's ascent from the empyrean.

Erato threw a hololith array up into the fore bridge-space, collating it with the astropathic screeds burbling from the shackled star-dreamers.

'Word from the *Suzerain*,' he reported. 'They have their targets and are moving to engage. I warned them to hold, but still they are moving.'

'Of course,' murmured Konenos. 'What else?'

Erato's lips twitched, snagging the stitches at the corner of his mouth. 'Three incoming formations, moving fast on the Memnos convoy.'

Konenos leaned back. The III Legion's warfront had become vast beyond all reason, stretching out in a huge arc across the galactic plane from Taras to Morox. Resupply had become erratic, plagued by warp-loss and counter-strikes from the fragments of Loyalist Legions that remained to contest the shrinking borders of their Imperium. Bulk carrier convoys had been hit repeatedly, the vessels either plundered or destroyed, slowing the relentless grind towards the Throneworld and drawing combat units away from the cutting edge.

It could have been any number of raiders. It could have been the dregs of the Legions they had broken at Isstvan. It could have been elements of the Imperial Army, still so vast that trillions remained alive despite more than four years of relentless culling. It could have been xenos, though precious few of those degenerates remained to draw breath.

'Him, then,' Konenos said.

'Yes,' agreed Erato.

Jaghatai. For years uncounted the White Scars had been an irrelevance, something to be reminded about in-between greater endeavours. Now, though, with the might of Ultramar contained behind the galactic fracture of the Ruinstorm and Dorn's praetorians leashed to their master's fortifications, only the unregarded V Legion still remained in sufficient numbers to trouble the Warmaster's main onslaught.

'You have analysed the attack?' asked Konenos.

Erato nodded. 'Yes, but–'

'The convoy is not the target.'

Erato inclined his head in agreement, and Konenos found himself distracted by the patterns of wire across golden flesh. Konenos had seen Erato shred enemies using the power of sonics alone, and death amid such a vortex of divinely honed sound was a fine thing to witness.

'They will strike *there* first,' said Erato, his soft eyes locked on the hololiths. 'They will hit the convoy, but that will be to draw us out. They are trying to pull the fleet together, away from where they truly desire to hurt us.'

'And where would that be?'

Erato smiled. 'There are a hundred targets, orchestrator. Would you like me to select one at random?'

'It will become apparent. The hawk's tricks are growing old. Signal the *Suzerain* that we will send three destroyers to their position. If they wish to preserve the Memnos convoy that is their choice, but I will not commit a greater force until we have seen the true hand of the enemy.'

Erato bowed. 'And then we inform… him?'

Konenos rose from the throne, feeling the tug of the barbed nails that had been inserted under each rib of his fused organ-cage.

'We do it now,' he said. 'It was never a good idea to keep the Soul-Severed waiting.'

THE SHIP WAS the *Proudheart*, and the name had once been deserved. Its commander had never truly relinquished the reputation it proclaimed, not even in death, which was less of an impediment to continued service than it had once been.

The battleship's flanks had been as deeply changed

as any other war vessel of the III Legion, and now
swam with colour like spilled oil. Its hull was
enormous – a Dictatus-class carcass, studded with
silver-mawed weaponry, powered through the abyss by
ancient engine-furnaces. The scars of a hundred cam-
paigns still lingered on its gilt-edged flanks: Jhoviana,
Apt var Aption, the Dalinite Nebula, Laeran, Murder,
Isstvan III, Isstvan V. Once, those old plasma-burns
and solid-round impacts would have been scoured
from the adamantium plates post-action by whole
armies of void drones; now they were left in place,
picked out, made into decoration by gangs of indentured artisan-slaves – years of warfare recalled in a
vast metal tapestry.

Deep inside the *Proudheart*'s outer shell, the corridors echoed to new sounds. Frenzied cries came
from the bowels of the ship endlessly, filtered and
directed through transit shafts all the way to the
exalted heights, every shriek resampled and reworked
by banks of auditory processors until the walls shook
from the overlapping layers of curated anguish. The
mirrored panels of the interior were streaked with
blood, left in place to turn darker, lit up by floating
lamps of paper, wire and pearl. Nothing was erased,
everything was savoured, all was illuminated.

In its past, the *Proudheart* had been like other Imperial battleships. It had employed a day-night cycle
based on the patterns of its Legion's home world,
bringing a rhythm of light and dark to the vastness
of the city in space. Now the lumens were never
doused, and the clamour of an eternal day was never
stilled. Menials had their eyelids sewn shut and their
ears excised to keep them from going insane amid

the eternal brilliance of it all, though many still succumbed; those who did were replaced by vat-enhanced analogues, built from the embryo to withstand the cacophony, the flamboyance, the terror.

Striding among that misshapen horde were the vestiges of the Emperor's own – once the most unsullied of Legions, but which had flown closest to the sun. They had purged their ranks of waverers on the bloodied fields of Isstvan III and now numbered only the devoted among their number, the brothers who embraced the new path, who revelled in it, who strove for sensation with all the zealotry they had once reserved for martial exactitude.

What they had lost in dignity, they had gained in pain-wracked power. Gifts came with mutilation, changes that once they would have shrunk from but which now made them conduits for a greater deadliness. Their armour had warped, cracking and blistering as the flesh and iron within twisted into new shapes. They toyed with their sacred gene architecture, willingly submitting to the knives of their Apothecaries, who in turn had become the most exalted of their number – a priest-caste of flesh-artisans commanding power over life, death and the various charted states between and beyond.

For Von Kalda, one of that cadre in addition to being equerry to the Lord Commander Primus, the elevation had been a mixed blessing. He strode from the *Proudheart*'s under-bridge antechambers and up the winding glass-stone stairways. His fingers still glistened from the medicae-slabs, sticky under the inner film of his battle-gauntlets. The armour he wore bore the ivory sheen of his old order, though lined now with purple lacquer. His strangely childlike face remained creased in concentration as he went, locked in the one task – the sacred task – he had set himself while elbow-deep in the entrails of his subjects.

And yet, when the Soul-Severed demanded attention, the summons could not be ignored. Von Kalda crested the stair's summit and moved across a crystal courtyard overlooked by burnished images of dead-eyed serpents and eagles. Ahead of him, the gates to the lord commander's sanctum slid open soundlessly.

The chamber inside was cloaked in shifting shadows, lit by vein-blue lamps that hovered soundlessly on cushions of anti-grav. Metal bulkheads above creaked and flexed as if caught in a strong wind, though none stirred in that filtered atmosphere. The *Proudheart* was a home to more than mortal souls now, and in every crevice and fall-shaft the echoes of empyrical denizens hushed and slithered.

The Soul-Severed, like all of them, had endured a long period of flux. He sat on a throne of fluid bronze that melded to his armour-clad bulk. The Lord Commander Primus had eschewed a gorget and helm, exposing the long scar on his neck that he seemed to take as a sign of strength. To be killed – by the primarch, no less – and then reconstituted by the command of the same executioner struck many in the Legion as a symbol of the new gifts they had won with so much labour. Eidolon was the first of the immortals, the first of those to show that death and life were mere facets of a deeper existence.

At first he had been known as 'the Risen'. That moniker had quickly begun to feel insufficient in its description of him.

He gazed down from the throne with the dull-eyed, listless mien of the Chemosian aristocracy. Every look, every gesture, implied *ownership*, the kind of acquisitive superiority that brooked no argument or dissension. In what remained of the III Legion's military hierarchy, that still counted for much, although there were many, Lucius perhaps foremost, who had treated it with a contempt that came from equal ambition.

Von Kalda had no idea why Eidolon had been brought back. Perhaps it was a whim born of a newborn god's boredom. Whatever the reason, the Lord Commander Primus had not remained long by Fulgrim's side, and had taken nigh a third of the entire Legion's strength under his own direction, giving no indication that he was following anyone's orders but his own. Such was the way of things now – a galaxy of confused and overlapping loyalties, obfuscated by the clamour in the warp and the impossibility of long-range communications. They were all fighting in the murk, clawing their way towards Terra like blind men scattered by the wind.

'Konenos makes contact,' Eidolon said, gazing languidly at Von Kalda from his high seat. His voice was a rasp, still tight from where his throat had been cut.

'What has he found?' asked Von Kalda, bowing formally.

'The Memnos convoy has attracted warp-wakes. It will be hit.'

'He asks for ships?'

'No.' Eidolon's irises had been replaced by iridescent jewels, and they glinted now with a tactician's enthusiasm. 'He reads it aright. This has the stink of barbarism.'

As he spoke, a silver dream-font slid up from the marbled deck. Von Kalda stepped back, allowing a five-metre-wide column of bone and lattice-inlay to rise to its full height. The water's surface began to ripple, and a faint hiss echoed around the throne-chamber.

'Too long since we were given a chance to take him by the throat,' Eidolon drawled, watching the water's surface slide.

The dream-font was a recent addition to his arsenal of arcane devices. Astropaths and daemon-bound psykers had been drowned in the machine, locking their visions into the water. Now it only reflected the dreams of the souls quenched within it, vomiting out their desperate nightmares when the waters boiled.

'This thing cannot be trusted, lord,' warned Von Kalda.

'True. But what can?'

Water spilled over the edges, frothing as the torrent cascaded through twists of bone. Reflective light angled up into the chamber's heights, dancing like marsh-gas. The hissing grew in volume, joined by the dying echoes of old chokes.

Soon enough, the images came. Von Kalda witnessed the ghostly orbs of worlds they had burned, the armies they had ground into the dust. Sigils snapped into focus briefly – the spidery motif of the forge world Ghorentes, the chevrons of the Knight House Praster, the endless imagery of Imperial Army regiments, now all destroyed. Cities drifted into view, planetary systems, deep-void installations, fleet-docks – all ruins, scoured down to ash by the remorseless advance of the Warmaster and his brothers.

'Tell me, what do you feel when you see this?' Eidolon

asked. His withered, rust-edged voice made him sound more than half machine.

'Only pride,' said Von Kalda. 'There will be more to burn before the end.'

Eidolon looked down sourly. 'And Terra is the crucible. Fabius has already drawn up the experiments for it. I have seen them.'

Von Kalda did not ask how Eidolon could have done so, nor what the Legion's Apothecary-general had planned. For the time being, Fabius remained with the primarch, who was far off, silent and sundered by the wrath of the warp. Instead, Von Kalda, who had plans of his own, concentrated on the dream-font's imagery, knowing that Eidolon placed faith in it even if he himself did not. So many bound souls of so many seers – it would tell them something, even if it did not deserve the name of anything like truth.

'An infinite universe to twist,' the Apothecary murmured, 'and still we cleave to this goal? Terra, the Throneworld, and nothing else matters.'

The shifting light of the dream-font played across Eidolon's scarred, haughty face. 'But that *is* all there is, my brother,' he said. 'We came from Terra, we return to Terra.' Eidolon's cheek twitched, exposing the tight skein of sinew that Fabius had painstakingly re-knitted. 'And besides, we are changing. Our pleasures will soon be our masters. While we remember how to order a Legion, we must make the most of it.'

The dream-font's visions intensified. More planets swam up out of the aether, many wreathed in cold silver flames. Von Kalda saw the worlds they had most recently subdued for the Warmaster – Lermia, Erwa Nha, Goball, Herevail, Mhoreb X. The orbs traced a scattered line across the physical void, a necklace of embers strung out in a trail unto the spinward curve of the galaxy. The bulk of the fighting was in the galactic west now, the most extreme edge of Horus' long warfront. Greater forces drove hard up the centre, grinding onwards under the leadership of the Warmaster himself.

'The Memnos convoy,' said Eidolon, his eyes narrowing. 'Where does it supply?'

'The Gheist Narrows. Materiel, troops, provisions. The Narrows are unsecured, only fallen for two months, Terran standard. If the supplies do not arrive–'

'Then nothing of importance will be lost,' said Eidolon. 'The fodder-carriers will be hit, that will draw a response, and then the real target will be chosen. But what? Where do they wish us to weaken ourselves?'

There were over a dozen garrison worlds within range, a hundred armed strongholds, twenty exposed battlefronts, all of which had their own strategic value.

Von Kalda saw no pattern. A loosening of the hold on the Narrows could be countered and draw little strength from the surrounding regions. It could be a token move – the telltale of an enemy that was running out of resources.

'Consider our enemy,' said Eidolon. 'Consider his strengths, his weaknesses.'

'The Warhawk,' said Von Kalda.

'None other remains. What is his position?'

'Dispersed. Strategos record nineteen strikes in three months, thirteen of which were repulsed. The tally of losses will be hurting them. He musters, surely now, for a final assault.'

'That would be against four Legions, and he has not

the numbers to take on more than one. If I were the Khan, I would be looking for a way out.'

'But he will not run.'

'He will have to. He wishes to see Terra before the end, just as we all do.' Eidolon pressed his fingers together. Von Kalda could see the old mind was still active, undimmed by the physical changes that Fabius had wrought. 'He knows the truth, even if you do not – this thing will be decided at the Palace, and he will not risk being cast adrift while we break the walls down. He needs to turn now, to get out of our pincer. See the void through his eyes, Apothecary. See what he sees.'

Von Kalda returned to the dream-font. He saw the channels of the warp, the paths embedded in the stolen minds of drowned Navigators. He saw the distribution of the Warmaster's forces, encircling, cutting off, stifling lines of retreat. Eidolon's battalions had not been the only hunters trying to run down the White Scars – a thousand salients jutted into the void, smothering all ways through the turbulent aether. They all had standing orders – eliminate the threat of the flanks, clear the way to the Solar System and hasten the coming of the End.

'Kalium,' said Von Kalda at last. 'He will attempt the Kalium Gate.'

Eidolon raised a stitched eyebrow. 'Tell me why.'

'The Memnos convoy remains deep in conquered space. Its loss will draw forces from three sectors of the advance-lines. If he provokes them fully, that will weaken the Garmartes Sector, but he will not assault that region, for it is laid waste now and has no value for either him or us. He may, though, use the

Garmartes margin to force passage under the galactic plane. The Kalium System can be taken if they move in numbers, placing the Gate in range, which remains clear of the aether-storm. If he can seize the subsector before a reply is made, he will have his passage home.'

Eidolon nodded slowly. The dream-font seethed, as if in congratulation. 'Good. And yet this is false hope, for the Gate cannot be forced – its foundations were broken by Perturabo and the storms now rage as wildly there as they do in every other sector.' Eidolon drew in a long, wheezing breath, making the sutures along his throat flex. 'But the Khan cannot know this. He makes the feint, and hopes to send us chasing after him into Memnos, freeing his path to Kalium.'

The Lord Commander Primus rose from the throne and drew himself up to his full, crooked height. Eidolon's movements had once been fluid, but were now those of an old man, made halting by the life-sustaining poisons that coursed through his ravaged frame. Only his voice still made him deadly – the swollen auditory augmetics and bloated throat-sacs that could unleash his flesh-ripping hurricanes of sound.

Von Kalda looked up at him with a kind of fascinated loathing. He would have loved nothing more than to put his master under the knives, to delve into the scars left by resurrection and uncover the secrets that had created such a glorious monster. The vision he had already endured would be augmented by such a subject, though *that* was impossible. Perhaps one day, when the war was done and there would be leisure to do so… But for now he merely bowed in supplication.

'Assemble the fleet and send word to Konenos,' Eidolon ordered, limping down the throne-dais steps to the chamber's floor. 'Send a token force to aid the *Suzerain*, then order rendezvous with all other elements in the sensor-shadow of the Gate. We will make passage to Kalium as soon as our brothers join us.'

'By your will.' Von Kalda followed Eidolon down the polished processional. 'And, if I may – the primarch?'

Eidolon shot Von Kalda a dry smile. 'If you can locate our beloved Father, then by all means inform him. Pinning the Khan down might drag him from his indulgences, though I doubt it.' He limped on, clearly still wracked by the pain of his transformation. 'There will come a day when we are not bound by the wills of those child-gods. For now, we must do as we have learned to – prosecute their wars, pretend we are the masters of our own fate.'

His gold-edged boots scraped against the marble as his feet dragged.

'But what dark jests this universe plays on us all,' Eidolon rasped. 'And what fools it chooses to tell them.'

ON THE BULK carrier *Terce Falion*, lead vessel of the III Legion's deep-void Memnos convoy, Shipmaster Eleanora Kulba pushed her way up to the observation bridge. A lifter-servitor blundered out of her path, snorting stupidly through iron mandible-guards. She reached the doors and thumped the access panel. The electronics clicked twice before the pistons finally released and the rust-pocked metal shunted open.

Fael Alobus, her second in command, was waiting for her on the far side, as was the sable-robed

Navigator Cavelli. Beyond them, the low curved roof of the *Terce Falion*'s bridge extended down towards rows of armourglass viewports.

'Gentlemen,' she said, crisply. 'With me.'

The three of them proceeded down the main gantry. A thin line of pressed metal hanging over pits crawling with indentured bridge crew. The space stank of corrosion, human sweat and machine lubricant. Ahead, the void peered down at them through the lead lining of real-viewers.

Kulba hated the sight of it. She spent most of her time lodged down in the inner cortex-hull of the bulk carrier, avoiding staring out into the infinity of nothingness that it was her curse to ply. She had never wanted to sail the void, but as the Great Crusade had sucked resources from every world in the burgeoning Imperium and stripped planets dry of those with any degree of capability or nous, eventually the summons had come her way and the agents of the Administratum had made it clear to her where her destiny lay.

To make it worse, she had discovered that she was good at it. Piloting a bulk carrier was a peculiar skill, a cross between spire administration and freebooting. She was tough, she had a healthy covering of fat, she was perpetually angry – all qualities that had served her well in the auxiliary fleets of the Imperial Army in its spread across the stars.

The old Army and its command structures were now gone, of course. Kulba's loyalty, for what it was worth, was to the Memnos Combine, which had long been in fealty to the sectoral command at Loeb, which had once been under the authority of the Terran prefecture of Phoedes but for two standard years now had

been subsumed into the growing hinterland of trib-
ute worlds harvested by the III Legion. Through them,
she supposed, her fealty now belonged to the supreme
authority of the Warmaster, but in truth it made little
difference where the orders came from. She made a
living, the food-cylinders kept coming, the ships were
repaired and kept in order. There was danger, but there
always had been. Her masters had always been distant, her goals obscure. She did what she did, the days
passed and other minds plotted the greater progress
of the Imperial dream.

The void remained hateful, though. Nothing would
ever change that.

'Signals, you say,' Kulba said, pulling a data-slate
from her grease-spotted tunic.

'Not from us,' said Alobus, scratching one of his
chins. 'Second-hand, out of the fleet.'

'Who in the fleet?'

'The *Suzerain*. A Legion ship.'

'Recognise it?'

'No. It's still incoming.'

They reached the main viewing platform. Above
them a crystalflex dome opened up, webbed with
metal and streaked with aeons-old void-grime. Kulba
took a deep breath and looked up.

Half her convoy was visible out there, hanging
above the *Terce Falion* in a procession of immensity.
Angle-sided and heavy-jowled, the big haulers stretched
off into darkness, their thrusters burning low orange.
Each ship was over fifty kilometres long, though almost
all that bulk was given over to colossal series modules, packed with ranks of shackled container units.
No human crew member went into those cavernous

spaces, for the only populated sections of the ships were the tiny blisters on the forward hull-ridge, where the cortex-bridges were lodged. Everything else was silent, enclosed, locked down, sealed in.

Kulba saw the underside of the *Revo Satisa* slide above them, and watched the rows upon rows upon rows of stowage modules pass in stately sluggishness. Beyond that ship was the *Daughter of Loeb*, and beyond that was the *Cold as Stars*.

'How soon until we break the veil?' Kulba asked.

'Three hours,' replied Cavelli softly.

Kulba didn't look at him. She didn't like Navigators either. They made her spine creep, with their third swathed eye and their parchment skin and their shuffling. Cavelli smelt bad, too; always had. The stench was something faint, undefinable, a pheromone or some other spoor of mutation.

'We could make the jump now,' she said.

'Then we would lose a third of the convoy,' said Cavelli, smiling apologetically. 'I do not have the manifolds for nine of the haulers.'

'And we have orders,' Alobus reminded her. '*Legion* orders.'

Kulba hawked up spittle and sent it sailing over the gantry edge. Void-nausea pulled at her innards. The stars glinted back at her from beyond the crystalflex bubble, malicious, eternal.

'How close are they?' she asked, resigned to more waiting in real space. The sooner the convoy pulled into the turbulent hell of the warp, the sooner they would know how many of them would make it to the Narrows in one piece.

Alobus consulted the snaked-head chrono-augur

embedded in the back of his hair-flecked hand. 'Less than... Well, I am mistaken. Getting something now. They must be early.'

That was when Kulba knew. They were never early: the III Legion were degenerating fast but they were still sticklers for detail, and if they had given a chrono-mark, they meant to keep it.

'Dispatch all pickets,' she ordered, narrowing her eyes, peering out into the dark. 'Tell them if they see anything on intercept, open fire.'

She pressed the alert bead on the inside of her palm and felt sweat there.

Alobus looked at her, uncertain. 'Ma'am, do you–'

'Say nothing.' Kulba saw the plasma bursts of thrusters firing as the convoy's escorts spiralled out to the margins, taking up fire-lattice positions. The bridge's lumens sunk down to combat-red, and flare-marks appears on cogitator consoles. 'If you wish to do anything now, double-check this Legion communication and hope it proves accurate.'

The void-behemoths made no course correction. It took hours just to calibrate them for a change of trajectory, and unless that was done they would keep ploughing along the same vector until the last supernova in the galaxy blew itself out. Their picket fleet, around fifty lance-bearing sub-warp corvettes, reached the perimeter of the defensive envelope and took up station.

Cavelli drew in a breath and closed his natural eyes. Kulba turned on him. 'You sense something?'

He gave her another one of those damnable half-smiles, but kept his eyes closed. 'I am an old man. In truth, I feel lucky to have made it this far with you.'

As he spoke, every cogitator console across the bridge suddenly went dark. Void-navigation sigils flickered out, and the lumens overhead began to fizz.

'Get them back on!' shouted Kulba, rounding on the hubbub of her crew down in the pits. As they struggled to restore command, the silent flash of las-fire burst out from the void.

The consoles cleared. Initially, three lines of text in standard Gothic scrolled down the screens, clear enough for Kulba to read even at distance.

OATH-BREAKERS.
YOU ARE NOW JUDGED.
WE ARE THE PUNISHMENT.

Kulba knew that every officer on every bulk carrier would be reading the same thing. 'Stay at your stations!' she bellowed, turning back from the real-view portals and striding down the gantry. 'Pull in manifolds! Prepare warp-cycle for ignition!'

That last order was a nonsense – even if Cavelli had initiated his preparatory studies, it would still have taken too long to key in the warp drives – but she had to say something. For the first time in her long and mostly hateful career, she was entirely at a loss.

Kulba made it five metres down the gantry before the first physical impact came in. She heard a hard smash somewhere high up in the cortex-bridge's anterior shield cluster, followed by the shriek of metal being torn.

The text on the consoles snapped out, to be replaced by an image: a stylised lightning strike across a horizontal bar.

'What is that?' demanded Kulba, reaching the nearest viewer screen and grabbing it with both hands.

More crashes from up above followed, and the oculus was riven with flashes of silver. Alobus was frozen with indecision, but Cavelli started chuckling.

Kulba pulled the screen from its housing and whirled to face the Navigator. She thrust the image at him. 'What *is* that? You know, don't you?'

Cavelli nodded. 'And if you had studied the livery of mankind's Legions, sister, you would know it too. But what does this matter? Any one of the Cartomancer's Twenty Visions would be more than enough for us.'

Kulba threw the screen down and grabbed Cavelli by his robes. The Navigator's old body felt like a sack of bones under the rich velvet. 'What does it mean?' she hissed.

Cavelli opened his mortal eyes, and gave her a steady look free of either fear or hope.

'Nothing made by the hand of man moves faster,' he murmured, lost in something like awe. 'They are magnificent. But let me tell you one more thing of them, for it is the last you will ever learn.'

He leaned closer to her, and his breath, scented with cloves, brushed against her face.

'They are still laughing.'

TWO

SIXTY SHU'URGA-PATTERN Xiphon interceptors screamed out from the hangars of the *Kaljian* and the *Amujin*, fell sharply to clear the wake of their motherships' main thrusters, then kicked into full speed. Behind them boomed twenty Storm Eagle gunships, slower but more heavily armed. The raiders spread wide, fanning out into hunting packs and boosting into pre-arranged attack paths.

The convoy lay ahead of them, wallowing, sluggish, surrounded by its protective shell of escorts. The *Kaljian* moved to a high-plane observation position, opening up with broadside volleys to hit the flanks of the distant leviathans. The *Amujin*, the smaller of the two White Scars attack frigates, fell away to take up guard position further back towards the local-space Mandeville point.

Shiban Khan glanced down at the spread of ships under his command, took in the velocities and the angles and the cohesion, and made his choices.

'Like sleeping cattle,' he voxed, pushing his interceptor into a corkscrewing climb.

Jochi, hurtling less than thirty metres from his starboard wing, laughed. 'Then we will wake them.'

The arrow-head formation of V Legion void fighters burst through the outer perimeter of guard-ships, far too fast to be tracked by the basic defence-nets of the picket vessels. Lance-beams scythed harmlessly above and below the diving interceptors, lighting up their bone-white chassis, the lightning strikes, the gold and crimson.

The underhull of the lead hauler loomed ahead, rust-red, lit with half-moon plasma thrusters. Its long series of armoured cargo-units stretched off into the dark like the shell of some immense creeping insectoid.

Shiban's squadron shot under the approaching lip of the rear engine-housing, swerving to avoid the blur of las-fire pumping from servitor track cannons. Targeting wireframes rotated and shifted across the cockpit's forward viewscreen, latching on to a thousand targets a second before isolating the most effective locus.

Shiban ignored the cogitated results and aimed the lascannons manually. Driving the thrusters to within a micrometre of their redlines, he strafed along the void-shield-warded flanks, watching fissures form at his weapons' impact sites.

'Bridge sighted,' Shiban voxed.

His fighter swung out from under the hull's shadow, then tore up the leading edge of the hull-plates, sending multicoloured static from the bulk carrier's void shields blowing outwards like spray from an ocean-speeder. The rest of the squadron came with him, staying tight on his wing.

'On my mark,' ordered Shiban, switching to his fighter's missile control system.

The Xiphon interceptors rolled into position, swerving around incoming las-fire, each one a blurred-edge smear of speed. Jochi went high, pulling a whole gamut of projectiles with him and leaving the attack run ahead thinned of flak.

The attackers cleared the last bulkhead, exposing the bridge complex perched atop the hunched spine of the bulk carrier.

'Mark.'

Rotary missile launchers sent streaks of neon-white tearing towards the metal-line horizon. Silent explosions rippled out, smashing through the vessel's shield generators. The interceptors ripped through a spray of burst armour-plates, tumbling away from the kaleidoscope of debris.

'*Hai Chogoris!*' whooped Jochi, pushing his fighter's angle steeply back towards the hunting pack.

All across the lumbering convoy, similar explosions lit up the void, each one taking out a bulk carrier's void shield coverage and leaving its heavy adamantium hull exposed. Pinpoint lines of las-fire and heavy-round cannons kept driving out from weaponised flanks, but none of it was close to hitting the mark.

Shiban wheeled away, choking his speed for just long enough to arrest the overshoot, then nudged the muzzle of his fighter towards the gaping maw of the hangar mouths.

For a moment, he thought he recognised the profile – the blinking marker lights, the chevroned warning livery, the vast cliff-faces of steel. He had hit a hundred such targets over past months, and they merged into one another. That had become life for them all now – hit-and-run scavengers, taking out the weak and the slow, hampering the mammoth warfront and pulling free before its enormous pincers could close on them. Every raid hurt the enemy, depriving him of the communication lines, materiel, supplies and troops that he needed, but it hurt them too, for the Warmaster had teeth of his own.

'Follow me in,' Shiban ordered, piling back into full velocity.

The approach was thick with glowing lines of las-fire. The bulk carrier's crew were attempting to lower blast-doors across the hangar entrance, and Shiban opened up with his lascannons. The piston-arms shattered, leaving the blast-doors half lowered. That left a gap of less than eight metres to thread through at near full tilt. The test made Shiban smile for the first time on that mission, and his fingers clenched a little tighter around his control columns.

We would do this for sport, in another age.

He pushed down on the throttle, and screamed low across the remaining ground. The hangar entrance swam up before him, and he slewed across its face before powering through the narrow aperture.

Inside, a cavernous void opened up, easily capable of housing ships a hundred times the size of his own. Enormous hauler claws hung from roof-mounted tracks, illuminated by the red fog of combat lighting. Ranks of landing platforms stretched away into the gloom.

Shiban compensated for the shift into the bulk

carrier's gravity well, switched to atmospheric drives and applied his newly cycling airbrakes hard. The Xiphon spun around over its centre and came down heavily onto the nearest platform, shrouded in vapour and ribbons of atomising plasma.

The fighter's cockpit locks blew, and Shiban pulled himself from his seat, taking up his favoured *guan dao* as he leapt down to the rockcrete. Defence servitors were already shambling towards him, levelling autoguns and limb-mounted carbines. Shiban burst into a sprint, smashing the heel of his blade into the steel-ringed throat of the closest attacker, pushing away and punching his blade through the stomach of another, whirling around to smash the legs out from under a third, before pushing out and beheading the fourth.

All across the hangar his brothers were doing the same – powering from their fighters and racing out across the echoing chamber. None of them moved like Shiban, though. Where their weapon-strikes were fluid, his were jabbing; where they danced and feinted, he smashed and careened. Their armour was the same as the Brotherhood of the Storm had worn since the first days of its inauguration on Chogoris: ivory plates, rimmed with red and gold and marked with three lightning bolts – the sign of the *minghan*. Only Shiban's right pauldron still bore those old marks, those old colours. The rest of his armour was a steely grey, pocked with shell craters and marred by the patina of combat. His plates were thicker than the others', knitted together with cables and clamps and fusion-locks. He called those things the Shackles – the damned Mechanicum devices that kept him alive, kept him moving, kept him fighting. Within them, his body was now a mongrel thing, part-superhuman, part-ruined.

Szu-Ilya had spoken truly to him, what seemed like a lifetime ago.

'In another Legion,' she had said, 'they tell me you might have been placed in a Dreadnought.'

A half-tracked servitor with iron pincers for hands rumbled towards him, and he leapt, using metal muscle-stimms lodged amid the sinews of his body. The guan dao whirled, tracing a perfect arc through the smog-laced atmosphere, slicing the man-machine's upper feed-cables. Shiban's momentum carried him into its embrace, and a crunch down from his clenched fist cracked its skull open, terminating the commands to its rudimentary impulse units. It was a move impelled by the embers of fury. It had never been that way before.

He shoved the twitching corpse aside and kept moving. Two hundred metres away lay the first of many doors leading into the vast ship's interior. The nine battle-brothers of his *arban* were close on his heels, only pausing to despatch the last of the hangar's defence force. They converged on the doors to a lifter shaft, their armour spattered with thin blood and viscous engine oils. All his warriors were helmed against the void, and their armour was covered with unique battle-marks – skulls, skins, signs of the vanquished – binding defeated souls to the armour of the one who had killed them.

Jochi was carrying the severed head of a mortal trooper in one hand, and let it thud to the deck.

'I do not think they saw us coming,' he said.

'They saw plenty,' said Shiban, mag-locking his blade

and pulling up a schematic from the wall-mounted cogitator unit. 'They are weak, not blind.'

He inserted a control wafer into the cogitator unit and the lifter access codes cycled down his helm display. He took control of the access shafts, the ship's shield subsystems, six other critical lattice-nets and the base level navigation grid.

'Anything, then, Tachseer?' Jochi asked, his enthusiasm reduced, shaking the blood from his blade.

Tachseer. They insisted on calling him that – all of them, now – and it was long past the time for resisting.

Shiban interrogated the augur-node implanted in his cranial interface. It caused him significant pain to use, just as every action – moving, breathing, killing – caused him significant pain. For a moment all he saw was the local-space tactical sphere, clogged with the burning shells of convoy pickets. The *Kaljian* remained in close, the *Amujin* further off. He was about to respond in the negative, to order the ascent to the bridge, when he sensed the first signal closing.

'Not far behind,' he murmured, as if that were something that had ever been different. He looked up, reaching for his locked glaive. 'They remain quick.'

'You have a ship-mark?' Jochi asked.

'What does it matter?' said Shiban, calling up the lifter platform and activating his glaive's disruptor. 'They will come, and we will end them.'

He paused before passing over the threshold. There weren't as many incoming signals as he had expected. That boded poorly for the opposite flank of the move. All the games were getting old, and perhaps even the Khan's mind could now be read by the enemy, just as they seemed to read all else.

A lifter platform shuddered into view on steam-wreathed metal columns, and the blast-doors ground open in a trail of sparks. A ship-ident flashed across his helm display, picked out in the Imperial Gothic runes that had once been a symbol of the dominance of humanity and now felt like the emblem of its folly.

Suzerain.

'Come,' he said, moving into the lifter shaft, his glaive glowing electric-blue against the dark. 'The debauched are on our heels.'

NO SHIP WAS suffered to break the veil ahead of the flagship. The *Proudheart* shattered the barrier between realms first, and in its wake came the outriders, pulling wide once the transition to the materium had been fixed and taking up pinpoint assault positions.

Eidolon, standing in the observation tower of his private hull-citadel, watched his fleet deploy, ship by ship. The capital vessels fell into the Chemos-authorised formations they had used since the earliest days of the Crusade, covering one another's trajectories, mapping broadside solutions to each other, sliding into the abyss like sharks through the ocean's swell.

They had lost nothing in precision. The purple-and-gold tide spread across the emptiness, hitting cruising velocity well within Legion expectations. Crystal spires glittered like frozen tears. Jewels reflected the light of the stars. It was beautiful, impressively beautiful.

The *Proudheart*'s main line deployment was joined, seconds later, by the arrival of Jewel Shard, Lepidan and three other battle-groups tied to the lord commander's will – four full line warships, many more support vessels, from hunter-destroyers to gun frigates, the kind of flotilla that would have once subjugated whole sectors, now running down those of the species who had refused the call to evolution.

Eidolon felt his new glands twitch. He raised a finger and traced the line of his swollen throat, the skin as tight as a drum. He felt the veins pulse rhythmically, tracing out the irregular pattern of two hearts.

Menials brought new armour-pieces to be drilled and turbo-hammered into place. A six-legged augmetic drone clattered across the marble, bearing Eidolon's swollen gorget in three iron pincer-claws. The armour-piece had been chased with silver, picked out with bestiary from Old Terra and Chemos, fluted finely, polished to the high sheen that had always been demanded. As the drone approached, Eidolon raised his chin, suffering its mechanical attentions like some old coiffured monarch. The gorget was clamped into place, and Eidolon felt filament-needles slide into his distorted black carapace, locking fast and pulling ceramite hard onto flesh.

As the sonic multipliers made their interface, an echoing *snap* spun out across the arming chamber. It was only a feedback glitch, but it still blasted open the cranial shells of the servitors, leaving several twitching helplessly on the flags.

Eidolon turned to the tech-priests, raising an eyebrow. The closest of them, a hunched nightmare of cabling and wire-mesh cowls, bowed in apology. 'Refinements are still being made,' it muttered.

Eidolon raised his arms to the horizontal, and the surviving menials shuffled forwards to clamp the

plates into position. Every addition brought a surge of
fresh pain – a toxic blend of his gene-template being
twisted into new and unsanctioned forms. Some of
it he had learned to enjoy. Other sensations were less
welcome, but in time he would no doubt find a way
to turn the experience to his advantage.

We are not the finished article yet, he thought. *There
are still steps of sensation left to take.*

A rune flickered into life over his helm display, indicating the arrival of Azael Konenos and his ships.
Eidolon remembered the same marker lighting up
before Isstvan, when Konenos was not yet an orchestrator of the Kakophoni and he himself had only
experienced one lifetime. Azael's loyalty had been
complete and perfect then, just as it was now.

'Be welcome, my brother,' Eidolon voxed. All around
him, the drills whined as the bolts were dragged tight.

'*Lord commander,*' acknowledged Konenos, his voice
also distorted by the augmetics of his own ruined
throat. '*The barbarians?*'

'They will come. My equerry doubts it, but they will
come.' Out of the corner of his eye, through the crystalflex real-viewers, Eidolon caught sight of the *Ravisher* at
the head of the newly translated formation. The hunters were gathering. 'Take up position beyond the Gate's
leeward rim. Run silent, and wait for the charge. Have
you witnessed Kalium before, my brother?'

'I have not.'

Tech-priests limped towards Eidolon, carrying his
helm aloft on a salver of gold. It was twice the size it
had once been, chocked and studded with auditory
dampeners and channellers, inlaid with the filaments
that would slide into his inner ear and wrap around

his sinus cavities. They lifted it high, and Eidolon looked up into its miraculous interior.

'Then you are fortunate,' he said, just as the rim of the helm came down, sealing him within the carapace of ceramite. Fresh shards of pain burned as more wires slithered into bone-sockets. 'As we destroy what we once built, there are fewer wonders than there were. Feast on this one, and as we slaughter in its shadow, remember what we, the children of Terra, once dreamed to accomplish.'

No one knew who had made it. All records were gone, lost in the long strife that had engulfed the galaxy before the Emperor's coming. It was ancient – that at least was certain – raised in a time when the technology of humanity had run amok, designed by those who had no fear of the blasphemous union of mind and metal. Perhaps that had been its undoing – those who had placed it into the gulf of the void succumbing to the machine-spirits sacrilegiously burned into its arcane core.

The date of its abandonment would never be known. The Gate had lain dormant and charred for at least a thousand years before the explorator fleet of Rogue Trader Josiah Halliard had come across it while roving far ahead of the First Legion's obsidian war fleets. Halliard had searched it with his own forces, believing the structure to contain treasure worth plundering, but found only echoes and rust amid the dark. Frustrated, he had later sent missives to the Lion's command, which in turn had brought the Dark Angels to Kalium. They had claimed the entire subsector for Terra, sealing it off and sending in reclamator squads of their own. What they discovered was never made known, though records of transits from Kalium to Caliban were logged deep in the Navis Nobilite's archives on Terra, none of which carried official authorisation and all of which were buried.

In time, the Lion himself had arrived, fresh from conquest on a dozen worlds. It was said that when his grey-eyed gaze alighted on the Gate for the first time, he did not speak. It had been as if he could peer beyond its bulk, past the great curve of its inner mouth, and see into the maw beyond. When he had eventually stirred, the words had been typically few.

'Make this place fast. It guards many paths.'

Perhaps he had sensed what the Navigator Houses only later proved, or maybe he had just been fortunate in his guesswork. Either way, the Lion's judgement was sound. The Kalium System lay at the juncture of nine major routes through the warp. Great currents of pure aether surged about it, pushed by the vagaries of the Tempest Invisible. A fleet could enter the aperture into those deep streams and be thrown far across the galaxy's plane at greatly accelerated speeds. A journey of Terran months might take a similar span of weeks, something that was of great interest to the strategos of the Administratum as they planned the ever-expanding warfront of the Great Crusade. In this the Gate was not alone, for other such portals and cut-ways had been found in scattered wastes among the stars, but it was stable and within the Crusade's core expansion sphere, and thus of principal value.

So it was that the First Legion did not retain ownership of the Kalium Gate, but it passed instead to the direct control of the naval echelons of the Imperial

Army. More fleets arrived, first by established warp lanes, then using the arteries under the Gate itself. The old structures were secured and charted, and then built upon. Ancient bulwarks disappeared under new mountains of adamantium and iron. Strange harmonic vanes were replaced with batteries of macrocannons and void-lances. Shafts of unknown provenance were filled in with lead-lined cells, ready to take the thousands of menials who would soon be shipped in from surrounding compliant worlds. Mechanicum crawler-teams turned up and promptly disappeared into the depths of the core, emerging months later laden with locked caskets ready for unscheduled and undocumented return voyages back to Mars.

By the Crusade's high point, a hundred battleships were passing through the Gate every week, guided by fifty thousand naval staff installed within the new refit yards and fortresses and sensor-towers and docking berths. An artificial world grew like coral over the old foundations, obliterating the signs of an older civilisation, until only a few archivists and sector commanders ever knew that the mighty staging post had once been a creation of humanity's era of semi-remembered terror and hubris.

And yet, all knew, deep down, that the place could not have been made in any other epoch. Its size defied description – a colossal ellipse running around the neck of the warp inlet, nine hundred kilometres in diameter at its widest extent. From a distance, it resembled a glittering necklace in space, at once fragile and indomitable. Coming closer, an observer would see that the Necklace – as it had become known – was composed of hundreds of node-stations, each one linked to the next by heavy lengths of reinforced chain. Every one of those stations would have been a formidable star fortress in its own right, bristling with defensive weaponry and crowned with assault craft docks. All of them, though, were dwarfed by the pinnacle of the Gate's mysterious architecture: the Keystone.

The Lion had given it the name. At the apex of the great curve of the Gate's collar, the Keystone swelled out into the abyss, bulbous, bloated, superabundant. It had taken two years to chart the full extent of its labyrinthine interior, and even after the Army had assumed final command, large sections of it remained effectively mothballed and unknown. The docks were capacious enough to accommodate a star fort and its escort fleet, and the towers that clustered at its crown were the equal of any hive world's spires. Huge protective arcs surrounded it, enclosing inhabited sections within concentric rings of cannon-laced adamantium. Its shield generators utilised archaeotech far more efficient than standard Imperial void shield capability, giving the entire edifice a permanent cloak of translucent silver.

They had said that the Keystone was unbreakable. They had said that even a Legion fleet would be unable to penetrate that degree of shielding, and that, if supplied and manned and in prime condition, the Kalium Gate could be held indefinitely against any besieging force known to Imperial high command.

Perhaps some rumour of that boast reached the ear of the Lord of Iron, called Perturabo, master of the IV Legion, and perhaps that wore at his ever-fragile pride. When treachery came to the Imperium, right at its apogee, it was his Legion that took command of the Kalium subsector warfront. In those earliest months of confusion, rumour and counter-rumour, little was known, or could be known, of the movements of those primarchs who had cast their lot with the Warmaster, and so the Gate's defenders might reasonably have believed themselves as secure as any. In advance of firm orders from Terra, preparations were made, drills were run, the resident fleet cordon reinforced.

It was afterwards said that Perturabo took little pleasure in its swift and complete destruction.

'I desire the fall of only one fortress,' he was reported to have remarked, even as the outer Necklace still burned from the *Iron Blood*'s punishing fusillades. 'Until then, count no victories.'

When the IV Legion took to the void once more, they left the Gate a smouldering tomb, spinning gently on its enormous axis, stripped of life and rendered back almost to the dormant state it had been in when discovered by Halliard.

And yet, in all the tumult of a galaxy in flames, the Kalium Gate's destruction was just another statistic among a thousand other catastrophes. Amid the riot of intelligence and counter-intelligence, much was missed, and more ignored. Though the supply fleets stopped coming, and access to the great warp lanes was blocked by mines and the wreckage of the inner collar, few in the outer reaches of the galaxy would have known of its fall unless their fight for survival had demanded it.

And so it remained a prize for the unwary, a nexus that now led nowhere, a ruin whose possession gained the victor nothing.

But that had not stopped them coming. Even as the warships of the Emperor's Children took up guard positions over the summit of the dormant Keystone apex, new warp signatures registered out in the far void – dozens of them, moving fast, just as those of Jaghatai's Legion always did.

THREE

SHIBAN REACHED THE blast doors to the bridge, crouched low and waved Yiman forwards. His battle-brother sprinted ahead, clamped three krak grenades to the hair-line between the door's adamantium plates and set them to blow in sequence. Yiman retreated as the rest of the arban fell back, taking cover behind a line of low support frames five metres from the clicking charges.

Explosions kicked out, shattering the doors' locking mechanism and denting the heavy plates inwards. Shiban moved instantly, clutching his guan dao two-handed, but he was not the fastest – Jochi, Yiman and two others beat him to it, revelling in pure genhanced muscle rather than the hybrid mechanisms their khan now employed.

'For the Khagan!' Jochi whooped as he smashed his way through the jagged-edged gap, firing his bolt pistol.

Shards spun and bounced as Shiban followed him in. Beyond the portal, the bridge opened up in a fog of flickering lumen-strips. It ran for a hundred metres, rising slightly towards a crystalflex observation dome at the far end. Deep pits fell away on either side, crammed with terrified mortals and chittering servitors. Projectile fire skipped from the gantries that spanned the drop, aimed poorly by nervous hands. The bulk carrier's defenders were not even of the calibre of regular Imperial Army troopers – if Shiban had not been encased in his superlative armour he would still have had little to fear from such ill-directed shots.

By now, Jochi was nearing the observation platform. Shiban followed close on his heels, feeling the metal decking flex under his weight.

'Preserve the shipmaster,' he voxed.

Bolt-round echoes rang across the arch-roofed interior. Two warriors had leapt down into the pits and were slashing through the hordes with their curved blades. Two more had vaulted up into the heights, defying the weight of their armour to clamber into the metal spars that sheltered the snipers. Cogitator lenses shattered, throwing fizzing sheaves of crystal over the decking. The air rang with the stink of cordite, human fear and burst lubricant cables.

Shiban reached the platform under the dome. Twenty-three corpses greeted him, each one felled by a single precision shot. Jochi stood guard over the slumped cadavers, his armour barely dented, scanning around for anything still living. Others of the arban fanned out, still hunting, thirsting for more blood to wet their blades.

Two crew members had been spared. The mortal

shipmaster, a woman, was on her knees, trembling. Her Navigator stood beside her, unafraid.

Shiban stooped, lifting the shipmaster's fleshy chin with a single finger. 'Where are you bound?' he asked.

'The Narrows,' she blurted, eyes wide. 'My lord.'

'I am not your lord. What is your cargo?'

'We did not–'

'What is your cargo?'

The woman looked briefly lost, her pupils flickering from the armoured giant towering over her to the other ones who rampaged across her bridge. 'I... We do not–'

Shiban let her chin fall, and turned to the Navigator, who bowed floridly.

'A privilege to witness you fight, khan,' he said. 'My name is Cavelli. We carry nutrient supplies, battle-grade rations for nine Army regiments in service of the Third Legion. Some infantry weapons – ground attack craft, heavy assault gear. The remainder from standard supply ledgers, medicae equipment, parts, machine tools. Little of great import. In truth, I am surprised you came for it.'

Shiban studied the old man. The Navigator would be allowed to live, for such rarities were never killed needlessly. It sickened him, for the agents of the Navis Nobilite were employed by both sides of the war, untouchable even in treachery, their lives protected both by ancient precedent and the practical necessity of warp travel. The convoy would have two-score of such mutants on duty, at least one for each bulk carrier, and all would be preserved. Perhaps many of them had already served the Loyalist cause before; perhaps none had.

'How soon before you power your engines to full?' Shiban asked.

Cavelli tilted his head in what might have been apology. 'As I was telling Shipmaster Kulba, it will be some time until all ships are prepared.'

'You have one hour. Get to work. And I will have additional requirements.'

Cavelli bowed again, then stiffened suddenly. 'Of course, we may not have that long.'

Even as he spoke, Shiban received the same data over his comm-feed. He switched to the wide-range tactical augurs and picked up idents from all the units fighting in the battlesphere. Every bulk carrier had been boarded and every enemy crew had been immobilised. The last of the defence pickets were being run down, and the two White Scars frigates had pulled in close to the void-wake of the convoy to receive the fighters again.

But that was not all. Warp signatures had registered on the edge of sensor range – a dozen of them, coming in tight, skirting the very edge of safe Mandeville tolerance.

Jochi stomped back across the command platform. 'They are here?'

Shiban nodded, trying to gauge how long they had, what numbers were incoming, how best to marshal the forces given to him. The margins were getting tighter, the response times faster, the windows for operation slimmer.

'This is still my ship...' came Kulba's tremulous voice.

Shiban turned to see the shipmaster standing defiantly, her chin wobbling a little, a bead of sweat running down her cheek. She had not drawn a weapon, but her fists were balled in her gloves, and she had placed herself between Shiban and the command throne.

There was something noble in that. From the earliest days on Chogoris, when Shiban had been Tamu and the boundary of his existence had been the sky and the earth beneath it, he had always admired defiance.

His bolt-round hit her in the chest before she had even seen him draw the weapon. Kulba hit the back of the throne with a wet thud and sprawled across its arms, by which time Shiban was already moving, sliding his bolter back into its lock-position, ignoring the slick of blood that spread from the throne's base.

'Secure the Navigators,' he ordered, switching to the arban's channel. 'And look to the engines, as ordered.'

A crackling comm-burst brought in more information – Emperor's Children war vessels, as precisely configured as they had ever been, in numbers. So this encounter would be the test Yesugei had promised him it would be.

'Then make them fight,' he commanded, knowing that every warrior in the brotherhood was primed and ready. 'Blood them deep, for they are the oath-breakers, the destroyers of the dream.'

He activated the guan dao's energy field again and felt it surge within him – the savage, sharp anticipation of killing that now only came from taking on his own kind.

'For the Khan,' he breathed. 'For the Emperor.'

THE ATTACKERS CAME in primed for combat. If they had expected to find the Kalium Gate unprotected, its defences denuded to provide cover for the diversionary raids choreographed at Memnos and nine other scattered sites, they gave no sign of it.

The main assault was led by the Dictatus-class battleship *Lance of Heaven*, one of the Legion's core war vessels, the veteran of a dozen major engagements since they had learned about Isstvan. Its flanks were no longer spotless ivory, its lines no longer purest blood-red. Old plasma burns now ran along the length of its charred gunwales, patched up by hasty battlefield repairs and marred by repeat impacts. Its thrusters were black from incessant overburning, its bridge disfigured with the brown patina of lance-scorch residue. The only part of it that was kept undefiled was the great icon high up on the ship's crown that bore the Legion sigil: the lightning strike, the vengeance of heaven. That image was restored after every encounter, picked out in rarest gold and flood-lit across its heavy armour plate, for there would be no deception, no attempt to run silent or defy martial honour.

We are the V Legion. We are the ordu of Jaghatai, the White Scars of Chogoris.

We are the oath-keepers.

A million souls had died under the sigil's gaze in four long years of vicious fighting, each one dying with the gold and red of heaven reflected in their eyes. It had once been a joyous proclamation, an exotic statement of freedom amid the juggernaut of Imperial conformity. Now its aspect was bloody and furious, the mirror of the forgotten barbarian souls who etched it on stone, steel and hide.

Seven more warships emerged in the *Lance of Heaven*'s wake: the *Namaan, Khamanog, Bloodline, Celestian, Fate's Arrow, Umaal, Qo Ama* – all variants of the Legiones

Astartes battlecruiser, each heavily refitted, altered, patched-up, wounded, so much so that their original Martian classifications had ceased to deliver much meaningful information about their capabilities. The *Umaal* had once been the *Tenacious*, a Death Guard line-breaker. The *Celestian* had not changed name, but had belonged to a Word Bearers compliance formation. The white war-paint was thin on both those vessels, scraped over hulls that had once borne the liveries of different masters. The others had always been V Legion.

All seven ships stayed tight to the centrally placed *Lance of Heaven*, powering towards the Necklace at full tilt, their shields glittering. Escorts radiated out from the attack axis – destroyers, gun frigates, missile boats – eschewing protection for the punch of unleashed speed. Every movement was deliberate, taken at high velocity, mapped to deliver the most intense shock-hit of ordnance before a counter could be organised.

Four years ago, such tactics had reaped ruin on the Warmaster's advance. Accustomed only to the ragged assaults of Isstvan's hollowed-out dupes, the traitors had taken time to adjust to the Khan's more orchestrated counter-offensive. The Death Guard had suffered particularly badly, unable to match the voidmastery of the V Legion, but all of them – Fulgrim's chem-addicted sensation-seekers, Perturabo's obsessive engineers, Mortarion's grim foot-sloggers, even the Sons of Horus themselves – had taken their share of pain.

But that was four years ago. Every Legion was a living thing, gifted with commanders of infinite subtlety and tactical understanding. The Death Guard refined their fleet strategy, bringing to bear greater firepower against the Khan's wild riders. The Iron Warriors gave their fleet enough heavy physical anti-ship protection to turn their attackers into great lumps of plasma-laced slag. The Sons of Horus did what they always did, responding with such concentrated brutality and directed discipline that the two Legions, once close in understanding and sympathy, became blood-sworn in antipathy through accumulated atrocity.

The Emperor's Children had learned just as fast, and from their positions at Kalium they recognised the Chogorian deployment of the False Spear. They knew that the *Lance of Heaven* and its escorts were not as all-powerful as they appeared, and that the more ephemeral wings of destroyers and frigates had been loaded beyond design capacity. They knew that to meet the main charge with equal force would invite disaster, and that they had to respond to the full spectrum of the incoming flotilla – just as spread out, just as fast.

And so they did. The *Proudheart*, the battle-group's flagship, equal in displacement and heritage to the *Lance of Heaven*, emerged from the shadow of the Keystone with its cruiser-class escorts, the *Mortal Splendour*, *Excessive*, *Infinite Variety* and *Aquiline*. These heavy warships were outnumbered by the V Legion formation bearing down on them, but bolstered by the defensive emplacements on the Keystone and Necklace. Fixed cannon batteries opened up, spiralling glowing lines of armour-rending shells into the battlesphere. Threading through the spider's web of coruscation came the Emperor's Children escorts, each one prepared and engine-keyed for rapid-attack manoeuvres.

For the space of a human breath, the void between the two fleets remained intact – scored by projectile trails, as silent as the grave, bounded by movement, but pristine. Long-range guns opened fire, shield generator crews placed their last power feeds into immense promethium coils, bridge pilots made their final calculations of distance, heft, mass and velocity.

Then the gap closed.

Shells slammed into armour-plate, las-fire raked across the void, assault boats slammed into hull-lines, lance-beams fizzed home. Bulkheads smashed, plasma-conduits exploded, armourglass shattered, spine-ridges shook with impacts, transverse bracing dented. Vast blooms of fire lit up the void, punched through by more spears of iridescence. The flanks of the Keystone turned red, banishing the void's eternal shadow as the power of suns was kindled and let fly.

The ships became cauldrons of fire, ringed about by focal webs of destruction. Smaller vessels screamed around those nodes, hammering out their payloads. Mortal cries rang out, thousands-strong, unheard over the claustrophobic tumult within each vessel but relished in the deeper geometry of the immaterium beyond.

And so again the abyss witnessed the raging death of aeon-machines, as the finest of humanity set about, with the perfect efficiency they had ever been gifted with, destroying themselves in the fires of choler, ambition and vengeance.

CARIO ENTERED THE restraint cage of the boarding torpedo, placed his sword in its steel casing and felt shackles descend to press against his armour. The other four warriors of his unit were already in their places ahead of him, each one a dark profile against the subdued lumen-strips. Before the coffin-lid of the torpedo hissed closed, he noted the deployment of the *Suzerain*'s menials, their eyelids sewn shut and their movements governed by spatial cogitator stimuli. He watched the other torpedoes along the rack take on their payloads, and counted every one of his brothers as they took their places.

Most were like he was – still arrayed in the old armour of Chemos, their outlines much as they had been from the very start, sigils unaltered, blades straight, gold polished. Even among his brothers, though, the changes were beginning. A ceramite panel here, a helm-lens there, a frozen scream imprinted onto a vox-communication, a sheen of never-dry blood glossing a breastplate.

It would come. Their gene-father's mutation would spread like poison in a wound, and they would all become half-breeds, caught between the physical and the daemonic.

But not yet. Not while mortal perfection had yet to be achieved – the cleanest kill, the most perfect agony.

The coffin lid clamped shut, and Cario closed his eyes.

'For the beloved primarch,' he said softly, speaking by closed vox to the shadowy outlines within the boarding torpedo's chassis, as well as those in the other tubes. 'That we remain worthy of his immortal trust.'

From outside the torpedo, he heard the clangs of blast doors closing, followed by lifter hooks retracting. A boom and whine of escaping air was replaced by silence from beyond the confines of his armour – just the thud, thud of his hearts and the low pull of his breathing.

'In this thing, as in all things, be artful.'

The torpedo's interior went pitch-dark, and its chassis shivered as the rail took it clattering out to the launch mechanisms at the hull's edge.

'These are our savage cousins. Bleed them, just as in ages past we bled the dead to preserve the living.'

Cario felt the torpedo shift onto the ignition track, and braced himself for the sudden surge of speed. Just as he did so, he heard the old whisper again, dancing around the inside of his helm. The muscles of his left shoulder twitched, and he saw the flicker of an old image chase across his visual field – a horned creature, immense, seductive, beckoning him onwards, curling a long black tongue across fleshy lips of purest pink.

But not yet.

'So we remain now what we have ever been,' he said, banishing the spectres with a mental command. 'The true and only children of the Emperor.'

The torpedo's engines ignited, and the chassis exploded into straight-line speed. Cario was thrown back against the restraint cage and relaxed his body, letting his power armour take the strain. He felt the sudden shift in trajectory as the torpedo left the hull and plummeted down towards the battle-plane. It was jerked sideways violently by some huge detonation, then slewed hard back towards the attack run trajectory.

Data cascaded down his inner helm display, recording the progress of the entire brotherhood. He watched dispassionately as the torpedo bearing Brother

Ramarda's squad was taken out by heavy bolter-fire from a V Legion gunship, and equally dispassionately as the same gunship was flayed by a vicious salvo from the *Suzerain*'s close defence grid. He could trace the progress of the entire engagement through that data – the hulking cargo vessels attempting to pull clear to enter the warp, the two White Scars frigates harrying the incoming fleet, the nine ships of his own Legion closing in inexorably to prevent the convoy's escape.

Then the torpedo reached its target, and everything smeared into a juddering crash of static.

Cario was shunted forwards, rocking as the torpedo punctured through plates the width of a man's arm and careened onwards through a fusing mass of melting deck-plates.

Even before it had finished its grinding progress, Cario activated the release rune. Melta-blisters on the torpedo's outer flank ignited, burning a cocoon clear around it. The internal lumens switched on, and the shackles of the restraint cage snapped free. The coffin lid slammed back, ushering in a howling flood of heat laced with the smell of burning metal, and the Palatine Blades sprang from their transport.

Cario retrieved his sword, mouthed a word of blessing over the long steel edge, and rose from the torpedo's rocking corpse. His helm display instantly switched from the wide-angle assault range to an interior tactical readout, isolating the positions of his brothers and marking their ingress routes.

He shoved aside a burning spar and hauled his way clear of the torpedo's wreckage. Behind lay a long gouge in the bulk carrier's outer hull, terminated by a smouldering ring framing the naked void;

ahead was a contorted mass of broken struts and the flame-wreathed discharge of escaping oxygen.

The squad of Palatine Blades strode through it, cutting out with sword-edge where the path was blocked. They reached an intact transit passage with working void hatches, and closed the seals, cutting out the tempest. They met up then with a second five-man squad and started to run, their longswords crackling. The twin kill teams passed into the bulk carrier's sepulchral interior, watching the feedback energy-snarls from their disruptor fields flare up into the darkness above.

As he sprinted, Cario watched the support columns soar away, towering above container-stacks over five hundred metres high. They reached a lifter shaft that ran into the heights, still operative, but exposed. They ignored the turbo-platforms and clamped on to the inner drive-tracks, climbing them hand over hand. They ascended quickly, gaining the approaches to the bridge without firing a shot or using a blade.

Only towards the end, as they crested the shaft's summit and blasted through sealed environment barriers, did any sign of the recent carnage show itself. They went watchfully then, going stealthily from bulkhead to bulkhead, swords held ready. Cario remained at the forefront, the hairs on the back of his arms rising with anticipation. A long, wide chamber ran away from them, studded with branching portals every five metres. On either side, bodies lay in piles on the decking, heaped together carelessly under the rows of arches, their limbs bent double and their unseeing eyes gaping up towards the vaulted roof. The narrow lumens flickered, leaving deep shadows to fester in the perma-dark.

The Palatine Blades silently adopted a diamond formation, Cario at the leading tip, followed by the sub-prefector of the second squad, Avanarola. Haiman was next, followed by the rest, with the taciturn Urelias covering the rear. Their helm lenses sent pools of light rippling over the heaped corpses in the vaults, exposing motley expressions of terror, surprise, shock, nausea. The bulk carrier's crew had been slaughtered far beyond what was necessary to control the ship, then shoved out of the way like slabs of meat.

Cario studied the auspex scans ahead. At the end of the chamber, a stairway rose to meet a braced pair of doors bearing the rusted griffon emblem of the Memnos Combine. Beyond that was hard to gauge, but he detected heat sources and movement, and the trace signal of energy weapons.

Without breaking stride, he issued battle-signals to his brothers, and the diamond gave way to a double line. The first squad would hit the doors, destroying them and laying down penetrating fire. Those five would give way quickly as the return volleys came in, but their screening would allow the second rank to storm the chamber beyond, where they could deploy their true strength – the charnabal sabre, aristocrat of blades.

Cario paused at the foot of the stairway, bolt pistol in one hand, ready to give the command. Just as he was about to act, his eye was caught by a face in the shadows to his right. He turned his head a fraction and saw a mortal woman's body atop a corpse-pile. She had been killed by a blunt blow, leaving most of her features intact.

A spark of unease suddenly struck him.

'Fall ba–' he managed to say, before the chamber exploded in bolter-fire.

Cario threw himself to the deck, feeling the hard thump of rounds against his armour. He scrabbled forwards, staying low, firing blind with his bolt pistol.

His brothers were all doing the same thing, scattering out from the centre of the chamber, trying to find cover, returning fire as best they could. Raffel was not moving, his body riddled with bolter impact craters, and several others registered hits.

Cario broke for the stairway, trying to orientate himself. They needed to get out of the chamber's open ground and fight their way towards the vaults where the bodies lay in their heaps, but that was impossible – the bolter-fire was *coming* from the corpses.

He reached the lowest steps, twisted around and wedged himself up against the nearside railing, firing steadily. All around him, stonework smashed and buckled, throwing a screen of dust into the gloom of the chamber.

White Scars were emerging now, pushing aside the corpses they had hidden under, their armour streaked with gore-sheen, their bolters pumping. Another of Cario's squad went down, pulverised by the weight of incoming fire.

But the shock had faded. Cario's squad fought back, keeping their discipline. Their armour absorbed the bulk of the hits, just as it had been designed to, giving them precious seconds to fight their way towards cover. He pushed clear of the stairway again, weaving out of the path of more shells, picking out a blood-armoured White Scars legionary amid the wheeling shadows.

There were nine of them in total. Even with two

of his own squad down, those were odds he could live with.

You do not know who you are taking on, he thought, closing into blade range.

The warrior he advanced upon fell back, switching to his own curved sword. Cario hit him on the downward sweep, letting the weight of the sabre carry it into contact. The two blades snarled together, dragging a line of sparks down the cutting edge. His enemy responded well, moving quickly, letting the impact subside. They traded more blows, their swords whirling, clanging on the strikes and flexing away.

It took five strikes for Cario to gain the measure of the legionary. He feinted left, just a fraction, playing on his opponent's marginal pull the other way, waited for the conscious correction, spun out of the contact and lunged point-forward.

The tip of his sabre blazed as it slid under the breastplate, delving into his enemy's stomach and slicing clean through tissue. The warrior staggered, trying to keep his footing, but by then Cario had already withdrawn the blade, hauled it round and whipped it across, decapitating the warrior and sending his helm bouncing bloodily across the deck.

He was about to launch into the melee further down the chamber when the doors at the top of the stairway juddered open and a figure in steel-grey plate bearing a disruptor-shrouded combat glaive powered through the gap. This one's movements were different – jerkier, with machine-heavy strength behind them.

Recognising the master of those he fought, Cario saluted in the old fashion, a swift lowering of the blade before guard was taken once more.

'Brave, to remain in safety while your warriors die,' he said.

His enemy lumbered into close range, swinging for the strike. All across the long chamber bolt-rounds continued to snap and boom, punctuated by the rasp and ring of blades in contact.

'You come too late,' the glaive-wielder said, his voice heavily accented with strange rhythms across the Gothic words. 'These ships will soon be in the warp.'

Cario made his final assessment, drinking in information from the way his opponent carried himself, the tenor of his speech, the hundred subtle signs that gave away strength and weakness.

'Then let us not waste the chance,' he said, grinning under his helm-mask. 'Show me what I came here to best.'

FOUR

EIDOLON WATCHED THE ships burn and die, though not with the eyes he had once owned. He saw the world in richer colours now, and savoured its agony through a more delicate sensibility. His armour did nothing to impede that – the things the fleshweavers had done to its ancient mechanisms amplified the flood of sensoria, channelling it, filtering out the ephemera and leaving only the core of it to relish.

He stood on the cusp of his teleportation chamber, unwilling to enter the energy-lashed precincts while the observation portals let him witness the truth of what was happening across the Kalium Gate.

Fifty kilometres away – a mere speck in the geometry of naval warfare – a White Scars destroyer plunged towards the Keystone, its back broken and its flanks aflame. Gunships harried it, ripping up what scant physical plate remained along its hide. The destroyer kept firing all the while, maintaining

the barrage while its structure melted and shimmered into atoms.

Eidolon could feel the terror coming from that ship.
He could smell the raw fear bleeding out of it, sweated
from the pores of the gun-crew menials and the mortal bridge officers as they did their duty. He mentally
placed himself in their position, under those collapsed
decks, crushed and maimed, the air escaping through
a lattice of shell-ripped gashes.

It made his breath quicken.

I wish it were me, he thought. *I wish all these things
were mine.*

All around him, his brothers were arrayed for
battle. They wore the same armour – what would
once have been Mark IV plate, limned with Legion
gold, but which now defied all description. Their
gorgets and upper torsos were grotesquely large,
linked by snaking cables to amplifier clusters lodged
amid overlapping sheets of richly decorated ceramite
plate. Each warrior carried the same weapon-type –
exemplars of the Kakophoni, massive organ guns
with bloated echo chambers and psychosonic reso-
nators. Even now, the guns hummed with a deep,
deck-shaking harmonic, making loose matter around
them jump and tremble.

The sonic cults had been the creations of Mar-
ius Vairosean in the beginning, but had now spread
throughout the entire Legion, growing in popularity
as their ruinous gifts became more clearly apparent.
Eidolon himself, who had embraced the mutations
more completely than any other since his resurrection, bore a thunder hammer in his heavy gauntlets,
its snarled head flooded with arcane psychic matter.

It cast a sick green sheen across the iron of the chamber's outer gates, strobing in rhythm with the beat of the idling organ guns.

Still he waited. Beyond, in the void over Kalium, more ships were torn apart and their inhabitants cast into the vacuum. He watched the foremost White Scars run the gauntlet of fire, and saw what it cost them. He saw the ever-loyal Konenos break from the cover of the Necklace's shadow and enter the dance of ruin. He watched torpedoes scatter like broken glass amid the whirlwind, and knew that every one of them carried a cargo of living warriors.

He closed his aching eyes, and listened to the sounds. Void or no, they still came to him, ushered across the aether by daemon-whisperers.

–old the line! Hold the line! Keep up that– By the Emperor! Nadir! More pow–

–ty-five points about. Release secondary barrage. Watch for counter-strikes from–

–nnot take this for much longer, lord. The shell will break, the prometh–

–o! No! Not yet! What is it? What devils are the–

They were woven like threads, those voices in the depths, each one animated by lusts and desires that were chaff on the face of the immaterium. Soon those speakers would be submerged back within its great tide, no more than fodder for the intelligences that hungrily swam there.

'*Lord,*' came Von Kalda's voice over the comm.

Eidolon already knew what his equerry would say, but let the creature speak. 'Yes?'

'*They will break the cordon,*' Von Kalda reported, reluctantly. '*They are losing ships, many ships, but we cannot prevent them landing. The Keystone is reinforced, but if he is among them…'*

Eidolon recognised the faintest catch in his equerry's voice, and marked him then for sanction. A primarch was a primarch; they were fallible, they had been killed.

'Peace. I will translate,' Eidolon told him, marching at last through the iron gates and into the heart of the teleportation chamber. As he took his place, the Kakophoni around him saluted, their movements already slurred from combat-stimms, their helm lenses swimming like burnished mother-of-pearl. 'What do you fear, Von Kalda? Destruction?'

'We lose troops here, my commander,' Von Kalda replied. *'We know they cannot use the Gate. Should we not let them–'*

'Every one of them we kill here strips Terra of another defender,' replied Eidolon, sensing the build-up of aetheric power in the chamber. Snarls of cold lightning flickered up the columns around him, distorting real space. 'And besides, you omit the crucial point.'

The air shivered, tensing for the explosion that would turn reality inside out and thrust a living spear of the warp into the realm of the senses. Eidolon hefted his thunder hammer, anticipating the temporary release of translation – the fleeting respite from the living agony of his existence.

'Which is?' Von Kalda asked, his voice growing faint as the teleport charge built to the apex.

Eidolon smiled. 'That we *live* for this.'

Then the chamber filled with light, the sensations snuffed out, and the Kakophoni were sent across worlds and minds and into the howling heart of battle.

✠ ✠ ✠

SHIBAN CRASHED THE guan dao down, relying on its weight to smash the sword clear. His opponent parried expertly, heedless of the disruptor sparks showering over his armour. All around them, spread out along the chamber's shadowed edges, the fighting continued, now brutal and close-range. Beneath their boots, the *Terce Falion's* engines were whining to full pitch.

His enemy was powerful. Skilled with the blade, orthodox as all sons of Chemos were, but intelligent with it. Their weapons clashed again, yielding no advantage. They spun apart, moving warily, each looking hard for the chink in an otherwise perfect defence.

'What is *wrong* with you?' asked his enemy, glancing at his angular limbs, his awkward armour-plate.

Shiban said nothing, keeping his mind focused. He slashed out, adding venom to the gesture, aiming to take the swordsman at the neck. The Emperor's Children champion retreated, evading the strike, returning quickly to bring his sabre to bear.

'You move like a machine,' his enemy said, dancing back into range with a flurry of strokes. 'I have killed many of your kind, and they fought more like humans.'

'We have all been changed,' Shiban grunted, starting to admire the doggedness in his enemy. This one was a step above the other legionaries he had killed – a master of his chosen weapon, an artist.

'All of us, aye.'

They crashed together again, taking strikes on their armour as the guan dao and sabre ricocheted from one another.

Shiban punched out with the heel of his staff, missing the target by a hair's width. Then he had to defend, keeping out the sabre's edge only marginally. He took a step back, creating space, making use of the motive power his augmentations gave him.

I, too, used to fight with art. I, too, used to make it beautiful.

'You are not in sickness,' Shiban observed, the words slipping from his lips almost unbidden.

In sickness. That was what the ordu had come to call the multifarious mutations and self-mutilations practised by the Traitor Legions. So many were now more beast than man, their genhanced bodies wracked and tortured, a willing hell of constant invention.

His enemy laughed – a cruel sound. 'Like my brothers, you mean? No, not yet. It will come.'

Shiban continued the retreat, letting his enemy come after him. From the corner of his eye, he saw his warriors doing the same, just as they had discussed, giving up ground towards the command bridge.

Below them all, the engine whine grew in volume.

'I will never understand it,' Shiban said.

A snort came from his enemy's face mask. The sword blurred around his armour-profile like a silver gauze. The blades hit again: *clang, clang, clang.*

'What can you not understand, savage? That we should wish for something greater? You were offered the gift, and you were too simple to see it. You fight for something already gone – all you have before you is limitation.' The weapons spun around one another, weaving, darting, hammering. 'For us, though... For *us*, limitation has ceased to be a factor.'

Shiban reach the foot of the stairway. He felt the strain in the muscles he still retained. Sweat ran down the inner lip of his gorget. His enemy was faster, stronger, more subtle and he worked the sabre as if it weighed nothing.

I would have been faster, before. I would have been stronger.

The surviving White Scars fell back further, retreating up the stairway, step by step. The Emperor's Children pursued them, all fighting as perfectly as their master. Stone smashed around them, flung from the balustrades by stray strikes. The engine whine throbbed into a grinding wall of sound, flooding up from the deeps.

'So why did you not seize the chance?' his enemy asked, sounding genuinely curious. 'You could not have loved Terra, not like Dorn's drones. You really had a choice.'

Shiban started to breathe hard. The glaive felt heavy in his hands, like a bar of lead. He was taking hits now – peripheral ones, chipping away at the margins of his defence. 'I made my oath.'

The laugh again. 'Your oath! I make an oath with every breath.'

The portal to the bridge beckoned now – a wide arch, crested with the Memnos griffon. Beyond that was the gantry, the bloody servitor pits, the corpse of the shipmaster in her own throne. Shiban saw Jochi fighting hard, now at his shoulder, just as they had been in the canyons on Chondax. There, too, they had been overmatched.

'You make no oaths,' Shiban rasped, working hard as the sabre whipped in. He was dimly aware of the roof opening out above him, soaring up towards the crystalflex dome of stars. He heard a muffled cry of pain – one of his brotherhood, succumbing to the enemy, another soul lost. 'Not like we do.'

A hiss of irritation came from his enemy, who pressed closer, scenting the end. Their weapons locked again, buzzing with feral energy fields.

'Yes, yes, you are finer than we,' said the Traitor, caustically. 'We have done what we did because we are weak and vain, and only in you, the doomed defenders of this rotten Throne, is there virtue.'

They swayed across the gantry, fighting all the time, ceramite flakes now flying in circles around them.

'Your words,' grunted Shiban, working hard not get his throat cut out.

'*Your* arrogance,' blurted his enemy, stepping up the assault into a new pitch of cold fury. 'My master now walks with gods. You have been lied to, and you know it, and still cleave only to ignorance.'

The charnabal blade shivered down the glaive's shaft, grating up against the weapon's shoulder. Shiban staggered, nearly going down. He was then forced to parry – a crossways brace across his throat as the sword whistled in again.

'Then why not take your new god's gifts?' Shiban spat out, falling back again. 'What are you scared of?'

His enemy snapped his blade down, pinning the guan dao into Shiban's guard. Their helm-masks were a hand's breadth apart, underlit by seething disruptor excess.

'I will take them, and with both hands, when the hour comes,' the Emperor's Children champion said, his voice savagely earnest. 'Until then, speak not of things you do not understand.'

'We know what it is to change,' Shiban said.

'You know what it is to die.'

'True enough. But not this day.'

At that, the engine whine reached its full pitch, making the walls of the bridge shake. Shiban heaved with his arms, throwing his enemy back by a single pace. The Emperor's Children legionary reacted instantly, bringing the point of his sword into range, poising to strike into the heart of Shiban's off-balance defence.

But the blow never came. The crystalflex dome above them shattered, showering a cascade of glittering shards across the entire bridge expanse. The air-bubble within burst outwards, thrusting into the void and taking the corpses of the old crew spinning with it.

The White Scars, prepared for the move, let the tempest carry them. The Emperor's Children, acting on instinct, activated the grav-locks on their boots, keeping them clamped to the vibrating deck. The two duelling forces were separated, cast asunder by the racing atmosphere.

Above them all, hovering over the jagged edges of the broken dome, hung a V Legion Stormbird, its twin-linked bolters pumping out more shells into the ruined bridge-space.

Shiban twisted his body, reaching out for the open crew bay, his fingers clamping on to the edge. He pulled himself to safety, as did Jochi and two others – all who had made it out. When he next glanced down, for a moment he saw nothing but a swirl of bloody corpses, bumping into dislodged debris from the command levels, all of it blown out into the void as the atmosphere streamed into the abyss.

Then he saw the swordsman, braced against the command throne, staring up at him.

'White Scar!' the champion shouted over the maelstrom,

disgust evident across the open vox-signal. *'I had heard tales of your bravery.'*

Shiban said nothing, but dragged himself inside. The Stormbird pulled clear of the disintegrating bridge, back into the heart of the void-war beyond.

'How many of the convoy are taken?' he asked the pilot, clamping his glaive wearily to the wall-mounted rack.

'All are now in the hands of the enemy,' came the emotionless reply.

Shiban nodded. Across the far side of the crew bay, Jochi leaned against the inner wall, breathing heavily through a damaged vox-grille.

'Signal all units to withdraw to the frigates. We make for the void.'

He considered moving back to get a final glimpse of the warrior who had bested him so easily. He might have been tempted to salute, or offer some word of defiance.

Not now. I am sick to my soul.

'Enough, then,' he snarled, hitting the controls to raise the ramp. 'Power the engines. Get us out of here.'

PERTURABO HAD DESTROYED the Keystone's impregnability forever, but the defences subsequently installed by the Emperor's Children remained formidable. Chain-linked cannons spat out from radial spans placed across the face of the docking levels, clogging local space with interlaced lines of las-fire, which joined the glowing trails of ship-hunting missiles.

The V Legion had sent their void craft diving and angling through the hail of projectiles. The interceptors came in first, staggered waves of them raking gun-placements as they swooped and tilted. The pilots hugged the curving flanks of the Keystone's armoured walls insanely tightly, screaming across adamantium plates while letting loose with their rotary launchers. Soon the outer shell was aflame, crackling out into the vacuum as gunnery magazines ignited and fuel-lines were kindled.

After the softener runs came the heavy gunships, each one carrying a cargo of infantry. Thunder-hawks, Stormbirds and Fire Raptors thrust through the defensive cordons, their bolters hammering and down-thrusters flaring. Many were destroyed, smashed apart by shells launched from the static positions, but dozens more got through, blasting their way under the shadow of the great ship-docks.

Once past the portals, the Fire Raptors unlocked their own close-range armoury, and the enemy posi-tions were momentarily lost behind rippling waves of neon-white. Thunderhawks powered through the whirling debris, sinking down across the colossal docking-plates to unload breacher squads. Stormbirds, with heavier armour and heavier payloads, pushed on further still, absorbing concentrated fire to reach their deployment points. Transporters set down behind the beachheads, disgorging assault tanks, troop carriers and mobile gun platforms.

Bolstered by the building torrent of fixed ordnance, fast-attack squads of White Scars legionaries raced out from their embarkation points, charging through the juddering rain of defensive fire. They broke the first bulwark circles, storming gun-pits and pushing onwards, clearing room for more squads to move up and contribute to the onslaught. More heavy guns were swung down from the gaping holds of the hovering transporters, and the rain of artillery from deeper inside the void port was answered by punishing fire from the attackers. Every strike was fast, hard, relentless, coordinated – just as the Legion had always enjoyed, albeit now tempered by years in the crucible of grinding civil war.

Docks Four and Five, the outermost tendrils of iron reaching out into the abyss, were swiftly taken, their berthing-zones overrun and strongpoints established. Dock Three was soon severely contested, though savage resistance from dug-in Emperor's Children legionaries halted the advance. Fighting soon spread to the refit yards equipped for void-going behemoths, lighting up the towering grav-cranes and railheads. Immense flying gantries and lifter-coils were lit by the flash and flare of munitions, then obscured by the roiling palls of smoke coiling up through the docks' atmosphere-bubble.

As the Emperor's Children deployed extra forces to Dock Five, opening up a second front along the right flank of the White Scars' advance, the wild riders of the V Legion launched their planned second-wave assault – squads of grav-speeders and jetbikes, held in reserve during the initial impact and now let loose. The speeders shrieked out across the burning quays, streaking past advancing infantry and breaking deep into the maw of darkness beyond. More heavy transports braved the halo of anti-ship fire to reinforce the growing beachhead. Land Raiders were dropped from the caged hulls of Thunderhawk transporters, hitting the deck-plates heavily before trundling forwards, their lascannons spitting beams deep into the heart of the enemy lines. Sicaran battle tanks thundered to attack speed, rocking wildly as they smashed through the smoking ruins of static defences. Ever more attack speeders were dropped into position and shot off immediately, swerving and skidding through the oncoming barrage.

Soon the fighting reached the Inner Dock Gates, six aquila-crowned maws, gothic-arched, each one large enough to take an escort-class void ship deep within the precincts of the Keystone's innards. They were all burning now, their soaring pillars cracked and their outer blast bulwarks underlit red by repeated mortar-strikes. As the V Legion closed in on their target, the full weight of the installed infantry defence was loosed against them – Emperor's Children Tactical squads, reinforced by mortal battalions taken from Traitor Army regiments, supported by their own hastily landed tank groups and armoured walkers. Lapis-crowned Devastator squads took up vantage points on either side of the Gates and swiftly turned them into scrap-choked kill zones. Battle-hardened III Legion infantry groups crunched their way into close contact with the advance units of the brotherhoods, and a front of hand-to-hand combat broke out under the very shadow of the looming portals. Amid the whine and boom of the artillery barrage, the older weapons of blade and bolter reaped their toll in a vicious, eternal symmetry of murder.

The V Legion gained the most traction here, pushing towards the entrance halls into the Keystone itself, seizing gun-point after gun-point and turning the cannons against the defenders set further back. Phalanxes of Land Raiders thundered down the centre of the

battlefield, crunching over the corpses of the vanquished and running down those fleeing the vortex
of slaughter. In their wake, ever more infantry poured
into the breaches, searing with flame what had not
already been obliterated by lascannon fire. Assault
squads soared across the smouldering killing planes,
their jump packs whining on a shimmering heat-haze,
before the warriors slammed to earth, lashing out with
chainsword and bolt pistol.

And yet, just as the vanguard looked to gain the first
of the Inner Dock Gates, hoarfrost spears slammed
down, riven from the skin of reality and twisted
into the physical forms of lightning and stormwind.
Deck-plates were pulverised. Radial shock waves
boomed across the battlefield, hurling warriors from
their feet and sending armoured walkers staggering. Forks of snaking aether-residue blazed out and
green-edged clouds of plasma bloomed against the
fires.

Purple-and-gold warriors strode from the heart of
the unnatural storm, moving purposefully and without haste, slowly fanning out, making no attempt to
avoid the ranks of armour grinding their way to their
positions.

The newcomers bore the ancient livery of Chemos,
though in more ornate patterns than their Tactical brethren, and their plate shimmered from the
retch-inducing stink of the warp. Each warrior held a
pendulous organ gun shackled by linked chains and
glistening cables. As one, the baroque mutants of the
Kakophoni reached their allotted positions, lowered
the muzzle of their devices, picked their targets and
fired.

What emerged did not deserve the name *sound*.

There were no words in the tongues of mortal men adequate to describe what could now be unleashed by Fulgrim's disciples, for the instruments of hyper-sensation created more than just auditory hell. Acting in concert, massed sonic blasts smeared across the artificial atmosphere of the void port in reality-distorting waves of molecular annihilation. The advancing V Legion outrider squads were thrown back, flung clear of the exploding cover all around them. Troops too close were obliterated instantly, disappearing in spiralling whirls of blood and armour-flecks. Landing plates cracked, tilting crazily as grav compensators whined, straining to fight the terrifying forces raging across them.

Advancing armour formations shuddered to a halt, lodging amid what shelter remained and launching everything they had at the Kakophoni spearhead. Second-wave Tactical squads advanced behind the uncertain tank cover, their helms automatically dampening the mutilating levels of distortion washing over the battlefield. Even that was not enough when the sonic weapons scored direct hits, in which case power armour was ripped clean apart, warriors stunned into a bloody coma even as their helm lenses imploded and internal organs ruptured.

The Emperor's Children Assault squads launched a counter-attack, protected by the voracious screen of psychosonics radiating out before them. The White Scars were driven back, losing numbers across ground only newly won, their advance blunted by the hell-shock of such unnatural weaponry. More aether-spears smacked into the ruptured rockcrete and adamantium, each one smashing itself apart to reveal a fresh wave of elite warriors.

From the greatest rift of all strode the glittering outline of the Soul-Severed, his armour blazing with after-light from the realm immaterial, his thunder hammer shimmering, his golden helm a miasma of dancing illumination.

Lord Commander Eidolon, the proudest of his proud breed, turned his pitiless helm across the ruined detritus of the tank advance, opened his agonised throat and *screamed*.

The devastation surpassed anything unleashed by his brothers. Reality split open, seared from its foundations by the release of physics-defying warp harmonics. Eidolon had grown since his resurrection, his might augmented to match his ancient arrogance. The brutal shock wave tore out, driving a path of annihilation through whatever stood in its way, bisecting the hulls of stranded tanks, cracking armour, smashing skulls and bursting blood vessels. The entire deck level reeled, casting warriors from their feet and causing grav-speeders to plough into the plunging metal. Palls of smoke swelled up from the carnage, underlit with racing fires and shredded by follow-up blasts.

The assault might have foundered then. Faced with such elemental ruin, the beachhead might have crumbled into nothing, hammered back to the ingress points and hurled into the burning void beyond. However, the forward push had won the V Legion enough time to bring *Lance of Heaven* within teleportation range. Even as Eidolon laid waste to the docks, the immense profile of the battleship loomed up from the fires beyond, its gunnery banks thundering against the swarm of enemy craft about it, its prow yet bearing the white and gold.

More shafts of other-light coiled and spat, this time amid the ranks of the beleaguered White Scars. Columns of pure aether-essence roared into existence, each one silhouetting the form of a warrior within. These were greater in stature than any yet, standing tall in pearl-white armour embellished with swirls of gold and red. One by one, they took their place, wielding power glaives whose hooked blades of purest silver burned with electric-blue light. Their ivory plate gleamed in defiance of the blood and muck around them, and was adorned with the tribal marks of Lost Chogoris and decorated with fluttering prayer-scrolls.

As they emerged from their cocoons of fire, the massed legionaries of the ordu thrust their tulwars into the burning atmosphere – a glittering sea of steel.

'*Khagan!*' they roared. '*Ordu gamana Jaghatai!*'

The greatest of the new arrivals, resplendent in his ornate, gold-chased dragon-helm, said nothing, but angled his fire-wreathed blade into the heart of the maelstrom. About him materialised the *zadyin arga* of the horde, those whom the Imperium had named Stormseers, the bringers of the tempest. They hoisted their skull-staves against the tumult, and the sound-tortured storm was rent asunder as the two cataclysms slammed into one another. Amid those ranks of bone-white psykers marched one who was set apart, whose armour was crimson and whose gauntlets ran with black-edged flame. About him the tearing winds blew strongest, and when he lifted his arms to contest the sound-madness, the explosion of countervailing warp-mastery levelled the terrain for fifty metres.

With his final strength gathered, the dragon-helm finally spoke. Even as the hurricane of noise poured across the battlefield, his voice pierced the cacophony, as sharp and clear as the sapphire skies of the Altak.

'You have sight of the enemy,' he said, breaking into the heavy charge that would carry him to the lord commander. 'His neck is bared – now *sever it*.'

FIVE

CARIO REMAINED MOTIONLESS, frozen with cold fury. Shards of armourglass tumbled around him, bouncing and skittering amid the tempest of the Stormbird's passing.

Eventually one of his squad managed to locate the bridge's atmospheric seals. The raging storm of oxygen cut out, leaving nothing but vacuum in its place. The last of the body parts and cogitator housings thudded, silently, back to the deck.

He slowly let his sword arm relax. Haiman walked over to him. The warrior looked as if he had barely taken a scratch, which was more or less how he looked after every contest. 'I expected more of them,' he voxed over the internal channel.

Cario drew in a long breath, then nodded. He stirred himself, sheathing his sabre. 'Aye,' he agreed. 'Why go to the trouble of taking these ships, if not to keep them?'

He walked over to the few auspex lenses that still functioned, arranged at the edge of the command throne platform. Tactical displays were still flickering across the dark screens, picking out the trail of the bulk carriers amid a swirl of war vessels. The general pattern was evident enough – the White Scars, heavily outnumbered and outfought, were pulling back to their frigates and making for the Mandeville point. They had lost swathes of gunships in the withdrawal, but both warships had managed to stay intact.

It was only as Cario watched the points of light slide across the crystal that the first twinge of unease struck him.

'These haulers were powering for warp jump,' he murmured, remembering his opponent's words.

Haiman nodded. 'I sent Vorainn to deactivate the sequence.'

The beat of the engines had been growing in volume ever since they had arrived on the bulk carrier. Towards the end, it had sounded like no preparatory sequence he had ever heard. Now, in the vacuum, it was impossible to gauge if it had kept on rising.

Why go to the trouble of taking these ships…

He turned on his heel, staring back up through the broken jaws of the observation dome. The vast hulls of the other bulk carriers were still visible, barely touched by the extreme violence unleashed about them. The Emperor's Children were on every bridge. The battles to reach them had been swift.

…if not to keep them?

Cario started moving. Six members of the boarding party still lived. 'All with me,' he commanded. 'Contact Vorainn. Get him back up here.'

The squad followed immediately, and they began to move swiftly back the way they had come. As they passed through the atmosphere seals at the rear of the bridge and back into the pressurised zones, the whine of the engines surged back into hearing. It was deafening, and throttled, like a mad beast caged in the depths and raging for release.

'Priority signal, all kill squads – withdraw! Withdraw to the void.'

He started to run. As he did so, Vorainn emerged from one of the many side chambers and joined them in the sprint.

'How long?' asked Cario.

'Seconds,' replied Vorainn, calmly.

Cario cursed. They were a long way from the hangars, and in any case the White Scars would not have left their boarding craft waiting there to be taken – they would have been either retrieved already or destroyed. He ran harder, picturing the path he had taken to get to the bridge, recalling every aspect of it.

There would be saviour pods. Close by, for the bridge crew.

As he went, the floor shuddered. The noise of the engines transmuted from a throaty grind into something akin to a shriek, resounding from the high chamber ceiling.

Cario reached an intersection with a transverse corridor – one leading right along the path he had taken to reach the bridge, the other leading left into unknown regions.

He went left. As he did so, the first explosion went off, smashing the walls in behind them. Urelias was caught in the blast and crushed between two colliding wall sections. The rest of them picked up speed, racing along the imploding corridors as flames spurted from between blown-clear panels.

Echoing booms rang out, overlapping with one another. Cario had an uncomfortable image of all those munitions nestled deep in the holds.

'Saviour pod arrays,' reported Vorainn.

As soon as the words left his lips, the ceiling above him collapsed, smashed downwards by a bloom of fiery plasma. He and three others were lost in the wreckage, sent plunging down into the ship's depths as the floor dissolved into burning flotsam.

Cario and Haiman, alone now, could only attempt to out-sprint the engulfing carnage, racing to stay ahead of the rolling tide of destruction. Beams snapped and bent, hazy amid the shake of extreme heat. The inferno surged after them, snapping at their heels.

They broke into a narrow chamber marked by a long row of capsules embedded in the far wall. Most were smashed, either by the explosions taking place all round them, or perhaps by those who had primed the engines to cycle so wildly out of control.

Cario and Haiman sped along the row, scanning for intact units. By the time they reached the end of the series, it was clear what remained – a single one-man pod, already burnished with the first flickers of flame. In a few seconds, as the ship entered the last stages of meltdown, it too would be gone.

Cario snatched a quick look at his fellow warrior.

Haiman drew his sword and placed it in the fraternity's salute position. 'Children of the Emperor,' he said, dryly.

Cario returned the salute. 'Death to His foes.'

Then he was scrambling through the pod's airlock and activating the docking clamps. From the outside, even as the bulk carrier's environment was turning into liquid fire, Haiman worked to prime the release locks manually, ensuring a clean escape for his prefector.

Cario pulled the restraint chains about him, activated the blast sequence and sent the launch command.

The pod's engines kicked into life, flooding the chamber behind him with plasma. Cario thought, for a microsecond, that he heard Haiman's cries of agony, before the hull-plate doors slammed open and the pod was hurled into the void.

The speed was crushing, as fast as a boarding torpedo but less controlled. For a few seconds, Cario was completely disorientated as the tiny ball of adamantium flew crazily into the abyss. Through the circular real-view portal he had fleeting impressions of huge fires wheeling the void, broken by the silhouettes of broken warships.

Slowly, he brought the spin under control, using the pod's scarcely functional thruster array. He took a deep breath, trying to get his bearings. A vast wall of rust-red metal ran away from him, rapidly shrinking as the pod powered clear of its old housings. He saw the icons of the Memnos Combine and the marks of old Imperial shipping lane guilds, all punctured by pinpoints of leaking plasma.

Then the *Terce Falion* exploded.

The impact was immediate – a rolling wave of immolated metal racing out from the epicentre, blocking out all else in a vortex of spinning debris. Cario had time to brace himself against the restraint cage before the bow-wave smashed into the pod, sending it careening again, buffeted between searing plumes of superheated gases.

Though Cario could not have known it, every bulk carrier in the convoy had been rigged to explode at the same moment, turning the entire train of massive vessels into miniature suns. Space itself seemed to ignite, to rage, to transmute into a burgeoning storm of heat and light and tearing speed. All he could see through the wheeling real-viewer were tumbling masses of red and orange. The cargo ships had been enormous, far bigger even than the mightiest Legion battleships, and their death-throes were like the ending of worlds.

By the time the worst of the tumult had blown itself out, Cario's pod had been hurled far from the core of the battlesphere, its viewers cracked and its thrusters burned out. Though its heavy plating had absorbed the worst of the shock waves, warning runes were already flickering along the inside of the narrow chamber, picking out the many ways in which the structure had been compromised.

'*Suzerain*,' he voxed, wondering if the ship still lived.

For a while, nothing but hissing answered the comm-burst. Then, after several more attempts, the link crackled open.

'*We have your position, prefector*,' came Harkian's voice.

Cario let his head sink heavily back against the metal collar of the inner cage. 'Status. What of the frigates?'

'*One destroyed. The other damaged.*'

Cario smiled coldly. He knew, *knew*, that the steel-armoured warrior would have made it back to the surviving one. 'What was its ident?'

'*The* Kaljian, *lord.*'

'Did we retain any of the haulers?'

'*Negative. Three ships lost in the explosions. Casualty figures are still being–*'

'*Kaljian.* Record the name, and tell every scryer we have to cast for its marker in the aether. Let it be known that there is a debt of honour to all fraternities that will only be satisfied by its destruction. Summon the Apothecaries and tell them to devise agonies.'

There was a hesitation at the other end. '*It will be done, lord.*'

'I will see him again!' Cario cried out loud, though no longer speaking to Harkian. The saviour pod rotated onwards, carried by momentum.

He was intact. His blade was intact.

The enemy had been bested, but not yet killed. That could not be allowed to remain the case – all things had to be made complete before he could give in to the whispers of the Legion's destiny.

He half saw the many-horned vision of his dreams then, stronger now, lascivious, confident. It would be strengthened by this, using every setback to make the case for sublimity.

Cario closed his eyes. He entered the combat-meditation designed to drain his anger and restore the cool command of the duellist. He rehearsed what he had done, and where he had erred, and determined to learn from it, to become more incisive, more controlled, ever more perfect.

The pod rolled further out, spinning like a shell-case into the violent abyss.

'I will see him again,' Cario said, knowing it to be true.

✠ ✠ ✠

SENSATION.

Sensation.

The rush, the swell, the gorge, the joy, the *infinity* of it.

There were no words, no images, no possibility of explaining the fullness – all there was was to *live* it, to let the flood rush into your veins and fill them with the fire that was pain and joy and forgetting.

The pain never left. It ramped up, it became excruciating, so much so that his screams were real screams, let fly from shredded lips and birthed in bloody vocal cords. But that mattered not, for pain was what reminded him that he lived still, and the numb cold of the hereafter had been spited for another lifetime. Every breath he drew was testament to that – it vindicated him, made him greater, fuelled the hell-furnace that had been lit in his engorged, straining hearts.

Eidolon waded into battle. Every sweep of the thunder hammer, every explosion as the metal head struck and slew, every recoil from the heavy shaft as it broke bone and armour; it all redounded into the melange of raw experience.

And he wanted more.

More.

He crashed onwards, his vision a blur of colour, made jagged and hyper-exposed by the extreme inputs assailing his ravaged armour-senses. He could feel his mortal body operating far beyond its original genhanced tolerances. Fabius' stimms were raging through his system now. They would one day kill him, if the enemy failed to, but he loved what they did to him all the same.

This was the reward. The many thousand agonies of

his new existence found their prize in these moments. Fulgrim had been no fool. He had been neither weak nor deluded. He had seen it before any of them had – the horizon of experience, extending far beyond what the lies of Unity had prepared them for. *This* was what humanity had been created to unlock – to remake itself, to grow, to take up the mantle of something better. If the darker fates were cruel, they were also the altars of creation, turning receptacles of poor flesh into vehicles for new and dynamic deities.

We are not degrading, Eidolon thought as the hammer-head whirled, ripping through the blown chest of a reeling White Scars legionary. *This is the perfection we were always denied.*

Blood splashed across his helm-lens, casting the world into filmy crimson. He could smell it in his flared nostrils – rich with hyper adrenaline, thick with nutrients, the matter of the False Emperor's biotechnological genius.

We are improving this. Eidolon laughed out loud, and the sound was enough to shatter glass and dent lead. *We are improving* this!

He lurched onwards, grinning wide, overcome with the tide of emotion. Once unleashed, myriad sensory possibilities engulfed almost all else, and he had to fight to retain his grasp on the here and now.

The wall of noise was ripping apart, torn like a great curtain. Something was opposing the Kakophonic Aura, blunting its edges and pushing it back.

Eidolon blinked hard, forcing himself to regain self-mastery. He saw Terminator-plated warriors advancing towards him, flanked by warp-weavers in bone-pale armour. He saw wild energies coursing through the blood vessels of those ones, glowing like phosphor in the dark.

They are mighty, he noted, reminding himself not to be surprised. The White Scars' shamans were powerful – like the rune-readers of Fenris, only more honest.

'*Go back!*' he screamed, and the world blazed from the glory of his death-shriek.

And yet still they came on, weathering the hurricane of destruction that the psychosonic blast caused, leaning into it, shrouded in the arts of their strange magic and the physical majesty of their war-plate.

The greatest of those fighters wore a gold-crested dragon-helm, which to Eidolon's swimming vision looked alive, its jaws snapping and its eyes blazing gold. That one, taller than all the others, fighting with a corona of beauty, weathered the sound-tempest as if born to it, and his long curved sword burned with reflected fires.

Eidolon laughed. He was vaguely aware of his brethren charging headlong into contact, the two Legion elites slamming into one another. Heavy armour clanged from the impact of pressed steel and the air fizzed from raging aetheric release. Wild magic exploded around them all, igniting as it impacted on the running waves of daemon-screams.

His enemy waited for him, driving his curved blade through those who came against him with almost lazy perfection. There was something striking about those movements – a freedom none of the Chemos-born would ever have allowed themselves.

Eidolon hefted his hammer, gauging distances through the fog of noise and colour. Distorted tactical readings told him of the wider battle unfolding across the docks – whole squads burning, gunships downed, walkers annihilated. The onward drive had stalled. The assault was grinding into the mire of dug-in combat. This enemy could not take the Keystone. For all their aggression, they had not come in sufficient numbers. It was only a matter of time before they were forced back.

Eidolon smiled, feeling the skin of his lips crack. 'A brave attempt!' he called out. 'Yet you have lost your way here.'

His enemy said nothing. Prayer-banners lashed around his ivory battleplate as he whirled into the attack. So fast, so unfettered.

They came together. Eidolon hauled his hammer-head up to meet the incoming strike, and the two weapons smacked against one another. He reeled backwards, pursued by the fire-flecked blade. He screamed again, making the air shake, but the dragon-helm pushed through it. Their weapons swung, smashing into one another again.

This time, the impact hurt him. Eidolon fell back, his vision laced with dark veins. They traded more blows – earth-breaking blows, ones that smashed the decking up around them, dented the ancient armour and made the burning atmosphere blister.

'You cannot escape through the Kalium Gate,' Eidolon spat, tasting his own blood alongside that of those he had already killed. 'This door is closed to you.'

Still no response. The dragon-helm towered over him.

Coil, hit, withdraw, coil again. He is astonishing.

Eidolon fell back, bludgeoned into retreat even as his troops held their own ground. Perhaps, then, the assault had all been for this – to end him again, to deprive the III Legion of its greatest tactical mind.

Hammer and tulwar smacked against one another, shivering from the hits, spraying disruptor-discharge in all directions. Eidolon's bloated breastplate cracked, disgorging white noise freely from damaged amplifiers. He fell to one knee, watching as the dragon-helm came to deliver the final blows.

As the shadow of his enemy fell across him, Eidolon cracked a wry grin. To be slain by *two* primarchs – how many could claim that honour?

And yet, as the fire-streaked storm howled, augmented by the cries of the dead and the dying, rocked by the explosions of mortars and krak charges, the truth came to him suddenly.

'But you are not *him*,' he said, clutching the thunder hammer tightly. 'You cannot be, or I would be dead already.'

He shoved himself back to his feet, thrusting the hammer before him two-handed. The weapons crunched together again, flexing from the deadening, repeated punishment. This time, Eidolon's desperation made him stronger, and he forced his enemy back by a fraction.

The race of sensations returned, as if rewarding him for the realisation. Eidolon laughed again. 'So why did he send you? Do you know not who you fight against here?'

His enemy redoubled his efforts, matching Eidolon's ensorcelled, stimm-frenzied strokes with ferocious counters of his own. He was graceful in his speed, fighting with a looseness of limb that was almost xenos-like in its manner.

'You are but one of his champions,' rasped Eidolon, forcing his enemy back. He could half hear the growing volume of discord around him – the Kakophoni were forcing the Stormseers to cede ground, just as the Emperor's Children all across the docks were recovering broken terrain.

Eidolon launched a savage back-hander across at the dragon-helm, catching the golden mask and sending the warrior staggering. He seized the initiative, hitting him again, smashing the hammer-head deep into ridged plate. The tulwar bit deep on the counter, catching him on his leading arm and severing clean through ceramite, but it didn't stop the furious assault. Eidolon jabbed upwards, connecting with the dragon-helm's vox-grille. The gold-and-ivory mask was sheared clean apart, ripping free from the face beneath.

Eidolon lashed out with his free fist, crunching a balled gauntlet into his enemy's exposed face. More punches fell, a flurry of them, to his neck, his shoulders, his throat. He was fighting in the primordial way now, hands clenched, his raw strength unleashed. They grappled like beasts, and the dragon-helm slipped at last, his boots dragged across the bloody decking.

Eidolon leapt atop him like a leonine atop its prey, thrusting his masked face against the ruin of his enemy's.

'Bested, Chogorian,' Eidolon whispered. 'A wiser Legion would have given up long ago.'

For the first time, his enemy seemed to be trying to speak. Through his broken faceplate, the jagged scar running down his cheek was just visible.

Eidolon lowered his face further. 'What is it?'

The words were lost – a hoarse whisper. Eidolon,

losing patience, pressed his fingers against the naked throat, and prepared to squeeze.

'Know that the Gate's path is destroyed,' Eidolon told him, speaking as softly as his augmetics allowed, watching thick blood pool over his purple-glazed gauntlet. 'Even if you had prevailed here, it would have been for naught. You cannot escape to Terra. All ways are watched, all ways are guarded.'

Still, his enemy tried to speak. Eidolon squeezed harder, choking the life out of him.

'You have failed here. Know this. You *have failed*.'

And then, despite everything, the warrior spoke, forcing the words out through his broken jaw.

'It kept–' he rasped.

Intrigued, Eidolon relaxed the compression.

'It kept–'

Booms rang out, distant echoes of more destruction. The docks were being ripped apart, berth by berth.

'Say it!' hissed Eidolon, staying the killing strike for just a moment longer.

The White Scars warrior managed to focus on him – clear brown eyes amid the ruins of a tight-skinned face, still unafraid, still with that infuriating serenity.

'It kept you… away from… Herevail.'

At that, Eidolon stood bolt upright, releasing his grip. He felt suddenly unsteady, as if the roar and echo in his ears had addled his mind.

He knew that name. Or did he? The stimms throbbed in his throat, making it hard to remember. *Herevail.* A warrior? Another warp conduit?

Yes, yes. He did know it. A *world.* But Herevail, surely, was nothing – a planet they had conquered months ago. It was heavily garrisoned, secure and

far from major warp routes. But he *had* been there:
assets had been drawn from the sector, for the Memnos response, for the other raids, for this.

'What is on Herevail?' he asked, crouching down
again, half speaking to the downed warrior, half to
himself. The blurs of colour swam before his eyes. He
reached down for the warrior's neck again, intending
to seize him, to haul him up. He was still alive. He
could be shriven, given pain beyond mortal imagining. Even now, he could be made to talk.

Just as Eidolon's fingers reached for the shattered
gorget, though, a shock wave caught him, hurling
him away and driving him bodily across the burning
docks. His boots ground deep into the churned-up
deck-plates as he righted himself, and his thunder
hammer's head kindled back into spark-laced life. He
whirled back around, scanning for the source.

Across the expanse of the smoke-clouded docks, the
battle had tilted firmly in the III Legion's favour –
whole formations of White Scars legionaries were on
the retreat, supported by heavy incoming fire from
hovering gunship formations. The Inner Gates continued to blaze, but had not been taken, and more
Emperor's Children Tactical squads were on the march
now, filing up out of the inner sanctums and onto the
void-berth level.

A crimson-armoured psyker – a Legion Librarian – remained before him, holding position even as
his battle-brothers slowly pulled back. The Librarian
stood over the body of the downed dragon-helm, his
armoured outline crackling with black-edged silver,
his feet planted firmly.

'No,' the newcomer said. 'Not for you.'

His voice was unlike the others – cultured, easy with the Gothic words, a less pronounced Chogorian inflection. For a moment, Eidolon couldn't place it, before he finally put the armour's livery and its owner together.

'Unexpected,' he murmured, gathering up the energy for the death-scream that would shatter the Thousand Sons legionary's armour and burn his body into fiery skin-strips. 'I rather thought your kind were on our side.'

The sorcerer carried no weapon, but his gauntlets fizzed with distortion, as if they were half immersed in another world. Even amid the fog of chemical stimms, his power was plainly evident – a witch of Prospero, somehow transported from the ruins of his home world and fighting now amid bands of void barbarians.

'Make no claim on him,' the sorcerer warned, 'or your thread ends here.'

Eidolon found himself smiling even before he started to move again. The death-scream built up in his augmentation chambers, swelling in his chest and ready to spill into the ravaged atmospheric bubble. 'Ends *again*,' he corrected him, drawing in the initial breath.

But the sorcerer had already moved. The gesture was hard to track, as it had been conceived before any of them had spoken, prepared out of time and now brought into the present, faster than thought. His shimmering gauntlets shot out wide, swirling with visual interference, sucking the light and form out of reality.

Eidolon unlocked his throat, just as everything

exploded. He was flung high into the air, his head slammed back hard against his inner helm. He heard fresh roaring in his ears, the thunder of racing winds, before he crashed back to the deck, thirty metres from where he had been standing.

Groggily, he lifted his head, scrabbling to gain purchase. He had lost his thunder hammer, and he could feel blood sloshing all across his carapace. His helm display crackled with a zigzag pattern of static, making the battlefield lurch and jump.

He caught sight of the sorcerer one more time, now alone amid a circle of nothingness. The psychic blast had flattened a whole swathe of the battlefield, scattering the Kakophoni and turning adamantium plates into a landscape of smouldering scrap. Aftershocks still pulsed out of his mind-blast, radiating from his clenched fists like heartbeats.

Eidolon tried to open his throat, but the resultant wet waves of sheer pain almost made him gag. He looked down to see the cascades of blood across his chest, and saw just what a mess had been made of his pristine armour. Bare flesh glistened between jagged edges, pallid even by the light of the promethium fires.

Wincing, he pulled himself to his feet, just in time to see the sorcerer teleport away with his wounded charge, no doubt pulled back to the interior of one of the huge warships still holding close position in the void above the Keystone. All across the berthing zones, White Scars formations were being lifted to safety by disciplined flights of landers, bolstered by a continual barrage from the numerous void fighters strafing the quays.

III Legion assets were responding, redeploying units

and artillery to bring as many down as they could. They had some success, and their opponents' losses continued to be heavy, but it would not be enough to halt the withdrawal.

'This is what they do,' Eidolon muttered to himself. 'Never a solid target – they come, they go, like birds over carrion. But for what?'

Reports began to filter back to him as his armour systems reacted to the shock. He felt the combat-stimms dropping quickly now that the enemy had been snatched away.

Konenos was signalling. Von Kalda was signalling. The hunters were straining at the leash, urging their master to give them leave to pursue the savages back into the void.

Eidolon ignored it all. He looked out over the burning docks, up to where the supermassive bulk of the Keystone rose away in perfectly constructed curves. He could imagine the thousands of mortal souls, those under his command, those sworn to end him, all locked in movement and counter-movement...

They had all been feints. The feints at Memnos had concealed nothing but more feints over Kalium. The Khan had shown his right hand, then his left, but still the blade was hidden.

Eidolon licked his lips, barely noticing the flavour of his hyper-rich blood.

'And what, then, is on Herevail?' he mused as the docks burned around him. 'What can he have seen there that I did not?'

SIX

Veil felt like he had been running for a very long time.

Perhaps he had always been running, first from his scarce-remembered home, then from Alatalana, then from Terra, then from whatever had emerged from the black maw of the void and turned everything to hell. Damn it, Veil was not even his own name, but he had been given it by Achelieux, and so it had stuck, and even now he had trouble remembering the old one.

For all the practice, Veil was still no good at running.

He was old now, and his health had been poor for a long time. They had almost rejected him from the Collegia Immaterium, and back then he had been as fit as he had ever been, conditioned in the scholam, hardened by auxilia officer training, well fed, well kept.

But that had been many, many decades ago. His lungs were old, caked with the grime of a dozen worlds, which was eating away at his insides like the ballast-vermin of an old galleass. He felt the rims of his eyes clog up from the poisons in the air, and wondered how Achelieux and the others had coped with it. They had always been so careful about hygiene. They had to be – he understood that. He had always endeavoured to serve them, and for a long time he had believed that service to be of benefit, something to be proud of.

Veil stopped running, pressed himself up against the algae-smeared walls, and tried to catch his hacking breath.

The sky was orange still, lit up by incendiaries. He could feel the tremors under foot, the afterglow of the earth-breakers. Walls soared up into the night around him, rain-streaked, stinking. He did not even know the name of the city he was in, and had only discovered the name of the principality – Navanda – two days ago. The security detail had been with him then, at least those who'd made it out of Vorlax, and they been running together, moving at night, trying to blend in amid the general fog of panic and movement.

One by one, though, the detail had been whittled away. They had died as they had been trained to die – hurling themselves into harm's way, taking the rounds meant for him. They had all been so well drilled, so fanatical in their devotion to the House. Some of it was training, some breeding, but that could not have been the whole story. Achelieux had inspired love. He really had. It could be unnerving, sometimes, to see how completely he did it. Even now, Veil could not quite bring himself to hate him all the time, despite all that had happened. Not all the time.

Veil felt his heartbeat begin to slow, his straining

throat start to clear. Rain sleeted down, worming under the collar of his robes, making him shiver. The buildings on the far side of the street were ruins now, still hot from old bombing. The eaves he sheltered under were mere façades onto empty blown-out husks. Everywhere was hollow, or home to the hunted or the dispossessed.

He had seen the refugee columns heading north in the early days, when the Administratum announcements had first passed on the orders to leave the urban centres, and wondered how they would survive out in the stone-wastes, where the air was a soup of toxins and the earth burned with rads. Pieter Achelieux had left standing orders before he departed, telling them, at all costs, to remain at their stations. They had trusted Pieter, for he was an Achelieux, *the* Achelieux, and so they had all remained in place until well after the vox-horns had fallen silent and the orbital barrage was under way.

Too late to run then, but they had tried anyway.

Veil shivered. It was impossible to get warm. He hadn't eaten for three days, and the foetid rainwater was making him ill. He pushed clear of the wall and out into the street again. Some of the sodium lamps were still operative a few metres towards the manufactorium sector, and he skirted around their dirty pools of light.

He had seen them himself, days after the first assaults. Most of the cities were aflame by then, their suburban zones rendered down to slag and rubble. The core spires had been preserved by void-shield generators, and so the enemy had landed troops to clear them out. They had come down in gilded caskets,

dropped from the heavens to spear into the heart of
the reeling world. Monsters had emerged from those
caskets – Space Marines, the Angels of Death, such as
he had only seen from afar on the ceremonial days
in different liveries.

But this time they came bearing weapons primed
to unleash not upon the enemies of the Imperium,
but upon *them*.

The noise had been the worst thing – they were
cloaked in a rolling wave of shrieks, laughs, maddened
roars. He had seen rockcrete burst into powder from
it, and witnessed men with blood running from burst
eardrums, eyes staring, mouths gaping in pure, abject
shock.

By then they'd all ignored Pieter's commands. They'd
dismantled the security cordon and began to run for
themselves. The security teams had come with them –
thirty troopers for the senior magisters, twenty for the
technical cadres. Veil himself had commanded over
forty of them, each pledged to defend him to the last.
He'd seen them die, most of them in the first fire-fights
getting out of Vorlax. Just one of the legionaries came
in pursuit then, arrogant in its invulnerability, smashing through the crackling streets, hunting for prey.

Horaff, the security detail's commander, had taken
half his men, the best-armed, the best-armoured, to
take it down.

Veil had tried to talk him out of it. 'You can't stop
it,' he'd said. 'Not one of these.'

Horaff had nodded, perfectly aware. 'We'll slow it,
magister. Give you time to get out.'

'Better to run.'

'Take the grav-transports west. Do not follow the

crowds. This atrocity will be overturned. Restitution will be made.'

This atrocity will be overturned.

He wondered if Horaff had really meant that. His last memory of the commander was of him and his men charging off into the shadows, determined to bring down the monster that hunted them, probably knowing that it was futile.

For himself, he'd just kept running. He hadn't even heard the screams. He'd gone with the rest of the detail, now led by Horaff's junior officer, Ariet, a burly woman with a brawler's voice and manner. By the time they'd reached the grav-transport bunkers, most of the big bulkers had gone or been destroyed. Ariet had commandeered one, turfing out its terrified passengers at carbine-point and shoving him on board. Then they'd set off, out across the stone-wastes, going fast. So Horaff had done at least what he'd promised – given them time.

After that, it had been city to city, trying to keep ahead of the tsunami of destruction. The monsters were ever on their heels, ravening, pulling everything apart. He'd never been able to make any sense of it – they were not there for conquest, just annihilation. He'd seen terrible, terrible things – whole settlements with their inhabitants eviscerated and left to die in the open, blood running ankle-deep through the slurry levels of burning hive spires, endless shrieks through the long nights, noises even an animal wouldn't have made.

Pieter should have warned them. Had he known this was coming? It was hard to imagine he hadn't. He had always given the impression of knowing everything.

'This will collapse soon,' Pieter had once told him, back when their work had just been starting up. 'The system is unstable. I do not think he can control all the elements.'

Veil had not understood that, and had learned never to ask. Pieter could be inscrutable – that was the price of his genius, but he had also cultivated the aura.

Now, twenty-seven days later, something was still following him. He had begun to listen out for the treads behind him. Now that he was alone, there was nothing between him and the monsters, not even Ariet, who had been the last to die protecting him.

It had been hard to keep running with her cries echoing in his ears. They did not just *kill* you, the monsters. They defiled everything they touched. Something horrendous had happened to them, some-thing from the very pits of species-nightmares, and the canker spread in their wake. Herevail had always been a hard place to live on. Now it was a living purgatory.

'Damn you,' he breathed, pulling his cloak tight about him, thinking of Pieter. Pieter must have known. There were no secrets for men like that – they ate and drank them like lesser souls took on food and water.

Then he was hurrying off again, scampering weakly through streets stripped of life and now home only to the echoes of old screams, knowing that they were only a few steps behind, and knowing too, with per-fect certainty, that they would catch him soon.

NIGHT CAME, BUT it made little difference. Orbital destruction of the scale that had come to Herevail blocked out of the light of the sun, masking it in sooty cloudbanks that stretched from horizon to horizon. Veil eventually hunkered down in the shell of an old meat-packing plant, the floor greasy with what he hoped was the remains of its old work.

He was shivering hard, sliding down onto his haunches and pressing his elbows against his thighs. The robes he wore had never been designed for the permawinter ushered in by the war, and were in any case torn to ribbons. As his teeth chattered, he stared nervously out over the plant's deserted packing floor. Dim illumination, burned orange, glowed from blown-out windows, exposing the outlines of rusting heavy machinery. It was hard to imagine such things ever being used now, though just a month ago the whole complex would have been operating at full tilt, absorbing the efforts of a thousand menials, producing nutrient-packs for millions.

He felt a hot pressure at his temples and recognised the first signs of fever. Exposure was killing him faster than his pursuers would, and he had few resources to fight it. He was no true soldier, despite the training he had undertaken half a lifetime ago. He had not been successful in his scavenging. His stomach ached emptily, and his dry mouth throbbed.

He needed to sleep. The heavy weight of fatigue sank down, vying with the cold for control.

If he slept, he knew he would dream. That was almost the worst of all – he would see the faces of those who had died. The acolytes were surely all gone, the House guard, the indentured thralls. They had come to Herevail three years ago to be free of the dead hand of the Nobilite, its agents and its poisonous feuds, so Achelieux had told them. They had come to pursue matters of importance, in which isolation was an advantage.

When the nerve-bombs had started falling, for a moment Veil had thought it might have been some scheme of Pieter's, the result of one of the deeper researches. Pieter had long been off-world by then, of course, but they had expected him back. It was essential that he came back. Had some trick been played? Was he dead? Was he behind it? You never knew, not with him.

We alone see the world behind the veil, he remembered, reciting to himself the words of inculcation of House Achelieux. *Pity those that do not. Scorn them not. We are their guides.*

His shivering became unstoppable, a jarring rhythm that scored the open sores on his back.

What had happened? What had turned the Emperor's Legions against the worlds they had carved out for humanity? Of all things, it was frustrating to know that death would come for him before he could seek out the answers, and before he had had a chance to accomplish his goal. A man could accept his demise, particularly one who had lived for as long and seen as much as he had, if only he knew why it came.

Veil pulled his robes tighter. As he did so, the darkening skies flared up in dull streaks of red again. He felt the earth shake, and heard the distant crack of the drop-caskets again. That was strange. He had believed that the enemy had landed all that they needed to land. There was precious little left on Herevail to kill; to send more torturers to prolong its terror seemed profligate.

He let his eyes close. The far-off tremors continued. Those strikes were like final stabs into a cooling corpse, and just as pointless, but they went on and on *and on*, staving off the sleep he knew he needed.

But you couldn't sleep when those noises were ringing out. They were the hammer-blows of fate. They marked the end of old visions, ones that had been nurtured for centuries before his birth. He knew something of them. Others knew more. Perhaps that was why the legionaries had come to Herevail. Perhaps they had been sent to punish ambition.

All gone now, anyway. All taken away.

'Scorn them not,' he breathed soundlessly as sleep crept up on him, trying to still his cold-locked jaw-line, to understand, to forgive. 'We are their guides.'

He awoke suddenly.

Moving his shoulders sent cold spears running down his curved spine. Veil opened his mouth gingerly, rolling his tongue around parched gums. Slowly, very slowly, he uncurled his limbs. He must have finally lost consciousness while propped up against the metal wall, hunched over tight.

The light hadn't changed much – perhaps a fraction less clouded than it had been. Weak shadows barred the floor, spread from the giant processors that stood sentinel around him. It must have been dawn. He could taste the faint change in the air – the slight increase in heat, the dulling of the night's killing edge.

He tried to clamber to his feet, and the pain in his joints made him grunt aloud.

Then he froze, listening hard. Something had stirred with him.

He waited, motionless, breathing lightly, fully alert now, his pulse thudding.

No further sounds broke the dawn silence. Through the jagged frames of smashed windows, he could see the scudding cloud-cover outside. A broken lumen at the far end of the processing hall flickered intermittently.

Carefully, painstakingly, he nudged himself from the wall, rising to his haunches. He could feel sweat starting to bead on his palms.

He cocked his head, listening intently. He couldn't place the sound he thought he'd heard – a dull machine growl, just on the edge of hearing, instantly stilled.

He started to creep forwards, pulling himself up to his full height. His legs prickled as sluggish blood returned to them, and the frigid air made him shiver again. He clamped his teeth together.

He had made it to the edge of the city the night before. Ariet had told him to keep heading out, beyond the rad-barriers and into the wastes beyond. That would be no good for his precarious health, but then the monsters weren't either. He might be able to scrape survival there for a few days. Whether that was better or worse than a quick death in the city was something that he hadn't asked her – nor indeed what purpose was served by staying alive just a little longer.

It was just instinct, in the end.

To keep going. To keep dragging in the breaths, to keep the cold from sapping his strength and making a corpse of him.

Veil edged closer to the hall's exit gate, peering hard into the gloom around him, hugging the inky shadows of the processor-columns. As he passed under the gate's lintel, high and wide enough to admit a

grav-crawler from the distribution hubs, the city's out-
lands stretched away from him – a jumble of low-rise
habs and manufactoria, hazy in the rising dawn mist.
The orange sky above throbbed like a wound. Thin
columns of smoke snaked up from the eastern horizon, black and sour.

He crept outside, surveying the streets ahead. The
widest led down a long incline, flanked by empty
warehouse fronts, a trickle of oily water bisecting
its length. Others branched out into the warren of
inter-block transit ways. He chose to take the smaller
thoroughfares – those routes at least had some cover,
even if they would keep the warmth of the masked
sun from his chilled back.

And then, as he moved off, he heard the machine
growl again, closer this time. His limbs locked. He
snapped his head around, and saw what he had feared
ever since leaving Vorlax.

It stood twenty metres away, watching him. It was
massive, far bigger than he had thought any of them
ever were. Its armour-plate was purple and gold, in
an orthodox Mark II configuration and bearing standard III Legion iconography. The residue of killing was
draped across it, clinging like sinew. The noise Veil
had heard earlier came sporadically from its armour's
power-pack, which hunched the warrior's back, and it
went helmless, exposing a pale, sickly face.

It did not move. It just watched him, smiling hungrily. Its pure black gaze made him want to scream
and scream until his throat was vomited out from it.

Somehow, drawing on reserves he had thought long
depleted, Veil managed to run. He scuttled awkwardly
into the nearest alleyway, heart hammering. He heard

it set off after him – heavy thuds in the dust, a lazy stride, a throaty hiss coming from between its teeth.

Veil stared frantically around him, searching for some escape, some hole he could squeeze through. All he saw were blank rockcrete walls, some blasted apart, most charred from old fires. Empty windows passed by, opening out into deserted hab-chambers. He thought he heard crashes from further back in the city, and more cracks of munitions going off.

More of them, he thought, bitterly. *By the Paternova, there are more of them...*

He reached the end of the alley, where it switched left between two teetering, bombed-out habitation towers. He could hear the monster's breathing at his back. Sprinting, given speed by fear, he skidded around the corner, nearly slamming into the far wall. He lost his footing, and grazed his knee in the dust.

A gauntlet fell across his shoulder, pinning him. Even through his robes, the touch was like an insect-sting, and he cried out.

The monster reeled him in, dragging him from the ground and turning him. He found himself staring directly into the creature's ruined face. Vestiges of an old humanity still lingered, but sacs now pulsed at the monster's neck, translucent and quavering. Its eyes were like pits into the void. Its breath was sweet, sickeningly so, and he gagged from it.

'You had help from others,' the monster said, squeezing tighter. 'Why was that? Who are you?'

Veil would have answered. The creature's voice cut through him, crushing his will to resist.'

'I am–'

Those were the only words he got out. The world suddenly burst into a cascade of hard golden light, throwing him clear into the air. He landed heavily, feeling his collar-bone snap. A rush of dizziness made him reel, and he saw nothing clearly – just a blur of movement amid the dazzling luminescence. He caught the vague impression of a monster of similar size wading through the curtains of gold, this one encased in ivory plates. The two creatures fought, and their blows made the dust jump and scatter.

Veil tried to crawl away, but the pain in his neck became unbearable, and he curled up into a shivering heap. The first monster was finally smashed across the far side of the street, its armour broken open and crackling with a blinding aura of gold. The second creature strode over to finish it off, bearing a heavy staff, skull-topped, festooned with strips of leather. The heel of the staff came down on the monster's neck, punching through the sacs of flesh, driving it down into the dust. Its gauntlets clutched for a few moments more, furious but impotent. The life was choked out of the monster, and it expired in a messy froth of blood and clear fluid, cursing in a language that Veil did not understand.

He could feel himself losing consciousness. The pain was crippling. His heart was racing out of control, fluttering like a trapped bird. When he felt the hand on his shoulder his first instinct was to pull away, but even that was beyond him now. He looked up to see – with shock – a human face, half hidden behind a rebreather mask. It was a woman, old, her grey hair pulled back severely from thin, fragile features. He had not even noticed her, amid the combat of such horrific beings. She bore the aquila on her breast, pinned to the grey-green uniform of an Army general.

She looked worried.

'Achelieux?' she asked, trying to keep Veil from falling. 'Where is he?'

He might have laughed, if he hadn't been in such bad shape.

Who knows? Who knows where that bastard ended up? If I knew, do you think I'd still be here on this hell-world?

But he couldn't speak. He slumped against her arms. The dizziness rose up over him like a smothering blanket, and he felt himself fall away.

For a moment, he wondered if he was dying. If so, that might have been for the best. What was left now, out of all they had been trying to do?

Then his vision went black, the pain fell away and he slipped into blessed unconsciousness.

SEVEN

SHIBAN LOOKED DOWN at his limbs, stripped of their armour now, illuminated by the light of ceremonial candles. Censers burned slowly in the duelling chamber's alcoves, each scented with sacred oils. The guan dao, powered down, hung loosely in his grip.

Metal glinted between the slabs of exposed muscle, grafted onto the margins of his black carapace and still thick with scar tissue. The white shift he wore exposed the full toll of his augmentation – forearms gone, calves gone, thighs studded with pistons and braces, his neck a mass of interlocking valves. From far below, the *Kaljian*'s engines churned and boomed, powering through an aether that was always in turmoil.

Calligraphic banners hung in the gloom, each one marking battles fought by the brotherhood. The ritual names charted early glorious victories, culminating at Chondax, through to the decisive crisis at Prospero. Thereafter, the marks were more often of

defeat, or pyrrhic charges that in the long run conquered no ground. To witness them was to witness the
slow degradation of a once proud and wild heritage.
The banners would have been created with almost
infinite care in the past, but now no time existed to
produce them properly, and so the lines were hurried
and imperfect.

All things were done as they had ever been done,
but the soul of them was gone. The censer-smoke was
empty of spirits, the cold air empty of songs.

Shiban shifted the guan dao again, rehearsing the
moves he had made against the III Legion champion.
He had done so a dozen times already, trying to find
the error he had committed. So far, he had discovered none. His enemy had simply been better – faster,
stronger, more instinctive.

There was nothing much to learn from that, only
an acknowledgement of weakness.

He could guess what Yesugei would have made of
it. The Stormseer would have given him a disapprov-
ing glare, and that alone would have forced him back
to the training arenas, again and again, until the flaw
was corrected. Qin Xa would never have been bested
so easily. Jubal either, nor Jemulan, had he lived to
see such days.

There had been a time when Shiban had aspired
to match the deeds of those names, to become one
of the greats of the ordu. Prospero had ended those
chances, and brought him the Shackles instead. Such
was war, such was fortune, and there were no longer
prizes to be grasped from the mire.

The guan dao swirled through the dark, carving the
air. Shiban stepped into the attack, fighting through

memory an enemy who no longer stood before him. He had done that, years ago, on Chogoris, with enemies drawn from the archives, for hours at a time. His blade strokes then had been as free and precise as the strokes of his calligraphy brush, back when he still dared to pen verses in the old tradition.

Shiban had not written a line since Chondax. None of the old scholars had, as far as he knew. The words were no longer there for them.

Tachseer, they called him now, the Restorer.

He had grown in the favour of the Khagan, and his brotherhood had swelled, taking in recruits from the brotherhoods of shamed khans. Along with Jubal, Ghinak, Ohg, Yesugei and Qin Xa, he had risen high in the counsels of the primarch, sharing in the *kurultai* that plotted out the strikes against the ever-encroaching warfront of Horus. Only the damned of the *sagyar mazan* had taken on more dangerous assignments, and their losses were purifications.

The blade angled, dipped, pulled back. Shiban adjusted his weight, compensating for every shift of the glaive. As he dragged his leading foot away, one of the mechanical conduits in his ankle snagged – just a microsecond delay, barely detectible, but enough.

He held position, gauging how far such micro-delays left him vulnerable.

A Dreadnought-shell at least would have made me stronger, he thought. *Damn our superstitions.*

Slowly, he relaxed. The censers guttered, making the banners waft a little.

There was nothing more to be done. The Legion champion himself was most likely dead now, caught up in the convoy's cataclysm. That was scant comfort, of course, for it would have been finer to have killed him face to face, in the way of the plains.

Shiban let the glaive's tip fall, and turned from the centre of the duelling circle. As he did so, he caught the outline of an observer in the shadows, hovering outside the light of the candles, waiting patiently.

Jochi would never have held back before. Before, he would have called out earlier, sharing in the appreciation of the art of bladeplay.

'You have tidings for me,' said Shiban, breathing a little heavily, moving to where his glaive's rosewood case hung.

'The star-speakers have completed their scrutiny,' Jochi said, bowing. 'We have orders from the Khagan and are to pull back to the inner circle.'

Shiban nodded. He placed the guan dao into its felt-inlaid casket, pulling the leather straps tight. 'What of the other raids?'

'Three convoys were taken and carried into the warp. One was a personnel detail, so there are new recruits for the fleet crews.'

'And the others?'

Jochi paused. 'Heiyu is taken. Xian Kamag is silent. Our losses were heavy, khan.'

Shiban moved towards the duelling chamber's exit, and Jochi fell in alongside him. 'Such is war,' Shiban said.

'It is, but...' Jochi shot him an uncertain glance. 'It has been like this for a long time, khan. The *Amujin* is gone.'

'We did what we were ordered. Many Traitors died.'

'More of us.'

Shiban reached the curtains barring the exit. Soft

lumens in the corridor outside bled over the paper floor threshold, illuminating the lines upon lines of inked script. 'We are no longer fighting xenos. Our enemy is as deadly as we are.'

'My khan, I must speak.' Jochi held his ground, refusing to cross the barrier. Shiban paused, then inclined his head. 'At Prospero, more than four years ago, we made the vow for Terra. Much was sacrificed for this. And yet still we are here, out in the void, bleeding on the blades of an enemy that cannot be defeated.'

Shiban listened impatiently. None of this was new to him.

'We try feints within feints,' Jochi went on. 'We lay them trails and hope to gain slight advantage, but they know our games now. We should have had many more hours with the convoy before the enemy arrived. They barely sent enough ships to contest us, and still it was enough. How many cruisers did we divert from Kalium? Did Qin Xa take the Gate? Do we know that yet?'

'Not yet.'

'The Traitors outnumber us. They are four Legions to our one. So we must kill four of them for every warrior we lose, and still it will not be enough.'

'We slow the advance,' said Shiban.

'In the beginning, yes.' Jochi's brown face was intense in the candlelight, marked by the ritual scar on his cheek. 'Yes, I could see that. But do you believe it now, my khan? Tell me truly, and I will believe it too.'

Shiban drew in a long breath. His own opinion, which he had come to hold firmly as the blood tally had lengthened, was of no consequence. The Legion's strategy had been set by the Khagan, and only he would change it. Even as the Hordes were brutalised, beaten back, bled white, they would not go against Jaghatai's ordinances. Not again.

'So what would you have me do, brother?' Shiban asked.

'You have the ear of the Khagan.'

Shiban snorted. 'You think so?'

'Tell him–'

'Tell him what?' Shiban blurted, feeling fatigue catch up with him at last. It had been hours of solid practice since Memnos. Three days since he had slept. His mood was already choleric; this did not improve it. 'We are *fighters*. Our Khagan throws us into the jaws of the beast, and we rejoice in it. We are broken, and we laugh to see it. We are given no rest, no respite, and it cleanses our soul. That is it. That is all there is. Or did you hope for me to find you somewhere safe to shelter?'

Jochi flushed. His fingers twitched, just for moment, as muscle memory responded instantly to the impulse to draw a weapon. 'You know that is not what I seek.'

Shiban looked away, already regretting the words. There was no lack of valour in the brotherhood – just the long slow grind of weariness, hammered in over continual retreat. He had voiced the same doubts in the privacy of his own meditations, even then castigating himself once they had formed in his mind.

We might have made the journey, once. We have left it too late. The enemy surrounds us, biting at our heels. All there is left to do is to cultivate our hatred.

'There will be kurultai,' Shiban said. 'The losses will be recorded. When the hour is right, the Khagan will rule.'

Jochi bowed. His frustration had not gone away. 'I know it, and yet… There are those who…'

Shiban looked hard at him. 'Speak, brother. No secrets between us.'

'They say the numbers are now critical. That is what the star-speakers report. We cannot hold even our core. There has been talk of… changes.'

Shiban studied his deputy. Jochi had always had an honest face. On Chondax, when they had fought freely for the last time, it had been as clear as the skies, prone to the laughter they had once been famous for.

'The oath-breakers, khan,' Jochi said, looking back at him sidelong. 'They will be summoned back.'

Shiban took him by the arm, gripping with a mechanical fist. 'The sagyar mazan paid for their crimes in death,' he said, his voice low. 'All payment has been made.'

'Not all.'

'How do you know this?'

'Those who can bear arms are being mustered again,' said Jochi. 'All of them.'

Shiban forced a smile, though it came out more like a grimace. 'You heard wrong, brother. The aether is turbulent. Star-speakers dream badly when the tempest rages.'

Jochi looked equivocal. 'Still, the talk runs.'

Shiban held his gaze. 'Then hear this new talk, from me, your khan. Do you suppose I know nothing of these gutter-rumours? And do you think, for a heart's single beat, that I would allow them back, the ones who forgot their loyalty? This thing will never happen. Better to die alone than with the sagyar mazan.'

Jochi's eyes dropped. Shiban released him.

'But, see, you did well to speak to me of this,' said
Shiban, trying to give him something. 'Know that I
have no feud with you, brother – nor with those who
always ran under the sign of the minghan, who held
their loyalty when lies spread through the whole fleet.
I could never have. We two swore once, here, on this
ship. You remember? That is what remains.'

Jochi nodded.

'But the oath-breakers are cast out,' said Shiban.
'They do not come back from that.' Even as he spoke,
Shiban felt a fresh spasm of pain – a numb jolt from
the Mechanicum machines that kept him alive. That
was a reminder of what that treachery had cost him –
his speed, his joy, his future.

So much was already destroyed, and the Traitors of
the ordu had played their part.

'So they do not come back,' Shiban said again, turning away from the duelling circle. 'The price will be
paid. If other souls waver in the collection, be assured,
I shall see to it myself.'

THE WALLS SHOOK, hit by repeated flank strikes. Even
deep within the battleship, ringed by layer upon layer
of reinforced decking, those impacts reverberated.

Revuel Arvida hurried down the corridors of the
Lance of Heaven, heading for the main apothecarion.
His limbs still burned from the discharge of warp
power. He could feel the flare-up now, and knew it
would be worse over the next cycle. Already his eyes
burned, his hearts laboured. It would have been best
to retire to his chamber, to fight the change, as he
had slowly learned to do, in the cool calmness of his
sanctum, but these tidings could not wait. Even as

the battered White Scars attack group fought its way to the Mandeville point, harried by Eidolon's fleet, other matters had become pressing.

He reached the portals, guarded by two hulking warriors of the *keshig*, and pushed past them.

Inside, many figures clustered around the main medicae-slab. Most were mortal, drawn from the battleship's standard crew. Less than half of those were Chogorian, for the turnover in human specialist staff had been particularly savage, and the majority now came from scavenged and pressed technicians from other Legions and Army regiments.

Jubal Khan stood at the head of the slab, his helm removed, his arms crossed. His face was bloody, and his topknot hung limply over his shoulders. Namahi, Qin Xa's protege and second-in-command, as well as others of the keshig and the khans of many brotherhoods, were there too. They parted to allow Arvida access, and he leaned over the slab.

Qin Xa had been cut from his battleplate. His body was exposed under the medicae-lumens – a mass of churned flesh and broken bone. His face was held together with a criss-cross of pins, and nutrient tubes gurgled as they entered the many lacerations made by Jaijan, the battleship's *emchi* Apothecary. His armour had been heaped to one side, bloodied and hollow like so much scrap. Atop it all was the dragon-helm, now in two pieces.

Qin Xa saw Arvida approach through his one working eyeball, and the blood-trails around his mouth bubbled into a weak smile.

'Sorcerer…' he rasped, barely above a whisper.

Arvida leaned closer. It was dangerous to use the warp

again so soon, particularly when surrounded with the Legion's elite, but in this case there was little choice.

+Do not weaken yourself,+ he sent, placing his mind-voice within Qin Xa's. +Speak to me this way.+

For both of them, the apothecarion dissolved in a white haze, and then they were facing one another, their bodies restored.

The mind-image of Qin Xa laughed. Freed of the horror of his ruined body, it sounded just as it always had done in life – sonorous, good-natured, preternaturally calm. All the old guard of the plains had sounded the same, though Qin Xa was the last of them, save Yesugei – the last of those who had fought with Jaghatai on Chogoris, braving Ascension beyond the customary age, and surviving.

We failed, Qin Xa's thoughts proclaimed, matter-of-factly.

+It was an impossible task.+

I would have driven them out of that place. I would have seen them run, just as we made them run on Peressimar.

That had been two years ago now. A great victory, driven by surprise and speed, perhaps the last of them.

+You did your duty, *keshiga*. That is all he will want to know.+

In the mindscape, Qin Xa's craggy features wrinkled in a smile, as if the too-bright sun of the home world glared back from the endless grass. *He will blame himself. It will seem to him that we have stayed in the void too long.*

Arvida nodded. +If he speaks to me, I will tell him otherwise.+

All the ways were watched. Even if we had wished to, we could not have broken through.

+He knows this.+

He has been a just master, all the years I served him. Blame is now of no use, for any of us. The search must continue.

+Ravallion said she knew of a way. This is why we did these things. She may yet be proved right.+

Whether or no, Qin Xa sighed inwardly, *he made the oath over the ruins of his brother's realm, and it will drive him. He must reach Terra.*

+And if no path remains?+

Qin Xa's outline grew more vague. The wind became chill, and the sky deepened to night-blue. His smile disappeared, to be replaced by growing pain. His soul was shearing from its foundations, pulling free of the body. *Do you not see one? You are the fate-scryer.*

Arvida did not know how to respond to that. He could not even see his own future-skein, except for the visions that came while in the warp, and those were not ones he wished to recall.

And yet, there were times when truth was a cruelty.

+The road will be found,+ he sent, confidently. +If Ravallion is wrong, another way will be made. The Khagan is a force of the universe – we both know this. He will not be denied by it.+

Qin Xa tried to smile again, and failed. The pain of the real world became etched on that of the imagination, and the old warrior's once-hale face began to dissolve. *You neither, sorcerer. Now take this final command – cure yourself, before you cure any more of us. Promise me.*

Arvida stiffened. How much did he know?

+I no longer make promises,+ Arvida sent. In the real world, moving blindly, he took up Qin Xa's smashed hand, and pressed his gauntlet against it. +The hunt will be eternal for you. And I swear this – your name will be remembered on Terra.+

And then the mind-images dissolved, and the spartan apothecarion reasserted itself around him. Qin Xa spoke no more, whether in the mind or in the real world.

Arvida found himself gazing down on a mangled heap of scorched organs and skin-scraps. Jaijan and his attendants had already moved away, cleaning their instruments, turning off the blood-cyclers, preparing the narthecium.

For a moment, Arvida was still. 'You remained unsullied, right to the end,' he said softly, remembering their first shared battle amid the glass dust of Tizca. Then, to himself, he murmured, 'I may yet come to envy that.'

He stirred, and straightened. Namahi was looking at him, as was Jubal, as were all the others.

'The sound-weapons,' Namahi said, disgusted. 'No blade, no matter how fast, parries them.'

Arvida was struck by the edge of grief in Namahi's voice. The Khagan's own brotherhood were as close to one another as blood-kin. And there was more: another link to the sundered home world cut. The strands were becoming frayed.

'What did he tell you?' asked Jubal.

Jubal was different. He had been far away from the Legion during the upheaval on Chondax, carried into the furthest reaches of the galaxy at the head of an *ikhan*, a great hunt that had arced beyond the galactic plane in pursuit of the xenos mjordhainn raiders. By the time his strike force had returned bearing the head of the xenos' controlling patriarch on a silver shield, the Imperium was turning in on itself, and he had been thrown into the heart of combat with no opportunity to ask why.

A lesser warrior might have succumbed to fate in the confusion and void war that had followed, but Jubal had always been a spirit of fire, and all the traps laid for him were broken. The Lord of Summer Lightning he had been on Chogoris, a capricious spirit who had defied restrictions even by the standards of a Legion that placed little value on them. Almost alone among the White Scars, his name was known across the wider ranks of the Great Crusade, whispered alongside the most exalted company, held up as a legend of elusive renown on worlds that had never seen a son of the Altak. That he had lived to fight his way to the Khan's side again was one of the few causes of joy in an otherwise harrowing campaign, a sign that their most vital soul had not yet been quenched.

Regarding him now, Arvida saw just how different Jubal was to Qin Xa. The keshig-master had been quiet in voice, solid in manner, his strength coming from within like a deep well sunk into bedrock. Jubal was the other side of the Legion's soul – flamboyant, artful, unfettered. Somehow he had retained that during the long retreat, his guan dao still flashing defiantly as blood flowed across worlds.

Perhaps his time had come now. Perhaps this was the age of wildfire, of the Master of the Hunt rather than the Horde.

'Little enough,' Arvida said, no longer wishing to talk of it. 'He died well, with his spirit laughing.'

Jubal held his gaze for a while longer, searching. 'We

could have died alongside him if we had chosen. We could have held our ground. They would have made verses of that.'

Arvida did not question his judgement. It was not his place – he was the outsider still, suffered to fight with the ordu, but never one of them. He had made sure of that himself, retaining the marks of his old order, refusing every offer to take up the ways of weather-magic, the arts of the plains-shaman.

'We did what we came to do,' he said, evenly.

'But the price was high, this time.'

'When has it ever not been?'

Jaijan returned to the slab then, his narthecium already whining. His attendants began to prepare the body. From the rear of the medicae chamber, menials entered bearing white ceremonial robes, each marked with the calligraphic glyphs marking the passage into Eternal Heaven, the wide arch of the sky, the hawk's flight.

None of the khans moved. Jubal looked at Arvida.

'We will give him *kal damarg*. You may stay, sorcerer.'

He would have done. If he had been able to choose, he would have watched the Chogorian death-rite as he had done so many times, giving honour to the master of the Khan's own elite, sharing in the privilege that almost none outside the ordu had ever witnessed.

But the flesh-change had got worse. The pain sang around his collar, bleeding up into his neck and across his chest. He could feel his limbs press up against the inside of his armour, hot with blood, seething like squalid nests of insects. He had already lingered too long – the edge of peril had crept up on him, worsened by the use of his mind-voice. That was the curse of his home world, one that had pursued him into the void even after his rescue from Prospero, dragging him back towards the fate of his old Legion.

To reject the offer made him feel wretched, but Qin Xa's last command still resonated.

Cure yourself.

'He was your Legion's champion,' Arvida said, bowing stiffly. 'He is yours to mourn.'

For a moment, Jubal didn't hide the slight. The offer, once made, would not be made again. 'As you will it,' he said.

By then, though, Arvida was already moving. He left the way he had come, feeling the flesh-pressure mount. Only when he had reached his own chamber, ringed with the wards he had created himself using the last of the knowledge he had taken from Prospero, did the pain begin to sharpen into curative agony. He knelt within the circles and pentagrams, knowing that the worst was yet to come, and that soon he would be crying aloud, lost in the visions that came with the change and his fight to prevent it.

He screwed his eyes shut, balled his fists, trying to recall the words of the Corvidae litanies. All he saw was Qin Xa's face, and then the sky over Tizca, and then Kalliston's death, and then the ghosts that had always been there within the shafts of sunlight and the crystal refractions, waiting for them, waiting for them all.

'Damn you,' he hissed. 'Not yet.'

And then the screaming started.

THE WORLD WAS a black sphere of silver-veined iron. Its distant star was white-blue, casting its every surface with ghost-pale edges. Once it had possessed oceans, but these had boiled away a million years ago, leaving open pans of ebony rock naked to the heavens. Its cloudless sky was black to the void, revealing the torso of the galaxy, strung like a trail of jewels against the infinite dark.

Spectre, the place had been called by the first explorators to make planetfall.

The rock had been charted, surveyed for minerals, assessed for habitation or cultivation, and rejected on all counts. Chill winds ran across its empty plains now, curling at the edges of crystalline rock towers. Strange lights flickered and glowed in the frigid skies, glinting from mirror-pure chasms below. For a long time, the hush of those winds had been the only sound on Spectre, repeated through the centuries in overlapping, moribund murmurs.

But now the winds raced from a different cause. Ancient dusts were stirred up, skittering across cracked rock-plates. The sky's purity was broken by the heavy thunder of landing thrusters. Vessels, dozens of them, made atmospheric entry, powering down on columns of thick smog. Most were Legion gunships, fitted for fleet-escort duties, switching from orbital to atmospheric engines as they plunged earthwards. Their flanks were a dark sea-green, all emblazoned with the eye of their primarch.

The gunships extended across the plains in all directions, setting up a cordon around the centre of a wide circular expanse, itself surrounded by ranks of towering stalagmites. Where they set down, Sons of Horus honour guards emerged, all wearing ceremonial cloaks and carrying heavy power spears. Once the cordon was complete, a lone Stormbird made planetfall in the centre. Down the steam-wreathed embarkation ramp trudged warriors in ebon-faced, bronze-encased Cataphractii plate – the Justaerin, most feared fighters of the most feared Legion. They marched with a perceptible martial arrogance, the confident tread of those habituated to ascendancy.

The Justaerin had always made their armour their own, marking it with heritage-tokens extending back to the gangs of Cthonia, but now the alteration of their Legion-issue plate had accelerated. Blood-brown bones clanked from chains set about their waists, and their pauldrons bore iron spikes set amid more glistening eyes. Sigils had been daubed across shell-chipped ceramite, signs of potency now taught to them by their consorts beyond the veil. Spectre's thin air shimmered as the Justaerin waded through it, repulsed by the name-forms that flickered in its austere light.

Once in position, the honour guard waited in silence, weapons held in static salute. They did not move even when the skies above them were sundered a second time. More landers cut their way down from orbit, this time bearing the white-and-green livery of the XIV Legion – named the Dusk Raiders by the Emperor, renamed the Death Guard by their primarch. Their own elites, the Deathshroud, clanged down the ramps from their Stormbird, each one a match in stature with his Justaerin equivalent. Bearing power scythes two-handed, they lumbered into position, and the two sides faced one another across the glass-dark rocks.

The Deathshroud bore no new sigils on their pauldrons, and their armour remained much as it had been throughout the Great Crusade and its aftermath – rime-filthed, battered, plain. No daemon-whispered signs had been scratched on their vambraces and greaves, just the accumulated muck of an endless campaign, staining a livery that had never been pristine, even upon leaving the forges on Barbarus.

They remained thirty metres apart, those two forces, making no move to close the gap. No hails were issued and no challenges laid down, for those killers were not the reason that Spectre's long isolation had been disturbed.

The first to emerge from his transport was the Death Lord, limping into the open from the Stormbird's gaseous interior, leaning heavily on his reaper, Silence. His face was hidden under a battered cowl, his verdigrised armour swathed in the tattered remnants of a fine cloak, his iron boots plastered with the caked soils of a hundred worlds. Vapour trailed after him in curls, expelled from intestine-like coils of cabling. His breath rattled, his back was curved and his stance was crabbed.

And yet, there could be no doubt of the power cradled within that savaged shell. Even in his seeming decrepitude, he somehow dominated all around him. Every dull ring of his scythe's heel against rock echoed heavily. His great shoulders spoke of an almost infinite endurance, an ability to withstand forces that would have laid even his brother gene-gods low. The sickly pallor that hung over him was not weakness, but the spawn of a long-gestated bitterness that extended back to the toxic world of his scattering, one that made him almost infinitely capable of enduring punishment.

As he reached the centre of the circle, the Justaerin

bowed as one. The gestures were not the perfunctory bows of diplomacy, but the recognition of a paramount lord in their midst, one who had overseen the slaughter of entire systems at the head of a Legion whose pale ships had become a byword for implacable, silent, inexorable murder.

If he noticed that, Mortarion gave no sign. He came to a halt, his rebreather clicking between hisses. A pair of yellow-green eyes peered out from the shadow of the cowl, heavy-lidded, windows onto a soul that had always been marked to suffer.

Then, slowly, achingly, the Death Lord moved his weight from the reaper's haft, pushed his mottled cloak to the side, and sank to one knee. His great head lowered in obeisance, followed in due course by those of his own retinue.

Mortarion had only ever bent the knee to two souls in creation. One he had since sworn to destroy; the other now emerged from the facing Stormbird.

He, like his Legion, had grown far beyond his allotted bounds. The old dynamism, the almost unconscious flair that had made men love him and armies pray to be given to his command, had been strangled long ago. The gold and white of his armour had stained and darkened, the furs had thickened, the ceramite plates had fused into new and tortured forms. His agility had been swallowed up by a new, horrific, cloying bulk. His armour-hood rose high over his head, lit from within by a seething cushion of blood-red energies. His right arm terminated in the immense, industrial outline of the Talon, which even at rest seemed to snarl with barely contained killing-lust.

When he moved, it was as if the matter of the galaxy

itself hastened to clear his path. He had become immense, obscenely so, an elemental force even among those who had been gifted with the Emperor's divine touch. The gold-and-ruby eyes that festooned his baroque armour seemed to gaze out with wills of their own, scrutinising, judging, testing.

And yet it was his own, mortal, eyes that were the greatest horror of all. Where once they had been vital, questing, alive with pleasure, they were now dark, ringed with ridges of pale flesh. They were the eyes of a soul that had peered into the epicentre of the abyss and faced the shape of reality in all its abject, cruel majesty. Nothing reflected from those orbs now. They were like black holes, greedily sucking every scrap of light into their unfathomable depths.

Horus Lupercal, Warmaster, came to a halt before Mortarion, and extended his left gauntlet.

'My brother,' he said, 'kneeling does not suit you.'

Mortarion looked up, his expression, as ever, impossible to read behind the mask and the cowl. 'You must accustom yourself to it. Soon we shall all kneel, *sire.*'

Horus beckoned him upwards. Heavily, awkwardly, Mortarion complied. Then they embraced as brothers, and for a moment it was as if the lesser primarch were swallowed up in the mauling embrace of the void.

Horus released him, and Mortarion looked around. 'Ezekyle not with you? I thought he was your shadow.'

'I thought Typhon yours.'

Mortarion hacked a contemptuous cough. 'Who knows what Calas does, or where he is? I seek him myself. If you should run across him, be sure to tell me.'

Horus' gaze flickered then. His eyes, those grey-ringed

eyes, moved strangely, as if witnessing things that were not there, or things that ought to have been. 'You know why I wished to meet.'

'You have a thousand worlds under your heel. You have ringed the Throneworld with fire. The galaxy is severed, barring Guilliman and the Angel from reaching our Father's side. These things are all now done, and the stage is set.'

Horus did not smile. His once-easy humanity had drained away from him, replaced with the distant, distracted grandeur of a different plane. 'In my mind, this thing had been done by now. Every day sees our advantage slip a little.'

Mortarion shook his head, wheezing. 'Then give the order, brother. Set it in motion.'

Horus gave a wry smile. 'And that is all there is to it,' he murmured. He looked up, his bleak gaze sweeping the crystal-sharp starfield arcing above them. 'We did not bring all of them with us. They are out there, still, fighting against the webs we have placed them in. That is the problem.' His expression hardened. Even in those minuscule movements, the projection of incipient command was always lurking. 'Lorgar's storms will not last forever. They can be broken, given the will, given the strength. And what then? All those we have sealed away from our Father's side, racing back to add their banners to His.'

'Then give the order.'

Horus turned back towards him, a brief flash of irritation rippling across his bloated features. 'We do not speak of some petty warlord, scraping a living on a backwater rock. Even in His weakness He is unmatched. You know what made Him. You know why He and He alone could lay the foundations of all this. Can you compass what it is to even *conceive* of killing such a one? To *do* it, to do it properly, so that He cannot escape the blade's cut and cling to His shrivelled soul... You do not see the full peril.'

'Since Molech, brother, you have lost your good humours.'

'Since Molech, there are *no* good humours. I am become vengeance, the destroyer of creation. So, no, I do not laugh as I once did.'

Mortarion sighed. 'Shall I say it a third time? No more delays. Launch the assault. My Legion stands ready.'

'No doubt.' For a moment, there was a kind of gratitude in those ruined features. 'Dorn is accounted for. Russ has been crippled at Alaxxes, and wastes himself in dreams of bringing me to his strange form of justice. Corax is lord of an empty Legion, and Ferrus and Vulkan are dead. That only leaves one who could hurt us.'

Mortarion looked wary, and said nothing.

'I had resolved to command the Phoenician for this,' said Horus. 'He and Jaghatai always despised one another. I would have enjoyed the sight of Fulgrim teaching the Warhawk a lesson in humility.'

'Then ask him.'

'If you can find him, then you may do so yourself.' Horus flexed his Talon instinctively, a gesture of impatience. 'Come, we both know this – Fulgrim cannot be trusted. He performed his one great task on Isstvan Five, so do not look to him for anything more.'

Mortarion shook his head, making the jars of toxins hung around his neck rattle. 'I will not do it.'

'You thirst for vengeance, do you not?'

'He did not best me.'

'No one says that.'

Mortarion slammed the shaft of Silence against the rock, sending shuddering lines of forces snaking across the dark plates. 'I *will* be at your shoulder,' he hissed. 'At the forefront. I have kept my sons pure. I could have twisted them like the others, but they still answer my command, and they still hold their discipline.'

'You shall be with me, just as I promised.'

'I will not be left behind.' Mortarion's speech was thick with long-bottled suspicion. 'I have as much thirst to see our Father kneel as you. More, I would claim, if all be reckoned.'

'And as the Palace burns, you shall be at my side.'

'Then why place the Khan before me now?'

'Because I can *trust* you,' Horus said, exasperated. 'Do you not see it? You look for slights in every shadow, waiting to be cheated, and yet you, my jealous brother, are only one I have left.' He laughed out loud, bitterly. 'Behold, the tally of my rebellion. Angron has made himself mad – I cannot charge him with the simplest tasks. Perturabo – by the gods, Perturabo. He would be left standing while the Khan's savages ran rings around his trenches, and the Scars have no fortresses for him to lay low. Alpharius is silent, and ties himself up in knots of his own devising. The list grows short.'

Mortarion listened cautiously, his filthy armour-systems cycling and gurgling.

'I come to you,' said Horus, softly, 'because I have no others. The Khan remains on my flank, his Legion intact, his fury undimmed. The storms keep him hemmed, but he will find a way to break them. He cannot be suffered to live – you know this. Once Jaghatai has been destroyed, the last barrier falls.'

Horus loomed over his hunched brother and grabbed him by the neck, one claw on either side.

'And then,' he breathed, drawing Mortarion's scabrous face close to his own, 'it shall be we two at the spearhead. You *have* kept your Legion pure. You do not disappoint. We approach the nexus now.'

Mortarion's suspicion never left him. His eyes flickered, the dry skin of his lips twitched. 'You were true brothers, you and Jaghatai,' he said. 'You were as close as mingled blood.'

'We were all brothers. Do not think I will regret one more death.'

'Or is it this – you do not do it yourself, because you *cannot*.'

At that, Horus hesitated. 'You really think that?'

'Have you not considered it?'

The Warmaster said nothing. He released Mortarion from his grip, and withdrew. 'I do not think there is a living soul I would not be able to slay now. Not since I saw… what waits.' He looked back towards his gene-brother, less assured now, his visage haunted. 'When the moment comes, when I have *Him* in my grasp, I will not hesitate. I know this at least.'

Mortarion listened, breathing heavily. Even after all that had happened, considering the very end of the enterprise was uncomfortable. They all had blood on their hands, rivers of it, but killing mortals was one thing. Slaying a living god, however false and sickened, was another.

'My gaze cannot waver from Terra,' Horus went on. 'You cannot imagine what a burden that is. Even as we bring the other-realm into this one, and the ancients respond to my lead like whipped dogs, there still remain the old soldier's curses – munitions, ledgers, schedules. I cannot deviate. Every wasted day narrows the lens of the future.'

Still Mortarion listened.

'We reach the inner rings of iron now,' Horus said. 'The first of Dorn's defences, arraigned on a hundred worlds. Each one will fight until the last breath is choked from them. Even with Perturabo, even with *me*, these will not be easy victories.' The Warmaster looked back intently at his pallid brother. 'So I need the Khan destroyed.'

'He has his Legion, I have mine. This, too, will not be an easy victory.'

'You will not be alone. Eidolon hunts him even now. You are to join him.'

Mortarion laughed savagely. 'Ah, I can see how that would appeal to you – me and that… thing. Perhaps all your humours have not yet been bled out after all.'

Horus did not smile. 'Fabius has made him deadly.'

'Yes, yes, we are all deadly.' Mortarion hacked again, shifting his weight, looking uncomfortable. 'Then Eidolon knows where the Fifth Legion musters?'

'He has their scent.'

'So it is still a hunt.'

'What else could it be?'

Mortarion smiled darkly. 'Aye.' He sighed, and flexed his gauntlet absently. The great dents and scores in his armour made on the crystal dust of Prospero had not been excised – they were the badges of a contest that had not been concluded. In Mortarion's exposed upper face, something like eagerness had kindled – the desire to finish what had been started. 'I am not the same as I was, when we last met,' he said.

'You have not taken your full quota of gifts.'

'Not yet, not ever. I am not like you. I do not wallow in this corruption. I *use* it. I control it. I set bounds on it.'

Horus did not reply. His black-within-black eyes reflected nothing.

'Then I have your word,' said Mortarion at length. 'You will wait. We shall assault the Throneworld together.'

Horus held up the Talon to the faint blueish light, as if it now served as some kind of pledge of surety. 'Have I ever lied?' he asked. 'Even to my Father? A time will come where there can no longer be lies, for truth and falsehood have no currency in the realm of dreams. I bring this time to the galaxy – that is why you follow me, just as you once followed Him.'

'Not as I followed Him.'

'But, yes, you have my word.'

'Then you have mine.' Mortarion seized the Talon with his own gauntlet, and its surface was subsumed within the massive lightning claw. 'He will be caught, he will be slain.'

If that news pleased the Warmaster, he showed no sign of it. He merely nodded – a fractional gesture, the mark of one more task achieved, one more obstacle to the Throne cleared away.

'Tell me when it is done,' he said, releasing Mortarion's gauntlet and letting the Talon fall. Above them both, Spectre's icy winds eddied. 'All I need is the word. Then the final assault begins, and you will be there with me to lead it.'

PART II

EIGHT

ILYA RAVALLION SUNK down to her haunches, shaking. She pressed her back against the wall behind her and wrung her hands together. Herevail was *cold*. She should have brought an environment suit, not just her old fatigues. But then, it had become important to her to wear the old colours. Once it hadn't mattered, but now it did – all the colours, all the symbols, all of vital importance.

She didn't fill out the old uniform well any more. She had shrunk, and the material had not shrunk with her. Age was cruel, taking away the very faculties that had made her useful. She wondered if the Legion noticed her diminishment. If so, they never mentioned it, though perhaps, she thought, they had become even more solicitous.

She closed her eyes and tried to stop shivering. From far away, crumps of artillery broke out, marking the steadily moving northern front. The III Legion troops on Herevail were some of the most debased yet encountered, but they could still fight. Even outnumbered, taken by surprise, they resisted with all that incredible tenacity every Space Marine possessed.

It was perhaps the most loathsome thing about them. She even found it loathsome in those who warded her. A warrior of the Legions was a killing machine, devoid of fear, devoid of self-pity. Place one in an impossible situation, one that would have crushed the soul of any non-Ascended, and he would just keep fighting, trying everything, using all the near-infinite resources at his disposal with every scrap of guile and invention he possessed. To end them, you had to physically cut their throats into ribbons. To end one of Fulgrim's grotesques, you often had to do more than that.

And they took pride in it. She had heard the brotherhoods telling themselves the same things, over and again.

We do not yield. We are the faithful. We are the oathkeepers.

There were times, when she was tired and exhausted – which was often – when she wanted to scream at them.

'You are not *better* for that!' she wanted to shout. 'If you had the slightest imagination, you would be *running away.*'

She never said that. And they never changed. They remained as indomitable as ever, though they smiled less. They were weary now. They were rehearsing the old rituals of happiness, perhaps in the hope it would stop being a sham in some unforeseen future, or perhaps because it was all they had left.

Lost in those thoughts, eyes shut, it took her a while

to realise that she was not alone in the chamber. Even Yesugei, who could do many things, never seemed able to keep his armour from making a noise when he moved. And there was his smell, too – years of incense, stained into the ceramite.

She didn't open her eyes. 'How goes it?' she asked.

She felt the Stormseer come close, stoop over her. She sensed his concern, and it irritated her.

'The city falls within an hour,' he said. 'Others being secured.'

Ilya nodded. Another battle over. At least they had won this one. 'Did they have any warning of us?'

'None.'

'And any word of the Gate?'

'None yet.'

Sighing, Ilya opened her eyes at last.

The Stormseer Targutai Yesugei stood before her. He had taken off his helm, revealing his weather-lined face, which was full of concern. His armour was splattered with the stain of old blood, masking the many charms and trinkets that hung from the ringed plate. But that was too cruel – they were much more than trinkets, and Ilya had seen just what he could do with them.

'You found what you seek?' he asked, his voice cautious.

It was the question she had dreaded. This had been her initiative. She had finally prevailed upon the Khagan, and a fifth of the Legion's entire strength had been diverted. Seven convoy raids had been orchestrated, clearing the ground for a major assault on the Kalium installation, all to prepare the way for the invasion of Herevail.

'He is not here,' she said, bluntly. She found it helped a little, not to mask the truth.

Yesugei nodded, and there was not the slightest blame in his eyes. 'And the one we find in the city? Will he live?'

'Yes, he will live. He has been taken to the *Sickle Moon*.' She ran her hands through her wiry hair, noticing as she did so how brittle it had become. 'He knew him. He was wearing the robes of the House.'

'Then that is good, szu. He may know more.'

Ilya shrugged. 'There will not be any more survivors now. I ordered Hoi-Xian to scan the spires in Vorlax. Nothing. They killed everything.'

'That is what they do.'

'Yes, that is what they do.'

The distant crack of munitions carried on, steadily diminishing as the V Legion front established itself. More drop pods would be landing soon, bringing in the second wave of Tactical squads. Herevail would be scoured for the presence of the enemy. When the last of them were hunted down and slain, then the world would be abandoned again, its surviving facilities scuttled and any retrievable resources plundered for the use of the fleet. There were no thoughts of *taking ground* now – such considerations belonged to the past.

'So, szu, do you require medicae attention?' Yesugei asked.

Ilya smiled wanly and looked up at him. 'What would they do for me?' Yesugei started to speak, but Ilya waved him silent. The time when she had crept around the *Swordstorm* in a state of petrified awe was long gone – the White Scars were like family to her now, a boisterous clan of younger brothers, no matter how lethal they could be when the mood came upon them. 'You have no cure for age, I think.'

As she said the words, the unwelcome realisation hit her again, one that had occurred to her with uncomfortable regularity over the last few months.

I will not see the end to this war. And, even if I did, what would be the use of it? I was trained to serve in another Imperium, and that has gone forever.

Yesugei lowered himself to her level. It was a clumsy manoeuvre in power armour. 'Do not blame yourself,' he said in his halting Gothic. 'This worth trying. It may yet bear reward.'

The optimism could get wearing. Even the ranking troops of the Legion had stopped mouthing platitudes at her, but Yesugei never lost faith.

'How long before we can leave?' she asked.

Yesugei paused, consulting his retinal feeds. 'Forty hours, if fate with us.'

'I would prefer to move sooner.'

'That risks leaving some alive.'

Ilya grimaced, and looked up at the grimy ceiling of the narrow chamber. 'And you absolutely have to kill them all, don't you?'

Yesugei withdraw his hand. 'Yes, we do.'

'I suppose that is what you have become good at. And they are getting better at it too.'

'Szu, you are tired.'

'We could have made it!' she cried, rising from her crouch, anger briefly driving out exhaustion. She balled her fists, futilely. 'Two years ago, even one, there might have been a way. You could have left this slaughter and made it back to Terra. But no, that would not have satisfied *honour*. You had to keep going after them, again, again, again.'

Yesugei remained on one knee, his expression never changing, waiting for the storm to abate.

'He should have retreated earlier,' said Ilya. 'None of you told him. Tachseer just wants to keep fighting until something ends his agony. He needed to be told, *then*, that it was pointless to get hemmed in. This enemy is not stupid. Hell, it is the least stupid there ever has been. Did you not think Horus could have engineered this?'

'We have discussed this before,' said Yesugei, calmly.

'Yes, and you did not listen then either.' Ilya felt her cheeks flush, and forced her choler down. She was angry with herself as much as him. Her limbs felt like lead, her head hammered and her breath came in snatches. 'After this, he will have to hear. If there is a way, *any* way, you must take it. When they counsel another raid, another offensive, then you must speak against it. They will listen to you.'

'The Khagan has slowed the enemy.'

'Yes, and at what cost? A third of our fighting strength?' She shook her head. 'Where are his brothers? Where is Lord Dorn? Where is Lord Russ? You are doing this *alone*, and *it is killing you.*'

Yesugei looked at her, and there was nothing but benevolent concern in his scarred face. She knew instantly what he was thinking, for he had told her many times before, and it made her want to scream out in frustration.

We will sacrifice ourselves, if it gives the Throneworld another day, another month, another year. We were made to do this, szu. We were made to die. You find this upsetting.

But he did not say that.

'It was you, who bring us to Herevail,' he said. 'You find this man. That is something. It will lead to something else.'

Ilya let her fists unclench. She suddenly felt foolish, standing before Yesugei's implacable reasonableness. Alone of them, he had not degraded. He was just as he had been when she had met him on Ullanor, back when the galaxy was laid open before humanity's advance and all talk was of triumph.

'Yes,' she said, weakly, with no further strength to argue. 'Yes, it may lead to something.'

Yesugei reached out to her, placed a hand on her upper arm, supporting her. His dark skin cracked in a weak smile. 'Judge not my brothers too harshly,' he said. 'This thing wears at souls. I had my own trial, on *Vorkaudar*. I failed it. In my dreams, sometimes, I see what I become. This is all of us now. He make them fight, because they need it. If they do not, fury devour them.'

She leaned against his arm. She was so physically weak now. It had been five years ago when she had set off from the Munitorum sector headquarters, hunting the elusive primarch. It felt like twenty.

'If we can leave this place sooner, we will,' Yesugei told her. 'Then we take the prize back to *Swordstorm*.'

She nodded. She needed to sleep. She needed, just for a few hours, to forget. Herevail was a hateful charnel-world, just like every world was on the bloody path to the Throne, and the stench of it made her sicker.

'I just hope it was worth it,' she mumbled, feeling sure that it would not be.

✠ ✠ ✠

THE CLOUD-HAMMER RAN ahead of them, belching
soot. Above and below it, Klefor's atmosphere glowed
in celestial splendour – a striated mass of fleshy pinks,
pale greens and blues. Cirrus flecks spiralled away to
the magnetic north – one of the few points of visual
reference in a translucent, hazy ever-sky.

'*It is very ugly,*' voxed Sanyasa.

'It is,' Torghun agreed.

'*I think we should end it.*'

'I think you are right.'

The cloud-hammer airship was still holding course,
giving no sign it had detected them. It was a big
one, fifty metres long with a vane that hung down
in the shimmering airs. Its eight air-turbines burned
white-hot, keeping its iron-clad bulk aloft on a broken cushion of superheat. Its gunnery blisters cycled
idly, scouring the eye-watering infinity of Klefor's gaseous atmosphere.

It was still far from its target. Once in place, the
cloud-hammer's hull would split open, revealing the
rows of sleek bombs nestling in their racks, ready to be
sent whistling down through the kilometres of steadily thickening air before striking far-off solid ground.
Such weapons had been deployed remorselessly on
Klefor, beating the fortress-cities of the Loyalist Ale-
gorinda Stoneguard close to submission.

But not this one. It had just a few minutes of active
service left before it was suddenly, and quite unex-
pectedly, to be taken out of commission.

Seven jetbikes spun out of the glare of the suns,
keeping high above the cloud-hammer's backwash.
All were a dirty white, with blunt prows and outsized
atmospheric engines. Once within visual range of the

behemoth ahead of them, they split up, racing to get ahead of the rear gunners before they could draw a bead.

The cloud-hammer picked them up and fell away to its left, lumbering awkwardly on swathes of down-draught. Projectile rounds pinged past the incoming jetbikes, aimed from the spherical gun-pods strung along its iron hull-plate.

'*Hai!*' shouted Sanyasa, swinging lazily away from a cloud of flak and burning in fast. Holian, Wai-Long and Ozad shot out beyond him, drawing more fire before pulling in close themselves. Inchig and Ahm came along with Torghun on the opposite flank, getting closer with every blurred second.

'Remember what I told you about the engines,' Torghun voxed, training his helm reticules and syncing with the jetbike's underslung heavy bolter.

'*They are most dangerous,*' Sanyasa replied earnestly, ducking under another incoming burst.

The cloud-hammer loomed above them as the jetbikes dropped down as one, falling like stones.

'And hence…' supplied Torghun.

'*…must be taken up close,*' finished Sanyasa, kicking in the last ounce of boost to carry him ahead of the hunt-pack.

The jetbikes angled up again, arrowing in on the cloud-hammer's churning bank of motive thrusters. They were lost in a shaking mass of air, wreathed with afterburner plumes. The heat was detectable even through power armour, and they were still sixty metres out.

Four of the seven jetbikes pulled alongside the cloud-hammer, raking its gunnery points. Torghun,

Sanyasa and Ozad remained in the engine-wake, fighting hard to bring their jetbike prows under the immense lower lintel of the thruster-housing.

Torghun crouched low in the saddle, ignoring the flickers of flame catching on the chassis of his mount. His targeting reticules danced wildly, knocked off centre by the buffeting thunder, so he turned them off and used his eyes.

Sanyasa fired first, followed by Torghun, with Ozad a fraction of a second behind. Three streams of bolt-rounds shot directly into the heart of the furnace, smacking and cracking against the inner curve of the thrusters and splintering the metal into slivers. Debris flew out, clanging and wheeling as it broke from the substructure. Torghun dropped lower, firing all the while as a sickle-shaped slice of burning steel shot over him.

The main thruster blew, exploding around its circumference and shearing from the cloud-hammer's underbelly. As the entire unit came away, the three jetbikes angled steeply, pulling clear of the disintegrating engine assembly. Huge bursts of exhaust-smog vomited out from the ruined feeder-lines, laced with sparks. The cloud-hammer's trajectory dipped. With a squeal and clank of tortured metal-plate, the machine began to list, beginning the plummet that would take it down through the atmosphere-layers and into Klefor's distant core.

Torghun spun away high, scything through desperate scatter-fire from the gunnery blisters. It would be pleasing to watch the thing burn, though its demise would still take hours and there were other targets to hit.

'*Darga*,' voxed Inchig from his vantage on the high-right flank, using the Khorchin sergeant rank-equivalent. '*Pull to my position.*'

As Torghun wheeled away right, he saw what Inchig meant – a juddering rain of return bolter-fire emerging from the hunched spine of the cloud-hammer. Wai-Long was hit, and his jetbike careened erratically away, leaking promethium-smoke.

Torghun's helm zoomed in, revealing bare steel power armour emerging from a hatch on the cloud-hammer's aft summit. Even as the airship lost altitude, the crew were coming out of it to fight.

'Scrape them off,' he ordered, zeroing in on the lead figure. He unlocked the heavy bolter again, sending a trail of impacts snapping down the cloud-hammer's roof before they smashed into the legionary, slamming him from his footing and sending him sailing out into the clouds, limbs cartwheeling.

But more crawled out of the interior, setting up fire-points and opening up against the jetbikes that circled around the carcass of the machine. Sanyasa smashed one apart, making armour-segments fly as a power-pack exploded. Another managed to erect a tripod-mounted beam weapon and punched a hole through Gerg's jetbike-muzzle, but the array and its operator were blown away by a vengeful Holian following close behind.

As the cloud-hammer plummeted further, only one defender remained exposed on the airship's roof – a heavy-plated warrior wielding a chainsword. That one remained exposed even as the jetbikes circled for the kill, brandishing his close-combat weapon and bellowing challenges into the buffeting wind.

Torghun detected the targeting beads locking on the warrior and dipped his jetbike towards the swaying metal below.

'Leave him,' he ordered, aiming his mount across the bucking airship-roof. 'He is mine.'

As the jetbike skidded into contact with the cloud-hammer's hull, Torghun leapt clear, his power sword fizzing. His enemy charged towards him, negotiating the swaying terrain with perfect balance. He was clad in an old armour variant, crusted with reinforced cable-housings and ridged greaves. Oily smoke oozed from his damaged power-pack, and his slatted helm was marked with dirty yellow chevrons.

Iron Warriors were rarely given to battlefield oratory, and this one did not depart from the pattern. He swayed into close range, his chainsword growling. Torghun met the first strike two-handed, absorbing the hit and throwing the whirling blade back. He darted in, moving with the tilt of the plummeting deck, reacting faster than his iron-heavy counterpart.

'I like your spirit,' Torghun voxed, trading more blows with the scything chainblade. 'Though not your stench.'

He lashed out, hitting the chainsword at full strength in the middle of the blade. The angle was perfect and sliced clean through the rotating teeth, sending chain-links flying free in bouncing lengths. The Iron Warrior clenched his fist and punched out, but Torghun had already pulled left, jerked the blade back, then slashed out again, hitting under his enemy's gorget point-first. The disruptor-charged steel pushed on through, severing both flesh and armour-links.

Torghun wrenched the sword upwards, tearing the Iron Warrior's head free. The ruined chainsword clattered away, careening down the slope of the cloud-hammer's carapace. Its owner's corpse joined it soon after, dragged along the reeling roof-plates.

By now the airship was pulling over close to thirty degrees, and the spine-sections were quickly turning into flank-sections. Torghun sprinted up the slope to where his jetbike had auto-anchored, its engines still gunning. He threw himself back into the saddle as the cloud-hammer's carcass fell away into its death-dive, consigning any crew still within to a long, spiralling descent.

He pushed clear of the wreck, sheathing his blade as the jetbike whined into altitude. As he did so, Sanyasa's mount streaked past, dipping its wing-stubs in amused salute.

'*Necessary, darga?*' Sanyasa voxed.

'The only way they learn,' Torghun replied, catching up with the rest of the squadron. The cloud-hammer was now a hundred metres below them and picking up momentum. Its stabiliser vanes cracked, and the lifter-turbines started running wildly out of tolerance.

Klefor's gaseous heights gleamed around them, suffused with the light of its suns and scrubbed of the churning toxicity of the airship. Even the engine-trails of the jetbikes seemed cleaner, vaporising to interlaced lines of pale white over a blushed screen of colour.

'Then this was good hunting,' said Sanyasa, boosting ahead.

'It was,' said Torghun, powering after him. 'And there's more to come.'

✠ ✠ ✠

TWELVE HOURS PASSED before they terminated the raid. They rendezvoused with the lifter, stowed the attack bikes and pulled clear of Klefor's upper atmosphere. Then they docked with the system-runner *R54* and headed out to the void.

Wai-Long did not join them. His jetbike had exploded on an uncontrolled plummet following the bolter-hit, instantly destroying him and his mount. That was their only casualty, though they would mourn him, for he had been a good fighter and a good soul. The sagyar mazan were battle-brothers twice-over – once for the Legion, once for the kinship of enforced exile.

They had started out with twenty-two. Torghun had been the only khan among them; the others had been drawn from the ranks of brotherhoods that had contested control of the capital ships over Prospero. They came into the squad as individuals, each sundered from his old comrades, for errant units had been carefully broken up by the Legion commanders.

Many sagyar mazan had taken to the abyss in conjunction with other Legion units – Iron Hands, mostly, though some had travelled with Salamanders and Raven Guard. Torghun's squad was purely White Scars, an even mix of Terran and Chogorian. They had taken the assault boat *Hooked Arrow* into the abyss, shot far ahead of the main Legion formation and had been charged, as all were, with a simple task: to erase their crimes through death in service.

The *Hooked Arrow* had lasted two years, finally being destroyed in a sustained action against an Iron Warriors patrol off the Periclan Shoals. They had lost six of their number in that one encounter, but still death did not come for the rest of them. Those who remained commandeered a sub-warp corvette, scratching around for several months on inter-world comms-runs, before the opportunity of taking a faster vessel came along, and they seized *R54*. That gave them a proper berth for their retained jetbikes and an armoury ready to restock with seized trophies. It was a battered old ship, once a minor escort in service of the XIV Legion, now barely capable of surviving a medium-severity warp storm and as slow as the oils that seeped from its leaking enginarium. Still, it had a Geller field, a functioning gunnery array and a happy knack of keeping them alive for *just one more* attack run.

Sanyasa had wanted to rename it. Like all Chogorians, he found non-poetic designations for warships offensive. Torghun had not let him.

'It would be bad luck,' he had told him. *Luck* was something that had come to obsess him since Prospero, something that had never been the case before. 'We will be nameless soon – let this keep its old one.'

One by one, more battle-brothers had died. The squad was whittled down to ten, then eight, then seven. Wai-Long's death made it six, barely enough to crew the system-runner even with a skeleton mortal complement and servitor assistance. Torghun had seldom used his khan designation before, and henceforth did so even less, taking on the role of darga of an arban – the least of all divisions.

Still, they ran ahead of the warfront. The main V Legion formations had long since dispersed, splitting their attacks into isolated strikes to avoid total annihilation. The surviving sagyar mazan units pulled back too, while staying for as long as they could in harm's way. Their only tactical consideration was to remain in contact with the enemy – to disrupt his lines, to hit his communication routes, to go after his commanders.

All of the penitential death-squads, via one tortuous route or another, had heard the stories of Dwell. That had been close. It would have been the crowning achievement of them all, one worthy of acknowledgement even in the upper echelons of the Legion. Hibou Khan's position was now unknown, swallowed up by the vengeful Sons of Horus counter-offensive. Word of the Iron Hands commander Meduson still filtered back from time to time, though with him it was always hard to separate truth from rumour from misinformation. A shifting hinterland of half-snatched tales and deed-rolls for the fugitives had taken hold, fuelling ambition and keeping despair from overcoming those doomed to die.

And so they lived a twilight existence, forever on the brink of their rightful death, riding the bow-wave of the enemy offensive, snapping at it like gadflies for as long as they could before its remorseless momentum caught up with them. That day would not be a cause for grief, for by the laws of the Altak their sins would be expunged by it, just as Wai-Long's were – just as all the other penitents' had been.

Back in the system-runner, Torghun sat on his chamber's metal bunk, holding Wai-Long's old glaive in his hands, running a finger along the rune-carved stave. Wai-Long had been of the plains, and his brothers would wish to give him a plains ceremony, burning the weapon, warding his spirit for the journey across the arch of an empty sky. If there had been a body, it would have been stripped of its armour and committed to the void, in imitation of what they had once done when warfare was a matter of mounted equines.

The Path of Heaven, they called it: the bridge between the world of souls and the world of flesh, something Torghun had never studied as much as he should have done. Few Terrans had. In the beginning, it had all been rationality and anti-superstition. Then, when that changed again, they had ushered in daemons rather than gods, and the virtue of keeping the immaterial locked away in ignorance suddenly became more clearly apparent.

They had been so close to the edge. None of them had really known, not fully. At times, Torghun would wake from nightmares, his body sheened in sweat, remembering the voices that they had listened to on the *Starspear*.

Since then, the consequences of failure had become all too obvious. He had fought Emperor's Children legionaries with their self-mutilations, and warriors of the Sons of Horus in league with *yaksha*, and Word Bearers apostles with robes still sticky with mortal blood. That was the future he had been steered away from. Compared to that, death in combat felt like reward beyond price.

Outside the chamber, Torghun heard the tread of armoured boots. He placed the glaive back on the rack, just as Sanyasa ducked under the mortal-scale door-hatch.

'This came before we entered the warp,' Sanyasa said, handing him a data-slate. 'Sent direct.'

Torghun looked down at the crystal-faced slab. It was a Legion communication, not an astropath signal.

These were sent over encrypted sub-warp routes, stepping-stoned from kill-squad to kill-squad. That method reduced the message-range by many times, but increased speed and security. The last such missive had come two years ago, warning the death-marked to clear out of the path of an offensive run by the ordu. After that, nothing.

He thumbed the entry-rune and waited for the retinal scan. Sanyasa stood just inside the doorway, making no attempt to join him.

Torghun read the communique. Then he read it again. Then he erased the contents and data-scoured the slate's storage coil.

'When do you wish to perform kal damarg?' he asked, tossing the slate onto the altar-top beside him.

'When we next drop out of the warp. What did it say?'

'A sector-avoidance command. We are to stay away from Lansis and Gethmora.'

'We are months away from either.'

'That is fortunate. How fares the ship?'

Sanyasa looked at him for a few moments. Then his eyes dropped back to Wai-Long's racked weapon. 'Well enough. Ozad has picked up something on the augur. Might be something worth pursuing.'

Torghun stood up. 'Good. I will look at it.' He moved to the doorway, and Sanyasa stood aside to let him pass. 'Klefor was a victory, brother. It was noble, to die for that.'

Sanyasa nodded. 'May our fate be the same.'

'Indeed,' agreed Torghun, heading out and up to the bridge. 'We can but hope.'

NINE

KONENOS STRODE THROUGH the corridors of the Keystone, kicking aside the last detritus of combat. Muffled cracks still rang out from the lower levels – White Scars suicide squads, left behind to hamper the pursuit. They were proving tough to eliminate, though the end would come within the hour. Kalium's docks had been retaken, purged of residual booby-traps, and made serviceable for III Legion landers to bring in constructor details.

It had been a well-fought defence, one that had severely damaged the enemy. It ought to have been satisfying.

Konenos entered the Hall of Images, barely looking up at the statues of the Imperial Virtues, abstract representation of things that had once been aggressively promoted: Resilience, Reason, Industry, Thrift. The artistry was shocking – the kind of numb, talentless dross that the Offices of Propagation had churned out in industrial quantities during the Expansion Phase.

Even before enlightenment, he couldn't imagine Fulgrim tolerating any of that filth on a III Legion warship. As it was, his troops had defaced those in the Keystone fortress, replacing the heads of the statues with the bloodied heads of White Scars warriors, hacking the outstretched arms off, replacing other body parts with various obscenities. Altogether, life was more rewarding under the new dispensation.

He reached the portals leading into the facility's Mirrored Sanctum, where Eidolon had chosen to place his command centre. The sentries, two legionaries wearing gold-and-sapphire aquila helm-masks, bowed as he passed.

The walls beyond glittered with reflected light. The fighting had not penetrated this far into the Keystone's superstructure, and so all was intact. Even so, sensory-thralls had been busy polishing, refining, re-equipping. Silken drapes hung from the high ceiling in layers, gauze billowing from the clouds of powdery incense pumped out of hovering aroma-units. A hundred mortal slaves bowed as he passed, their heads pressed against the chequerboard floor, waiting motionless for orders. Most had been changed – elongated, compressed, blinded, given extra eyes, whatever whims the fleshweavers had felt like indulging. Legionaries lounged among them, some polishing blades, some in a post-combat stupor.

Eidolon himself sat atop a throne of lapis lazuli and hammered bronze. Its armrests were carved into the form of two rearing serpents, the back moulded into a depiction of an open maw lined with curved teeth.

Within the creature's mouth, hellish visions writhed, moving subtly by the light of the many candelabra, or perhaps from other sources.

Eidolon slumped in his seat, toying with something in the palms of his gauntlets. His helm was gone, and he looked maudlin.

Konenos knew why – he felt the same. Combat-withdrawal was harder now than it had ever been. The stimm comedown was harsh, and only partly ameliorated by lower dose adjustments. The world outside the battlefield had become almost permanently fuzzy – a low-volume, soft-edged dreamscape.

At least we can survive its withdrawal now, he thought, perfectly aware of where this direction led. *That may not always be true.*

'Orchestrator,' said Eidolon, lifting his bruised chin a fraction. 'Your armour is disordered.'

Konenos smiled. The last White Scars legionary he had killed had managed to crack his pauldron open. The resultant vox-scream had burst the warrior's head, but the loss of symmetry had still been annoying.

'It will be replaced, lord,' he replied. 'The order is already with the artificers.'

'You will have creative suggestions, no doubt.'

'There will be… Chogorian inspirations.'

Eidolon's eyes drifted over to the silk drapes. His movements were even more sluggish than expected. Perhaps he had dosed himself too vigorously. 'I had hoped *he* might be with them. The Warhawk.'

'Then we would have lost.'

'Probably.' Eidolon looked thoughtful. 'But how far have we been elevated now, do you think? To slay a primarch… That would disturb the equilibrium.'

Konenos said nothing. Eidolon was entitled to fantasise – he'd probably earned that with the kill-tally he'd reaped out on the docking-plates. Of all of them, all those gifted with psychosonic hell-weapons, he was by far the most proficient.

And so, who knew? Perhaps he was even right. Perhaps Fabius had indeed made him a match for a Legion progenitor. Or maybe that was just the old hubris, placed in a new vessel.

'We have reports from other raids,' Konenos said.

'I know them,' replied Eidolon, disinterestedly. 'Some we won, some we lost.'

'We blooded them deep.'

'Surely, and yet I deem their heart was not truly in it. Tell me, do you know the name Herevail?'

'Capital world of the Telgam subsector. In counter-compliance for two months. Now in the final stages of reduction. Why do you ask?'

'What is there, on Herevail?'

Konenos had to think. 'Medium-grade industrial output. It was populated, and there were plans to raise regiments. Beyond that–'

'Yes, yes, so dull, so much I already know. It was their real target, you know this? They were prepared to surrender Kalium, all to protect their attack there. They knew more than we did. It was our world, one we owned, and we missed something.'

Konenos frowned. 'I can send scrutiniser teams.'

Eidolon laughed lazily. 'By the time they get there, the Scars will be long gone. You know them.'

'Then we go after them.' Konenos felt a last spike of combat-chems flare up at the thought. 'They are running, lord. We can cut them down as they flee.'

'You are not the first to counsel this. Take a look.'

Eidolon tossed a slate at Konenos, who caught it one-handed. It was a standard command-tablet, used for storing astropathic interpretations. The runes on its crystal surface were in two levels of cipher, then disguised further with references from Chemos mythology. The dream-scryers who had taken this message would be dead by now – any transmission from such a source would have been very carefully protected.

It took him a moment to unlock the content. 'The Warmaster,' he said eventually. He left unsaid his immediate response. *So he takes more interest in our doings than our own gene-father.*

'Interesting, is it not?' remarked Eidolon. 'The Lord of Death hastens towards us. Somehow, Lupercal has got it into his head that we would work well with the Fourteenth Legion. I do not really think that likely, do you?'

'Come, my lord, this is what you wanted,' said Konenos, studying the command-scripts closely. 'Sanction to take on the Fifth Legion entire. With the Death Guard, it could be done.'

'I had sanction before. I am not some witless menial, nor a Son of Horus, to be commanded by that warp-swollen abortion.' Eidolon's gaze kept shifting over to the gauze-layers, as if he had buried something behind them that intrigued him. 'So I am not inclined to follow this command. I have had my fill of barbarians and wish to find other souls to torment. Do you not enjoy it, when we toy with Ferrus' sons? They die so slowly, and in such rage.'

Konenos was about to reply when the great doors at the Sanctum suddenly slammed open. The body of a blood-masked door-guard skidded through the gap, his weapon knocked from his grasp. Konenos whirled around, grabbing his own bolt pistol. All around the Sanctum's margins, legionaries levelled bolters.

A lone figure strolled in, clad in the armour of the III Legion, no weapon in his hands. He went helm-less, exposing the sculpted features of the Chemosian aristocracy. A pair of ice-blue eyes surveyed Eidolon's court with cool contempt.

'And now,' Eidolon murmured, 'we have this to torment us.'

'My lord!' Ravasch Cario called out, stepping around the struggling door-guard and striding up to the throne. 'I had heard it said that the Soul-Severed still prosecuted the war. End my confusion, and tell me why you are not already in the void.'

Eidolon gazed at the intruder, intrigued. Slowly, those around the hall's edges relaxed their grip on their weapons, though muzzles remained angled at Cario's head.

'A Palatine Blade,' Eidolon said. 'A singular honour. But where is your troupe, prefector? Surely you did not mislay them en route.'

Cario came to stand before Eidolon, and Konenos watched him all the way. The blademaster's bearing was immaculate, his poise impeccable, but the absence of flesh-improvement was disappointing. It spoke of a lack of ambition, and fate had a way of punishing that level of pride.

'You sent us a tithe of what we asked for,' Cario accused, not bothering to acknowledge Konenos. 'If you had answered the summons, I would be here at the head of a salvaged supply convoy.'

'*Summons*,' said Eidolon. 'Is that what you call it?'

'We have warp-wakes. You have means of divining them.' Cario's fury was artfully contained, and as cold as marble. 'Let them go now, and let go the last of your paltry honour.'

'Now, then, brother. I did that a long time ago.'

Cario glared up at the throne. 'Find them.'

'You have bolters trained on you from every angle,' said Eidolon. 'Prefector, I do not think you are in a position to give many orders.'

Cario had moved before the last syllable left Eidolon's mouth. Konenos opened fire immediately, missing by a fraction. All the others fired, also too slowly – the post-combat narcotics in their blood, the lethargy, it all combined.

Cario reached the throne in a single leap, boosting up from the dais and swinging his drawn blade up at Eidolon's fleshy neck. He pressed the sabre's steel into the white-grey skin, clamping down on the Soul-Severed's shoulder with his free gauntlet.

'No further!' Eidolon cried, addressing his troops, now clustering towards the throne. Konenos, who had trained his pistol on Cario's exposed temple, held his finger against the trigger.

By then the Lord Commander Primus was breathing heavily. His eyes sparkled. 'By the gods, you are fast.'

'And you are grown fat.' Cario's eyes stayed narrow. 'Death-shrieks will not be heard in the void. There is still a need for the blade.'

'So you have proved. But withdraw now, please – against expectation, I find I do not wish to kill you.'

'Then end this sham. Order the pursuit.'

'I do not enjoy being instructed at the point of a sword.'

Watching the theatrics unfold, Konenos allowed himself a dry smile. Every indication spoke to the contrary.

Slowly, Cario withdrew the blade's edge. He pulled back from the throne. The anger remained, though, and he did not sheathe the charnabal sabre.

'For shame, brother,' said Eidolon, his sutured cheeks flushing as he adjusted his position. 'There was a time when we would debate our strategy with fine words.'

Cario looked distastefully up at the silks, the twisted slaves, the puffs of incense. 'There was a time when words were enough.'

'But what makes you suppose I have any means of finding the Khan?' Eidolon was still enjoying himself. 'He has a reputation, you know.'

Cario stepped down from the dais and strode over to the lengths of silk. With a twin strike of his blade, one-two, he slashed the curtains aside.

Behind them, suspended on golden chains far above the chequerboard floor, hung a side of meat. Once it had been more than that – a superhuman warrior clad in ivory ceramite. Now it was mere flesh and sinew, quivering, kept alive by pain-machines clamped to its brain-stem, its spine, what remained of its face. A fixed, silent scream was locked on its skinless face, looped through the coils of agony amplifiers. Psychically attuned plates had been set on either side of its temples, each one feeding cables that looped up to the incense-clouded ceiling. Despite its lack of eyes, it sensed the removal of its silk shroud, and twitched.

'Learned much yet?' Cario asked.

Eidolon shrugged. 'We have made a start.'

Cario finally scabbarded his sabre. He turned back to

the throne. 'Do this thing, and word shall go to every Palatine fraternity in the sector. If you grow weary of the game, consider at least the aesthetics – we can do this to all of them.'

Eidolon eyed the prefector hungrily then. That was the key to him, Konenos realised: the Lord Commander Primus no longer fought for the cause, for the primarch, even for himself. He fought to keep himself amused.

'The Death Lord burns through the warp,' said Eidolon. 'He has been ordered to join with us. Did you know this?'

Cario fixed his blue eyes on his nominal master. 'It changes nothing.'

Eidolon smiled. 'It changes everything.' He turned to Konenos. 'And you would be in accord with this, I take it?'

'Always.'

'Yes, always.'

Eidolon sat back in the throne, his eyes fixed on Cario. 'I needed something to stir my blood again. Perhaps you are it.'

The prefector turned away, unconcerned. 'Whatever you need,' he said, his voice low. 'Just get me close enough. I ask nothing more.'

A FLEET MUSTER was a critical time.

For most of the years-long campaign following Prospero, the White Scars had been dispersed. Chondax had been an aberration – a rare instance of the entire Legion operating as one. As the forces of the War-master had pressed their advantage, the V Legion had reverted to type – splitting up, forming autonomous battalions, using their speed and void craft to stay one step ahead of destruction.

Now new orders had been given out – the ships were pulling back, squadron by squadron, battling their way across the turbulent aether-seas to join with the command group in the Aerelion System. Those that had already made it now hung in high orbital anchor above Aerelion III, a giant of indigo gas-swathes and violent electrical storms.

Large-scale void war was always hard to prosecute with any certainty. In the absence of any reliable detection systems working over supra-system scales, fleet commanders had to judge enemy positions via a mix of warp-wake soundings, uncertain espionage, psychic reading, or blind luck. Galactic wars were not fought to conquer contiguous territorial zones; they were battles over the thousand points of light amid the endless dark – fortress-worlds that could be attacked from any direction at any time. The existence of 'fronts' and 'salients', though widely referred to by strategos, was in the strictest sense inaccurate, since physical void extension was only erratically mapped to the underlying currents that governed the immaterium. Before Horus had launched his run to the Throneworld, no such assault, not even at Ullanor, had truly deserved to be described as a single battlefront. Only the Warmaster's advance, through its sheer scale and audacity, carried the volume of destruction necessary to amount to a coherent line of ravaged worlds, and even then the gaps were far larger than areas of compassed, controlled space.

Nonetheless, placing all major Legion assets in one place was a risk, particularly as the enemy outnumbered the White Scars many times over. The Khan had studiously avoided massed engagement throughout the years of open war, knowing that it would end him. Only as the net closed in and the policy of targeted raids became less effective did the strategy change.

The process was perilous from beginning to end. Astropathic messages could be intercepted, encryptions deciphered, physical comms broken. It would have been safer to linger at Aerelion for just a few days, but it would take far longer than that to assemble the sundered Legion warships, during which time their location was always liable to be uncovered.

A policy of misinformation had been triggered alongside the true communications effort, something made easier by the difficulty non-Chogorians had in understanding Khorchin inflections. False gatherings were seeded into astropathic screeds, incorrect names mingled with true instructions. Suicide squads had been sent out to far-flung locations to lend credence to dummy musters, each trajectory carefully rigged to resemble the real thing.

Now, all that could be done had been done. The ordu was drawing itself back together, preparing for the exercise that would see it fulfil its vows or destroy itself in the attempt.

Every serviceable frigate had been placed on the perimeter of Aerelion's gravity well, and an ever-shifting sphere of fleet pickets now patrolled far into the system reaches. All approaches to the Mandeville point had been heavily mined, save for the one clear path left to allow ingress and egress for ships with the requisite code-chains.

From a private observation chamber at the summit of the *Swordstorm*'s command tower, the architect of the policy observed his fleet coming into coherence. He watched the sleek lines of the *Qo-Fian* slide past the immense shadow of the *Lance of Heaven*, with the *Tchin-Zar* some way off, having only broken the veil two hours previously. Every battleship bore heavy damage. Those that had recently made the warp-stage from Kalium were the worst, and were now surrounded by heavy shells of void scaffolds, over which swarmed Legion repair teams and Mechanicum overseer details.

No lumens had been lit in the Khan's chamber. Two candles burned, each one scented with oils from Chogoris – one was *iryal*, the anointment given to those about to head into battle, the other *gagaan*, that smeared on the foreheads of those who had died. Between the candles were the two pieces of Qin Xa's dragon-helm, his blood still stained across the inside curve.

When that helm had been brought before the primarch, he had said nothing. He had sat on the command throne of the *Swordstorm*'s bridge, the pieces in his lap, his dark eyes focused on the metal, as if by boring into them he could somehow reverse the fate of its owner.

None had dared disturb him for orders, and the flagship's crew had held silent station, breath caught, waiting.

Eventually, the primarch had lifted his severe profile from the broken helm and given the order he had put off for too long.

'No more. Order the muster.'

And so they had made for Aerelion. The Master of

the Horde had withdrawn to his private chambers, and none had broken the sanctity of his meditation-space.

It was the same space in which he had received his Father the last time the two of them had been alone together. Back then, they had both stood before the great crystalflex ports, watching as the night curve of Terra had rolled slowly beneath them. They had exchanged few words prior to separation, for words were ever hard to come by between them. They had skirted around the issue that divided them – the Imperial Truth – for neither had wished to part on poisonous terms.

And so the Khan's most lasting memory of his gene-sire – more profound than the great displays of power on Ullanor, more lasting even than the first, glorious descent to the plains of Chogoris – was of a very human awkwardness.

He had attempted to speak of the *Swordstorm*'s majesty, to highlight what a superlative ship his artisans had made with what they had been given. 'Nothing is faster,' he had said. 'Nothing serves you better. We have poured our hearts into this, and made it perfect.'

His Father had understood that. He had appreciated the ingenuity of the changes. More than any other, He comprehended the ancient technology at the heart of His Imperium's war vessels, for His genius lay behind the ancient templates, just as it lay behind all else that was significant in the expanding galactic empire.

And yet, He had not praised His son for his labours, for that had never been His way. His proud face, so hard to perceive clearly, so ineffable and so severe, had never moved from consideration of the stars beyond the armourglass.

'And even these,' the Emperor had said, 'are fleeting.'

What had that meant? There was no good in asking, for the Master of Mankind never explained. At the time, the Khan had taken the remark to be a reference to the *Swordstorm*'s speed, but later on he could no longer sustain the illusion. Everything in his Father's demeanour had suggested impatience – a desire to move on from what had been done, to what might yet be done. The Emperor had been talking about something else, something to come after what He had built amid the ruins of Terra's past, something that had not been revealed.

Now, when all had been cast into the flames, the Khan returned to that moment more and more. There were nights when it gave him hope, for there was always the chance that the Emperor had somehow foreseen this great rupture, and that it meshed with His designs in some way – and such would not be completely impossible, for His genius in the beginning had been untouchable, accepted even by those who had fought futilely against His rise.

But he could not sustain that hope for long. With every defeat, every astropathic-tiding of another ravaged world, it became clear that the great designs had been derailed, and that Horus had acted for reasons that were entirely his own. For all the centuries in the planning, the Emperor's vision had proved fallible, open to assault, apt for destruction.

What were You intending? the Khan asked himself, watching the shadows of his great war fleet preparing themselves. *You were never a fool. You knew the risks of leaving the war to Your sons. There must be something else.*

Perhaps Magnus had known. Perhaps those who had been closest to the Emperor in counsel – Dorn, Guilliman, Fulgrim – had done so as well. The Khan had never been close. He and his Father had been different in all things, servants of different creeds, with as much innate sympathy as the nomads had always had for the settled. If there was a reason for the Emperor's decisions after the Triumph, then the White Scars would not have been told of it. They would have been let loose, just as they had always been, to take the war to the outer margins of the empire, to be forgotten until they were needed again, feared, disregarded, as unwholesome as Russ' berserkers but without the predictability.

So I fight for a Father who I never loved, against a brother that I did. I defend an empire that never wanted me against an army that would have taken me in a heartbeat.

And yet the oath had been made. The promise could not be broken.

Seeing Mortarion's fall had been enough, as had the visions of ruin on Prospero. Horus had swapped one tyrant for others, ones that would eventually devour him. If it had been a mistake to pretend the warp never existed, it was an even greater one to believe the words of those who dwelled within it.

The lines had been drawn. All that remained was to put each side to the test.

Jaghatai turned away from the vista, back towards the candlelit chamber. Silhouetted under the arch beyond Qin Xa's memorial altar was the outline of Jubal Khan. He had not moved, waiting for the command to approach, until then standing as still and silent as stone.

'Come,' ordered the Khagan, walking past the altar and descending a shallow flight of stairs. Jubal fell in alongside him, and together they entered another chamber below the observation level. There, rough-cut sandstone walls were hung with calligraph-scrolls. Fires burned in lined circular pits, just as they had done in the old Talskar realms. The lightning strike of the Legion had been inlaid in gold over the far wall, and the metal glinted from the dancing flames. Hides hung tight from wooden racks, scraped clean, as taut as sinews.

'Did you see him fall?' asked the Khan, reaching for a goblet of *halaak* – the fermented lactose that only a Chogorian's constitution absorbed without challenge.

'No, Khagan. We were sundered by battle.'

'He was brought home by the sorcerer.'

'He was.'

The Khan took a long sip, savouring the acrid taste. 'They tell me the Kalium Gate was mined.'

'Fleet augurs detected them once we were close,' said Jubal, standing stiffly before his master, his hands by his sides. They looked similar, those two – the hooked nose, long oil-black hair, earth-dark skin. 'We could not have used the portal.'

'So you called off the attack.'

'The numbers were too great. If the Gate had been intact, then–'

'You would have fought on further, hoping to turn the tide. And still lost.' The Khan had already studied all the battlefield reports, and had gauged every tactic employed by every detachment. 'Just as you said – the numbers were too great. It was well that you withdrew when you did, for they are getting better at reading us.'

He stared into the depths of his goblet. The murky liquid gazed back.

'Khagan, are you angered?' Jubal asked, cautiously.

'Angered?'

'It was another loss. The keshiga…' Jubal trailed off.

The Khan felt a spasm of pain, and paused before replying. 'Qin Xa took a thousand souls with him. He more than accounted for himself. That is all we can hope for, is it not?' He looked up directly at Jubal. 'We could huddle together, hoping to avoid danger in numbers, and perhaps the war would pass us by. Or we could strike at the enemy where he travels, trusting to fate to guard our souls.' His lips pressed together, as close as he got to a smile, though he did not entirely hide the hurt. 'The wind blows east, the wind blows west. Our fortunes will change.'

He moved over to two stools, arranged as the Altak war-chief would have had them – low to the stone floor, criss-crossed lengths of wood, slung with cured hides. Each one was far larger than the old mortal-scale warlord-thrones, built for the outsized bulk of the Legiones Astartes. The Khan gestured towards one, and sank down into the other. His long limbs, clad in a crimson kaftan, stretched out lithely over the leather.

Jubal did as he was bid, though uncomfortably. Like most of the ordu, he preferred to stand, or take the saddle.

'I need a new keshiga,' the Khan said.

'Namahi is a fine choice.'

'I have not yet spoken to him. I wished to speak to you.'

Jubal looked even more uncomfortable. 'Khagan, you do me too much honour.'

'Too much honour?'

'More than I deserve.' Jubal looked up to face him. 'The Master of the Keshig is your right arm. He is your sword. He must know your mind like none other. I was not on Chondax, nor Prospero. There are others with better claim.'

'Hasik is gone. Jemulan is gone. The list is shorter than you think.'

'What of Tachseer?'

'What of him?'

'There are many in the brotherhoods who would wish it for him.'

'My warriors wish for many things. I am not bound to grant them.' The Khan took another sip. 'Shiban was a poet, Yesugei tells me. Now he does not write, he does not sing, and he does not laugh.' He swilled the cup around before him, watching the play of light on the rim. 'I guard more than the ordu's fighting strength, Jubal. There are those under my command who fight with the sun of the plains in their eyes. There are those who reflect the darkness of the enemy, for it has entered their blood. Both will kill at my command, but I take no joy, and never have, in killing without artistry. Do you see what I am saying?'

'It will not sit well with those who name him Restorer.'

'And that disturbs you.'

'Not at all. So long as you know.'

'Let them whisper.' The Khan put the goblet down. 'So we have it, then? You will not outright refuse me. I give you this honour and you will accept it, grudgingly, your feet dragged to my side like a whipped lad.'

Jubal laughed, despite himself. 'You reject my

counsel, so what remains? My blade is yours, Khagan, as it always has been. But grant me one thing – I will not take the title. Qin Xa was the only Master of the Keshig you have known. I will not live in his shadow.'

The Khan inclined his head. 'So be it. You are the hunter, the slayer of beasts. Thus I name you *Ahn-ezen*, Master of the Hunt. How does that sound in your ears?'

Jubal rose to his feet, and bowed low. 'Khagan, it is fitting.'

The Khan rose in turn, and drew his tulwar. He held it before him, letting the curved shadow fall over Jubal's flame-lit face. 'I shall hold you to the name. No more the Lord of Summer Lightning, but my hunts-man. My wide-ranger, my bringer of trophies. You will bring honour to the Horde, even as the darkness falls.'

'Be sure of it.'

The Khan placed the sword's edge against Jubal's cheek, balancing it perfectly, resting it on the edge of the raised scar. 'Let there be no illusion, the way ahead will be dark.' Then he drew it away, flashing the steel against the firelight before placing it back in its ivory sheath. 'We are running out of room, Ahn-ezen.'

'All must change.'

'Aye, it must. The storms hem us, we cannot run these raids any longer. I bring the ordu together, even those who once broke the law of the Altak. We shall meet this thing united.'

'Then can you tell me, yet?' Jubal asked. 'What is your purpose?'

'Not yet. I await tidings from my counsellor,' said the Khan, a wry look on his scarred face. 'I sense him now, he is close. In truth it was for him that I sent my sons into peril. If he brings the tidings we hope, then there may yet be a way to my Father's side, and to the walls of Terra.'

'And if not?'

'If not, then we cannot leave the void,' the Khan said, bleakly. 'We shall die here, but we shall yet make it such a death as songs are sung of.' He reached for his goblet and drained the last of it. 'But the galaxy will know, before long,' he said then, 'one way or the other, that defiance yet exists in this crooked house of lies.'

TEN

SHE WATCHED HIS eyes open. They flickered, then the lids parted, and he was looking straight at her.

The lumens were set low, but he still winced. For a moment, he clearly had no idea where he was, and the panic reaction set in.

She waited. He was secured to the bunk, there was a legionary stationed outside the cell on the *Sickle Moon*, and Yesugei was on the ship somewhere within mind-reach, so she had nothing to fear. For all that, her mouth was dry. This was the final chance to salvage something from what had been her counsel.

Once the man's disorientation had subsided, and he realised he was on a starship, and that the woman before him did not obviously intend to harm him, he swallowed painfully and blinked.

'Who are you?' he croaked.

Ilya passed him a canister of water. 'General Ilya Ravallion, Departmento Munitorum. Who are you?'

He drank greedily and handed the canister back for more. 'You don't know?'

Ilya refilled it. 'Tell me your name. It will be easier if you answer the questions.'

He shrank back against the wall of the holding chamber. Ilya waited again. The man had gazed into the eyes of a corrupted Traitor Marine. His dreams would likely be bad for the rest of his life.

'I was...' he said. 'I was called... Veil.'

'Veil. Nothing else?'

'He gave us names he liked. That amused him.'

'Then what were you called before that?' He looked panicked again. 'It matters not. I shall call you Veil.'

Veil drank more. He smelt foul, despite treatment in the apothecarion for the worst of his exposure. He had suffered several broken bones and severe mental trauma. It was unlikely he had slept for several days while on Herevail, and the pollution of that world was acute.

'When we took you, you were wearing Nobilite robes,' said Ilya. 'House Achelieux. Can you tell me what your function was?'

'No.'

Ilya sighed. 'Veil, whatever bonds of secrecy were placed on you are now gone. Your world is now gone. You will need to reconsider who to confide in.'

Veil's hands began to shake, and he looked up and around the walls of the cell like a hunted creature. 'Where am I?'

'The Fifth Legion frigate *Sickle Moon*.'

'And what... were *they*?'

'Your world was attacked by the Third Legion Astartes, the Emperor's Children. Traitor Space Marines.'

At the mention of the name, Veil shrunk back further, as if he could press himself through the metal walls. 'They were...'

'Do not think of that now. See, I am answering your questions. Now answer some of mine. What was your function?'

Even then, it took him a long time to answer. The Navigator Houses were honour-bound institutions, and bonds of confidentiality within them were laid down strongly. They were also repositories of secrets, buried deep and locked away, and it was rare for those secrets to be probed, even under the duress of war. This was the first time she had ever had occasion to quiz a magister of the Nobilite, and, in truth, she had little idea how far she would get.

Ilya waited for a third time. Veil would have to absorb what had happened and see for himself how far it nullified any orders he had been given in the past.

'I was an... But you will not understand the terms.'

'Try me,' she said.

'*Ecumene-majoris, in tabulae via speculativa*. Under charter from the Paternova. If you are in the Departmento, you should be able to find this information.'

Ilya smiled. 'That is a touching thought. How senior were you?'

Veil took another swig. He was a calming down, though his fingers still trembled against the canister. 'I have served ninety years. There are no more senior positions for those without the Oculus.' He lost focus. 'It was everything. The world. The Houses are like worlds. There is no *outside*, and–'

'Concentrate, please,' said Ilya, bringing him back.

'You have been given drugs for your pain. I need you to think clearly. Why were you on Herevail?'

'It was ideal.'

'Ideal for what?'

'Everything.' He brightened, latching on to something he could speak with authority about. 'It was a stranded world – you know this expression? No? High in the *stratum aetheris,* too high. Remember your fleet dispatch – your Navigator will have told you to break the veil a long way out. Perhaps it took you weeks to reach it. That cannot be altered. Herevail is remote from a portal absolute, and thus the harmonics are insignificant. Almost completely insignificant. When I first arrived, I could not believe it – they detected nothing, even Pieter could not. That was remarkable.'

Ilya listened. Much of what he said made no sense to her, but that was not important – he was talking now, that was the main thing. And, unbidden, he had already said the name she sought, which boded well.

'So, imagine you are doing what we are doing,' Veil went on. 'You could not wish for somewhere more suited. We were able to make great progress. There were charts, oh there were *charts…*' He broke off, looking confused. 'You destroyed the monsters?'

Ilya nodded. 'All killed. All those we could find.'

'And so you took back Vorlax? There was a spire, close to the edge of the outer city. It had a double-crown, the mark of the House on the eastern side. Did you retrieve anything?'

'All the cities were burned,' Ilya said. 'All the spires were ruined. I had explorator teams search Vorlax. There was nothing.'

That made Veil recoil, as if stung. 'So that is why they came,' he muttered, disgusted. 'To destroy it.'

'I do not think so. I do not think they came for you. If they had known you were there, they would have hunted you from the beginning, and you would not have evaded them.' She remembered the scale of the devastation. Even a relatively minor Legion-splinter was capable of turning whole planets into slag, and the dead on Herevail must have numbered in the millions. 'They are burning worlds, one by one, marking a route back to Terra. It was your misfortune to be in the way.'

'Misfortune,' mumbled Veil, numbly. 'Not just ours. All lost, then.'

'How long had you been working there?'

'Three years.'

'And before that?'

'On Denel Five. A Nobilite sanctuary world. Before that, Terra.' He allowed himself a blush of pride. 'Have you seen the Palace? I have. I have walked the streets of the Regio Navigens, and seen where the Paternova, exalted be his name, dwells in splendour.'

Ilya wondered what had happened to the Navigators' Quarter now. In lockdown, no doubt, surrounded by growing fortifications. The vast old mutant at the heart of it all was probably being watched by a hundred of Malcador's agents for the slightest twitch of insurrection.

And vice versa.

Like every element of the sprawling Imperial hierarchy, the Navigators were split in twain, their agents and lords straddling both sides of the great divide. How many of their Houses had gone over fully to the enemy? Was there any other institution, even including the Cult of Mars, that was less well understood by those outside its cabals, echelons and rituals?

Veil stopped talking and looked at her strangely. 'So how did you know?'

'Know what, Veil?'

'That we were being attacked.'

'We did not. At least, we could not be sure.' Ilya recalled the heated discussions with Yesugei, Jubal, the two *noyan*-khans. Only Qin Xa had been calm, accepting whatever outcome the Khagan adopted. It would be good to see him again, she thought, when they reached the muster-point. 'You must know little of what has happened since you left Denel Five, so let me inform you. The war has grown. There are no places of refuge left, and soon the enemy will be at the gates of Terra itself. You are now among the White Scars Legion, who are still fighting. As far as we know, we are the only full Legion still fighting, though unless we can break free and see our way into the open void, we cannot know anything with certainty.'

Veil took in the information soberly, sipping every so often from the canister.

'I hide nothing from you – we are trapped,' Ilya told him. 'Warp storms block the principal routes back to the Throneworld. Four Traitor Legions are tracking us, and have closed a ring of steel around us. Every attempt we make to break this ring has failed, and our room to manoeuvre grows narrower. The Khagan, the primarch, he has made an oath to reach the Emperor's side before the final assault comes. That means a great deal to this Legion – they will die rather than leave an oath unfulfilled, but the universe has made it difficult. So every course is tried – we are fighting, not just for survival, but to reach the Solar System before the Warmaster closes the approaches.'

'You speak of the Great Fracture,' said Veil, nodding. 'We tracked the course of the storms. We knew they were coming. Even he did not know how they did it.'

'Yes, they are part of the problem, so our Navigators tell us. The enemy has other powers over the wider warp, and allies within it – that is the other part. And so we are hunting for the narrowest path to Terra.' Ilya leaned forwards, crossing her legs. 'Listen, Veil. When I was serving in the Imperial Army, I had many contacts in the Houses. I knew one Novator in particular. We served jointly during the Crusade and achieved much together. I assisted him with some logistical matters, and he disclosed more to me than was common for your kind. I came to understand that he was close to high-ranking figures at the Imperial Court, and that the things I was assisting him with were part of something much larger than he could tell me. I did not press him then. We remained friends, and I admired his work, and that was that.'

Veil listened to her intently. His lower lip hung down by a fraction.

'But I knew enough,' Ilya said. 'I knew that some great project was being enacted, and that he was a part of it. Perhaps only a very small part, but even that was so heavily guarded that I was left in no doubt of its importance. We parted ways long before the onset of the war, but I never forgot. The last I had heard, he had been due to take a posting at Denel Five. Eight months ago, we were there. It was deserted, all life erased, all spires empty. But it had not been invaded, for the war was at that point a long way off. Denel Five had been destroyed by its inhabitants. Why? I do not know. Perhaps you do.'

Veil gave no sign.

'That might have been the end to it,' Ilya said. 'But there are those within the Legion who are adept at decoding hidden signs, ones that would have been invisible to me no matter how long I looked at them. After much toil, the Stormseers gave me a name – Herevail. It was clear that he had gone there. We did not know why. We did not know when. It took me a long time to persuade the primarch to permit an expedition, and in order to achieve it we had to combine it with a dozen other raids lest our intentions be read. That has no doubt exacted a cost in lives. It is important, then, that it was not done for nothing.' She looked directly at him. 'I had hoped to find this man again, for I believe that if anyone could guide us out of the tempest, he could. You know of whom I speak. You have already named him. Pieter Achelieux. Veil, you must tell me if you know – where is he now?'

Veil chuckled sourly. 'I wish I knew. Well, I *do* know, but it will do you no good.'

Ilya pulled back, giving him space.

'He was never on Herevail for long,' said Veil. 'He came and went, like they all do. Perhaps you have never seen a Navigator House's own vessels? They are like nothing you have ever sailed in. He would embark on journeys that should have taken weeks, and be there in days. He could read the Seethe like a mortal reads a chrono.'

'The Seethe?'

'The immaterium. The warp. Achelieux was the best

of the long generation, they told me, and having witnessed him scry the tides, I cannot dispute it. Some
had already marked him for Paternova, given a few
centuries more. Who knows? There is always gossip.
But he was good. By the Cartomancer, he was *good*.
And he left it all behind, all for the greater purpose.'

'Which was?'

'What we were doing on Herevail. How can I explain
it to you?' He pressed his fingers together and frowned.
'There are schools of thought in the Houses. Different methods of engaging with the Seethe. Some treat
it like a beast – an animal, to be tamed or ridden.
Others as a ritual, a kind of dance. Or an artwork,
even – can you imagine? But there is a third doctrine – that the warp is nothing more than a mirror,
one that can be charted just as real space is charted.
They believe the paradoxes can be overcome, and that
one day living maps will be created, ones that predict
the storms and give reliable guides to the aether-flux.'
Veil smiled absently, remembering. 'That was what
we were doing in Vorlax. We were topographers,
psycho-sounders, aether-readers. We were attempting
to compass the stratum aetheris. All of it. It was the
work of generations.'

'Did you succeed?'

'We were nowhere close. We kept going because
he was so sure, and he demanded it, and he had a
way of making you believe that it was possible. But
there were other things, too – places he would go
to. I wasn't privy to all the secrets, but we did know
about Dark Glass. Just the name. I never saw it, never
knew where it was. He'd gone there, but this time he
never came back.

'You heard nothing?'

'Not a thing. We kept working. We thought he'd return. When *they* came, at first I thought it might be something to do with him. Throne of Earth, we were so unprepared.' Veil shuddered. 'Not that we could have done much if we had known.'

'What is Dark Glass?'

'I do not know.'

'You must do.' Ilya felt her frustration rising. 'The name must mean something.'

'It was a component of the project. A place. That is all.' Veil looked distressed. 'If I had known more, do you not think I would have gone after him? He was close. He was a Novator – they bind their secrets within secrets. I was desperate to find him – we all were.'

'Anything – a system name, a subsector.'

Veil looked genuinely frustrated. Ilya had interrogated many subjects in her time, and had a good sense for deception. Right then, she detected none.

'He hid his tracks,' said Veil, pulling his robes about him and shivering. 'I would have followed him. But all I have is the name, and that would not have got me far.'

'Nor us,' said Ilya, grimly. 'You cannot tell me anything else?'

'Lots of things,' said Veil, brightening. 'I can tell you of the warp's wonders, the arts and sciences of its delving. I know things even the Oculi do not, for what they see with their Eye I have had to scour from the depths of Nobilite manuals. I know all these things. I can tell you them all.'

Ilya felt her heart sink. If he truly could not follow

Achelieux's route, then the raids were all for nothing. Tachseer's counsel would prevail, and the Legion would erase its oaths in death, achieving nothing but a little more delay to the Warmaster's offensive.

'Keeping talking,' she said, trying not to let her despair show, trying to hold on to diminishing hope. 'Tell me everything you know.'

THE LAND BEFORE them smouldered in columns of rust-tinged darkness. Trenches scored the charred earth, each sodden with oily water. The sky was occluded, apart from savage flashes of white as massed las-barrages kicked out.

Far ahead, more than ten kilometres to the north east, a column of armour smashed its way towards the besieged walls of the Imperial bastion-city Craesus, demolishing haphazard lines of razor wire and iron-cross tank defences. In the wake of the mechanised spearhead, ranks of masked troopers marched, lasguns and carapace-shredders hoisted onto their shoulders. Their visors glowed ghost-blue in the drifting night.

Across the cloud-barred horizon, greater explosions hammered out, underlighting thunderheads with flicker-patterns of illumination. The dirty trails of Thunderhawk backwash criss-crossed the light show, overseen by the hazy shadows of orbital bulk landers lurching their way to planetfall.

Another world was being carved apart, city by city. The IV Legion had arrived, as just one of a thousand operations undertaken by that vast host of siege-breakers. The precise denomination did not concern those who darted under the shadow of the oncoming vanguard, though, wheeling amid the gloom like unlocked stars, for life and death meant precisely nothing for those who had sworn it away.

Torghun was at the apex, closely followed by Sanyasa. The rest came behind in a wedge formation, crouched in their saddles, holding their machines low and tight to the earth. The jetbikes' mag-plates whined as they grazed the poisoned soils, underflying sensor-umbrellas and moving far too fast for tracker sweeps.

'*You did not speak the truth to me, khan,*' voxed Sanyasa, tilting to avoid a burning web of metal struts.

'When was this?' Torghun replied, arming his *holan* clamps and switching to short-range targeting.

'*When you took the communication from the fleet.*'

'Brother, this is really not the time.'

The jetbike formation hurtled towards the Land Raider column, still undetected, but now in visual range. Solid clunks rang out as every warrior of the squadron slotted heavy bolt-rounds into the in-line magazines.

'*Nonetheless. You did not speak the truth.*'

'Concentrate – they have seen us.'

Tracer-fire spat out from the armoured column, followed by the dance of projectiles. The Land Raiders were turning, pivoting heavily on their axes, and the troopers were rushing out, falling to the ground and angling their guns.

All too late.

'Now *take* them!' Torghun cried, piling on the velocity.

The jetbikes ate up the ground, driving furrows ahead of them with massed heavy bolter fire. The earth exploded upwards into a rolling tide, punctuated by the diced internals of the mortals caught up in the hurricane.

Then they were over the tanks, and every rider loosed their holan clamps. The star-shaped mines flew out, slamming into the adamantium hulls of the Land Raiders and locking fast. In a fraction of a second, the jetbikes were on the far side and gunning hard, pursued by a hail of return fire.

The clamps went off. Two Land Raiders blew up, their hulls destroyed by the dozens of explosives latched to their exteriors. Three more were rocked to a standstill, grinding down into the mire with their smokestacks churning. Seven more received glancing damage and came after them, trundling across pitted ground, las-beams stabbing out into the night, their own bolters thundering.

It was still too slow. The sagyar mazan whooped wildly, pulling clear of ground-level, putting distance between them and the vengeful armour. They burned across the wasteland, ducking and slewing, riding the hail of laser-light like mariners on the waves.

Soon they were beyond pursuit, haring back to the rendezvous with the lifter. Their presence had been detected now and the entire planetary attack force would be converging on them. They had perhaps seven minutes to make it off-world before the pincers caught up.

'So what did it say?' voxed Sanyasa, driving hard.

'I told you,' voxed Torghun, irritated.

'*The Horde will never attack Lansis. It will never attack Gethmora. I regret this, but you are lying to me, darga.*'

Torghun glanced over at Sanyasa's speed-blurred outline. 'Say that with a weapon in my hand.'

'They have called us back.'

The wedge sped onwards, sweeping in a curve away from doomed Craesus, just one desperate chase on a world scored with a million other duels.

'And if they have?' replied Torghun. 'What would that matter? Penance through death. That is what we *are* now.'

'Not by choice.'

'It was all about choice.'

'That can change. We are still alive.'

'If you do not cease this, that too may change.'

Ahead of them, shrouded by heavy clouds of soot and drifting ash, the lifter was coming down, running dark, its presence only given away by forward short-range augurs. The jetbikes decelerated by the bare minimum, scraping up the open ramp and skidding into the lifter's hangar. As soon as the last one was in, the ship's atmospheric drives boosted back to full power and the void doors hauled themselves closed.

Torghun kicked his bike's power off, dismounted and strode over to where Sanyasa was doing the same. He caught the warrior by the chest and slammed him into the hangar wall.

'Speak to me like that again and I end you.'

Sanyasa did not fight back. He let his arms go limp. Around them both, the rest of the kill-squad assembled warily. 'I would follow you into the ice-halls of the underworld, my khan,' he said, calmly, reverting to the old rank designation. 'You do not need to keep this from us.'

Torghun held position for a few moments longer, then let Sanyasa go. He twisted his helm free, turned away and ran his gauntlet across his cropped scalp. 'Damn you,' he breathed. 'And damn them.'

Sanyasa removed his own helm. 'The need must be great for them to consider it.'

'Of course the need is great,' Torghun spat back. 'What does that alter? We are alone now. That was how they wanted it. We all took the trials.'

Muffled cracks made the lifter's hull shake. Something had trained weapons on them, and the vessel picked up speed.

Sanyasa mag-locked his helm and wiped sweat from his face. 'What did it say?'

Around them, the surviving members of the kill-squad clustered, all of them looking at Torghun. None had drawn a blade, but their faces were implacable. After more than four years, they wanted to know.

Torghun suddenly remembered his last sight of the *Starspear*, from the shuttle that would take him to the flagship for his interrogation. He remembered the shame of it. He remembered the Techmarines scouring the lightning strike from his pauldron. He remembered the looks on the faces of his judges. Chogorian faces, they had been. Alien faces.

Sanyasa did not move. The others did not move. The hull-shakes died away, indicating that the lifter had pulled clear of land-based attacks and would now make it back to *R54* in one piece.

So they would live to fight another day. They would live to take the war to the enemy one more time.

'What did they say?' asked Sanyasa again.

Torghun looked back to him, back at the still-proud face, the epitome of the plains-warrior even after being cast loose. Sanyasa had never stopped believing.

For himself, Torghun had never truly believed, not even from the start. That was always the difference, the one that had opened the door to weakness.

He took a deep, resigned breath. This could bring nothing but pain.

ELEVEN

THE FIRST VOID-SOUNDINGS came in at chrono-mark -52.13 from expected warp re-entry. It took the master of the watch on the escort frigate *Melak Karta* thirteen seconds to assess the augur-profile and pass the signals up. Algu Khan, legionary commander of the much-depleted Brotherhood of the Pennant Spear, was on the bridge before the chrono ticked over to -48.00, and gave the order to run.

All plasma engines were fired into overdrive, boosting the frigate past the top edge of its velocity envelope. Algu ordered it to push below the system's plane, giving the option to loop around the gravity field of the iron-core giant Revo to gain momentum for an early return to the aether.

Behind them, the enemy gained quickly. The Death Guard cruiser *Implacable* was already operating its far more powerful sub-warp drives at full pitch, and its six thrusters left dirty smudges of red afterglow as they thundered.

'Rear fusillade,' ordered Algu, watching the onset calmly, knowing it would do little to halt the enemy's advance.

Torpedoes shot away aft, streaking into the void in a scatter pattern of bright white. The *Implacable* responded with a fore-shot mix of void flak and tracker torpedoes of its own, the bulk of the fusillade disappearing in a rippling wave of explosions. The remainder of the *Melak Karta's* volley was absorbed by its pursuer's fore void shield array.

Algu watched the enemy's response, using the experience he had gained in over a century of void war to gauge their intentions.

'Void-seal armour,' he voxed to his warriors stationed across the frigate's decks. 'Prepare for boarding.'

The order was probably unnecessary. Most ship actions of this sort came down to a boarding manoeuvre in the end, and so his troops would already be preparing. If it caught them, the larger enemy vessel was probably capable of destroying them, but in a war that had extracted such a fearful toll on the fleets of both sides, and which had slowed new vessel production from the forge worlds to near zero, it was more usual for commanders to try to take over enemy craft for their own use.

That made things interesting. Algu had eighty-two battle-brothers aboard, plus several hundred mortal auxiliary troops. The frigate was still well-stocked with close-range weaponry, and would reap a heavy toll on boarding-tubes if they got in close.

But it was still better to run. The *Implacable* likely contained twice that number of XIV Legion warriors, and there were few better exponents of close-confines fire-fights: other Legions might have a more developed tactical sense, but it took a lot to put down every single Death Guard warrior, and in a tight space with few options for flanking moves, that mattered.

'Coming within range of Revo's gravity well,' reported Idda, the master of the watch. All across the bridge, the crew were working hard to extract more power to feed the main drives, to calculate the slingshot angles, to find a balance between the hundred competing demands on core power.

'Can you outpace them?' Algu asked, absently checking the energy readout on his chainsword.

Idda took a few moments to reply, his face buried in a nest of angled augur-lenses.

'Perhaps,' he replied, a dry smile on his weather-beaten face. 'If you risk the main reactor it might be done.'

On another occasion, Algu might have stayed to fight. Odds could be overcome, and they had been in the past. Revo's enormous, space-distorting bulk could be used, as could the myriad tricks they had picked up since the proud tradition of Legion warfare had descended into the brutal post-Chondax era of scrappy civil war.

Not this time. The Khagan's muster-orders were still lodged in his armour's internal buffers, giving precise coordinates and timing windows. Better to decline a battle in order to make the war.

'Do it,' he ordered, deleting all mission-critical data from his armour's systems with a series of retinal movements. 'Purge all bridge cogitators of input data over the last standard week and reset encryption on the rest. Then run the reactors ragged. Get us out of here.'

The orders were conveyed, cascading down the ranks, enacted efficiently. The enginarium crew keyed the main drives, the navigation stations plotted the main route, the pilots jinked and danced through the *Implacable*'s long-range probing fire, and the colossal dirt-grey sphere of Revo entered visual range.

'Entering slingshot perimeter,' intoned Erya, mistress of sub-warp navigation, rocking in her station-throne as the enemy gunners began to find their range. 'Velocity increasing.'

'Keep us steady,' ordered Algu, watching the magnified ocular scopes carefully.

As he spoke, something hit the rear void shields hard, catapulting the *Melak Karta* over to starboard. The frigate's structure shuddered, and the echoes of explosions could be heard filtering up from the decks below.

Algu's stance flexed with the movement. Warning runes spread like a rash across the bridge's comm-stations. The hurtling run continued, and Revo loomed ahead of them, its circular outline now clear against the blackness beyond.

It was then that the first uneasiness came.

'You have run a forward scan of the planet?' he asked.

Idda looked up. 'Why? It would be pointless. The core is too dense.'

Algu turned to Erya. 'Then pull us out.'

Uncharacteristically, she hesitated. 'My khan, if we–'

'Pull us out.' Algu expanded the range of the tactical scope even as his navigation crew struggled to alter the incoming angles. 'Get us away from it. Now.'

The *Melak Karta* swung down and around, straining

hard against the sudden course correction. More hits came in from the pursuing cruiser, strafing the rear thruster-banks and causing the plasma-trails to spit and writhe.

Idda swung around in his harness, confused. 'My khan, we cannot pull clear on this course.'

'We never could,' said Algu, grimly. 'And they never wished to catch us.'

As the last word left his mouth, the truth became apparent – a battleship emerging from Revo's distant horizon, a mere speck of light against the iron arc, but already close to the limits of its long-range weapons. Ident-runes began to scroll down the *Melak Karta*'s cogitator feeds – scanned and cross-referenced against sighting and fleet databases.

It was Gloriana-class: the *Endurance*, flagship of the XIV Legion's primarch. Survival had just gone from being a matter of difficulty to one of near-impossibility.

'Keep running,' ordered Algu, watching the battleship sweep into full view, thinking back to the times he had pulled a similar manoeuvre on his prey. 'Find some speed from somewhere. Ignore all limits – just get me speed.'

Idda complied instantly. The entire bridge complied, and soon voices were raised as every section frantically searched for some way to boost the already perilous levels of engine-overburn.

Algu watched them for a moment. Some had served with him for decades, and he knew they would find a way, if one could be found. It would at least fill their minds with something productive and stave off the paralysis of fear.

As for him, fear was not even an option. He gripped

the hilt of his chainsword tighter, feeling the weight and balance of it in his grasp. It felt good – in peak condition, recently refined by the Techmarine Xiang, already humming with the thirst for combat.

That was well. Unless a miracle occurred, it would be in use within the hour.

MORTARION DID NOT oversee the running down of the frigate. He waited in the depths of the *Endurance* for notice to reach him that the ship had been disabled and boarding squads sent in.

During that time, he surrounded himself with the things he had taken from Terathalion, and from Xerxes IX, and from the dozen other worlds he had laid low. After Prospero, where his last encounter with the Warhawk had taken place, his path through the void had become meandering, and the destruction wrought unfocused. There had been matters to resolve, and that had taken time. The fading embers of the Prosperine empire had been the victim of that destructive period, and he had absorbed the last of its secrets in a bid to settle the doubts that the Khan had kindled in his mind.

The residue of that quest remained in place. Heavy glass jars lined the walls of the broad chamber, glossy with syrupy preserving oils, each one containing the atrophied remnants of semi-formed things. Great leather tomes, their hide covers mouldering in the humid atmosphere, were stacked up like towers in the semi-dark. Three great weapons had been placed in stasis fields, their iron-dark blades inscribed with xenos scripts.

Mortarion stalked amongst it all, running rheumy

eyes across the esoterica of fallen civilisations. Such
a collection would have been laughed at by the truly
determined jackdaws of the Great Crusade, by a Lorgar or a Magnus, but the Death Lord had come late
to study. He devoured learning now with the fervour
of the long-famished, reading feverishly for days at
a time, suffering no interruptions. All the time, he
remembered the words of the daemon Lermenta, the
one he had captured, taking her from the ruins of Terathalion and holding her here until the truth of her
came out.

By the gods, you learn fast, she had told him.

He had killed Lermenta's mortal shell, but that
would not end her animating spirit. It lingered in
the shadows, perhaps goading him, perhaps assisting, always there. And all the time, the span of his
knowledge widened. The sum of spells at his command grew, gifting his already deadly Legion another
weapon. The stronger he became, the more clearly
the intelligences on the other side pressed against the
membranes of reality. He heard them speak to him
in his rare sleep-periods, gifting him visions of the
past and the future, though intermingled within the
truth were falsehoods so blatant that even he could
see them.

At other times, he would cast the books aside, rip
their pages free and burn the scripts contained within.
He would smash the jars and storm from his sanctum,
pledging never again to immerse himself in the filth of
proscribed wisdom. In such times as those, the menials
aboard the *Endurance* would look up from the bilge-decks
and gunnery halls with dread, waiting for the crash and
roar of their master's rages.

There had been lapses. Molech was the worst, in which he had given in so completely to the stuff of the aether that it had seemed there was no way back from it. And yet, just as on Barbarus, an old, deep stubbornness prevailed. The abomination Grulgor was contained again, sealed down in the darkest oubliette of the flagship and bound tight with wards and hexagrams gleaned from desolated grimoires. His warp-spawned toxins had been replaced with the forbidden bio-weaponry developed in the years before the Crusade – just as destructive, but at least confined to the physical.

What he had told Horus was true – he had kept the Legion pure. His warriors fought with their blades, bolters, fists and nothing more. There had not been a Librarius in the XIV Legion for a long time, and never would be again.

But what of Typhon? That element, at least, had eluded his control. Calas emerged ever more often in Mortarion's fevered dreams, marching at the head of Legion detachments he barely recognised. There would have to be a reckoning with Typhon before the assault on Terra. The Legion had become too distributed, too caught up in the sprawl of the burning galaxy.

And so the order to bring the Khan to heel had been well made. It would be a work of glory, something to set aside the deeds of Fulgrim and Lorgar. Mortarion would march to Terra with the mantle of *primarch-slayer*, just as his Chemosian brother would.

Until then, the study continued, the immersion into the lore that both disgusted and fascinated him. If he noticed the degraded appearance of those about him, the gradual accumulation of grime and war-patina, he never spoke of it. Sickness ran through the mortal crews of the line battleships, making the echoing holds ring to the cries of the afflicted, and nothing was done.

I will comprehend, became the mantra, repeated into the deeps of the endless nights. *This at least will not be denied me, not as the other things have.*

When notification eventually came through that the V Legion frigate had been broken open and lay ready for his arrival, Mortarion cast around him, rooting through the vials and specimen crystals. Having found what he had been searching for, he trudged from the chamber, leaving it to the chattering whispers and the slow-ticking dark.

He passed through the winding inner ways of the *Endurance*, and all fell back before him. Legionaries bowed; the mortal crew fell to their knees, not daring to look up at his cadaverous face as he swept past them. He reached the Stormbird hangars, where his Deathshroud honour guard waited.

Once in the void, on the approach, he could assess the prize through the real-viewers. The enemy frigate was scorched, as if it had been plunged into a lake of fire. Clearly the *Endurance*'s gunners had enjoyed their work.

The Stormbird entered the frigate's hangar, dipping hard to avoid a collapsed entry portal. It set down on a shattered apron, coming to rest amid hissing heaps of molten metal.

Mortarion emerged, passing through the still-burning interior like a shade of the afterworld, his entourage tramping behind. He crunched over the corpses of both White Scars and Death Guard legionaries, all

slumped across one another in bloody piles. The
sounds of ongoing conflict could still be heard
from far off – the crack of bolter-fire, the clang of
sword-edges – but that would soon be over. His troops
would not have permitted him to enter a ship that
had not been made safe, its enginarium and bridge
secured and all weapon systems disabled.

The place smelt foul. Some barbarian-world incense
or other had been strewn across the once-gleaming
surfaces. The interior was too bright, emblazoned with
lines of red and gold, and he found himself adjusting the filters on his helm-lenses to compensate. For
a long time, the interior of all his Legion vessels had
been miasmic.

By the time Mortarion reached the bridge, the devastation was complete. The enemy had clearly barricaded
themselves behind the last set of blast doors at the
end, fighting hard for the final stages. Just as many
Death Guard armour-plates were mingled with the
ivory of the Khan's sons, testament to a resilience that
the Chogorians were not necessarily known for.

Only one enemy combatant remained alive. All
others – the Space Marines, the mortal crew, the servitors – had been slaughtered at their stations, making
the bridge reek of copper and charcoal. The lone survivor, the ship's master, was held up by two Death Guard
legionaries, his helm ripped off and his long black hair
hanging in matted clumps around a mottle-red head.

Mortarion approached, and the other Death Guard
on the bridge retreated, forming a circle around the
primarch and his prey. The shattered bridge equipment continued to crackle sullenly, sending curls of
smoke into the vaults above.

'Look at me,' Mortarion commanded.

The White Scars legionary lifted his head with difficulty. His eyes struggled to focus.

'You have been caught up in this,' Mortarion said, drawing close, studying the warrior's wounds. He reached out with a brass-clad finger and traced the line of the scar down his left cheek. 'You fought well, but there are no alternatives now. You were on course to meet your master. Give me the coordinates.'

The warrior grinned, exposing a smashed jaw-line. Then he spat a bloody gobbet into Mortarion's face.

Mortarion let the acidic spittle slip down the outside of his rebreather-housing. 'Very good,' he said.

He reached down for the casket he had taken from his chambers. It was no larger than his forearm, a little wider, capped with iron at either end. In between, shrouded behind frosted glass, something swam fitfully. As he lifted it higher, black tentacles lashed against the inside of the armourglass, briefly sucking to it before whipping free.

'See. This is a *djemdja falak*. A mind-eater. It will kill you, but not for many long hours. During that time, it will devour your mind from the inside. For the period you remain conscious, you will scream out anything I ask you. If you knew the secret of the Khan's movements, his allies, his weaknesses, you would tell me it. Is that not a strange thing? Is this not a strange creature? I hunted long for it, for they are rare beyond price now. But I have this one, and be sure that I will use it.'

The warrior looked at the canister with contempt. 'Yaksha,' he rasped.

'Daemon? No, not on this occasion. There are monsters

in the universe other than those in the warp. But come, there is nothing served with stubbornness. Tell me where your master is, and you may yet die with honour.'

The White Scars legionary couldn't take his eyes from the creature that thrashed inside the tube. After a long, agonised pause, he lifted his bloodshot eyes back to Mortarion.

'Then I… will tell you,' he said, his voice wet with his own blood.

Mortarion listened patiently.

The warrior grinned. 'Over your corpse. Laughing.'

Mortarion smiled thinly. 'I fear he has missed his chance for that.' He indicated to the two Death Guard, and they forced the warrior's arms out at right angles, which pushed his face closer to the stooped primarch's. 'We shall talk much now, but while your mind is still your own, know this – you are beaten. Every battle you fight, you lose. You were built for speed, and this war is the slow grind of long attrition. You bleed for a creator who no longer knows whether you live or die. I gave your master a choice on Prospero – glory or futility. As your mind rips apart, as the agony seeps into your soul and you hear yourself give me everything I want, remember that. *He* did this to you.'

The legionary closed his eyes, and started to mumble some kind of mantra.

'*Er Khagan, eran ordu gamana Jaghatai. Tanada Talskar. Eran Imperatora. Er Khagan, eran ordu gamana Jaghatai…*'

Mortarion let him babble. He held the glass tube up against the warrior's face, and with a single twist broke the seal. There was a flurry of black scales, a snap of skin, a sluice of oil, and the thing leapt for the warrior's head, punching through his closed eyes and wrapping barbed coils around his temples.

Mortarion strolled away, discarding the broken canister as the screams started. He briefly looked around him, at the broken bridge, at the twisted ranks of cadavers, at the blood dripping down from the perimeter walkways, and sighed.

'Let us begin, then, and see how long this takes,' he said, turning back to the struggling legionary, his writhing forehead now lost behind the flex and pulse of neurotoxin-glands emptying. 'Tell me, where is the Khan?'

TWELVE

THE SICKLE MOON broke the veil a long way out from Aerelion, driven off-course by a brutal warp squall just before making for the planned exit vector. Yesugei had felt every beat and hammer of the aether-storm during the passage. The surges had pushed against the fragile outer shell of the vessel, swamping it, pressing down on it like piled earth against a rotten wall.

He had flown through worse, but the endless torment of the heavens took its toll. The ship was in little better shape now than when it had rejoined service immediately after Prospero, and then it had been barely voidworthy. Everywhere he looked there were the signs of stress – bulwarks cracked down to the decking, the taste of leaked promethium, the continual flicker of lumens.

Locked away in his personal chambers, he recited the mantras of homecoming, shutting out the turmoil for just a few moments. He stood, eyes closed, before an altar over which hung the calligraphic *tiang*. Wisps of sandalwood smoke curled upwards from golden bowls, glistening from the light of three drifting suspensor-lumens.

He felt fatigue lying heavy on his limbs, and went through the long-established muscle-relaxant exercises. Those disciplines predated his Ascension to the Legion and were designed to work with mortal limbs, but he had never got out of the habit of using them. If they had little effect on his genhanced physiology, the repetition of old rites soothed the disquiet in his mind.

The warp made it worse. To one with his gifts, piercing the centre of the storm was a mental challenge. On some nights, he could not escape the visions – the stretched faces clustered against the hull, the fingers scraping down the adamantium, the deep, thundering howl of infinite voices circling over the abyss.

On the altar-top rested the tarot pack he had been given by Arvida. The deck of esoterica had once belonged to Ahriman, lost equerry to the Crimson King, and had been retrieved from Tizca by its last living son. Arvida had passed it on to Yesugei a long time ago, having rejected the chance to formally join the V Legion, and since then it had sat, barely touched, in the Stormseer's chambers. Only in recent months, as the storm-ways had closed about them, had he reached for the symbols.

Even with his eyes closed he could see the pictograms last turned over: the swordsman, the one-eyed king, the fiery angel. The signs remained opaque. Perhaps the tarot only answered to its old master. Or perhaps Yesugei was just failing to see something, letting his fatigue get the better of him.

In any case, scrying the future had never been his

talent. His was an elemental gift – power over the ways of matter, the stuff of the physical. Prophecies and soul-delving, that had been the preserve of the others, the ones who had dug too deep.

But still he turned the cards, one by one. From time to time he felt he was on the edge of something, just on the cusp of seeing a pattern, and those moments would spur him to research further.

Then he smiled to himself. Even he was capable of weakness, of the human vice of *just a little further*. That was the root of it all, all this damnation – the satiation of curiosity, the pushing into the darkness. There was no unlearning it. It was written into the genetics of every one of them, the seeds of species destruction, as permanent and furtive as a virus.

He opened his eyes. The suspensors glowed to full power, flooding the chamber with daylight-equivalent illumination. He moved over to the altar, and took one final card from the deck, turning it face-up.

The Hierophant.

Yesugei placed the card on the stone. The card still showed its old artwork – a delicate ink and wash over thick, gold-edged material. The depicted prelate held his hand up, two fingers angled towards the heavens, two curled into the palm, extending earthwards.

Yesugei's smile died. The deck was mocking him and he was not in the mood to indulge it. He turned and left the chamber, the suspensors following him like trained dogs. Doors hissed open and closed three times, tracing a route deeper inside his private rooms. Every surface was thick with glyphs, all drawn by his own hand – some were wards against yaksha, others magnifiers for weather-magic.

The final set slid apart to reveal Ilya's guest, now restored to something like health, clad in clean white robes and sitting at his ease, alone, in a hull-facing cell. The warp shutters on the porthole had withdrawn, giving him a view of the approach to Aerelion through the real-viewers.

He didn't turn to greet the Stormseer. Alongside everything else, he seemed to have recovered his Nobilite hauteur.

'So the woman has discovered all she can,' the man, Veil, said, dryly. 'And now they send for the soldier.'

Yesugei joined him at the viewport. At that stage the destination was just a larger star amid a whole swathe of lesser stars. They would encounter V Legion outriders long before the planet asserted itself as more than just another pinpoint of cold light.

'No, I am not soldier,' said Yesugei.

'You are a legionary. You may dress it up in as many totems as you like, but you still kill for the Imperium.'

'Many who kill are not soldier. You have killed, I think, in your own way.'

Veil turned to face him. Yesugei saw a creased, pale face. The man's cheeks were still hollow, his eye sockets ringed with black.

'I cannot tell you what you wish to know,' Veil said. 'She has asked me many times.'

'Then tell me of your work.'

Veil shuffled away from the viewport. 'What do you wish to know?'

'Everything.'

Veil laughed. 'That would take a long time. Longer, I think, than you have to spare. They are hunting you, she tells me.'

Yesugei felt a small but significant sense of disappointment. The man's voice was arch, the kind of cultivated Terran accent that spoke of entitlement and boredom. It was hard to square with the terrified, famished soul they had rescued from Herevail.

'All wars can be won,' Yesugei said. 'This no different.'

'No, I think this one is very different.' Veil shot him a cold smile. 'The woman–'

'Her name is General Ravallion.'

'–told me of your predicament. You are a Legion Librarian, not a fool, so I do not need to pretend with you. The warp is home to more than storms. If they can speak to those things, then they can hem you in. You will not be going home.'

'The Khagan has ordered it. It will be done.'

Veil looked incredulous. 'You truly think that?' He turned on the Stormseer, jabbing his bony finger for emphasis. 'He may be a primarch, but he does not command the tides. This is how they work – they are movements of souls, of minds, caught in patterns set by the living while they still draw breath. You cannot force a path – if you try, the aether responds. The great conduits will thicken, the lesser ways will wither. Your enemies will slide through the dark as if through water, while you wade through pools of the dragging mire.'

'I do not know the warp as you do,' said Yesugei. 'But I know is not that simple. Otherwise, no movement is possible at all.'

'There are layers,' said Veil, impatiently. 'Yes, there is stratum aetheris, the shallow ways. There is stratum profundis, the greater arteries, plunging deeper. There is stratum obscurus, the root of the terror. How does this help you? No living man can navigate the deep ways. Even he could not.'

'But you try to map it.'

'It could not be done.' Veil shook his head with frustration. 'He was wrong about that, at least. It is not a mirror. It moves like a living thing. It *is* a living thing. Touch it, and it trembles.' He briefly lost his certainty. 'I do not have the Eye, but still I have seen things. I have studied what they study. The complexity is... immortal.'

'Try to explain.' Yesugei spoke softly. 'I am fast learner.'

Veil exhaled, his eyes widening. 'The Seethe is an ocean. All know this – it has currents, it has depths, it has storms. Near the surface, you can see the Cartomancer's light. You can follow it. You can use your Geller aegis, and you are kept barred from the Intelligences. But even then, you are just below the upper limits. Go deeper and the aegis shatters. The lights go out. The Eye is blinded. When men say that they traverse the warp, they boast, for no mortal does more than skim across eternity's face, like stones thrown by a child. We do not belong there. It is poison for us, and the deeper in, the worse the poison.'

'Achelieux try to go deeper?'

'Who knows? Maybe. He did not succeed. Do you know why not? Because it is impossible. It takes the power of a tormented sun just to puncture the shallowest shoals. No energy in our arsenal could possibly pierce further. String the reactors of a dozen battleships together, double their potential, and still it would not be enough. So no, he did not succeed.'

'General Ravallion had trust in him.'

'She should not.' Veil looked disgusted. 'Believe me, she should not. They are all the same, the Oculi. They spend too long gazing into it. You know what they say? About the abyss?'

Yesugei did not reply at once. He studied Veil carefully, noting every tick, every mannerism. The man was not being deceptive – Ilya was right about that. Still, there was something. He had spent a long time inside the Nobilite's counsels, and that left a mark. He might not even be aware of it himself. Every moment with them had left a trace, perhaps even one that could be detected.

'I do not doubt you, Veil of House Achelieux,' Yesugei said at last. 'We do not belong there. I often consider, in the night, wisdom of building empire on such foundation. But there was no other way, no?'

Veil shrugged again. 'Not one that worked,' he mumbled.

Yesugei held his gaze for a few moments longer, then released him. 'You educate me, so I do not despair yet. Ilya was right to chase down this man.'

'You still think you can find him,' Veil said, irritated. 'How many times must I tell you – I do not know where he is. Break me, if you choose. It will not help you.'

'I would not break you. That is not our way. But there may be another.' Yesugei looked back up to the real-viewer. Far ahead, six points of light were moving across the starfield – escorts racing to engage them and take them into the heart of the fleet. 'I have not skill to seek traces you have forgotten. This is mind-work. But I have a friend. He has these things. When we arrive, I shall introduce you.'

Yesugei caught Veil's wary expression, and laughed.

'Fear not,' he said. 'He is last survivor of a world too. I think you and he will find much to talk about.'

BY THE TIME the *Kaljian* reached the outer edge of the muster-system, the bulk of the fleet was already in position. The great white warships prowled high across Aerelion III's stormy troposphere, circled by packs of their hunter-killers and formation-breakers.

Shiban had planned to take his ship into tight alignment with the *Swordstorm*, in the expectation that he would be summoned to the flagship within a few hours of arrival. Instead his path was blocked by an inter-fleet shuttle. Once it became clear that the interloper had no intention of standing down from the *Kaljian's* incoming vector, hails were issued and met by a standard Army protocol burst.

Once he had heard that, Shiban gave the order for full-stop.

'Bring it in,' he told the ship's master. 'I will meet her in the forward tower.'

Then he waited, alone, up above the great command bridge facade. Narrow real-viewers gave a glimpse of the foredecks, long and rangy like all ships of the class, ridged and rigged for gunnery. He paced across floors of stone overlooked by walls marked with Chogorian runes. A long crack ran up one side – evidence of the structural stress caused by the flight from the Emperor's Children. That might get repaired before the fleet was deployed again, though most likely it would remain a mark of battle to add to the hundreds of others.

He was not waiting long. As ever, she made her way

efficiently from the hangars, escorted by an honour guard from the brotherhood. They left her at the door, bowing before sealing the two of them in together.

She looked painfully thin. Her frame, always spare, now barely filled out her uniform. Her grey hair had whitened, and the lines around her tight mouth had deepened into dark cracks.

Shiban bowed low. 'Szu-Ilya,' he said.

She made the aquila in return. 'Tachseer.' Then she looked his armour up and down, like a mother appraising a wayward son. 'I always wondered, could they not have painted it white?'

'I asked them not to,' said Shiban. 'It is not battle-plate. It is a machine.'

Ilya smiled. 'You people and machines. You use servitors. You fly starships.'

Shiban tapped his gauntlet against his chest. 'Not in here. That is the difference.'

'Then wear Legion colours.'

'I will. When I can wear power armour again.'

Ilya said nothing.

'So then, why are you here, general?' Shiban kept his voice amiable. 'Do you not have a thousand tasks? We are still a rabble of disorganisation, are we not? There must be matters to set straight.'

'I arrived here just before you did,' said Ilya. 'I have my work before me, to put the muster in its order.' She looked around her, at the scars of battle on the chamber walls. 'By the looks of things, it will be needed.'

Shiban laughed lightly. 'Just what did we do before you came among us, szu?'

'Just what you are doing now.' Her voice was harder than it had once been. 'Killing yourself for no reason.

Wasting potential that could be used where it is most needed.'

Shiban lost his smile. 'I think I do not understand you.'

'You understand perfectly.'

'I lost brothers in the last action. I would not have ordered them to fight if it were not worthy.'

'Once, perhaps.' She looked at him straight-on, her tired eyes never wavering. 'Now you would fight at every turn. You would fight while the stars went out, brawling over a universe empty of joy. If the orders did not come, you would find some way to seek them out and hunt them down.'

'You describe a warrior,' Shiban said, softly.

'You were once more than that.'

'Since you have known me,' he said, gesturing to his exoskeleton again, '*this* has been everything.'

'You had a life before, so they tell me.'

'Szu, with respect, I asked you why you were here.'

Ilya's glare never wavered. Her body might have weakened, but her spirit clearly had not. 'You know he will call the khans together for kurultai. You will speak, just as the others will. I come here to ask you to change the counsel you give him.'

Shiban turned away and walked over to the real-viewers. As he did so, the pistons in his right leg clicked – they would need to be re-aligned. 'If you think I have the power to sway his judgement, you are mistaken. He will already know what he wishes to do.'

Ilya followed, hovering at his side, coming up to little more than chest-height against his posthuman bulk. 'Tachseer, I do not speak to you with disrespect, so do me the same courtesy. You command factions all across the ordu. Twenty brotherhoods would follow you to war against their own noyan-khans. Yet more heed what you say and weigh the words.'

Shiban listened. He had once found her voice – mortal, breathy from age – almost endearing. Now it sounded merely shrill.

'We have been making these arguments for more than a year,' she went on. 'To maintain the resistance, or find a way back. You have kept up the campaign to fight on, pushing him harder, pushing your brothers. They remember what you did at Prospero, and they listen. But it cannot go further, not now.'

Shiban smiled, though with little warmth. 'Then you have an alternative?' he said. 'If you do, speak now. If you do not, what else remains?' He drew closer to her, looking down at her tight-drawn hair, noting how her hands shook when they moved. 'You know us by now, surely. We made oaths. We swore over the blood of our slain brothers.' He felt the beginnings of the rage stir again, so quickly now. 'That is why we were created, szu. I believe this now. We are the judgement of the free on the corrupt. We are the vengeance of heaven. While one of us lives to wield a blade, they will not know peace. And that is enough, for it is all that remains.'

'No.' She remained defiant, fragile and stubborn. 'There is the Throne. There is the promise your primarch made himself, the one that will bring us back to it.'

'Ha! You think he cares a damn for the Throne?'

'He is of Terra. Why do you always forget this?'

'And we are of Chogoris.' Shiban found he had involuntarily curled his metal fingers together, and forced his hand to relax. 'If we could not defend our own world, the world we were forged on, what matter the world of emperors? We have *lost our home.* It lies beyond the fleets of the Traitor, and no one is saying let us break all vows of honour and return to our own lands, and drive the enemy from our towers, and purge his filth from skies that were once the purest of all skies claimed by humanity.'

Ilya waited for the words to stop spilling out. When he had finished, she looked up again, wearily. 'If I could bring your home world back, I would. If the Khagan gave me the order, I would break open heaven and hell to bring the fleet there. But your lord is not a fool. He knows that it cannot be done, and if he sent his sons into that furnace then none would return. I have seen him plan for your survival, Tachseer. I have seen him garner every last scrap of strength he possesses to keep the Legion alive while the greatest warhost ever assembled hunts it down.'

Shiban shook his head. '*Alive* is nothing. We were not made to grow old. We were made to ride, to chase our enemies to exhaustion and burn their high places.'

'Yesugei told me the same thing.'

'Then you should have listened.'

'He also told me, a long time ago, that you did not have a centre. That wherever he was, that was the centre.'

That was indeed just the kind of thing Yesugei would have said.

For a moment, Shiban was back at the walls of Khum Kharta, long ago, with the hot wind of the summer on their faces, he and the zadyin arga. They had spoken there, before the great change, when Shiban's body was a half-formed bridge between man and super-man.

I can only imagine Terra, Shiban had said.

You may yet witness it, Yesugei had told him.

Then, they had felt like empty words, the kind of thing said all across the galactic empire of humanity that would never come true. Then, the grassland had rustled in a shimmer-pattern of blue and green, the wind making the pennants snap, the sun baking the mud bricks of the monastery walls into cracked shells.

Then, his limbs had been clean, smooth, tanned. Then, he had laughed easily.

'I will go to kurultai to listen,' Shiban said. 'If he asks me, I will speak. That is how it works.'

'We are striving to find a way out,' said Ilya, insistent now. 'The chance is faint, but we only need time. Yesugei believes in it.'

Shiban locked his gauntlets together. 'It is in his nature to believe. We cannot all be like him.'

'More's the pity,' muttered Ilya.

Shiban smiled at her. 'Do your work. Make your case. If you sway his will, then I will fight for you just as I fight for any cause I am ordered to.'

Ilya finally let her eyes drop from his, shaking her head. 'You do not see how this has changed you. You used to preach this virtue – *ukhrakh, utsakh.* Withdraw, but then return. I never hear that said any more.'

Shiban recognised the Khorchin, spoken strangely by a Terran. It had been a long time since he'd mouthed them himself. 'Those were words for another age.'

'So you keep telling me, but I no longer believe you. You *relish* this. You see the war shattering everything you have built, and part of you longs for it. I can see it when you go into battle. It is the easier path, Shiban Khan. I have seen mortal men succumb to it, but the harm you can do is greater.' She reached out to him, placing her frail hand on his forearm. 'Remember yourselves. It is not yet all ruined – if Terra is saved, the Imperium can be remade. The storms can be compassed, the way made straight. We *have* to be there.'

She really believed that. Seeing that, Shiban hardly knew what to say to her. He might have told her what had been apparent to him for a long time – that it was all gone, that a noble dream dreamt by other minds had been ripped open to reveal the nightmare beneath, and moreover it was a dream that they had had no part in, which had barely included them from its inception.

He took her hand in his, and gently removed it from his arm. 'I will do what he orders,' he said.

'But what will you counsel? Has anything I said made any difference?'

It was too late for that now, and she ought to have seen it, but he had no wish to hurt her further than the truth already had.

'I make no promises, szu,' Shiban said, turning away.

Von Kalda listened to the hum of the *Proudheart*'s engines. He pressed his fingers to the slab before him and felt the vibrations radiate through his arm.

'Do you hear it?' he whispered, lowering his head towards the mass of flesh and sinew below. 'Do you hear that sound?'

It was unlikely. The subject strapped to the medicae bench no longer had ears, nor eyes, nor lips. Its face, which had once been mortal, was a mass of bloody wire, punctuated with red-rimmed holes ready for the insertion of sense-units.

Von Kalda stroked iron-tipped fingers along a trembling ribcage. 'We are back in the warp. That is what it tells me. The lord commander has his quarry.'

He reached for a scalpel. All around the operating table, menials worked in perfect silence. Their faces were a study in variety – hairless, grille-mouthed, masks of iron with glittering compound eye bulges, grafted with the mouths of beasts, or as smooth and featureless as eggshells.

Von Kalda lowered the implant towards its receptacle, and feeder wires splayed like spider's legs towards the fixing nodes. Just as the needles lined up for slipping under skin, he heard the low thud of power armoured boots.

He looked up. Konenos had entered the apothecarion.

'Something I can do for you, brother?' asked Von Kalda, holding the implant steady.

'When you are done. Do not trouble yourself.'

Von Kalda drew in an irritated breath. He had hours of work ahead. Captured V Legion mortals were hard to subvert, and their blood chemistry differed subtly from Chemosians. Many had died before being improved, so there remained much to learn in order to give Eidolon the extra crew cohorts he wished for.

The implant slipped into the empty eye socket, clamping tight to the bone. The subject pushed against its bonds, no doubt in excruciation, but no longer with vocal cords to scream. Von Kalda finished the insertion, wiping blood from the neat cut. The microsutures went in, dotting neatly across the join.

Then Von Kalda stood up again, returning the instruments to the salver next to him. 'Monitor vital signs,'

he said to the nearest menial. 'Do not let this one die.'
Then he looked over to Konenos, who had started to
wander down into the chambers beyond. 'A moment,
brother. Be careful, if you please.'

The apothecarion was crowded with gurneys, medicae slabs and claw-shaped operation cradles. The
gleaming surfaces were thick with steel instruments,
vials of gurgling nutrients, coils of translucent tubing.
In the midst of that Konenos was like a giant let loose
in a treasure cave, blundering past fragile tools with
his every movement.

'This is impressive,' Konenos said, appreciatively.
'You learned all this from Fabius?'

Von Kalda caught up with him as he passed down
a winding stair of white veined stone. Gurgled grunts
of pain echoed up from deep spaces below, filtered
through shafts that led down the pits the apothecarion. 'Some of it,' he said, defensively. 'He is not the
only fleshweaver in the Legion.'

Konenos flashed him a rictus-like grin. Free of his
helm, the orchestrator's throat and face were a great
tumescent mass of sound-chambers and emitters. His
eyes gleamed, as pink as a rat's, out from the cranial
folds of glistening skin. 'No, he is not. But you have
been busy since we last spoke.'

They descended slowly, stepping around the
blood-cyclers and organ-columns. The war had placed
many demands on the fleet's apothecarions, and every
space, every surface, was cluttered with the debris of
body-augmentation.

'It is good, truly, to see you here, brother,' said Von
Kalda, brushing past a line of glass tubes, each the
size of a man. Some were empty, others were occupied

by dark shapes, thrashing against the edges like fish on a line. 'Yet you know, of course, that we are busy.'

Konenos continued to look about him with a kind of enthusiast's wonder. Glossy things hung from the roof on chains, twisting and buffeting under the glare of medical lumens. 'And you know that our commander has the course-bearing he needs.'

Von Kalda nodded. 'He sent me word.'

'And every ship he could signal is in the warp. A third of the Legion. Imagine that.'

'And the Palatine Blade?'

Konenos shot Von Kalda a weary look. 'Eidolon remains taken with him.' They entered a long, low room. Its walls were ellipses of iron, ribbed and studded with inward-facing spikes. The air became hotter, throbbing out from dull red mesh panels. 'The commander is always taken with novelty. It will wear off.'

Curls of steam rose up from filters in the floor, twisting like entrails. Strange noises echoed from up ahead, no longer the agony-echoes from human torment, but more like barks, or bestial rasps.

'You know him best,' said Von Kalda. 'But it might be wise not to assume too much. Things are not what they were when the primarch was in command.'

Konenos headed towards a circular door at the far wall, ringed with iron and inscribed with old variants of Chemosian runes. Just as he neared the release mechanism, Von Kalda reached out to pull him back. 'Be wary, brother.'

Konenos' eyes never left the portal. 'Why? What lies beyond?'

Von Kalda moved towards the outer seal. 'My realm,' he said, flatly.

Konenos looked up, then back, taking in the arcane architecture. 'There is a direction of travel,' he said, musingly. 'A decision made. We will better ourselves. We will experience all there is to experience. We suffered for that decision, and others will suffer for it.'

Von Kalda said nothing, but the foretaste of violence suddenly sparked in the narrow chamber, like fear-musk. His fingers moved a fraction closer to his holstered bolt pistol.

Konenos moved back towards the door. 'I would have that direction of travel reinforced. I would not have any regrets, when the time comes for reckoning. You do not only twist flesh, my brother. You twist worlds. You tear the veil.'

Von Kalda tensed, judging how quickly he could move. 'I do nothing without–'

'Hush.' Konenos turned back, placed his finger against Von Kalda's lips. 'You and I are of the same mind. Truly. Show me what you have done.'

Von Kalda hesitated. Even now, even after all the primarch had done to settle the issue, there were still risks, for ancient proscriptions died hard, and a Legion that had learned treachery could birth it within its own ranks easily enough.

Then he moved his hand away from the pistol, and reached for the seal.

'Tread carefully,' he said. 'Watch where you look.'

He entered the pass-sequence, and steel bolts shot back. With a hiss of escaping air, the portal swung open.

Beyond was a thick haze of lilac, heavy with complex scents. The muffled barking faded away, replaced by a low, lisping hiss. Von Kalda and Konenos went inside, and for a moment the gloom across the threshold baffled even their enhanced eyesight.

When the haze cleared, it revealed a circular space marked by runes painted in red-brown all across the walls. A bronze-lined pit opened up before them, barred by thick armourglass just like the body-tubes up in the apothecarion. The base of the pit was full of corpses, piled a metre high, a heap of cracked bones protruding from hunks of raw meat.

Above the corpse-pile squatted something that was almost impossible to see properly – a false reflection, a shaft of misdirected moonlight. Only when it moved did broken aspects flit across the visual field: a crown of thorns, whiteless eyes, a full-lipped mouth with a lashing tongue the length of a man's arm. At times its flesh resembled that of a human woman, at others a man. As the two legionaries approached the glass, something lashed across the barrier at them, blurred with speed.

'Ah, beautiful,' said Konenos, nodding appreciatively. 'Where did you get it?'

Von Kalda hung back. There were still times when he doubted the wisdom of this work. 'It is not ready. None of them are.'

Konenos gave him a sly smile. 'There are those, they tell me, who are not yet committed to enlightenment. They cling to older disciplines. They do not see the benefit of improvement.' He edged closer to the protective glass and something like a crab's claw snickered, *click-clack*, in the shadows. 'Yet this is our future, these are our allies. That is why you did it, yes?'

Von Kalda felt nauseous. He always did, when in the presence of the things he had summoned into captivity, their ephemeral presence kept anchored by the continual sacrifice of the living. 'Cario's favour is high.'

Konenos swept around towards Von Kalda, catching his face between his gauntlets. He drew closer, and Von Kalda smelt the sweetness of his breath. 'And, in that, you have your answer. The Palatine Blade is as damned as we – he hears the whispers just as we do. This thing may even hasten them, and I would enjoy that.' He looked back at the writhing shadows, and his pink eyes shone. 'Forget making more menials. This is your task now.'

The thing behind the glass thrashed at him, whipping strands of something nearly-physical in a vicious down-stroke. Something, either the thick armourglass or the mystic signs daubed across the dark metal, held it back.

'This order is from the Soul-Severed?'

'You did not wait for that before.' Konenos licked his cracked lips. 'He will tire of his swordsman in time, but time is not something we have in infinite supply, so make these answer your call, and when we next take the ships into war I want them with us.'

He released Von Kalda and moved back towards the armourglass. The creature within responded, and a pair of violet eyes, greater than a human's, almond-shaped and cruel, flickered into life amid the shadows. Konenos watched it move, mesmerised.

'They are contagious,' he breathed. 'It is time that we hastened the pace of infection.'

THIRTEEN

BEFORE THE MAN Veil was brought in, Yesugei took Arvida aside.

'Are you in pain, brother?' the Stormseer asked him, concern evident on his tattooed face.

Arvida might have smiled. He was always in pain. The flesh-change bubbled away under the skin, though the discipline helped, as did the deep void. Every so often the hiss in his ears would abate and the terrible heat in his blood would ebb, but it was only ever temporary. Using his craft brought it right back to the surface, and using his craft was what he had been retained by the Legion for. Every time they asked him, the pain got worse.

If this had been what had driven his Legion to dabble further than they should, if *this* had been what had brought the Wolves to Prospero, then perhaps he could begin to understand. Magnus had always been an indulgent father, and he would not have been able to bear suffering on that scale.

To be slain for that crime, all of them, was a harsh judgement, but then the universe was a harsh place, and the Thousand Sons had flirted with destruction ever since their founding.

'No more than usual,' he replied.

'We do not have to do this.'

'You would not ask if it were not important. Who is he?'

Yesugei gave a look that said *I wish I knew.* 'We are not successful on Herevail. The man we retrieve is only link to the one we sought. He knew target, but he does not know location. However, they work together for years. There may be a way.'

As the Stormseer spoke, Arvida's heart sank. Yes, it might be done, but it would take its toll. Of all his arts, scrying potential futures from dimly imprinted pasts was the hardest, the one that involved the deepest immersion in the corrupting swirls of the Great Ocean.

'You spoke to him yourself?' he asked.

Yesugei gave a rueful look. 'I do my best. As far as I see, he speaks truth. He is proud, like them all.'

That was their reputation, but Arvida had never associated much with Navigators. Vessels in the Thousand Sons fleet had often been guided by their sorcerers on short voyages, leading to friction between the sanctioned Nobilite agents and ship commanders. In no other Legion were the gifts so overlapping and intermingled, and thus the source of so much antagonism.

'There will be a cost to this,' Arvida warned. 'You trust Ravallion's instincts? She has not swayed many yet.'

Yesugei spread his palms in an equivocal gesture. 'What else we have? Our options narrow. If things were not as they are, I would not chase this name from a mortal woman's past, but death now circles us like wolves around fire.' He looked up at Arvida, and his golden eyes – still so strange – glinted in the soft light. 'We have tried everything else. And yes, I trust her. I trust her since we first meet.'

Arvida nodded, steeling himself inwardly. Yesugei liked to believe the best of those he mentored, but he was no fool. 'Very well, though I give no promise of success.'

Yesugei clapped him on the arm, pleased. 'When can we ever? Come, he is waiting.'

They passed from the antechamber, high up in the *Swordstorm*'s bridge level, along the corridors to the secure interrogation unit. As they went, menials hurried past them, bowing hastily before racing off to perform whatever duty they had been given. The entire flagship hummed with energy. Khans from long-sundered brotherhoods had returned and now stalked the crew levels, bringing tidings of long defeats or brief victories, seeking out comrades, taking soundings, testing the ground in advance of the great gathering before the primarch. On another occasion, some might have gawked briefly at the owner of the crimson battleplate in their midst, but none did now – all minds were on the choice that needed to be made.

'They say you preserved Xa's body,' said Yesugei as they passed down through the decks.

'What remained of it.'

'That will not be forgotten.' Yesugei shot him a grateful look. 'The Khagan will not forget it, either. If you change your mind, ask for Legion colours, they be happily given.'

Arvida winced inwardly. He had made his decision a long time ago, and now there was no going back on it. In any case, parts of his body had fused to the inner curve of his armour-plate, gradually pressing into the mechanisms of the ceramite units. He could no more escape its embrace than he could extract his own skeleton.

'One day, maybe,' was all he said. 'Not today.'

They reached the interrogation units, guarded by legionaries on either side of two heavy iron doors. Most cells were empty. Capture had become harder, and less useful, and it was difficult to restrain victorious khans from slaughtering every enemy they came across in retribution for earlier atrocities.

Veil had been placed in one of the lighter, drier, less uncomfortable units. He had access to clean water, regular food, a modicum of privacy, but no one had pretended that he was not being kept secure. As the two Librarians – one shaman, one sorcerer – entered the cramped space, the man rose and bowed floridly.

'See, another comes to try his luck,' Veil observed, looking Arvida up and down. 'But you are a curiosity – I heard that your kind were all destroyed.'

'Not all,' said Arvida. 'Obviously.'

Arvida sat on a metal bench opposite the mortal, and Yesugei did the same. Veil remained standing, though his eye level was now more or less on a par with theirs. He looked agitated, like a cat confined for too long in a wire cage.

'So, what shall we talk of?' he asked, his gaze jumping between the two of them. 'More on the Heisen Vortices? The lore of the Seethe's screaming? Tales of old Navigators who made it home to Terra, now rocking themselves to sleep in the eyeless halls of the Paternova?'

Arvida watched all the man's movements. Some of them were for show – the outrage of the noble falsely kept against his will. Some of them were real nerves, as if he did not trust the good faith of his captors.

'There is not much you could teach me of the Ocean,' Arvida said.

'Oh no?' Veil looked at him scornfully. 'You spell-casters, you hex-makers. You were like children cupping their hands to the waves. You only waded in knee-deep, and it was enough to doom you. Trying swimming where the sunlight does not reach. Try staying alive where the leviathans hunt.'

Yesugei said nothing, though Arvida could sense his presence beside him – observing, taking stock.

Arvida leaned forwards, and Veil recoiled.

'Give me your hand,' Arvida asked.

The Nobilite operative thrust his bony hands into long pockets in his robes, petulant as an infant. 'Do not seek to compel me, witch. I am a–'

+Give me your hand,+ Arvida commanded.

Veil complied before he had a chance to realise it, proffering both hands palm-up. Arvida took the right one, forcing the fingers apart. The flesh was calloused still, tinged grey by a lifetime amid books and star charts.

Veil was at least astute enough not to struggle in the Librarian's grip. He fixed Arvida with a look of pure loathing. 'I am of the Navis Nobilite, high in the favour of the Houses Magisterial. Know that my rights are sacrosanct under ancient treaty and custom.'

Arvida felt the panic running tight under the surface

of those words. For all his bluster, this was just one
more terrified soul cast adrift amid the war.

'Fear not,' said Arvida, aiming to relax him suffi-
ciently for the future-cast to bind. 'This will not cause
you to suffer.'

Tentatively, his opened his mind to the aether. It
surged up within him, far too fast, swelling like a
foaming flood, and he clamped down on it again.
Veil's outline became translucent, as did much of the
cell around him. Only Yesugei remained firm, his own
soul half shackled to the stuff of the underverse.

Veil's hand started to shake, but he held position.
Arvida probed a little further, and his mind began to
fill with ghost-images.

*He saw the reflection of shadowy halls, filled from floor
to ceiling with leather spines, then a great dome containing armillary spheres and orreries, then men and women
in dark velvet robes walking among whispering galleries.
He saw infants rocking gently in rows of iron cradles, all
with swathes of fabric wrapped across their foreheads, their
young eyes fixed on charts hung above them, picked out in
silver on ebony, bewildering in complexity.*

*Then the visions rushed into other, far-off worlds – ocean
planets with orbital rings constructed of adamantium, floating telescopes circled with silver-prowed warships, vessels
with vanes and sails and pulsing, underslung spheres. Amid
those sights were intermingled glimpses of mortal-scale
events – a ceremonial ball under lumens shaped like swans,
thronged with elegant figures in damask and ermine, moving around one another like Platonic spheres. Ancient
words were exchanged, of contract, of fealty, of alliance.
Agents slid among the courtiers and magisters, their eyes
darting, carrying messages of binding or breaking.*

+These are your people,+ Arvida sent. +Now take me to Herevail.+

It took a moment for the visions to align. Veil did not resist, but nor did he know how to comply. Eventually, the cell filled with landscapes of a burned-out planet, its spire-stumps throwing smoke into a sky made red from the residue of a thousand orbital lances. Arvida watched the cities imploding and thought how familiar the aftermath looked.

Then they were racing backwards, to the time before the III Legion had arrived, to the bustle and chaos of a major hive-complex, stuffed full of human life and dirt and splendour. Arvida saw officials swarming across glass floors, their faces part hidden behind glittering augmetics. They were scribes, loremasters, scholiasts, all clad in the heavy furs and rich silks of Achelieux's Magisterium. Only a few carried thick bandanas over their foreheads, edged with gold and draped with jewelled webs. They were the Oculi, the ones with sight into the Ocean, blessed mutants whose origins stretched back into the fractured horror before the coming of the Emperor and whose webs of influence now stretched into every corner of known space.

One of them came to the fore – a young man with old eyes. He too wore the bandana across his forehead, stained with henna and encrusted with sapphires. He was slender, his skin olive. He floated in and out of focus, laughing, talking. He carried a long ebony staff tipped with a white stone.

+Follow.+ Arvida was no longer addressing Veil.

The images shifted, moving from Veil's memories, tracing a line out from them and hunting down the soul-warmth of this new man. Arvida's mind swept down darker corridors, floating through sealed doors. He saw more great charts engraved on marble, etched with snaking tracery and marked *with the names of many worlds. He saw plans, devices, and heard voices raised in argument. Strange faces came in and out of view – bloated, black-eyed, curious and malign.*

Dimly, he was aware of some commotion back in the world of the senses, but by then he was too deep to care. The olive-skinned man turned back and smiled, revealing juvenat-pristine teeth. Another chart hung on the wall, lined with gold. Arvida saw the spidery tracery on it, backed with obsidian, carved by the man's own hand. There were attendants there too, black-robed, wearing masks that obscured their faces. The smell of incense – musky, heady – filled his nostrils.

The man was gesturing, but it was hard to follow the movements. The trace was weakening. Soon it would be gone. Arvida focused on the wall, on the chart of gold. He saw words carved against the stylised void, crafted in runes that leaked their age into the vision like smoke.

+Dark Glass,+ he sent, recognising the script. *There were others, a string of worlds along a warp-conduit. He saw more lines of gold, picking out a pattern down through layers of the Ocean, heading back towards a young yellow sun. Something about the pattern was familiar, and it set his teeth on edge.*

Then the man turned again, looking straight at him. He was still smiling, but the expression was cold.

+You do not belong here.+

Arvida snapped back, and the visions tumbled into clouds of grey. That should not have been possible – he was observing events of the past, glimpsed as reflections of reflections, sealed into the timeline like insects in amber...

He reeled, feeling the ground – the real ground – lurching. He heard cries of pain, muffled and distant. 'Release me!'

He couldn't open his eyes – it was as if they had been welded shut. The pain of the flesh-change thundered in his temples, and blood boiled up in his chest.

+Brother,+ came Yesugei's mind-voice, lancing through the confusion, cutting out the tumult. Arvida latched on to it, clinging like a drowning man to flotsam. +You are hurting him.+

Someone was screaming now. Arvida fought his way back to the surface, clawing away from the visions that clustered around him. Right at the end, as he felt the images fade and ripple into nothing, he saw a shadow gazing up at him from the depths – *an immense figure, crimson-maned, one-eyed, stumbling blindly amid the disintegrating walls of aether-magick.*

Then he was out, panting, flushed, his vision shaky. The mortal was on his knees, crying with pain. Arvida realised he still held his hand, but his gauntlet had crushed it. Blood welled up from the burst mass between his armoured fingers.

He released his grip instantly, and Veil collapsed, cradling his broken hand. Arvida got to his feet, his head hammering, his breath still short. Yesugei was also standing, looking at him with concern.

'What is wrong?' he asked, but Arvida was not listening. He fell back against the cell wall, staring around him as if seeing them for the first time.

'I thought I saw...' he slurred.

Yesugei came up to him, grabbed him by both shoulders. 'What? What you see?'

Arvida blinked hard. He swallowed back the vomit that had risen in his gorge. He felt the Change subside, frothing like sea-foam as it sank back into quiescence.

He had seen so much. The world of the senses

solidified around him, bringing the pain back with it, driven like spikes into his now-open eyes.

'What you see?' Yesugei asked again, more firmly. Veil whimpered in the corner, ignored.

For a moment, Arvida had no words for it. It felt as if his mouth would shatter if he opened it. He stared at Yesugei's scarred face, and it briefly seemed as if his gene-father stared back at him, superimposed on the wind-beaten Chogorian features beneath.

'I know,' he croaked, tasting blood at the back of his mouth.

'What do you know? *Tell me.*'

Even then, he could not utter that truth. But there was another truth to impart, the one he had been sent to delve for.

'I know where he is,' he said, committing the star chart to memory before the image faded. He swallowed hard, pushing all else down, away from where it could cloud his judgement. 'You want this man Achelieux. I know where he went.'

THE ENDURANCE BROKE the veil with its customary brutality, slicing apart the matter of the universe in a blaze of cascading silver. After-ripples of violence juddered across the void, leaking plumes of crackling aether-matter amid trails of dirty smog. The immense warship thundered into full physicality, row upon row of heavy gunnery sliding through the abyss. Seconds later the others came, punching through like thrown spears amid the seething clouds of real space entry.

Mortarion strode to the edge of the bridge's command dais. Ahead of him, the cathedral-sized viewport unfurled its warp shutters, exposing a crowded view of local space. War vessels had assembled, hundreds of them, all bearing the death's-head sigil of the XIV Legion on their pale prows. As the *Endurance* came among them, idents began to flicker into life across cogitator lenses – the *Indomitable Will, Reaper's Scythe, Moritatis Oculix, Stalwart.*

Mortarion did not need to watch the runes to know who had answered his call. He recognised the hull of every battleship in his warfleet, and scoured the void ahead for those he had summoned. The vista was clogged with detail – minor escort wings casting shadows across the flanks of the greatest beasts, tenders ferrying supplies from carriers to line battleships, refit shuttles in Mechanicum-red hovering around colossal engine clusters and thruster rings.

'Where is it?' he asked.

Below him, in the pits and channels of the *Endurance*'s command bridge, masked thralls kept their heads down. The Deathshroud stationed around the edges of the throne dais said nothing, as ever, but stared silently through their slanted armour-masks. Great coils of green-tinged smoke drifted up from rusted brazier-columns standing sentinel over the teeming crew-stations, and the air stayed humid and close, thick with screens of dust.

'Where is the *Terminus Est*?'

More idents scrolled down the lenses, now picking out the new arrivals – commandeered ships from other Legions, older Barbarus craft pressed into service, auxiliary vessels with Army regiment insignias scoured out and replaced with the death's-head emblem. The fleet was enormous, the greater part of the entire Legion pulled back together from a hundred

different separate engagements. Even as the augurs
added to the muster-list, yet more emerged from the
Mandeville points and steamed across real space to
join the throngs.

No one on the *Endurance*'s bridge could answer the
primarch. Ulfar, the ship's master, ordered extra scans
but offered no opinion. Trangh, the master of the
watch, looked up from under his cowl, but shook his
head. The Navigator transmitted nothing from her
cloistered chambers, and shut the comm-links down.

Only Marshal Gremus Kalgaro, Siegemaster of the
Legion and successor to the fanatic Rask, standing
less than three metres from the primarch's side in his
bloodstained artificer plate, grunted audibly.

'First Captain Typhon may not have received the
summons, lord,' he said, his voice a low growl.

Mortarion shot him an acid look. 'Oh, he received
them. This is the first order he has actually defied.
What do I make of that? Has he recanted his choice?'

Kalgaro lowered his eyes. 'Unlikely,' he muttered.

Mortarion limped stolidly across the dais, thudding
Silence's iron heel across the adamantium deck. 'Then
summon those who deigned to heed.'

All across the comms-level, cable-shackled crew hastened to obey. One by one, ghostly green outlines of
Legion commanders shimmered into view, arranged
in a rough semicircle around the primarch. Some wore
their helms, others showed their battle-scarred faces.
All were dour, heavy, rundown.

'Know that I do not take you from your duties without cause,' Mortarion told them, pacing among the
luminous spectres. 'The Warmaster prepares the final
approach to Terra, and demands the elimination of

the Fifth Legion on our flanks. This honour he gives to us. We have their coordinates, which are being sent to your ships as I speak.'

None of the hololithic faces so much as twitched. The commanders were all of Barbarus, stolid and inured to total war even before the coming of the Emperor. They had trained their guns on their own kind at Isstvan, then slaughtered their fellow legionaries across the dark sands of the Urgall. They did not question orders.

'The Khan and his depleted Legion have admitted the inevitable, and drawn their forces together at Aerelion. You know he has avoided pitched battle, but now there can be no more evasion. The raids are over. We make for the warp within the hour – prepare your ships for immediate despatch.'

Even as he spoke, Mortarion kept checking the muster-logs. At any moment, he half expected the faces before him to be joined by one more – the greatest of his servants, the one who from the start had been the most loyal, the most diligent.

'There will be others in this armada. The Third Legion is due to join us, if they can keep pace. I know what that means to you, and I share your disgust. Swallow it. This alliance will not be lasting – with their numbers, we have the means to end the Fifth Legion cleanly. After that, we will be at the Warmaster's side. This he has promised me.'

Calas' absence nagged at him, spoiling like a poison embedded in wine. There had never been any explanation, just a sudden silence, echoing through the void. Typhon might have been killed, though that was hard to imagine. Even harder was the thought that he had turned to some other cause. That was surely impossible. What other cause existed for them now?

'Remember your vows. Those of you still consorting with the warp-fouled, cease. All licence for residual phosphex and bio-weaponry is given – you have your stocks, see that they are deployed in full. I wish to give my brothers a lesson here, not that I have much hope it will be heeded. We are flesh. We are mortal blood. This is enough. It will always be enough.'

Somewhere far below, though, Grulgor still drew foetid breath. The spirit of Lermenta haunted the ship's bilges, lingering over the treasures taken from the worlds of sorcerers. Every vessel in the fleet had its secrets now, monsters and daemon-spoor buried amid glyphs and rune-scripts. It was hard to recover that which had been unlocked – hard, but not impossible.

'We have not fought beside one another, all together, for more than two years. The galaxy has forgotten what the sons of Barbarus are capable of. It is time to remind them.'

But Typhon would have made it *complete*. His return would have removed the last scintilla of doubt.

'Now go, prepare your ships,' snarled Mortarion, pushing the irritation deep down. That would be the end of it – grand speeches were not his way and never had been, for the lure of fresh killing was enough. 'Arm every warrior and make ready every weapon. We leave within the hour.'

FOURTEEN

ILYA TOOK HER place in the chamber of kurultai, and ran her eyes over the throng, trying to ascertain how many warriors had made it and how many were missing. The khans of many brotherhoods sat in ranks, all facing a low stone-flagged platform. Flames burned in ceremonial pillars, and the banners of the old Chogorian realms and empires stood behind the platform, all traced in gold and red, hung from wooden poles and lashed in place with leather thongs.

The Stormseers sat around the edge of the platform, two dozen of them, all that remained of the entire Legion's complement. Yesugei was with them in the place of honour, as was Arvida. Ilya sat beside them both, given her position by the ever-respectful ordu. The commanders of the Legion sat on the other side of the semicircle: Ganzorig and Qin Fai, the two noyan-khans of the Hordes, Shiban Tachseer, Hai-Shan, Namahi of the keshig, Jubal Ahn-ezen. Other famed warriors, tempered during the long-running battles of the war, sat close by – Ainbaatar of the Brotherhood of the Night's Star, Khulan of the Brotherhood of the Golden Path.

Facing them all, seated on the old plains-chair, was the Khagan, the Khan of Khans, wearing the long kaftan and leather jerkin of the Altak. His unarmoured hands rested on his knees, his severe face gazing down from the high vantage, half hidden in the flickering firelight. His oil-black air was unbound and hung across his shoulders. For some in the chamber, this was the first time they had laid eyes on their liege-lord for years.

Ilya did not look at Shiban, sitting across the semi-circle of the hall from her, nor at Arvida close by. The atmosphere in the chamber was tense, fuelled by rumours and counter-rumours.

The last of the khans took their places. A gong sounded, the lumens faded and the flames reared up in their burnished bowls to compensate.

'My sons,' said Jaghatai in Khorchin, sweeping his gaze across the assembled throng. 'You have fought through fire and pain to reach this place. The road has been long. Many who ought to stand with us now are gone.'

Ilya felt her pulse pick up. After five years with the White Scars, she could follow their language with some ease, and thought it was never more beautiful than when spoken by the primarch. His voice, in that place, still had its old wind-burned resonance – low, measured, stained with quiet power. The khans, the zadyin arga, the lords of the Legion, they all listened intently. Even now, there were no guarantees, and none knew yet how he would rule.

'If time remained, I would give honour to them all,' Jaghatai said. 'But every hour we remain here is perilous. We must move again, but now the only question remains – to where? You all know the pattern of this war. The enemy bends the warp to his will with storms we cannot pierce. Our routes to Terra are watched, or blocked, all by forces that outnumber us many times over. We have tried to break free, and have been cast back every time. Survival has been secured by remaining asunder, by running apart, by deception. That cannot suffice any longer, for the noose has tightened. Only two choices remain – to attempt the Throneworld again, or to make our stand here, far from home, and hope to wound my brother so deeply that the sacrifice will not be wasteful.

'For, doubt this not, if we engage the Warmaster's forces here, there can be only one outcome. Many Traitor Legions ply their way towards Terra, supported and aided by their countless mortal armies. We are strong enough to draw his attention, but not to end him.'

That brought a low ripple of murmurs. Many of the khans would have disputed that, given the chance, yet none openly gainsaid their lord. Ilya felt her grip on her seat edge tighten.

'And if we honour our oaths?' Jaghatai went on. 'Are all ways barred to us now? Maybe so, maybe not. We have been pursuing one hope, little more than a rumour. In another age, we would not have stooped to such, but the times are straitened.' His dark gaze moved to Arvida. 'Sorcerer, you will tell.'

Arvida stood, turning to address the rows of khans. Ilya thought he moved awkwardly, as if carrying an old wound. Had he been hurt at Kalium?

'We have a name,' said Arvida, also in Khorchin. 'It is Novator Pieter Achelieux, known to us through the service of General Ravallion. Of all those of the Navis Nobilite, it is believed he holds the greatest chance of divining a route for us. The general vouched for him, and amid the last sequence of raids he was sought on the world Herevail. We did not find him there, but now we have a location: the Catullus Rift. To the best of our knowledge, there is nothing there worthy of attention from the enemy. It is an isolated place, of no strategic import and with no recorded activity. If we wish to seek this man out, that is where we must go.' Arvida looked back up to the high dais. 'If we wish to seek him out,' he said again.

The sorcerer resumed his place.

'So this is the sage's counsel, the one we have been fighting for,' said Jaghatai. 'It is in our power to reach Catullus. If this man exists, we may find him. And if he has the power over the aether we hope, that will give us our way home.'

'And if he does not?' Shiban asked.

Ilya's heart sank. The scepticism in his voice was plain.

'Then, Shiban Tachseer,' said Jaghatai, 'it may be as good a place as any to meet the enemy.'

Shiban smiled – a strained expression on his scarred face. 'Forgive me, Khagan, but this is kurultai, where all words may be spoken. Many have already fallen chasing this dream. Every battle we fight takes us further from where we need to be. There are other choices.'

'There are,' said Jaghatai.

'Our home,' said Shiban, turning to face his brothers and eliciting another subdued wave of agreement from the chamber. 'If we cannot break open the path to Terra, we may yet return to Chogoris. We know nothing of its fate. Perhaps its people fight on, or perhaps it is laid waste.' He looked up directly at the primarch. 'If it is honour we are to satisfy, then we should first tend to the hearths of those who raised us.'

'We cannot go back to Chogoris,' said Yesugei. There was no triumph in his voice, only sadness. 'It would be beyond our strength to try.'

'And yet Terra is not.'

'If Terra falls, nothing else remains.' Yesugei did not look at Shiban, but addressed the primarch, as all at kurultai did. 'The war would be over. Horus would be free to scour the rest of the galaxy, world by world.'

'There are rumours,' said Ganzorig, Hasik's successor. 'They say Ultramar still stands, that the Raven is still alive, in spite of everything. The Warmaster cannot be everywhere.'

'Not yet,' said Yesugei. 'But hand him the Throne and that will change.'

'This man, Achelieux, is but a mortal,' said Qin Fai, Ganzorig's counterpart in the Legion command. 'He may live yet, he may be dead. He may aid us, it may be beyond his power. These are weak strands to clutch at.'

'They are,' said Ilya, pushing herself to her feet. She did not like addressing the ordu in their own place, and she spoke in Gothic, not trusting her Khorchin to convey her thoughts aright. 'Weak strands indeed. It would shame me to bring them to you. If there were any other chances we had not tried, I would agree with your words, and with Tachseer's, and with any other counsel that said "Enough, we have run and we have hunted, but there is no path left"…'

The khans listened in silence. Ilya could feel their massed eyes on her – quiet, respectful, sceptical. They had always listened to her, right from the very start. That burden had been a heavy one, and the weight of it had never lessened.

'But you did not know this man,' she went on. 'A Novator of the Houses Magisterial is a great lord, and Achelieux was amongst the greatest of them. He had the ear of the Palace itself, and I saw his warpcraft enacted during the Crusade, when he brought fleets to war through storms of such magnitude they said the task was impossible. Be in no doubt: he is a magister of the aether, a true guide. '

'And yet, if he could find the path to Terra,' said Shiban, also in Gothic, 'would he not have taken it?'

'I believe he remained in the void.'

'Because he could not do otherwise.'

'Because his duties kept him there.'

'You cannot know that.'

Ilya felt her anger rising. Shiban's tone had become sardonic. 'No, Tachseer, I cannot. There is much that is guesswork – I have never hidden that.'

'Yet whatever the truth,' interjected Arvida, reverting to his fluent Khorchin, 'we know where he is now. I have seen it.'

'And we can gain this location,' added Yesugei. 'The ways are charted, and the journey is short. Perhaps that is fate. Or maybe good fortune – the first we have for a while.'

'Then you support this, zadyin arga?' asked Ganzorig. 'Is that true?'

'Because when has szu-Ilya ever led us wrong, noyan-khan?' said Yesugei, smiling. 'And because

we swore to gain Terra after Prospero, and to break
an oath is a sacred crime, punishable by the gods
themselves. And because it is the way of danger, and
discovery, and, as for myself, I am not yet done living, and wish to frustrate the enemy a little longer.'

That brought answering smiles from the assembled
khans.

'But it is not my order to make,' said Yesugei, bowing to the primarch.

All eyes turned back to Jaghatai. He had remained
silent throughout the exchange, listening intently,
his deep-set eyes giving nothing away. Ilya held her
breath.

'You answered the call,' Jaghatai said, addressing
them all again. 'You were faithful, even when treachery knocked on our doors from within. I know the
cost already borne, and until this moment, in truth,
I was not fully of one mind, for I yearn for nothing
more than to finish what was started on Prospero. I
am hunted by my brothers, and my blood runs hot
from the shame of it, and my wish is only to turn and
face them. Yet this is the easier choice – to become as
they are, and to counter rage with rage, and fight blind,
knowing that the greater cause will be lost.'

Ilya sank back against her seat. Once again, the trust
was there, though it felt to her, and had always felt,
that she had done so little to earn it.

'Distrust the path of ease,' Jaghatai said. 'That is
what we have been taught, is it not? So I give the
command – if we are to die, then Catullus will serve.
Return to your ships, make ready for the warp. Our
hunters are tight on our scent, so I wish us gone
swiftly. You have five hours.'

The Khagan looked at Ilya and inclined his head in what might have been acknowledgement.

'We will do what the sage counsels,' he said. 'One last throw of the dice.'

TWO HOURS BEFORE the *Swordstorm's* engines were primed to fire, the first signal came in. An outrider on the edge of the system picked up the dim fore-blip of an incoming ship, and initiated a deep-scour sensor-sweep. Significant ships were yet to join the muster, among them the *Melak Karta*, so all checks were thorough.

The gun-corvette *Xia Xia* received the signal and burned hard to close the distance, aiming to get a clearer augur-reading. Its crew managed to clarify the signal, but did not recognise the ident. They ran the scan again, cross-checked it, then upgraded the alert to a fleet-wide priority signal.

'*Fourteenth Legion,*' came the comm-burst, sent to every ship in the outer perimeter. '*Repeat, Fourteenth Legion signal incoming.*'

At that stage, the *Kaljian* had taken position closest to the likeliest incursion points. Returning in poorly hidden anger from kurultai, Shiban had ordered the attack frigate away from the main cluster of battleships, pulling high above of the lumbering void-monsters still undergoing preparations for warp jump in Aerelion's shadow.

'Can you be sure?' Shiban asked, moments after returning to the bridge to assume full command. The scarred flesh of his exposed face shone from exertion in the practice cages.

'No doubt,' answered Tamaz, the sensorium master.

Jochi was there too, as was Yiman, promoted to darga since Memnos, and many others of the brotherhood. All were armoured, their weapons powered.

'Launch intercept,' ordered Shiban, taking his seat in the throne. 'Full speed.'

Already primed, the frigate powered up to attack velocity, shooting clear of the other vessels in the local void-volume. By then the alert was still filtering through to the body of the main fleet, putting the *Kaljian* ahead of the pack.

Jochi moved up to Shiban's shoulder. 'My khan,' he said, warily.

Shiban looked straight ahead. 'Do not counsel caution, brother,' he said. 'The others will be with us in moments.' He felt the drum of the engines vibrating up through the decking. 'We can at least claim the first kill. These things have not yet been taken away.'

The *Kaljian* overhauled the *Xia Xia* and assumed point ahead of the other ships spreading out to intercept the rogue signal. Within moments, the first inbound vessel was detectable on the forward augurs.

'Arm main lance,' ordered Shiban. 'How many craft have emerged?'

Tamaz did not reply straight away. 'One, my khan.'

Shiban laughed. 'A brave one. He has broken formation.'

Tamaz looked up at him. 'No, my lord. Just one. No other signals. And we are being hailed.'

The rogue ship's details began to spill down the sensor-lenses, and immediately the oddness became clear – a system-runner, not a warship, barely capable of making warp jumps at all.

'Shall I relay the hail?' asked Tamaz.

The *Kaljian*'s lance remained trained on the incoming ship, now almost close enough to spy on the real-viewers. Almost without realising, Shiban ran through the pre-fire routine himself, visualising the flash of light as the forward lance fired. A ship like that would have no chance – a clean hit would implode it instantly.

'My khan?'

Shiban snapped back. 'Maintain course,' he said. 'Train macrocannons, engine-shots. Relay the hail to me.'

The audio, when it filtered through his helm systems, was thick with white noise. Even so, the signal was just clear enough, and from the first word Shiban felt a sudden, cold wash of familiarity.

'*Torghun Khan, five others, sagyar mazan kill-squad, responding to Legion muster as ordered. Awaiting command.*'

The voice hadn't changed much. Perhaps the Khorchin was a little better than it had been – a more Chogorian inflection. At least he had adopted the custom of the Legion now, and there was no more talk of 'companies'. The old Brotherhood of the Moon had been disbanded, its warriors assessed for loyalty before being dispersed under the guidance of other khans, so by rights he should not even have used the honorific.

By rights, he should have died. That had been the justice of it.

The two ships continued to hurtle towards one another, and the system-runner became a visible white dot in the far distance. Other vessels of the fleet came into range behind the *Kaljian*, their weapons primed.

At such a distance they might not have picked up the hail yet – a single shot would still end the situation.

'Khan, what are your orders?' asked Jochi.

One shot, from the *Kaljian* or from any other ship, that would do it. There could be no blame attached, and little enough loss.

'Khan?'

Shiban broke from the vision, and rose from the throne. 'Transmit stand-down notice to all following ships,' he said, striding over to where his guan dao had been hung. 'Select ten from the minghan, full-armour, battle-ready.'

He activated his blade's energy field, and it sparked into life as eagerly as it had once done on the bone-white plains of Chondax.

'Order the ship to come to full stop, shields down,' he commanded, his eyes locked on the steadily growing blob of light ahead. 'Say nothing, give them nothing. We are going over.'

TORGHUN WATCHED THE incoming ships. Merely laying eyes on them again was enough to make his pulse quicken. The ivory prows of the fleet had never been a source of pride, not even at the start, and now they also brought with them the heady nausea of shame.

Even after all had been made plain – that the Legion was re-forming for one final engagement and that all blades were needed in the defence of the ordu – the decision to respond to the summons had been hard to make. Sanyasa had been in favour, as had Ozad, Ahm, Gerg and Inchig. Holian had been the only other one to hold back. The two of them had resisted, and a khan's word had the greatest weight, but there were no certainties, not among those whose only purpose was to die in battle and who had been flung far from the heart of the Legion's ranks and honour-codes.

The possibility of deception had been raised. Perhaps, Holian had argued, the order was a ruse, elaborately disguised and used by the enemy to flush them out into the open. To die in open combat was honourable, but to be lured into a slaughter was pointless.

In truth, though, Torghun had never believed that – the codes were in order, the seals and counter-sigils perfectly aligned. The things that had prevented him from responding immediately were human things, mortal emotions that might have been purged a lifetime ago in another soul – pride, resentment, the burning guilt of failure, of a step wrongly taken.

So now he stood on the rusting bridge of his stolen ship, watching those whom he had once betrayed swarm out to meet him again.

He rested his gauntlet on the hilt of his sword, still sheathed and unpowered. A lone frigate had pulled ahead of the rest and was now demanding the lowering of shields and the opening of docking bay doors.

'Do it,' ordered Torghun quietly. 'Do anything they ask.' He turned to Sanyasa and the others. 'So here we are. We will meet them together.'

Sanyasa remained confident. The prospect of fighting once more among the ranks of Chogoris had reinvigorated him, fuelling an already vital warrior-energy.

They went down to the main docking bay – a cluttered space barely big enough for three landers and the still-functioning jetbikes. The six warriors emerged into the centre of the apron, in armour but helm-less and with no weapons in hand. It took a long time for the shuttle to clear the gulf between the vessels.

Eventually it arrived, setting down before them on a wash of filthy smoke from charred down-thrusters. The craft looked beaten up, almost as much as their own equipment.

Crew bay doors hissed open, and the embarkation ramp thudded to the adamantium deck. Eleven warriors of the V Legion emerged, ten in standard ivory power armour, all bearing glaives or power swords. The eleventh, their khan, was clad in a suit of gunmetal grey of a strange design, the only concession to the Horde being his pauldrons, which still bore the lightning-strike image, gold and red on a white ground.

As the boarding party approached, Torghun and the others bowed. No one said a word until the steel-armoured khan stood before them.

'Declare yourself,' came the command, filtered through growling layers of vox-enhancement and barely recognisable as human.

'Torghun Khan, once of the Brotherhood of the Moon,' Torghun replied. 'Five others of many brotherhoods, now joined to the sagyar mazan. We answer the call.'

This information had already been conveyed once, though the questioner seemed to want to hear it again. The steel-armoured khan said nothing for a while. The energy fields on his warriors' weapons snarled in the silence, casting an electric-blue sheen across the landing site.

Then the khan moved closer. Torghun could hear his breath scraping through a damaged vox-grille.

'This cannot be chance,' the khan hissed. 'This is just one more poor jest. There were never chances, not with you.'

Slow realisation dawned. Torghun saw the way the armour had been designed to keep its occupant fighting. Its owner must once have been horribly wounded.

'My brother–' he began.

'If it had been me, I would not have come back. I would have heard the order and ignored it. I would have remembered Prospero, and taken my blade and fallen across it. And even in that, I would have had no honour. There would have been no succour. No respite.'

Torghun's face flushed hot. He felt his gauntlets twitch and knew instinctively how quickly he could reach for his blade. He sensed the rest of the hunt-pack around him, uncertain now, making their own calculations.

'The order,' Torghun said, working hard to keep anger out of his voice, 'came from the Khagan.'

By now the steel mask was inches from his face. He could see scratches on the metal, the thousand marks of long combat, and could smell the lubricating oils and the faint burn of servos.

'Turn around,' the khan said. 'Take your ship. Go back to the oblivion that was reserved for you.'

All heard it. Out of the corner of his eye, Torghun saw the tight fury build on Sanyasa's face. The atmosphere in the hangar became febrile, as if thunder were about to break.

'The order,' Torghun repeated, softly, firmly, 'came from the Khagan.'

He had not quite finished when the first blow hit – a curled fist, rammed hard into his exposed face, sending him reeling. Torghun staggered away, tasting blood across his mouth. Another strike thumped into his temple, knocking him to his knees. He would have fallen, but a steel fist caught him by the throat, lifted him up and slammed him into the nearest wall. He hung, feet barely touching the ground, struggling to breathe.

'We have been *so weak*, for *so long*,' came the voice from behind the mask, seething with a deep, cold loathing. 'So many were lost. If all had stood firm then we would be winning this, not watching our strength bleed from us.'

Torghun clamped his hands onto the khan's forearm, scrabbling at the grip. His vision began to blur. He tried to speak, but could not force the words out.

'Do you understand what you did?' Amid the fury was pain, amid the pain, incomprehension. 'Do you truly see it now? Are you blind or merely a fool?'

Torghun heard the fizz of energy weapons igniting, and finally went for the hilt of his power sword. He was losing consciousness and needed to strike. His fingers wrapped around the grip, and his thumb slipped over the ignition stud.

Then he was falling, thudding into the deck in a heap, his temples hammering. He pushed himself back up, teeth gritted, ready to strike.

But the khan had let him go. He had deactivated his own blade, and was unclamping his helm-seal. Sanyasa and the others were being held back by the rest of the khan's entourage, unable to intervene.

Torghun watched the steel helm lift clear, his vision returning, his fist still tight around the grip of his sword. He could have struck then, thrusting upwards.

Shiban Khan's face emerged. At least, it was partly

Shiban's face. Half of it had gone, replaced by synth-flesh and metal plating. One eye had been replaced with an iron augmetic, and a forest of pistons and nerve-bundles protruded from the lip of his gor-get. The Talskar scar was still visible, preserved amid the overlapping steel scales, zigzagging across what remained of his cheek.

The last time Torghun had looked into those eyes had been on the *Swordstorm*, years ago. Everything had changed since – the augmetics dragged Shiban's fea-tures out of symmetry, fixing a permanent snarl onto what had been an open, pleasant visage.

Shiban lowered himself cumbersomely, his armour clanking as it compensated.

'Did you think I would kill you?' Shiban asked coldly. 'I have my orders.'

Torghun finally let his power sword go. 'And you never doubted them.'

'Never.'

Torghun spat a gobbet of blood on to the deck. 'Do not think I will beg, my brother. I came because I was called, not because I desired it.'

'I care nothing for what you desire,' said Shiban. His voice was the greatest change – it was harsher now, and not just because of the implants in his throat. 'You will not be slain by my hand, nor by any hand in the Legion. But neither will you return to the place of honour – I will see to that, if nothing else. Whatever duty is most shameful, that is where you shall serve. When the noose closes and we are fighting again, your blades shall be absent. If there is victory, you will have no part in it – your station shall be in the rear, the reserves, among the mortals and the mindless.'

Torghun stared up at him, his jaw set. Though he had suffered wounds too during the long exile, his face was intact, his armour functional. Of the two of them, it was he now who looked more the White Scars legionary. 'Then you would waste our coming here.'

'You will serve, but you will not atone. There is no atonement. You were sent away to die, and failed even in that.'

Shiban got back to his feet, leaving Torghun half kneeling at his feet. He turned on his heels, and stalked back towards the waiting shuttle.

'So is that it?' Torghun shouted after him. 'Is that why you came – to stage this show?'

Shiban kept walking. His troops fell in behind him.

'You would have laughed at that, once,' Torghun called out. 'You would have laughed to even *think* it.'

Shiban kept walking. The shuttle's thrusters keyed up again, flooding the apron with a tide of boiling smoke.

'You are not my judge, Shiban Khan. You have been judging me since the day I met you, but you are not the arbiter of this Legion.'

Shiban kept walking. As he went, he replaced his helm, covering over the puckered mass of scar tissue at his neck.

'What *happened* to you?' Torghun cried out, getting back to his feet.

Only then did Shiban halt, as if he would turn. He paused for a moment. 'The same thing that happened to all of us,' he said quietly, never looking back.

Then he carried on, up into the crew bay, and the ramp hauled back up. The shuttle's thrusters boomed into life, and the vessel lifted once more, turning tightly before blasting down the exit towards the void doors.

THE PROUDHEART LED the spearhead into the Aerelion system, closely followed by the rest of the fleet. The formation remained tight, arranged to give the forward lances unimpeded access. Only at the very margins did the escort-class vessels move away into wide positions, throwing long-range scans out into the void.

Signals flooded back immediately, hundreds of them, overlapped and mingled as the augur-beams calibrated on the mass of sensoria to be processed.

Watching it all, Eidolon felt the first stirrings of combat stimulation begin to build in his ravaged body. He limped back across the throne dais, prowling the limits like a beast yet to be loosed.

'Tell me,' he growled. 'Give me everything.'

The mistress of the watch could not turn from her station, since she had been stitched into it for the past three months, her eyes hidden by the burnished cables that fed directly from the flagship's sensor array into her narcotic-soaked mind.

'Multiple capital ship signals,' she reported in a stilted monotone. 'They are moving, lord, pulling clear to one-ninety-thirty. We are placed between them and the Mandeville vector.'

Eidolon grinned. His battle-group accelerated further. He watched data stream in from all sectors of the formation – gunwales unshuttering, macrocannons shunting out, lances hitting maximum energy, void shields snapping into full coverage.

Konenos would be leading the starboard flank, making the same calculations. Cario would be racing ahead, desperate to bring his retinue into contact first. The cohorts of Kakophoni, fresh from the defence of Kalium, would be imbibing the last of their combat-stimms. Whole companies of Tactical Marines would be drilling the last of their armour into place, pressing the plates down over enhanced flesh and whispering rites of exuberance.

'Bring me visual,' Eidolon demanded, ignoring the speck of drool that had gathered at his mouth's edge. 'Let me see them.'

The first images were grainy, shaking as the ocular feeds struggled with the extreme range. For all that, the visuals made his blood spike with pleasure – pale ships, already under way but far from warp-ready, out of formation, drifting at high anchor over the gas giant as if they had only just arrived.

'Sloppy,' Eidolon murmured. 'Worse than their reputation.' He stalked back to the throne, over to where his engorged helm waited to be donned. 'Attack speed, all quarters,' he ordered. 'Engage before they have the chance to come about.' He started to breathe more heavily, wetly, anticipating how the impact would go. 'Let none escape.'

The III Legion flotilla thundered up to full burn, each commander picking a target, each gunnery-master marshalling vast arrays of ship-breaking weaponry. Eidolon watched it all unfold from the *Proudheart*, placed at the vanguard of the charge, the first to strike, and sure to strike heaviest.

Then the first contrary signals were received. Disquiet ran down the sensor-pits like a wave, followed by consternation. Warning runes glowed into life, and officials raced from station to station to confirm the readings.

The mistress of the watch spoke first. 'My lord, we are too late.'

Eidolon turned on her. 'Are you blind?' he cried. 'I see them! I see them myself.'

He gestured wildly over to the great screens that hung above the command throne, each one linked via thick iron-rimmed cabling to the core real-viewers. The images were stabilising now, shaking down and losing the thick patina of interference.

For a moment, he did not want to believe it. He let the attack-run continue, hoping against hope that some mistake had been made and would yet be corrected.

In the end, it took the audio feed to shake him out of it.

'*Third Legion battle-group,*' came the grinding, unmistakeable accent of Barbarus over the inter-fleet comm-link, as unlovely and stolid as it had ever been. '*This is the* Endurance. *You are on an intercept heading, your weapons armed. I am instructed by my lord to inform you that if you do not assume a more suitable trajectory then you will be disarmed.*'

Eidolon remained motionless, poised as if to strike. He felt a scream of frustration boiling up within him, and clamped it down – released then, it would have skinned half the crew.

The fleet powered onwards. As the images resolved into further details, he saw the prow-sigils of the white ships become clear – death's heads, poorly painted on slovenly ship-lines.

'Order power-down,' he snarled, eventually. He turned away, no longer willing to even look at those he had taken for the enemy. 'Fleet-wide. Do it now.'

He heard the orders despatched, and each one was like a twist in the wound.

'More hails, my lord,' came the enervated voice of the mistress of the watch. 'The Death Lord demands your presence and has tidings from the Warmaster. How shall I respond?'

Eidolon drew in a long, pained breath. 'Tell him I will come.' He started to pace again, allowing the combat-stimms to ebb, his blood to cool. 'Tell him it will be an honour, a *true* honour, to parley with the Dread Liberator of Barbarus.'

He looked out again, into the void. The gas giant was an object of rare beauty, its hue both intense and varied. Such would be wasted on the savages who orbited it, and with whom he was condemned to work.

'Try to sound sincere,' he said. 'They tell me his pride is fragile.'

PART III

PART III

FIFTEEN

THEY NO LONGER played *go*. In less straitened times, Ilya and the Khan had passed many hours poring over the black and white stones, discussing the ways of the plains and the ways of the Imperial high command, considering the parallels between the patterns they created and the ones that played out in the void around them.

She could not remember when they had stopped. Perhaps it had been after the first truly heavy defeat, when a force of Iron Warriors had correctly predicted an assault on the garrison world of Iluvuin and wiped out two brotherhoods. After that, the mood throughout the Legion had changed. Now the stones remained in their ceramic bowls, untouched.

Now, alone with him again in his chambers on the *Swordstorm*, Ilya studied the primarch's features, trying to remember how he had seemed to her when they had first met, back on Ullanor after the high point of the Crusade.

He did not look any older, she concluded, but he looked wearier.

He had led most attacks himself, taking on the brunt of the enemy vanguard. On a few occasions, she herself had witnessed the engagements, usually by long-range pict relay, but close enough to get a sense of how a primarch wielded his power. She had seen him overturn Land Raiders with his bare hands. She had seen him take on howling battalions of frenzied horrors and annihilate them all. She had seen him cut through the heart of enemy elite formations – Terminator honour guard, Destroyer squads, veteran companies – all as if they were the rawest neophytes.

None stood before one of the Eighteen.

The Khan had slain and slain until his tulwar threw sheets of blood around it, and still it had not been enough. If his will to fight had been damaged by that, he did not show it. He spoke in the same cultured, measured way, balancing the lives of his warriors with the task of survival. It must have been the same for him from the very beginning, on a world of constantly moving warfare where borders meant little and speed meant everything. He did not understand pity, not for himself, not for others. He did what he had been created to do, just as all of the Emperor's loyal sons did.

And yet...

The primarchs were posthuman, but they were not automata. Though the Khagan had never cared overmuch for the Imperial mantras, nor for territory or title, he loved his sons, and too many had been cut down.

Now he stared into the firelight, toying with a long *kiril* dagger, his dark eyes heavy with thought. Ilya sat opposite him, lounging in a hide-bound chair, low-slung in the Chogorian style. She was tired herself, but had not been given leave to depart.

The Khan was pensive. She had learned to read the signs – this was one of the rare occasions when he wished for her counsel. Ilya was never quite sure what he gained from that, since the advice of lords such as Yesugei and Tachseer was of far greater value, but still, from time to time, the occasion presented itself.

'It was a success, Khagan,' she said.

He looked up, as if noticing her presence for the first time. 'Hmm?'

'The muster. Eighty-four per cent of known remaining Legion assets retrieved and in the warp. All capital ships in combat condition. You have your fleet intact, my lord. You have your army.'

The Khan nodded absently. 'A success. You are right, szu.'

'You could look happier about it.'

His mouth twitched, and on his lean face the half-smile looked ghoulish. He raised the blade up against the light, turning the steel one way then the other. 'If we had achieved the goal, I might celebrate. It is a faint chance that you offer me. Perhaps no chance at all. And then maybe that would not be something to mourn.'

'It would be something very much to mourn.'

'I have refused fights that I yearned to take. It is not easy, believe me, to run before the storm. I was made to embrace it.'

Ilya raised an eyebrow. 'Is that what disquiets you? My lord, you did what had to be done. A lesser general would have seen this Legion scattered to the winds

by now, and I know of what I speak, for I have served
under many lesser generals.'

'I gave us survival.' He mulled the word over for a
while. 'Not something to be cherished. I wish I had
hurt them more. And I wish...'

Ilya waited for the sentence to finish, but it never
did. She sighed, kicked back her chair and clambered
awkwardly out of it. The furniture in the Khan's
chamber had all been constructed for a primarch's
dimensions, and she looked almost comically small
within it. She shuffled over to the fire pit and flung
a log onto the pile. The wood – Chogorian *haelo* –
burned ferociously, spitting sparks as it caught.

'Achelieux will find us a path,' she said, more confidently than she felt. 'I know you doubt me, but no
soul knew more of the warp than Pieter.'

'So you told me, many times.' The Khan remained
seated, his limbs sprawled. Even recumbent, he
looked dangerous – a tempest momentarily stilled.
'If he does not, the enemy will be swift on our heels.
Do you sense him? I do. I hear his breathing in the
night, as harsh as it was on Prospero. He burns for
vengeance. He burns to take up the fight we were
unable to complete.' The dagger's blade flashed as it
turned. 'As do I, szu. There are nights when that is
all I wish to do. There are nights when I forget my
oath, and forget that my warriors look to me in all
things, and I only wish to cast off into the abyss and
find him again.'

'These things are said by your sons, too,' said Ilya,
quietly. 'You should listen to Yesugei, for he sees the
danger of it.'

The Khan chuckled – a sonorous, chest-deep sound.

'I listen to Yesugei. I listen to many voices. By the four winds, I even listen to you, if you choose to believe it.'

'I do,' said Ilya, returning to her seat. 'Of course I do – Achelieux was my counsel, and of all things I have cause to be grateful to you for, that remains the greatest.'

The Khan tired of his bladeplay and let the dagger fall to the tabletop beside him. He sat forwards, steepling his long fingers.

'The lie has always been present,' he mused. 'Right from the start. We preached the Imperial Truth to the masses, yet employed sorcerers and mutants to guide us through the heavens, and practised the very arts we pretended did not exist to sustain them. That was the great lie, and I could not endure that. It could never have lasted. And so here is the question – why was it allowed to happen?'

Ilya listened. She knew that the Khan only half spoke to her, half to himself, but these were rare moments – the opening of a mind that preferred to remain locked tight.

'My Father was neither a monster nor a simpleton. He did a thing only because it had to be done. Perhaps He could have explained more, but I will not believe, even now, that there was not a reason for His choices. He led us to Ullanor, then left. After that, He was silent, and only the words of the Sigillite emerged from Terra. What project could have kept Him from the Crusade that He instigated? Only one that was necessary for its survival. And so I have been pondering all His words to me, trying to find the ones that explain it, and I curse that we spoke so little, and that our minds were so unlike to one another.

'In the end, I come back to the same place. My Father hated the lie as much as I did. He knew the Imperium could not last as long as its foundations were knee-deep in the warp. It was necessary to use these mutants and witches, but they could not be allowed to endure. They would be passing tools, like the warriors of thunder that united Terra – blades that would grow blunt and be cast aside. We were always told that the Great Crusade was the end of things, and all else was subordinate to it. I believe this now to be false. The Crusade was launched to give Him something he needed – knowledge, perhaps. Maybe forbidden, maybe lost, maybe xenos, maybe dragged from the aether. But after finding it He went back, and put into place His scheme of eternity, and for the first time since the Ages of Strife His mind was no longer turned towards His creations. Thus they wandered. Thus they fell.'

Ilya had never heard the Khan talk like this before. She had never heard anyone talk in such a way about the Emperor, of whom the White Scars had always known – and had always cared – relatively little. 'What scheme do you speak of?'

The Khan inclined his head equivocally. 'I know not. I do not have His genius. But consider this – the Navigators are the last of the old mutants, the final throwback to our distant horror. They are the clearest and most potent exemplars of the lie, and for as long as the Imperium needed them it could never rest secure. If my Father were truly set on making the Imperial Truth a reality, they could not have been suffered to remain. There must have been another way. And others, perhaps in the Nobilite itself, must have known or guessed this.'

Ilya sank back into her chair. 'Then I understand now.'

'Understand what?'

'Why you allowed me to pursue Achelieux. You do not believe it possible to return. You wish to meet your end out in the void, fighting your brothers in the honourable way. To hunt this place – the Dark Glass – is merely for knowledge. Before the end, you would know whether you were right.'

The Khan smiled. 'No, szu, you judge me too harshly. My oath binds me – if there is a path to the Throneworld, I will take it.' The smile dissolved. 'But if there is not, and all ways are barred, then, yes, I would learn why my Father turned His back on us. This place may be the key, it may not. We risk these things, you see, as the end hastens.'

'So if the moment comes,' said Ilya, trying to hold his shifting gaze, 'if you have to choose death with honour, or to flee home, what course will you take? How far will your oath bind you?'

'To the end of time.'

'But you have sworn more than one, so which bears more heavily?'

The Khan did not answer. His aquiline face turned away from her, gazing back into the flames. 'When did you learn to ask questions so fiercely?' he muttered. 'I preferred it when your fear made you mute.'

'And what point is there in fear now, Khagan? After a lifetime of labour I have seen the worlds of man tear themselves apart and usher in the yaksha of ancient nightmare. I am old now. There is not much in the galaxy worthy of fear that I have not seen.'

'Do not be so sure,' said the Khan.

✠ ✠ ✠

OF ALL OF them, Sanyasa took it the hardest.

After the system-runner had been abandoned and
scuttled, the sagyar mazan were transported over to a
heavy crew transporter called *Xo Gamail.* The orders,
it seemed, had come from Shiban Khan, whom, Torghun learned, they were calling Tachseer now, the
Restorer. His name was spoken throughout the Legion
with a kind of reverence, though a wary one. They
knew what he had done, both at Prospero and since,
but they spoke the name of Jubal, Master of the Hunt,
with more joy.

Seventeen sagyar mazan squads had heeded the call
and made it back to the muster at Aerelion. The survivors in each varied, giving a total of one hundred
and thirty-two warriors – less than a brotherhood, and
thus not deserving of a khan. It was as Shiban had
told Torghun: they would be reservists, left to fester
while the loyal servants of the ordu faced the enemy.

The *Xo Gamail* was stationed towards the rear of the
fleet convoy, amid the supply ships and the munitions bulkers. It must have been in service for decades,
maybe much longer, and it had not been well maintained. Unlike a line battleship, the interior was dirty,
poorly lit, under-crewed and rust-laced. The shipmaster was a mortal, as were all the crew. They were
mostly Chogorian, and paid all homage to the warriors in their midst, but not perhaps quite as reverently
as they would have done for the faithful.

Torghun was the most senior of those who had
assembled. Several darga had survived, but no khans
of old brotherhoods. That in itself was a source of
doubt – in every sidelong glance he found himself sus-
pecting that they resented that. He should have been

first in the line of fire, just as their khans no doubt had been. To be alive at all was a kind of failure, one that even they themselves felt and amplified.

'So you were right,' said Sanyasa to him, two days into the first warp-stage.

They sat together in the mess hall, now scattered with sparse groups of occupants. From down below the clang and echo of the old engines could be heard, labouring hard to keep up with the main convoy.

'Right about what?' replied Torghun, chewing on a dried husk of meat-equivalent.

'We should not have come back. Just kept fighting. Waited until the numbers got too great.'

'You would have died unmarked.'

'It would have been better.'

But Torghun no longer agreed. The shame of meeting Shiban again had not yet burned itself out, but was giving way to anger. The scarred khan had surely been right – it was more than coincidence. They had dogged one another since Chondax, their paths criss-crossing over and over. That was fate, not chance.

'Fighting will come,' Torghun said. 'I have spoken to the others, the ones who arrived before us. They say the numbers are against us. The enemy has closed the Legion off.' He rolled the meat-stick around in his mouth. 'We will all be fighting soon, some way or another.'

'I do not believe he knows,' said Sanyasa, poking at his own ration.

'Who?'

'The Khagan. I do not believe he sanctioned this. Even those who took the death-oath were treated honourably. He would not have recalled us for this.'

Torghun smiled dryly. 'Maybe he does, maybe he does not. Do you think that every kill team in the ordu attracts his attention?'

'He would not have allowed it.'

'You seem sure.'

'I *am* sure,' said Sanyasa, slamming a closed fist down on the tabletop. He leaned in closer, his voice falling. 'We might petition him. If Tachseer is his adviser, then there can be no redemption for us, but if *he* sees us–'

Torghun laughed, shaking his head. 'Did you not notice it, brother? We are at war now, the Legion united. There is no time for this, even if it could be done.'

'It was done before,' said Sanyasa, warily. 'So I was told.'

So it had been. The *Kaljian* had made it in close to the flagship, aided by the *Swordstorm*'s bridge crew, right at the height of the Legion's confusion. Torghun remembered the flurry of orders beforehand, most from Hasik, bringing the *Starspear* alongside and forcing the confrontation that, once again, could not just have been chance.

'That was then,' Torghun said.

'It can be done again. Or is Tachseer greater than you in all things?'

For an instant, the barb stung. Then Torghun reached for another meat-stick. 'Do not attempt to sway me that way, brother.'

Sanyasa shook his head, smiling ruefully. 'Others here feel the same,' he said. 'The Khagan would never have sanctioned it.'

'You will not have the chance to put it to the test.'

Sanyasa reached for his own rations.

'Perhaps not,' he said, ripping a strand of synth-meat from the block.

MORTARION WAITED A long time. The system was searched from end to end, and nothing was found but wreckage – some older ships, scuttled before the V Legion had made for the warp. Augur-sweepers were sent out further afield, travelling as far as their sub-warp engines would allow before being recalled.

They found nothing – the Khan was gone.

That was neither unexpected nor something to be regretted. The fates had remained silent on the prospects of an encounter, and the esoteric tarot in his possession had similarly given him nothing. It was enough, for the moment, to know that his quarry had been at Aerelion, perhaps only hours before his own arrival. The subsequent presence of Eidolon only made the prospect of an eventual resolution more certain.

And so he waited, first in his private cells, where he consulted the arcana and returned to the grimoires. Then he studied the tactical data streamed to him by his bridge crew, and noted every morsel of it. Then he returned to the transcript testimony of the captured legionary, Algu, looking for anything in it beyond Aerelion. He did not expect to find much, but the steps had to be taken, in order, as steadily and thoroughly as he did everything.

By the time Eidolon finally signalled his passage to the *Endurance,* all preparations had been completed. The Lord of Death watched the glittering III Legion Stormbird make the short journey between flagships, accompanied by a wing of gunships and tracked throughout by the *Proudheart's* gunnery teams.

Even now, so little trust, the primarch thought. *This may be our gift from Horus for eternity.*

He received Eidolon in the dusty Chamber of Records, set deep in the flagship's forward carcass. It was a sombre space, hung with burned battle-standards and the long lists of the fallen, carved into black stone and embellished with Barbarusian glyphs. Lamps burned softly in the alcoves – pale green, luminous as marsh gas. Webs of black mould crept across the pockmarked stone.

The Lord Commander Primus entered alone, followed only by two of the Deathshroud, both of whom took up positions on either side of the chamber's great obsidian doors.

Mortarion took a moment to gauge his opposite number. He had known of Eidolon and had witnessed him on many prior occasions. He had been elegant in the past, lean, with armour that had been gilded and master-crafted but had not strayed into gaudiness. Some of that old poise remained, but much else was gone. His throat bulged obscenely, accommodated by new armour that swelled and curved like water. His heavy cloak was burnished with veins of gold and silver, woven into impossibly complex patterns that reflected and caught the lantern-light like prisms.

When he reached the primarch, Eidolon bowed clumsily, his movements halting and awkward. Pain was evident in every gesture, drawn across flesh that had once been pristine.

'For a moment back there, lord commander, I thought you might attack us,' the primarch said, his dry voice crackling through the rebreather. 'You noticed the sigils late.'

Eidolon gave a shrug. 'My troops are enthusiastic. We blooded the Scars at Kalium – you heard about that? They are a beaten force, and we looked forward to doing it again.'

'My brother would have been with them.'

Eidolon sniffed. 'So he would.'

Mortarion allowed himself a brief flicker of amusement at that. If this creature truly thought he was the equal of the Warhawk, perhaps the mental acumen of the Emperor's Children had indeed been damaged beyond repair.

'Lord commander,' Mortarion said, gesturing ahead, 'walk with me.'

The two of them passed deeper into the chamber. Graven images looked down on them from the shadows above – passionless statues carved of dark granite, their faces blank. The two sets of boots sent dull echoes ringing through the aisles, all drear, all empty.

'I have not spoken with your master for a long time,' said Mortarion.

'Nor I.'

'If you knew where he was, what his purpose is, you would not tell me.'

'No, I believe I would.' Eidolon showed little interest in the sepulchral surroundings. 'I thought for a while he was waiting for the Lord of Iron's wrath to wane. As for now, who knows? He does not choose to make his intentions known, but we trust that he has the interests of the war at heart.'

'But he will be at Terra, by the end.'

'One way or another, I suppose we all will.'

'Not the Khan.' Mortarion paused before one of the greatest statues – a twisted, many-headed beast that reared up into the dark like an ogre of his home world's past. 'He must not be on the walls of the Palace when the siege is set.'

'Be at peace on that score,' said Eidolon, casually. 'Every major transit and conduit is blocked or watched. The Warmaster's host has the measure of Dorn's outer sentinels. All we are doing here is chasing him further out into the void, along with Guilliman and those two damned Angels.'

'That is not enough. When I return to the Warmaster's side, I will bring his head back with me.'

Eidolon looked at him slyly. 'For Horus, or for you?'

'Our purposes are aligned in this.' Mortarion started walking again. From beyond the chamber walls, the many noises of a warship filtered through the stone – hums, snarls, clangs. 'But here the trail goes cold, unless you have spoor that I do not.'

'You would know these things if you made use of that which has been given to you.'

'I am unwilling to pay the price.'

'Yet you will allow us to,' said Eidolon, 'to give you what you need.'

'You embrace these things like children running after sweetmeats. There is no hardship for you in this.'

Eidolon chuckled, nodding. 'How well you know us. Or most of us, anyway. Give me time, and it shall be done.' Then he lost his smile. 'But you cannot defer the gods forever, my lord. You may build walls and you may issue laws, but I heard the reports from Molech – you cannot put back what has been taken out.'

'That has always been your philosophy.'

'Not just ours. They will come to collect, sooner or later.'

Mortarion kept walking. He had heard the threats breathed in the night for too long to be troubled by the same warning from a mutilated legionary's lips. 'Let them come. I fear neither them nor the one who made me.'

They reached the end of the chamber. A granite altarpiece soared up before them, crowned with chain-hung lanterns. A great skull carved from ivory rested on the top of it, its eyes empty and gaping. Once an Imperial aquila had been suspended there too, but it had been cast down and now lay in thick, dusty pieces.

'I suppose we are not natural allies, you and I,' said Mortarion, looking up at the mingled icons. 'But I am no tyrant. I do not command your allegiance, and do not attempt to wrest it from you. When this is done I will hold you in honour. Only one thing do I demand – that it is I who lands the killing blow. In all else, you may do as you wish.'

Eidolon stared at him for a moment, his expression difficult to read. Perhaps there was even something like admiration there, but that would be hard to countenance. In any event, it didn't last long – the Lord Commander Primus bowed again, as haltingly as before, and when his sutured face rose it carried the habitual air of disinterested amusement.

'I have no appetite for taking skulls, my lord,' Eidolon said, sounding sincere enough. 'It brings back painful memories. So, believe me, when the final blow is struck, no matter what else is done, his head can be yours to claim.'

SIXTEEN

THE JOURNEY TO the Catullus Rift was not long – three warp-stages, maintained in spite of the heavy contrary buffeting that the universe always sent against them. Two ships were lost, one of them a veteran destroyer with three dozen warriors of the Legion on board, and many other Navigators were wounded or slain on the crossing, their fatigue or mental exhaustion finally getting the better of them. Through it all, the fleet limped on, amalgamating crews and drafting in the last of the reserves to keep the void craft battling along their tortuous course.

At the end of the final stage, the fleet vanguard emerged into real space and powered towards the coordinates revealed in Arvida's mind-scry. As the warp shutters came down and the real-viewers were opened up, every soul on every vessel felt the same instant unease. The void was not black, peppered with stars – it was a dull, throbbing blue, shifting like dye thrown into water. More of the Navigators, even those in the big battleship cadres, suffered. Some drooled and clutched at their warp-eye; others simply slumped into their nutrient baths, blood leaking from their ears.

The *Swordstorm* quickly assumed the spear-tip. The flagship powered its way ahead, carving a straight path through the seething matter. Despite its vast displacement and powerful plasma drives, it was still rocked on its axis, shaken as if by seismic charges.

The Khan sat enthroned on the command bridge, watching the journey unfold through the great forward viewports. Yesugei, Jubal, Shiban and Veil stood close by, together with the flagship's own master of Navigators, the crone Avelina Hjelvos. Ilya and Arvida had taken position a little further off, and on the edge of the throne dais others of the Legion command assumed their stations: khans, Stormseers, fleet strategos.

Hjelvos leaned heavily on her staff, curling long brown fingers around the length of rune-carved steel. Her breathing came fitfully from under a heavily embroidered cowl. 'The void is polluted, lord,' she whispered, adjusting the fit of her bandana.

Veil looked both fascinated and appalled. Though he might not have shared Hjelvos' acute warp-sense, he clearly recognised the broad shape of what lay ahead.

'Lham harmonics,' he muttered, peering through the viewers intensely. 'Radiating widely. This is from a warp rift.' He looked up at the primarch. 'I urge caution, my lord.'

The Khan remained impassive. 'Proceed at cruising speed,' he ordered. 'Keep the fleet in cohesion. All void shields to full coverage.'

The *Swordstorm* ploughed on, its massive prow slicing through the thickening clouds. Slivers of light flickered and danced within the plumes, like gas flames caught within crystal vials. Soon the real-viewers clouded over, clogged with inky tendrils and stained with a filmy blue smear.

'Release augur-probes,' ordered the Khan.

A brace of spinning steel orbs shot out from the *Swordstorm*'s prow, tumbling away into the murk beyond. Screeds of data began to pour through the pict-feeds – topographical surveys, channel-widths, echoes of more solid material far up ahead.

The deck began to judder. Warning runes glowed into life, one by one, across crystal viewscreens. The deep rhythm of the plasma drives picked up in volume, as if the engines were struggling against a strong headwind.

'Slow to half-speed.'

The change in velocity improved things for a while, but as they made further progress the vibrations returned. Electric flickers broke out within the clouds ahead, scampering across a churning voidscape.

'This will damage us,' warned Hjelvos, twitching at each sudden sway of the deck.

Yesugei took a step towards the dais railing, his golden eyes locked on the light show outside the hull. 'What are we seeing here?' he asked, intrigued.

By then Veil was almost as agitated as Hjelvos. 'Something has punctured the *impedimentum realitas*. Something profound, up ahead. This must be done with caution, lord. Your ships do not have their Geller fields raised.'

'Quarter-speed,' ordered the Khan, and once more

the onward procession slowed. Violent streaks of sharp white slathered across the vacuum. They were strangely suggestive, those flickers. For fractions of a second it seemed that they displayed images – faces, or reaching limbs, or some other mortal aspect – but never for long enough to truly resolve.

'Probes report solid matter ahead, bearing five-six-one,' reported Taban, the sensorium master. 'Adjust course?'

The Khan nodded. 'Adjust, then maintain. Signal all ships to follow our lead.'

Ilya looked over at Arvida. Like the Navigator, he was breathing heavily through his vox-grille. 'Are you well, my lord?' she asked.

Arvida made no reply, but gripped the iron railing hard. Above them, suspensor lumens began to sway.

'There will be a centre to this,' said Veil, addressing Hjelvos, Yesugei and the primarch as he spoke, unsure who best to direct his commentary to. 'A source. You cannot take these ships into it.'

The Khan barely seemed to register. His gaze was now focused on the swirling clouds ahead, as if in recognition of something. 'We will not turn back.'

The vibrations continued to ramp up. Muffled, rhythmic bangs rose up from the lower levels, and the engines began to stutter. Damage reports from the lesser ships started to register on the fleet ledgers. In the vacuum ahead, the cobalt glow built further, strobing uncomfortably, spilling through every open real-view portal and making the interior of the bridge shimmer.

'My lord,' said Hjelvos, wheezing now and clamping one hand to her right temple. 'I counsel you, listen to the ecumene. The warp drives–'

'Are dormant,' replied the Khan, as quietly and firmly as ever. 'We proceed.'

The bangs grew in volume. A hair-line crack snaked its way across the ceiling-brace above them, worming through pure adamantium, slowly but surely.

Hjelvos looked like she was considering another protest, but said nothing. The engine pitch became strangled, and the bridge decking drummed. A low, booming thunder began to build, sounding – impossibly – like it was coming from the exterior. Soon the clamour resolved into deep, repeated clangs, like an iron fist banging on a brass door.

Even Jubal shifted a little then, just moving his weight from one leg to the other, the warrior's preparation for sudden action. The mortal crew in the pits below stole furtive glances up at the command dais, hampered now by the strangely occluding light that crawled and slid across every surface, blurring the controls and the pict-feeds. The breaking of glass rang out from higher up in the bridge galleries.

'My lord–' Taban started.

'Maintain course.'

The Khan never moved. Klaxons started to blare and a sensorium platform lost its bearings, collapsing into the underpit below in a shower of electric light.

'My lord!'

'*Wait.*'

Just as he said it, just as the final consonant passed his lips, the flagship broke through. It surged forwards, no longer fighting the headwind, and its pent-up power hurled it clear into the empty void. One by one, the rest of the fleet did likewise, bursting from the clouds of glittering azure and leaving long trails behind them as they struggled to re-establish control. All across the *Swordstorm*'s bridge, menials rushed to stabilise the onward tilt. The deck-level slewed as the opposing pressures radically altered, and fresh warning chimes resounded.

Behind them, stretching off in all directions, the vast wall of shifting plasma churned. It curved away into the darkness of space, an immense concave barrier. They were on the inside of a sphere – a colossal sphere, its far extremities lost beyond visual range. The enclosed volume might have been the size of an entire star system; both the chronos and the augurs were spinning wildly, giving no firm reading.

'I have heard theories on this,' murmured Veil, looking at the phenomenon with wide eyes. 'A lham shock wave, supermassive, thinning real space.' He turned back to the Khan. 'This is an aftermath. Something has been released.'

The Khan ignored him. 'Full ahead. Keep shields raised.'

The fleet picked up speed, clustering together, plasma drives glowing in the gathering dark. The walls of lightning-infused cloud slowly fell away behind them, and a starless abyss gaped ahead.

'I can sense it,' muttered Hjelvos, still agitated. She shuffled closer to the real-viewers, peering with her cloudy eyes. 'I feel it like heat from a flame.'

After what felt like hours, but might have been any length of time, a singular point of pale light appeared on the forward scopes. The point grew rapidly, swelling and spreading, until a second cloud-sphere appeared before them, wreathed in veins of lightning and illuminated from within by sporadic bursts.

'Seven hundred kilometres diameter,' reported Taban. 'Heavy radiation levels over physical and sub-physical ranges. Aetheric readings are close to that of a warp rift.'

'Full stop,' ordered the Khan. 'Send in another probe.'

The fleet powered down to a halt, strung out in a wide arc before the lightning-flecked orb. More augur-probes shot out into the void, their marker-lights fading rapidly as they disappeared into the distance. Images returned via pict feed were shaken and fractured by the electrical storms. Underneath the clouds, the surface of the sphere seemed to be composed of massive crystals, rolling and bumping into one another in a grinding orbital procession. There were gaps between the crystalline edges, giving tantalising glimpses of something darker and less sharply defined beyond. An eerie blue light bathed everything, swimming like myriad spores across the stately movement of the crystals.

'What are those?' asked the Khan, speaking to the two Nobilite representatives.

'I have never seen the like,' said Hjelvos.

'A consequence of competing energies,' said Veil, speculatively. 'Real space, stratum aetheris. A rift has been opened. You cannot penetrate that barrier – the active immaterium would rip your warp drives apart.'

For the first time, the Khan turned to look at him. 'What were your people doing here?'

Veil shrank back, clutching at his ruined, bound hand. 'I know not,' he stammered. 'Truly. I only interpret the signs.'

The Khan looked back up at the unfolding images from the probes. The gaps between the crystals were wide, several hundred metres at their furthest extents.

One by one, the augur feeds failed, just as the probes crossed the threshold. The last of them emitted a jumpy final feed showing a spectral image from beyond the barrier – a thin, dark outline, hazy from the blue sheen, extending down and down. Then nothing.

'The danger is to the warp drives,' the Khan said. 'What of standard propulsion?'

Veil looked uncertain. 'I do not know. There is the lightning, as you see, but–'

The Khan rose from his throne. Even as he moved, attendants made haste with his wargear – the dragon-helm, kin to the lesser helm Qin Xa had worn on Kalium, as well as the heavy tulwar blade the primarch had borne on Prospero. 'This is what we came to discover. I will see it with my own eyes. Yesugei, sorcerer, you will come, as will you, ecumene.'

He buckled his blade to his belt, and took the helm in both hands. 'Jubal Ahn-ezen, you have the fleet. Ready it for war – we will not remain hidden for long, even here.' He turned to Ilya. 'You will be needed here too, szu. If we find him, I will contact you first.'

Ilya nodded. She looked deeply wary of the visions playing out across the real-viewers.

Then the Khan lifted the dragon-helm over his head. Once in place, his armour was complete – pearl-white, lined with gold and decorated with the icons of the Qo Empire of Chogoris.

'Prepare the Stormbirds,' he commanded. 'We are going in.'

VON KALDA EXTRACTED his hands from the entrails, shaking the gore from them before reaching for a cloth. The pressure in the chamber was stultifying.

The menials around him made no sound. They were blind, these ones, and thus spared the sight of scattered body parts, the lumps of glistening fat, the stark protrusions of bone amid the slurry.

They were fortunate. Even for him, even after coming so far, there was a grimness to this work.

'*Halev erub mac'jerella,*' he intoned, marking the floor with blood. The last of the runes was completed, the characters from a language spoken by no living mortal, preserved only in dreams. This was not knowledge from Fabius, nor from the primarch – these were things he had discovered himself, melding the arts of the fleshweaver and the arts of the aether-diviner.

It made his head throb and his nightmares vivid, but the prize never disappeared. And now he had his orders – Eidolon had sanctioned it, and would be waiting.

He looked up. The iron chamber was swimming with red blotches now, hanging in the air like puffs of smoke. Every soul that had died in exquisite agony had thinned the curtain a little more, pulling apart the matter of the universe, strand by strand.

He hardly dared to peer behind the armourglass. Its surface was smoky, smeared with the desperate handprints of those he had eviscerated. A sooty substance curled and shifted within, shrouding everything on the far side.

Von Kalda shuffled forwards, his boots crunching through the bones on the floor. As he neared the container, he intoned again.

'*Malamennagorastica. Hovija. Khzah'tel arif negassamar.*'

They were nonsense words, far too long and cumbersome for human purposes. Only the deep places could have spawned such a tongue, crafted by the infinite for its own indulgent purposes.

He reached the glass and spread his palms out across its curved surface.

'*Gegammoror. Gegammororara. Shashak. Lethatak.*'

The eyes swam to the surface, startling him. He pulled back, but did not look away. Two violet orbs, almond-lidded, whiteless, swimming with pearlescent sub-colour.

So you found the path, it told him.

The voice was astonishing – a nightmare-whisper wrenched into waking but given no form of its own. Many voices were overlapped there, jostling with one another as if buried alive within some master rattle-bag of intelligence.

Amid the smoke and filth, limbs emerged, cleaner than they had been before. The flesh was pale and vivid, unblemished with wounds. A long barbed whip flicked back and forth around lissom thighs. In the background, the claws still snapped, clicking rapidly, a language all of their own.

'Not yet,' said Von Kalda. 'Just the beginnings. What do I call you?'

Master. Mistress. Or Manushya-Rakshsasi. This is what I was called in the Age before Anathema.

Von Kalda resisted the urge to look deeper into the murk. The violet eyes were unblinking, unsettling. It was almost overwhelmingly tempting to gaze into them, to prize out the hidden movements in their opaque innards.

'I would ask you a question.'

Ask, then.

'My master seeks the Great Khan. To track him

through the warp will take time, and every day wasted here delays us. Is his location known to you?'

These things are known to me. What do you offer in return?

'What do you wish for?'

The daemon seemed to smile, and a long tongue flickered across a wide, needle-toothed mouth. *You have read your spells and you have learned your rites. You know the ways of the dream. Give me something I desire.*

Von Kalda tore his eyes away from the shifting movement of the pale skin. It was harder, far harder, than he had thought. The musky aroma of old blood was mingled now with something else – a perfume of intoxication that slunk and crept around the entire chamber.

'Is it not enough to aid the Warmaster in his victory?' he ventured.

The daemon laughed then, genuinely amused. The laugh, though, was horrifying – a high-pitched shriek of pure malice, leavened by no joy, stitched together by mortal screaming.

Victory is for mortal minds. There is no victory for us. What is our goal? We have no goals. What is our peace? We have no peace. You already give us what we wish for, and we drink it in and thirst for more. Now all that remains is amusement. The eyes flashed greedily. *So amuse me.*

'You will feast on the souls of the Khan's sons,' Von Kalda tried. 'They are weary and hunted, and our forces outnumber them. I will feed them to you, one by one.'

Try again.

Von Kalda instantly thought back to the conversation with Konenos, and the object became clear. There were mutually reinforcing goals here, ways of accelerating that which had already been started. Other Legions had done it. Lorgar's had been the first, as in so much else, but the predecents had been set elsewhere too.

'There are other souls,' he said, cautiously. 'One in particular – one who would find union with the aether... hateful.'

Good. That game appeals more.

'It will take time. He is wary, and capable.'

All the better.

'Then you will give me what I want?'

The whip snapped across the floor of the containment tube. In the chamber, blood-runes began to boil. *A bargain made will hold you. These things, words, contracts, wishes in the dark – they reach out across the worlds.*

Von Kalda withdrew from the edge of the glass. His hearts were pumping.

'I know it. I do not deceive you. Payment will be made.'

The daemon smiled again, this time with some disdain, as if those words had been uttered in its presence too many times to count. As the blood-runes fizzed away, its warp-spawned outline faded again, melting into the plumes of smoke.

Then we shall speak again, you and I.

'And the destination?' Von Kalda asked. 'Just a word – that is all.'

The daemon was almost gone, and fading fast. With its passing, a hot and humid wind shuffled through the chamber, rippling the puddles of human waste that swam ankle-deep.

Catullus, it told him. *The Warhawk stands there, halted before the Road to Hell.*

Then the image ripped away, leaving only scraps of curling darkness. The containment column fell silent, marked only by a patch of condensation where the daemon had pressed against the armourglass.

Von Kalda stood motionless for a long time. For all his training, it was still a difficult thing to be in the presence of one of them. There would be others, too – the Soul-Severed demanded it, always pressuring, forcing the work to go faster, to take more risks.

But that was yet to come. The first question, at least, had been answered.

His breathing returned to normal. His secondary heart ceased beating. He shook himself down, turned and crunched his way back through the bones and the sinews.

'My lord,' he said over the secure vox, opening the link to Konenos. 'I have progress to report. Acknowledge, please, then indicate where we may meet. There are things we need to discuss.'

THEY TOOK FIVE of the heavy gunships, escorted up to the perimeter by two wings of void fighters. The Khan travelled in the lead vessel, accompanied by those of the keshig not taken by Jubal for the fleet-ordering. Namahi, the cadre's second-in-command, led the detachment. Three other gunships carried squads of White Scars legionaries equipped with breacher gear.

The fifth contained Yesugei and Arvida, alongside Veil in the rear chamber, and the last of the Tactical

Space Marine complement – more than two hundred warriors in total. The journey was not long, but it was violent, rocked by the elemental forces unleashed within the sphere's heart.

Yesugei remained close to one of the viewports in the crew bay, watching the lurid edifice lurch closer. Azure light skipped and slid through the armourglass portal, playing across the surfaces inside the darkened interior.

Next to him was Arvida. The sorcerer's breathing was coarse.

'If I ask you if all is well, my brother,' Yesugei said quietly, 'I believe I know what you will tell me.'

Arvida did not reply. He seemed to be rocking very fractionally, as if steeling himself.

'You will tell me yes, all is well,' Yesugei went on. 'You are weary, that is all. And who of us is not weary?'

Yesugei looked back out at the void. The great sphere now filled most of the view forward, and the edges of its constituent crystals were becoming visible. They were massive elongated octahedrons, regular in form and size, their facets perfectly angled and regular, as if cut by a las-beam. The spectral glow that coiled inside them was like the aether itself, ever-changing, writhing within a glassy prison.

'Perhaps is easier if I tell you what I know,' Yesugei went on, his voice soft enough to keep the conversation between the two of them. 'You are not a fool, but neither am I. You learn to put control on it, but you cannot keep it fully hidden. Your gene-father could not, so what hope you have? There is no shame. You have done well to keep it secret, so dormant, but is running away from you now.'

Still Arvida did not respond. The rocking grew more intense.

'It is the warp, yes?' asked Yesugei. 'It is worse, when you use your art. I encouraged you. If I caused you greater pain, then–'

'You are not the cause.' The sorcerer's voice was hesitant. Somewhere behind his helm, his features must have been stiff with suppressed agony.

Yesugei placed his hand on Arvida's forearm. 'What can I do?'

'Nothing.'

Neither spoke for a while. The Stormbird flight neared the sphere's perimeter, the craft buffeted as the first forks of lightning shot around and under them.

'Is it obvious?' asked Arvida at length.

'I do not think so. You have been careful.'

Arvida nodded stiffly. 'It will be worse. In there.'

'I know. You could have refused to go.'

'No, I wish to see it. These are the places where the warp was studied. Who knows?' Arvida sighed – a grating sound like filtering stones through a sieve. 'Chasing down diminishing hopes, grasping at the last of them as they gutter out. There are days when I think your Shiban is right. Force the battle. Get it over with.'

At the mention of Shiban, Yesugei felt a brief twinge of pain. 'If moment comes,' he said. 'If you cannot control it…'

'I remain the master.'

'Very well. Then I trust you.'

They neared the first of the apertures between crystals. The lead Stormbird angled away, pulling down across the face of the sphere. Crystal facets the size of destroyers swam beneath it, bathed in pale light, turning slowly. What lay beyond was still invisible, lost in the haze of shimmering aether-residue.

'We are all damaged now,' said Arvida, watching the approach. 'All but you.'

Yesugei sat back against the curve of the hull. 'No living thing is undamaged.'

'Yet you still smile. You still believe.'

'So do the rest. They need to remember, that is all. For now, all they see is slow defeat. They forget they have been... magnificent. They fight alone when all others are lost or manning walls far away. They come at enemy out of the glare of the sun. They have made him halt, turn back, come after us. They have forsaken the world they loved, have let it pass into ruin, all for this.' Yesugei thought of Qin Xa then, from whom there had never been a murmur of unbelief. 'They will remember, before the end. Other Legions have failed this test – they let their souls change.'

'Other Legions.'

'Forgive me, brother, I did not–'

'No, you are right,' said Arvida. 'My kind might have learned from the path you teach.'

'Ahriman and I discussed it, long ago,' said Yesugei. 'On Ullanor, and before. We were never of the same mind.'

You are too cautious, the Thousand Sons Chief Librarian had said. *Does anyone even know the gifts you have?*

'To teach the Path of Heaven,' said Arvida, dryly. 'To walk between worlds, never leaving a trace in either. To kick the fire over, never to build, never to delve. You practise your art like you practise your war.'

Their Stormbird was following the first one in now, travelling in its wake on half-thrust, negotiating the great arcs of power that lashed and slapped around them. The atmosphere in the crew bay seemed hotter, or closer, or charged with some kind of energy. The refracted blue light was all-encompassing, overpowering the onboard lumens and making everything blur with soft cobalt shadows.

'You were always greater than us,' remarked Yesugei. 'Even now your power greater than mine. Cure this… sickness, and yours might be the greatest power I ever know.' He smiled. 'There is weakness in limitation, as well as wisdom.'

Arvida did not respond to that. The threshold surged towards them, crackling and violent. A crystal lazily rolled above them, forming a moving lintel to their entry point. The Stormbird dropped in response, fighting to maintain alignment with the gaps ahead.

Aether-lightning surged, whipping and writhing, nearly punching clean through the Stormbird's thruster-housing. The pilot applied more power, and the gunship lurched under the shadow of the rotating facets, across the shimmering threshold, into the vortex beyond. For a moment, the viewports went blank, blazing with a cold, diffuse light.

Then they were through. The Stormbird swung about, holding position above the others that had already emerged.

Ahead of them lay the heart of the inner sphere, itself the size of a world. Its interior was dark like the true void, barely lit by the shell of lightning-crystals that orbited it. From below the gunships' position, at the nadir of the galactic plane, boiled a furnace of many colours – a whirlpool into the vacuum, kaleidoscopic and hard to look at. Both Yesugei and Arvida knew what those false colours signified – a rupture in the matter of the universe, leaking the stuff of the immaterium.

Neither of them, though, was looking at the rupture. They were looking at what was above it: vast, slender, as black as burned iron, underlit with faint points of red, bearing no marker, standing guard over the mouth of the abyss.

'Then there it is,' said Arvida quietly.

'Yes, brother,' said Yesugei, with equal wariness. 'Dark Glass.'

SEVENTEEN

ILYA COULDN'T SHAKE the headaches. Ever since they had entered the Catullus Rift, the pain had been excruciating, burrowing under her skull like gnawing worms, making her vision shaky. After the Khan had decided to investigate the crystal sphere, she had retreated to her quarters, grabbing meds from a cabinet and downing them. They kicked in swiftly, allowing her to function, but the dull pain refused to shift, lurking like some malign presence at the back of her mind.

For a long time she remained seated on the edge of her bunk, holding her head in both hands, fighting down the urge to vomit. Now she had seen the place, the absurdity of the quest she had instigated truly hit her.

For so long she had been desperate to find an escape, *any* escape, for a Legion she had drifted into feeling were her true kin – those she had been ordained to come amongst to guide away from their more destructive instincts. The hubris of it was laughable; any one of the White Scars was more than a match for her, physically and mentally. They had lulled her into her role, calling her the Sage, deferring to her, bowing as she walked past them. Had it all been some kind of obscure joke?

Probably not. All the same, the courtesy felt hollow now.

Achelieux was not there. They would surely have contacted her if they had found him, but just laying eyes upon the crystals, sitting at the heart of what had been some kind of enormous warp detonation, had already told her all she needed to know.

It had been futile. She had allowed herself to be seduced by a ludicrous hope, a whisper among whispers. Even if he had lived, there was no guarantee Pieter could have helped. He was a Novator, a Lord of Navigators, but not a god, and in such times surely only gods held the power to bend the warp to their will. Slowly, inexorably, all avenues were closing off, cutting them down, boxing them in. There was nothing her adopted Legion hated more than confinement, but there was now nothing else left for them.

For the last hour she had ignored the signals on her console summoning her back to the bridge. Eventually, though, the sheer number became too much. She reached for more meds, swallowed them painfully, then got back up, pulling her uniform jacket on and adjusting the flabby fit.

Jubal had taken command of the *Swordstorm* in the Khan's absence. The other Legion commanders had either left for their vessels or were preparing to do so.

The fleet had moved back from the outer rim of the sphere and taken up position closer to the great walls of turbulence beyond, morphing as they did so into a standard defensive formation. No doubt that was why they wished to speak to her – to check the ledgers off against her memory, to ensure that all had been done to her satisfaction, to make her feel useful.

Her place, then, was on the bridge, but it was not to the bridge that she headed. One item of organisation, in itself a small one, seemed to have slipped the mind of them all, perhaps even the Khan himself.

But not her. Never her. That was why they employed her, after all – to attend to the small things, the little snags at the edges of the great tactical dance.

It took her a long time to find him. In the end, she had to go down to the hangars where the inter-fleet shuttles set off to ply the void between the warships. They were places of furious activity now, with gun-crews and medicae details, and darga and khans, and fleet officers all racing to be where they needed to be before the riptide of battle subsumed them once again.

She located him waiting in the last great void-berth, his transport from the *Kaljian* coming in late, his retinue standing about him.

'My lord Tachseer,' Ilya said, hailing him from afar.

Shiban turned to see her approach. He was in his full armour, as ever, his expression hidden behind the dark metal mask. With a gesture, he indicated for his entourage to move away, and he came to meet her, bowing as they neared one another.

'Szu,' he said. 'Are you well?'

'I studied the logs,' she said, ignoring the hum of

pain in her head and neck. 'Did you think I would not notice? You had no authority for that.'

'I had every authority. They are renegades. They will be safer where they are.'

'We are undermanned. Every ship is short on crew. That is why they were brought back.'

'No time remains to integrate them, general. We cannot just take them back, not without screening. You are our one for procedures.'

'They have been fighting, on their own, for four years. Most died. If they were still traitors, do you not think they would have made their choice by now?'

'And how would we know?'

'You *know*, Shiban Khan.' The ache in her spine grew stronger. 'This is not about security.'

Shiban's blank helm-face remained impassive, unknowable. He didn't respond immediately, clearly choosing his words. 'They would have killed you, if they had achieved what they desired,' he said eventually. 'They would have killed us all.'

Ilya shook her head. 'That is why we had the trials. There is no spoiled blood in this Legion – they atone, they fight again.'

'They can still fight.'

'You penned them together, gave them a ship with no guns. What are they supposed to do? Shout loudly?'

'Szu, you are not well. I can see it. You should rest.'

'Damn you!' she cried, wanting to thump her fist against his ugly, stubborn armour-casing. 'This is an *old battle*. We have enough new ones.'

She suddenly felt faint then, and tilted forwards. Shiban caught her, holding her by both forearms. For an instant, it felt like the last time he had sustained her, racing across the warzone of the *Swordstorm's* bridge, taking the bolt-rounds that would have ended her. She wanted to push away, to forget that memory, but had enough trouble retaining consciousness.

'It is this place,' Shiban told her gently, keeping her on her feet. 'The warp. Others will suffer soon. The longer we stay, the worse it will get.'

'Then it was a mistake to come here,' she muttered.

'It was done. We will endure.'

She looked up at him, locked in an awkward embrace.

For a while after his recovery, they had spoken often. His deterioration had been slow, a product of the endless, mindless slaughter, so slow that she had never really noticed it.

'What keeps you fighting, Shiban?' she asked.

He started. 'My oaths.'

'No,' she said, sadly. 'That is not enough. Not any more.'

Her dizziness cleared. She pushed herself away from him. He made no move to prevent her, but shuffled stiffly away. They stood facing one another.

Out in the centre of the hangar, beyond the inner blast walls, a shuttle came down at last, doors opening, crew hurrying to meet it. A faint click inside Shiban's helm told Ilya that his summons had come. He would go back to the *Kaljian* now, to whatever duty he had taken on himself.

'Fight well then, Shiban Khan,' she said. 'I fear that is all that remains for you.'

Then she turned away and went back the way she had come, not waiting to hear if there was a reply.

✠ ✠ ✠

THE STORMBIRDS TRAVELLED under the lip of the station's upper sections, tiny beads of ivory against an unremitting mountain of beaten iron. Hails were issued, and met with nothing but the empty hiss of closed comm-channels. Eventually, hangar doors were located – twenty of them, set in a long line under the overhanging bulge of the main structure, all barred.

The gunships held position, allowing the Tech-marines on board to cycle through access codes. It gave time to take in the scale of the void station before them.

It was entirely black, the colour of deep-lode coal and ridged across all its surfaces. Every angle was a mass of over-thick plating, riveted and cross-braced. A great oval structure dominated its apex, ten kilometres in diameter at its widest point, as swollen and curvaceous as a jellyfish's body. No viewports were visible, just blank screens of blast-resistant metal, plate after plate of it. Occasionally, slivers of pale blue energy slithered across the empty surfaces, before dissipating into nothing again.

Under the heavy topmost edifice, the structure narrowed rapidly into a forest of angled shafts, each one studded with sensor fronds and augur-pods. A thick central column descended from the very centre of the station's underside, dropping towards the roiling mass of the warp rift more than a hundred kilometres distant. That spike of metal shot all the way into the heart of the slowly rotating tempest, silhouetted against it like a spear raised against sunset.

Perhaps the column anchored the station in place, or perhaps it was some elaborate probe – it was impossible to say from the outside. What was certain was that the open wound into the warp was still leaking huge amounts of raw aether-matter into real space. All the psykers on the Stormbirds, Yesugei included, felt it – a pressure at their foreheads, a heating of their blood.

The exterior of the station gave little clue as to its origin or purpose. There were no sigils displayed on the plates of black iron, not even the mark of the Navis Nobilite or the aquila of the Imperium. The place was silent, and it was dormant, save for a line of blood-red marker lights that still blinked *on, off, on, off* all the way down the impossibly long central shaft.

After failing to retrieve an answer to their hails or access codes from the station's central cogitator, the Khan issued the order to break a docking bay door open. Interceptors from the escort wing flew in close, balancing against the eddies and shifts emanating from the rift and launched a flurry of clamp-mines against the largest of the blast doors. The explosions rippled out silently, cracking the heavy plating, but not breaking it. A second run was needed, then a third, to breach the outer skin. The final explosions were cripplingly violent, as if suddenly augmented by secondary detonations from within, sending slivers of hull-plate shooting out at the waiting Stormbird wing.

With the way opened, two lead gunships thrust into docking range, scanning all the while, heavy bolters trained on the exposed interior. The hangar space inside was unlit, pitch-black, nearly empty save for a long void vessel secured by iron docking claws. Its design was much as the station around it was – heavy-plate, no obvious viewports, ridged and vaned, and prickly with sensor-spikes. On its flanks was the first sigil they had seen – a pictogram of a man dressed in gold, seated on a throne, holding one hand up and one hand down.

'House Achelieux,' noted Veil eagerly, watching on the pict feed.

The Hierophant.

'Then he was here, at least,' said Yesugei.

'Maybe. The House had many ships.'

The scan completed, showing neither life signs nor energy-signatures, and the Khan gave the order to advance within. The escort interceptors peeled off into holding positions, and two lead Stormbirds passed under the shadow of the jagged hangar entrance. Each touched down on the apron beyond and despatched their warrior complements, engines whining, ready to pull up at a moment's notice and unleash their full ordnance.

The White Scars breacher squads, led by Namahi, fanned out across the rockcrete, keeping low. The entrances were secured, fire-points set up, augur-relays deployed. The squads of warriors bearing storm shields and thunder hammers smashed their way into the chambers beyond the hangar's far walls, establishing fire-lanes down tributary corridors. All was done swiftly, efficiently, with no response.

'Hangar secured,' came Namahi's voice from within the station. 'No life signs detected.'

Yesugei's heart sank when he heard that. Ilya would be dismayed.

'Bring us in, then,' ordered the Khan, and the final three Stormbirds pushed off, drifting under the enormous curve of the station's upper structure.

They touched down onto the deck, each gunship settling far from the others. The empty space was colossal, as it was in all major Imperial facilities, dominated by ranks of black-sheened columns that swept up into a vaulted roof. The scale and armament looked to be roughly in the same class as a Ramilies star fort, but the configuration was like nothing Yesugei had ever seen.

By the time Yesugei and Arvida had disembarked, the Khan was already stalking across the apron towards them, his keshig entourage in tow. The hangar was silent and depressurised, although teams of Techmarines were already working away with arc welders and turbo hammers, trying to establish what was working and what was not.

'We have gravity,' remarked the Khan. 'That is something.'

Veil was the most incongruous of them all there, dressed in a bulky void-suit. He struggled to keep up with the others, who strode out confidently in power armour while he limped and lurched behind them. 'No power,' he muttered. 'Where are the lights?'

Arvida looked over towards the docked starship, suspended above them in the hangar's vaults. It looked to have a set of glassy spheres hung under its rear structure, rather than conventional plasma thrusters. 'A strange ship,' he said.

'This is all strange,' said Yesugei, looking around him at the oppressive architecture.

The darkness lay heavily on everything. Aside from the helm lumens of the White Scars, sweeping across the hangar in twin pools of stark white, nothing else was illuminated. A faint glow of dark blue slunk across the metal decking from the open void doors behind them, but the shadows ahead were those of perfect dark, the kind of pure oblivion only found in the deep void.

'You sense anything?' the Khan asked, speaking to his counsellor.

'I feel the warp beneath us,' said Yesugei, speaking carefully. There was not much else – a dull after-echo of old human activity, left like a fingerprint trace on every surface. The rupture was a long way away, though its corrosion was palpable, like the heat of a toxic, bleeding star. 'Nothing else.'

The primarch nodded. 'Perhaps it is dead. If so, we will not stay long.' He gestured for Namahi. 'Keep this level secure. Make contact immediately if you pick up anything.' Then he turned to the rest of them. 'There will be a command level. Ecumene?'

'Up,' said Veil, unconvincingly. 'It must be up.'

'Then we go up,' said the Khan, placing his gauntlet on his tulwar's hilt and waiting for Veil to move. 'This is your place. After you.'

CARIO STRUCK, SHOVING the blade point-first into the reeling White Scars legionary. He spun away before the corpse fell, crashing into the next one and swiping the head free of its ivory shoulders.

His brothers came on beside him, surging in a wave of steel and sapphire, pressing down the cramped corridor and driving the defenders back. They had made rapid progress, but still every intersection was contested. The Scars did not know when they were beaten.

A boom rang out from further up, shaking the decks. Frag grenades spun out of the smoke ahead, rattling down to zero as they tumbled.

Cario dived forwards, skidding under their flight,

then picked himself up and kept sprinting. The charges blew up behind him, sending shock waves shuddering down the confined space, but he remained ahead. The intersection neared, and he burst through, firing his bolt pistol with one hand while his sabre danced. Two more legionaries barred his passage, each one wielding a curved blade of his own. Steel clashed, sending blazes of light out between them, exposing in freeze-frame the insignias, the rank-markers, the bone-white helm-masks.

Then he was slashing, turning, cutting them down even as they reached out for him. He kicked out, sending one staggering, then pivoted and smashed a helm-clad face with a bolt-round at point-blank range. He went back for the first one, jabbing his blade down between helm and gorget – the cleanest kill, right through the spine.

More charges went off far behind him. Cario felt the massed tramp of armoured boots. He heard foul tongues raised in anger and delight – the enemy, whooping like animals, racing towards their oblivion with feral savagery.

'He is close,' Cario voxed to his surviving brothers, and they pressed on. Corridors sped by in a blur, all fought for, the duels processing in a bloody, hasty, chaotic sequence. His breath hammered in his helm, hot and wet. 'Faster.'

It was then that he felt the first stirrings, coming earlier than ever before. It writhed in his mind, the pink-fleshed thing, the horned presence, with the almond-shaped eyes, the black tongue.

My lord, it said to him.

He carried on, ignoring it. The next chamber beckoned,

clogged with smoke, striated with crazily-angled las-beams. He smashed into it, vaulting past the falling cadaver of another victim. Two more died to his whirling blade, both before they had even seen him. His brothers piled in after him, shooting from low grips, ripping the smog apart with bolt-trails.

My lord.

Then he saw the one, *him*, charging towards him, shrieking in that mechanical, damaged vox-burst, his gunmetal armour dully reflecting the carnage unfolding about them.

Cario felt a lurch of pleasure and readied his blade. He cast aside the pistol and held the sabre two-handed. It was only the two of them then, and the others mattered not. It was–

'My lord.'

Abruptly, the illusion shattered. The mind-impulse link severed, sending spears of pain into his eyes, and the inloaded cranial pattern de-shunted with a hard bang.

Cario cried aloud, scrabbling to reach for his sense-mask. He ripped it free and pulled himself up from his bench, furious.

There was nothing to hit. A hololith flickered before him, full-sized, displaying the translucent shade of Azael Konenos. The isolation chamber was otherwise empty – a lead-lined room deep within the *Suzerain*, brightly lit, stacked with Mechanicum mind-input devices.

Cario was still breathing heavily, flushed with combat mania. Blood ran down from his temples where the mask-edges had been torn away from the skin.

'I apologise for the intrusion,' the hololith said. *'How goes your practice?'*

Cario swung his legs over the edge of the bunk,

pulling electrodes from his forearms as he did so. 'How did you get into here?' he asked, rolling his shoulders to ease the ache. If he had had his sword to hand, he might have hurled it through the luminous green spectre, just in case.

'As I say, I apologise. We are in the warp, or I would have come in person.'

The entire fleet had been in the aether for hours. Such an unwieldy joint armada had taken time to stitch together, for the Navigators had to combine forces, the astropath choirs had to align, the battleship's protocol officers had to decide on the order of precedence. All of this had been of no interest to Cario – it mattered not whether they sailed with the Death Guard or any other Legion so long as they got there.

'And it could not wait?' grunted Cario, wiping the blood free.

'When we reach Catullus, the Lord Commander Primus and the primarch of the Death Guard have determined we will attack immediately. Hence, I contact you before we break the veil. The Suzerain is important to us.'

'Oh yes?' Cario cared nothing for that. He had already given the ident Kaljian to the sensorium crew, and issued his fraternity with their standing orders. His malice and energy were intact. Everything else was secondary.

'We are gathering allies,' said Konenos. 'We wish the power at our disposal to be overwhelming.'

'Allies?'

'I am sending you coordinates. You are to be at the spearhead, my lord. I hope that is a pleasing prospect.'

Cario fixed the hololith with a dead-eyed stare. 'You disturb me for this?'

'*I wanted to be sure you had them. I wanted to be sure you realised the import of them. Everything will be balanced. You will be advancing in tandem with the* Proudheart, *part of the Soul-Severed's first assault. Equerry Von Kalda will be at your flank.*'

At mention of the word *Proudheart*, the horned beast flashed across Cario's thoughts once more – a spasm, an after-flicker from the cranial simulation.

'Fine,' he said. 'Fine, whatever he commands. Send over the schematics.'

Konenos bowed, Chemos-fashion, palms crossed. '*I will do so. Once more, forgive the interruption. Train well, my lord. Perhaps we will fight together when the storm breaks. I would welcome that.*'

Then the hololith snapped out, leaving the chamber empty and silent. Cario blinked heavily, still adjusting.

Konenos was a narcotic-addled dullard, a walking advertisement for the benefits of avoiding entanglement with Fulgrim's perversions. The equerry was even worse, a sadist and a flesh-butcher. Only his brothers, the pure ones of the Palatine Blades, were a pleasure to fight alongside, and their number dwindled with every engagement.

Cario reached for the sense-mask and clamped it into place. He lay back, blinking to activate the impulse-unit. Almost immediately the visions rushed back into place, embedding him within a world of imagined combat, honing him, preparing him.

The real thing would come soon enough.

'Again,' he ordered.

EIGHTEEN

DARK GLASS' COMMAND station was a circular arena,
a hundred metres wide, ringed by concentric terraces
facing a single central branched column. Above the
column rose a huge dome, as black as everything else,
bisected by thick struts of iron. Hundreds of cogitator
stations, their screens blank, gazed across the empty
space. No dust gathered. Every surface was as clean
as when it had left the forge. The metal mesh floors
were pristine.

'Was this place ever used?' asked Arvida.

Yesugei nodded. 'There were many souls here, for
a long time.'

The two of them stood near the entrance to the command station, where a heavy blast door had earlier
been forced open. The Khan had moved off towards
an iron throne placed under the column's shadow, too
small for him to occupy but clearly the seat of command. Veil followed, hanging a few paces behind like

a kicked dog. The desertion of the station had knocked some of the arrogance out of him, and he looked around nervously, still cradling his wounded hand.

White Scars legionaries were stationed at every entrance, bolters drawn. Dozens more moved through the decks below, scanning for life, for records, for anything. Techmarines had discovered control chambers for the main reactors, all of which were now shot and unable to function. Back-up generators had been located further down, which had given them use of at least some flickery, unreliable lumens. Their light – sour yellow and weak – did little except expose how mournful Dark Glass was.

Arvida and Yesugei moved to catch up with the Khan and the ecumene. The pall of gloom was hard to shake off. There was nothing here.

'No power to these units,' Veil was complaining, rummaging through the cogitator valves with his good hand. 'No good. Without power, we cannot tell what he was doing.'

'If he ever came here,' said the Khan, idly lifting a lens, angling it towards the nearest lumen.

'He was here. He built this place.'

The Khan looked back at him. 'This is the work of generations.' He put the lens down. 'How was it kept secret? Who knew of it?'

'I do not know.' Veil's ignorance, as ever, sounded perfectly genuine. 'They were only rumours, things he let slip. He was close.'

'Yes, so you say. The crew here must have run into the hundreds.'

Veil shrugged. 'I know not.'

The Khan sighed and drifted aimlessly through the

rings of cogitator stations. 'There is nothing for us here, Yesugei.'

'We do not know that yet,' Yesugei replied, evenly.

'Whatever it was built for, it does nothing now.'

Yesugei looked up at the empty dome, then around at the poorly lit ranks of empty thrones. 'Or maybe just sleeping.'

Arvida, who had been exploring further up, slipped. As he fell, the echo rang around the vaults, resounding oddly, lasting longer than it should have done. Yesugei looked up at him, concerned that someone might have noticed the momentary weakness, but the sorcerer had already righted himself, and the rest of the search party were detained with their own work.

'I would explore further,' said the primarch. 'Yet to stay is not without peril. You can feel it, yes?'

Yesugei could feel it deeply. It was like an ache in his bones, a twitch in his jaw, a mote in his eye. Every gesture was clumsy, every thought sluggish. The entire station was bathed in the aftershock of what had been unleashed, and underneath that, the rupture below them was a constant, if invisible, churning presence.

'This was a control centre,' said Veil. 'There are decks below us, a hundred of them. We cannot leave, not yet.'

'You will leave when we do,' said the Khan absently, never looking away from Yesugei. 'Namahi tells me he found an armoury. It is empty. He tells me there are blast-marks on the corridors three levels down.'

'Bodies?' asked Yesugei.

'None found. He is investigating.'

'Something must have happened to the crew.'

'They were trained,' said Veil. 'They were Nobilite-screened.'

The Khan snorted a laugh. 'If we have learned one thing,' he said, 'it is how weak our safeguards were.'

From far below, a long, drawn-out creak echoed towards them, like metal stretching. It was followed by a faint series of knocks, fading away into nothing.

'Atmospheric pressure,' remarked Yesugei. 'The Tech-marines have done their work.'

The Khan wasn't listening. He pressed his hand against the central column, holding his gauntlet tight to the iron, as if by linking himself to the structure he could divine its history and purpose.

'Maintain the search,' he said at last. 'We have come this far – if anything remains, we will find it.'

'And if it does not?'

The Khan started to move, to head towards the gates that led deeper in. 'Maintain the search.'

REPORTS WERE COMING in from all across the fleet. They had started in isolation – a gun-crew captain not turning up for duty, a lumen-bank shattering suddenly for no reason, an unarmed torpedo loosing without warning. Then they had mounted up, startlingly quickly, coming in from all decks and all ships.

Jubal strode across the *Swordstorm*'s bridge, senior crew in train, all of them dealing with a flurry of inter-ship comms.

'How long until we reach the outer barrier?' he demanded.

'Less than an hour,' said Taban. 'We were delayed by the *Sunhawk*.'

That frigate had suddenly taken a wildly divergent

course during a come-about manoeuvre, nearly running into the flanks of the battleship *Lance of Heaven*.
Panicked comms had managed to establish that some
madness had run through the frigate's navigation crew,
only suppressed when warriors of the ordu had inter-
vened and disabled them all. Now the *Sunhawk* was
limping along with a weakened bridge crew and damaged engines.

Jubal felt it, too. First, a slight pressure behind the
eyes. Then pain, throbbing under the skin, making
his bones twitch. Then fatigue, sinking over them all,
making it hard to think clearly. 'Accelerate the movement,' he ordered, approaching the command throne.
'I want us into range within thirty minutes.'

Taban bowed, and hurried off. Jian-Tzu remained at
his side, ready to relay vocal orders over the fleet-comm.
Down in the pits, the work-rate had become punishing. All but the servitors were struggling now, fighting
against the deadening mental confusion that exposure
to the raw warp brought.

As Jubal took his seat, he caught sight of Ilya coming towards him. 'Szu,' he said. 'Where have you been?'

The general gave him a bow of apology. 'Something
I needed to pursue.'

'Jian-Tzu tells me the astropaths are all united – the
enemy has found us. I have augurs running at extreme
range, but this… *thing* makes it hard to scry.'

Ilya glanced up at the banks of pict screens, each one
dense with real space sensor readings. 'How stands
the fleet?'

'In position. And yet, the reports…' He shook his
head to clear it. 'You have seen them? I have ordered
us to pull out further.'

'Not too far,' said Ilya. 'The Khagan is still on the station.'

'I need my crews to operate. I need them to keep their minds together.'

Even as he spoke, a scream burst out from the pits. A mortal man in Legion uniform jumped up from his position, a blade in hand, shouting incoherently. He lunged towards the nearest of his comrades, going for his back, when a single bolt-shell speared down from the upper terraces, exploding as it struck him in the throat. The White Scars legionary who had loosed it trudged down towards the body, followed by several more. All around the corpse, the rest of the mortal crew went uneasily back to their work.

'My brothers stand guard over every critical sector,' Jubal said, watching the scene impassively. 'There are not enough of them.'

'This anchorage will not endure long.'

'He has not been in contact with you? No word of your target?'

Ilya shook her head.

'Then we wait.' Menials raced up to the throne, handing Jubal a series of data-slates. Most were troubling – reactor failures, weapon-systems malfunctions. The formation he had ordered was holding, but only just. 'Order the capital ships to move further apart,' Jubal commanded. 'Enhance escort spread, and double every comm-burst, just to be sure.'

More orders followed, one after the other, shooting out across the entire fleet in an attempt to keep it moving together, to keep the lance fire-lanes clear, to ensure each flank was watched over by all the others. It was a few moments before Jubal could return his attention back to Ilya. When he did, she was staring hard at the readings from one of the long-range augurs.

'What is it?' he asked.

'Have these been verified? Where did they come from?' She turned to Taban, who was returning to the command dais bearing data-slates of his own. 'Have you seen this?'

Taban's face looked grey, as if he were ageing before their eyes. 'I missed it,' he mumbled, distractedly. 'The error was mine, my khan. I missed it.'

Jubal stood up. 'Send a signal to the Khagan. Pull them off the station.'

Ilya pressed Taban. 'We need to know the angle of approach.'

'Under-plane, twenty degrees, rising to parity at forty-five-six-three. But we cannot rotate, not with the–'

Jubal pushed clear of the throne. 'Sound the alarm!' he roared, stirring even the most lethargic from their mental fug. 'Raise status to gold, arm all weapons!'

A gong began to hammer out, resounding dully throughout the vast bridge-space. Lumens dimmed, replaced by combat lighting along the paths between stations. By then the augur-screed had become apparent to all, and the tactical screens were thick with the light-points of incoming ships.

Ilya looked sick. Even the legionaries themselves, their armour-plate giving nothing away, seemed to be moving less assuredly. The poison could be tasted on the air.

'Open a channel to Tachseer,' ordered Jubal, reaching the edge of the dais and peering over the mass of humanity below.

'*Ahn-ezen,*' came the reply from Shiban, swiftly, as if it had been expected.

'We need more time, brother,' Jubal told him. 'Can you find me some?'

'*By your command.*'

Almost instantly, the local-range sensors showed Shiban's fast-attack wings breaking free of the main cluster and racing ahead, aiming to intercept the more sluggish signals still inbound.

After that, all that remained was to align the main defence-lattice, placing the heavy warships in positions where they could deal out the most damage.

'So here they come, szu,' Jubal said, watching the blips march across the pict screens.

The general nodded.

'Yes,' she said, her fragile features a mask of foreboding. 'Here they come.'

IT WAS FOOLISH to have ended up alone. Every part of his old training had screamed at him to remain within sight of the others, but then he had other things on his mind that clouded matters – the Change was far advanced now, a body-wide itch that had begun as an irritant but was now almost maddening. He had to keep moving, just to prevent the effect from overwhelming him entirely. Extending his limbs, forcing them into their habitual patterns, felt like the only thing preventing him from metastasising entirely.

As he walked, he recited the mantras over and over again. He barely noticed his surroundings, which passed in a dark procession of half-glimpsed shadows and swept light-pools from his helm lumens.

Going downwards helped. Every step he took away

from the command chamber eased the pain a little
more. At the start he had heard the thud of his brothers' movements as they had scoured the decks for signs
of life, but now they too had died out. The corridors
around him were near-silent, their tomb-like calm
broken only by the muffled knocks and ticks of the
station's deeper structure.

After some time – it was hard to gauge the passage of the hours – his senses began to return. The
pressure in his blood and body tissue fell, the hissed
voices ebbed away.

Arvida stopped moving and looked around him.
He must have come a long way – the walls were of a
different style – organic, almost, though still carved
from the hard black iron that all of Dark Glass had
been hewn from. He was in a circular chamber with
a tulip-shaped roof. Every wall-panel was decorated
with geometric shapes, overlapped and bisected with
criss-crossed lines of force.

He could hear a deep, distant roar, like foaming
waters, coming from below.

Below was where the rift circled. Below was the eye
into the abyss.

He reached for the wall to steady himself. It felt wet
to the touch – impossible, to have sensed that through
the armour of his gauntlets.

In the centre of the chamber was a raised octago-
nal platform, carved into a nest of writhing forms like
snakes. Its surface was polished to a high sheen. As he
looked at it, he could hear his own breathing inside
his armour, close and rapid.

'Yesugei,' he rasped over the comm. Nothing came
back. 'Yesugei,' he said again.

He felt light-headed. It was foolish to have ended up alone. Then again, he had been alone before, and for a long time. Even after they had taken him away from the ruins of Tizca, he had never truly been one of them. *Alone* had become the default, bereft of the company of true battle-brothers, of the kind of magisters he had once delighted to talk with, to learn from, to study.

Back in the time before the inferno, he had possessed a tutelary, Ianaius. The Intelligence had appeared intermittently as a faint and barely perceptible presence at his side, though it had disappeared long before his last fateful journey with Kalliston to Prospero. It had never been something of cardinal importance to him. In the years afterwards, he had never tried to summon the spirit to his side again, but just then, for the first time, he found himself missing the subtle warmth of its diaphanous shade.

He moved to the platform and leaned over it heavily, pressing his palms against the wet stone. If he kept leaning, leaning, leaning, he would topple forwards, plunging into it head-first. Perhaps then the surface would break, and he would submerge within the matter of it, becoming one with the bones of the station. Perhaps then the eternal pain would cease, cooled by the oil-dark liquid. Perhaps he would become a tutelary himself, a twittering afterthought to plague the dream-worlds of men.

'I would have fought the Wolves,' he breathed aloud. 'I would not have let them defile the sacred spaces.'

The air ahead of him, between his face mask and the platform's surface, trembled. It felt as if his fingers were sinking into the stone. He blinked several times and tried to push away, but failed.

Below, far below, the rift circled. It roared, on the edge of hearing. The waters foamed.

Things began to change. He felt warm in his every sinew. He narrowed his eyes, and the vision before him blurred and wobbled.

There was a world, dark, lashed with lightning in many hues. There was a tower, immense beyond physics, thrust clear of the plates of the earth like an erupting arrowhead. He saw Intelligences dancing in the starlight, spewing out their fragments of esoterica as jests. The land beneath bubbled and altered, morphing with every rapid sunrise into something new, something tormented.

He wanted to pull back then. A terrible fear caught him by the stomach, kneading it, making him cold again.

Below, the rift circled.

He saw fleets of ships, their prows sapphire and their flanks bronze, pulling out of the warp, drifting over the tower. He saw robed figures out on the planes, milling around the base of the tower. He saw the Intelligences clustering like angels in the night sky, drawn to the tower. It was all the tower. He could not take his eyes from it. His head dipped further.

He cannot live.

That was when he saw the reflection – broken up, like images in a hall of mirrors. The faces gazed in different directions, hazy through the facets of crystal lenses, antagonistic, unaware, as confused and as lost as he himself. All images had the one, lone eye – on some faces, ringed with fire, on another, a mournful human orb, on others, a daemonic pit of insanity.

He cannot live.

His brothers were on the world, walking across its lightning-glossed landscape, making pilgrimage towards the black gates.

'No,' he breathed, out loud, his head dropping further. 'They were dead. They were all dead.'

They stood in their crimson battleplate, their robes of azure, carrying staffs topped with rearing serpent-heads, insects, bird-beaks. They spoke to one another, mournfully, resentfully, and they looked up into the skies, searching for the source of their sudden transformation.

'I would have known it. I would have sensed it.'

The shattered god was not yet amongst them. He was only there in reflections, in dreams, in the gathering dust. They did not see him, not fully. They were working. They were studying. One of them led the others now. His armour was the most familiar, marked with the sign of the raven, as ornate as it had been when he had been magister templi and the greatest of them all.

'No, you cannot cure it,' Arvida found himself saying, desperately. 'No, not that way. Do not try that way.'

He reached out, as if he could pluck the figures from their world of spells and fling them back into the void. As he did so, the image sheared away, breaking into shards and spinning apart.

Beyond it was another vision, far colder, far more remote.

He saw a galaxy of a million worlds. He saw vast fleets ply the darkness, black with the patina of age, their plasma drives leaking toxic sludge across the void. He saw manufactories churning smog into rain-grey skies. He saw lines of huddled mortals, billions of them, processing into the grinning maws of immense cathedrals where frenzied hymns were sung to a skull-faced corpse shackled to the remnants of a pain-engine. He saw books being burned, tossed on to enormous pyres and denounced, even as the ancient vehicles that carried men through the stars faltered for lack of knowledge. He saw the tortures, the fears, the despairs, the endless grinding, wearing, deadening labour, the gathering might of xenos terror, and under it all, the gurgling chortle of voices from the deepest recess of the human mind...

He was Corvidae, of the caste of seers. This was not a vision like the other, removed only in space. This was far into the future, a future every soul around him was striving to build.

'No,' he whispered, and pushed himself away.

Below, the rift churned.

He struggled to breathe. He staggered clear of the platform, shaking his hands clean of the liquid that coated them. He blundered into the wall, snapping his head back.

Then he was at the portal again, somehow blindly through, limping out. The visions crowded his mind, driving out the fear of the Change, driving out everything.

'Not this,' he blurted, staggering into another wall, reeling away from it, limping onwards like a drunkard.

The further he went, the easier it became. His vision cleared. He saw the shadows ahead of him, inky and oblique. The warmth faded, settling down to the void-chill of the abandoned station.

He sank down, hearts beating, palms sweaty. He had to find the Khan, or Yesugei, or one of the keshig. He had to get off the station. They all had to. All that remained was the warp, the poison, the heart of all corruption, leaking up the long shaft and staining their souls to the black.

He lives.

The knowledge made him want to scream aloud. Every certainty was gone now, every allegiance. Could he be found? What price had he paid for clinging to life? And the others, the others...

They are all *alive.*

That was too much. He started off again, pushing to his feet and moving faster. The dark pressed in on him, smothering the thin light of his helm lumens, trying to choke him out.

He kept moving. He kept going.

Down below, uncaring as eternity, the warp rift wheeled in the dark.

NINETEEN

TORGHUN REACHED THE bridge after his brothers, disturbed from a meditation that had been difficult to sustain. The place was in disarray. Sanyasa had drawn his blade and was shouting out orders. Others of the sagyar mazan worked their way through the lower stations, examining every mortal as they went.

'What is happening?' Torghun asked. He felt thick-headed, as if he had not slept for many days.

'You did not hear the alarms?' Sanyasa was in full armour. All the others were in full armour. 'My khan, the fleet is on a war-footing, and we have a problem.'

Torghun stared up at the *Xo Gamail*'s overhead viewports. White Scars battleships were powering ahead, gliding through the void in wide formation. Their gunnery arrays were open and primed, their void shield aegis glittering. 'You did not summon me earlier?'

Sanyasa was striding over to a rank of sensorium stations. 'We have been busy, my khan.'

It was then that Torghun saw the bodies, three of them, lying face-down amid the many crew-stations. The ship's engine hum was strained, a throttled beat that missed its rhythm. They were already out of position – far in front of where they had been ordered to remain.

Torghun assumed the command throne and began to access the myriad data systems that shunted through the vessel's arteries. 'We are above the designated plane. Bring us down.'

Sanyasa turned back to him. 'You may try.'

'Do you not see the order-scheme?

Sanyasa didn't move. 'Study the wider picture.'

Torghun hesitated, then accessed the tactical hololiths, the system read-outs, the diagnostic relays. The *Xo Gamail* was close to the flagship, treading a dangerous path amid the weaving courses of the big warships. They should have been a long way back, out of harm's way.

Then he saw the engine readings. They were far into the red-zone. They were going far too fast, burning far too much fuel, wearing down the protective reactor-shell.

'This course will lose us containment,' Torghun said, seeing the danger. 'Shut it down.'

'We cannot,' said Sanyasa. 'The cycle has gone too far.'

Out in the void loomed the hunt-lean profile of the greatest warship in the fleet, the spear-prowed *Swordstorm*. It was coming about, ponderously, its immense lance configuration snaking with barely contained energies.

'Get us off this course,' said Torghun, looking for more options. 'Get us down further.'

'If it could have been done,' said Sanyasa, firmly, 'it would have been.'

Sanyasa was implacable, holding his ground. The others, Holian, Inchig, Ahm, stood with him, and they were making no attempt to find a solution.

The *Swordstorm* drew closer.

'They will not take us,' said Torghun, understanding at last what had been done. 'Not now.'

'I estimate the engines will burn out in ten minutes,' said Sanyasa. 'Then we will be dead in the void, target-fodder, even more than we are already.'

He was right. The *Xo Gamail* was on a suicidal course, out beyond the protective range of the main guns. Torghun could see the first glimmers of enemy location-markers, and could guess how quickly the battlesphere would envelope them. They had been condemned to a futile enough role before, but this was automatic suicide.

'You see it – there is no choice,' said Sanyasa, working hard not to sound as if he were over-pressing the point.

For a moment longer, Torghun resisted, searching for another way. Being manipulated was always hateful, especially from a subordinate. He had already made his decision, he had given his orders – they would not contest Shiban's directive. He did not want to become what he was accused of. Not again.

He slammed his fist into the throne's arm. There were over a hundred warriors to consider, each one needed, each one capable of killing in the Khan's name. They had proved that, a thousand times over. In all justice, they were already redeemed.

The *Swordstorm* had almost finished its turn, after

which the mighty thrusters would fire, taking it far
beyond range.

Torghun rose from the throne again, shooting Sanyasa a sour look. 'Give the order. Mortal crew to the
saviour-pods, warriors to the shuttle-bays. Do it now.'

Klaxons began to sound, instantly, as if they had
long been primed. The bridge erupted into movement
as menials, fleet officers and legionaries all began to
make their way, quickly but without panic, to the evac-
uation stations.

Sanyasa nodded his head in acknowledgement. He
had not moved yet – they would not stir until Torghun gave them their lead.

He regarded them coldly, but there was no time
left for questions, far less for investigation. Witchery
ran through the closed atmosphere, fizzing across the
cycled air, making him feel both febrile and dangerous.

'Signal the flagship,' he said, moving at last. 'And let
us hope they retain more honour than you do.'

THE DECKS PASSED, one after the other, always descending.

The keshig went first, their pale armour glimmering
in the dark. As he travelled, the Khan looked about
him, taking everything in, absorbing the detail, isolating points of danger and advantage.

The air tasted foul – filtered through machines that
had been inactive for a long time. Every so often he
tasted the tang of dry blood.

They had passed the bloodstained rooms already.
There had been no bodies, just long smears of dark
brown on the metal. In several places there were marks
made by carbines, plus the remains of spent cartridges,
but no weapons. A few levels further down, even those

signs dried up. The chambers were empty, every one of them, scraped clean of life and home to only the endless dark, the cold, the faint creaks of the structure's massive architecture.

The Khan entered a long hall. He moved his gaze across it, his helm adding in false colour to what the lumen-beams missed. Ranks of smooth-boled pillars marched away into the gloom, glinting as the lights flitted over them. Iron bookcases, many tens of metres high, filled the wallspace, each one stuffed with scrolls and leatherbound tomes. A heavy metal orrery stood in the centre of the floor, listing to one side on a broken axis. Its rings and dials were covered in algebraic script, and jewels marked the position of planetary systems.

Low, long tables sat under the pillars, some covered in the flaking remains of parchment maps. The Khan moved closer to one of them. He reached out to flatten the material, and it cracked along the folds.

Namahi joined him. 'There are many such rooms,' he said.

The Khan looked at the charts. The nearest was like no star chart he had ever seen – a riot of swirls and serpentine eddies, backing up, switching over, the courses merging into one another. Various labels had been applied in tiny High Gothic letters: Stratum Aetheris, Stratum Profundis, Viam Sedis, Ocularis Malefica.

'Warp channels,' the Khan said. 'Has the ecumene seen these?'

'He says they are like those on Herevail. He has pushed deeper.'

'Yesugei remains with him?'

'And his guard.'

The Khan nodded. He let the parchment fall and kept walking. 'Map-makers,' he said. 'That is what they call my Father, you know this? The Cartomancer. He was all things to all people.'

Namahi walked alongside him in silence. Like Qin Xa, he was a calm soul.

They reached the end of the hall. It terminated in a colonnade of thin, perilously tall columns. After that was a balcony, overlooking a deep shaft. The gulf was over twenty metres across, and its base was lost in the shadows. A stair led down into it, clinging to the near wall, zigzagging back and forth. On the far side of the abyss rose another iron wall, covered in a mass of overlapping pipes and cables.

The Khan stood on the balcony. As he peered over the edge, he felt a nagging sense of familiarity.

'I have seen this before,' he said.

Down below, a squad of White Scars was negotiating the stairs, the soft glow of lumens following them down. Their bootfalls echoed in the emptiness, gradually fading as they descended.

'Some light,' the Khan said.

Namahi reached for a flare, unscrewed the canister and threw it over the edge. The charge tumbled for a while, then exploded, flooding the walls of the chasm. It dropped away slowly, dragging its aura of short-lived brilliance with it to the bottom.

The pipework ran down a long way, hundreds of metres. The workings of enormous machines were embedded among the metalwork walls – pistons, flywheels, riveted gears. Massive chains clanked gently against one another, shackled to levers buried amid tangles of thick cabling. The complexity, even to one used to the spectacle of Imperial starships and hive spires, was impressive.

The Khan watched the flare fall all the way, capturing the outlines of further devices before it dropped beyond sight. As he did so, the familiarity suddenly became clear.

'I remember this.'

The far-off past, back when he had first been taken to Terra. He had walked the endless corridors of the Palace, exploring the city-world from its highest spires to its deepest pits. He had been free to roam, and none had dared hinder a primarch in his Father's house. During that time he had seen the Emperor only rarely, for He had been called away by the duties of the Great Crusade, and when returned to the Palace was habitually occupied with the thousand cares of empire.

It had been a day in winter, the flanks of the mountains white and glaring. The Khan had roved far into the deep places, treading the paths of the Palace foundations. Earth-movers were still active down there, gnawing their way through the roots of the peaks, hollowing out what would one day become the greatest and most secure of the Palace's hidden halls. The Sigillite's people were everywhere, mingling with squads of Legio Custodes in crimson robes and golden armour.

It had not taken much to elude them – Jaghatai had been doing that all his life. He kept travelling, ever further into the heart of the earth, the lights dying out, the rock unworked, the earthbreakers dormant and unmanned.

There had been a shaft there, just like this one. Cables had run down its entire length, just as they did here. Great energy coils had been sunk into the walls, feeding engines of unknown purpose and power.

At the very base of it all, thick with darkness, he had spied a last unfinished hall, immense beyond anything else in that assembled vastness. All the cables led there, terminating over an empty stage. Scaffolds straddled the edifice, lost in the dusty occlusion, heavy with haulage claws and chain-lifts.

He had not noticed his Father's presence until too late, for that was the way with Him – He would be there, then not there, like light on water.

'What is this place?' the Khan had asked.

'The end of the Crusade,' the Emperor had replied.

And that had been all he ever learned. Now, unimaginably far away, out in the furthest tracts of cold space, here it was again – the shaft, the machines, the power coils, identical in every detail.

He was about to give the order to descend, when his helm comm-bead crackled into life.

'*Khagan,*' came the message from Jubal. '*They are here.*'

So soon.

He curled his fingers over the balcony's railing in frustration. 'Understood,' he sent back. 'I return.' He closed the link and turned to Namahi. 'Yesugei continues?'

'He does.'

'Bring him back, the others too. There is nothing here for us.'

Then the Khan turned and started to march back the way he had come. There was no time left for

speculation – the docked Stormbirds were far off, and
Jubal would not have notified him if the threat were
not imminent.

Then he paused, looking back over his shoulder.

The end of the Crusade.

Dark Glass had not been made by House Achelieux.
It had been made by the Emperor.

Then he was moving again. The questions might be
answered, but not now, and not by him. Just as it had
done unbroken for every year of his centuries-long
life, battle called again.

WHITE SCARS FAST-ATTACK wings screamed out of the
empty void. Phalanxes of fighters – Fire Raptors, Storm
Eagles, Xiphon interceptors – scattered ahead of the
thundering passage of frigate-level warships. A full
third of the V Legion fleet had been deployed, every
void craft powered up to maximum velocity.

The *Kaljian* thrust ahead, foremost of the true
warships. Twenty more frigates fanned out in its
promethium-afterburn wake, thirty destroyer-class
escorts, hundreds of gunships and heavy bombers,
all snaking and diving among one another in perfect
synchronisation.

Faster.

Shiban stood on the edge of the bridge command
platform, watching his brothers burn towards the
inner edge of the aether-clouds – the extremity they
had pushed through in order to discover Dark Glass.

No one rides the void like we do, he thought.

'Signals!' reported Tamaz.

Ahead of them, the azure walls of turbulence
churned – the vast inner sphere of blue-tinged detritus,

unbroken, unscannable, crawling outwards from the epicentre with glacial slowness.

Shiban narrowed his eyes. Garbled visual signals multiplied ahead, obscure but tangible, hundreds of them. Every crew member on the bridge concentrated their attention forwards, waiting for the first break in the boiling matter. They knew where the enemy would emerge – a straight line from the Mandeville point – but only roughly, and they did not yet know numbers.

'Maintain full speed,' Shiban ordered. 'Fire only on my mark.'

The initial impact would be critical. Their pursuers would be sensor-blind, prone, vulnerable, suffering from the damage of the passage as they had done in their turn.

Then the first one punched through, shoving a plume of blue-edged plasma ahead of it.

'Swing to zenith!' roared Shiban. 'Calibrate all lances on that point!'

The ships powered upwards. The fighter wings angled sharply, boosting ahead, followed by the heavier gunship squadrons, then the lance-bearing vessels.

Shiban waited just a few seconds longer, watching the azure cloud-banks pucker with incoming ship-forms. The moment had to be timed, held back for maximum impact.

'Mark,' he commanded.

Every attack craft loosed its weapons, just as the first enemy prows jutted clear of the aether-storm. Torpedoes, las-beams, heavy bolter-rounds, cannonades – all smashed across the narrow void and slammed into the emerging ships. A curtain of immolation spilled across the sphere's concave interior, igniting against the edge of the turbulence and sending coronas of fire flaring wildly.

'Again.'

The gunships came about quickest, hammering at the flame-wreathed ships from their battle-cannons. More lance-strikes followed, splitting the void with white-hot intensity. Salvo after salvo hit home, cracking against void shields and slamming hard into the adamantium beneath.

In the face of that concentrated fury, even Legion armour would break. Enemy escorts shot clear of the cloud-banks, swathed in an aegis of drawn-out aether-spume and burning plasma. Like firecrackers they spat and withered, leaking promethium from a thousand cuts, their spines aflame with sequential explosions. They were III Legion outriders, nigh as fast as the V Legion craft that preyed on them, thrown hard into the maelstrom and taking on horrific levels of damage.

'Punish them,' ordered Shiban coldly, bracing himself as the *Kaljian* fired its main lance again, spearing the beam clean through the ventral flanks of a tumbling Emperor's Children destroyer. *'Again.'*

The mass of firepower ramped up another notch, turning the starless void white and gold. White Scars hunters wheeled and darted amid the carnage, swinging in wide arcs like the raptors of the old plains, piling on the waves of destruction.

The entire enemy vanguard broke apart, its formation shattered as commanders desperately tried to evade the concentrated barrage. Some plunged low, others tried to climb; a few desperately activated retro-thrusters to slow their emergence from

the encompassing aether-clouds. The Scars went after
all of them, running them down, harrying them with
a freedom they had not been able to indulge for years.

At the forefront, the *Kaljian* turned hard, exposing
its broadside to the burning morass of ships before it.

'All guns,' ordered Shiban, feeling exhilaration again.
'Fire at will.'

The frigate's macrocannons boomed out, hurling their payloads across the abyss in serried waves.
Two III Legion escorts were snared in the hurricane,
their shields annihilated, their hulls breached, their
fuel-tanks pierced. Seconds later they exploded,
spreading huge starbursts of raging plasma and tumbling debris in ragged blast-spheres.

But then the true monsters emerged, barging their
way through the barrier, their heavy-armoured prows
shoving aside thick tendrils of flame. The enemy
battleships thrust into contact like cetaceans swimming up from the deeps, their heavy guns already
firing. These were liveried in both purple and gold,
and dirty white – the combined main attack force of
the Emperor's Children and the Death Guard.

'Ready second wave,' ordered Shiban, watching the
giants push their way into range. There was still a tactical advantage, one that had to be pushed for as long
as possible. 'Select targets and run-out guns.'

The numbers were already daunting. Line-class
battleships roared into contention, one after the
other, all more heavily armed and defended than the
advance guard. They smashed their way up through
the shattered ruins of their own kind, already firing
back from main lances and soon to be in position to
launch their own ruinous broadside volleys.

'Now,' commanded Shiban, giving the pre-prepared signal to Tamaz. 'All ships, fire second wave.'

The *Kaljian* leapt forwards, its crew feeding a final boost-level to its straining engines. The frigate raced out under the shadow of the burning enemy wrecks, aiming for the blunt angle of a XIV Legion cruiser. Its speed brought it away from the potential of the forward lances and below the fire-arc of the macro-cannon batteries.

Every White Scars ship did the same, relying on superior momentum and position to race in close, avoiding the ship-killing lance fire-lanes and rushing in to raking range. Every commander switched power from fleet-range weapons to the close-killers. The gunship wings did likewise, swarming over the bridge-towers of the bigger ships and hammering them with concentrated bolter volleys. They flew fiercely fast, fiercely close, strafing along the spires of the Emperor's Children ships and the blunt watchtowers of the Death Guard vessels, breaking and burning. Fighter wings shot along in support, soaring clear to loose charges into the mouths of the opening hangars, destroying the enemy gunships before they could even get out of the hulls.

The *Kaljian* reached its destination, hurtling along the underside of the greater mass of the Death Guard battlecruiser and peppering it with targeted strikes from its upper-level guns. Just as it drew level with the far larger vessel, Shiban ordered retro-thrusters to fire, subjecting the frigate to a bone-aching drop in velocity.

'Flanking fire,' he ordered, watching the more ponderous warship struggle to come about. They were close in now, and he could see every panel of every deck-level, every comms-vane and every gunwale covering. 'Over hard.'

The tactical crew responded, sending the frigate swinging over on its central axis, rolling tightly and bringing its lateral broadsides into range.

For a moment, Shiban relished the sight – the target was just a few hundred metres distant, already burning, moving too slowly to do anything about it.

'Fire.'

The *Kaljian*'s broadside thundered out, vomiting its entire complement of loaded ordnance in a single bloc. The macrocannons slammed back in their carriages, barrels glowing hot as the shells sped across the void.

They hit in a rolling wave of plate-ripping devastation, impacts feeding from one another, birthing a raging cauldron of liquid fire across the battlecruiser's flanks. Its void shields blazed then buckled, exposing the hull-plates beneath, which were pulverised by the incoming waves of hard-round ammunition.

The battlecruiser was bodily crunched aside, spinning clear of the smaller frigate, its underside raging. The *Kaljian* rolled back the other way, rotating one hundred and eighty degrees to bring its other broadside gunnery to bear.

By then, Shiban was grinning. 'Fire!'

The second volley had the same intensity as the first, launched by weapons teams anxious to match the performance of their brothers, and the void was ripped apart again by the tempest of the battery launching as one. Mortars and incendiaries pierced the burning cruiser's shell, burrowing deep to strike at its vital organs – its engines, its fuel tanks, its warp reactor.

'Now away!' roared Shiban, detecting the first huge energy spikes. 'Get us out, then find another.'

The *Kaljian* kept firing even as its enginarium crew propelled it beyond the burning battlecruiser, out ahead, into the oncoming storm of ships. Just as it broke free of the blast-zone, the cruiser exploded, blasted apart by the horrific forces unleashed within it. It broke into three, plumes of raw plasma flaring into the tortured abyss, its constituent parts spinning wildly and sending clouds of burning metal flying. White Scars fighters flew exuberantly through the blazing wreckage, strafing the last of it before circling around to find new prey.

Shiban guided the *Kaljian* higher, pulling up across the expanding battlesphere. Every passing second brought a new ship into the void-theatre, a huge procession of Legion assets. Soon the numbers would become ridiculous – they would have to fall back to Jubal's position and consolidate ahead of the gathering storm. These newcomers were too huge and well-armoured to be troubled by the firepower he had at his command, and once they reacted to the sensor-loss and the damage of the passage, they would be able to deploy fearsome levels of retribution.

But not yet. For a few precious moments more, they were disorientated, plunging into a feverish nightmare of swirling fire and an enemy that was fast and savage, and had nothing to lose.

He almost laughed aloud, just as he had once done in every battle.

'The Khagan!' he roared, and the crew on the bridge roared back.

Then the *Kaljian* ducked and pushed ahead, its next

target located and fixed, its guns reloaded and its engines at full tilt. Every white-prowed ship in the fleet did the same thing, racing heedless into the maw of danger, unloading their wrath, out-pacing, out-firing, out-thinking, and bringing the long-nurtured vengeance of Chogoris to those who had dared to chase them down.

EVERY SHADOW HELD a flame of malice within it, curling away, rising from the blackened iron like heat-haze. The lower they went, the more acute it became. The surroundings gradually changed, from the utilitarian bleakness of the upper void station into something new – an almost organic profusion of curls and spirals, all sculpted from the same unyielding metal, glinting in the gloom like obsidian blade-edges.

'This place not made for star-mapping,' Yesugei said to Veil.

The ecumene nodded. 'Not completely,' he said, shuffling clumsily through the narrow corridor. 'Something else, yes.'

Ahead of them went four legionaries, blades drawn and casting flicker-patterns of electric-blue across the pressed metal walls. Behind them came two more, and after them the unbroken shadow.

Yesugei checked his comm. Nothing. No orders, no updates.

That in itself was strange. He was about to open a channel to the Khagan when Veil suddenly halted.

'Now, then. I recognise these things.'

Just ahead, the corridor opened up into a high, circular chamber, its walls clustered with ganglia of pipework. Long grilles ran away into the distant roof-vaults, screening narrow shafts that led out in all directions, and the floor was smooth and polished. Helm lumens rippled over valves and gauges, all linked to a byzantine clot of glass transistors. None of it was operative, but Yesugei could feel a faint afterglow of heat across the surface.

'What are they?' he asked.

Veil poked at the machinery with his good hand. 'So much power needed, impossible amounts. But they were trying here.' He turned back to Yesugei, and his face was a ghostly glow behind his void-suit's visor. 'We used machines like this on Herevail, and on Denel Five. They built one on Denel and it took years, and even then it was not enough.'

'For what?'

'To go beyond the shallows.'

Yesugei reached out and touched the machines in the walls. They were old. They looked barely human in origin – more like xenos constructs, designed by minds far removed from Terran limitations. Even the portals around the edge of the chamber were oddly shaped – fluid, with fern-like tendrils intertwining with the forests of cables.

Veil moved across to the far side of the chamber, held rapt by what he was seeing, studying everything. The legionaries remained at the doorways, on alert. Yesugei felt a gathering sense of unease. The air should have been colder – they were far from any heat-source, and yet the readings had started to climb. The silence was unnerving, and had been for a long time. Only his own breathing broke the grip of it.

Where was Arvida? Why had he not heard from the Khan?

He moved towards the chamber's centre. The poison was getting to him, making his thoughts cloudy. He had let it work for too long – arrogance had always been the great peril for his kind.

'Something is aware of us,' Yesugei said. 'Keep away from the machines.'

Just as the order passed his lips, the chamber suddenly flickered into light. Strip-lumens running up the walls flared briefly, then settled into an uncertain glare. A column of vivid blue light burst out from the floor, surging up to head-height, then disintegrated in a riot of cascading sparks.

In its wake stood a man, smooth-skinned, young-looking, wearing rich robes and a sapphire-draped bandana across his forehead.

'*Welcome to Dark Glass,*' came a cultured voice speaking Terran-accented High Gothic. '*I am Novator Pieter Helian Achelieux, House Achelieux, Cartomancer's Envoy. I am sure you have many questions.*'

TWENTY

EVERYTHING WAS DIFFICULT, everything was slow. The entire crew worked as if in a fog of insomnia, taking far longer than they should have to complete even the simplest tasks.

Ilya was not immune – she had to cram her fists into her face and rub hard to wake herself up. Watch-squads of legionaries were dispersed from their stations to oversee operations in the enginarium and on the gunnery levels. For a short while, that stopped the rot, but then the chain of command slowed again, and Jubal ordered more to move through the vast starship. They had licence to use their weapons, to force compliance, something that was hateful to all, for the White Scars had never been a Legion built on fear.

Despite it all, the fleet had responded. Alignment was almost complete, the defence-grids raised. Shiban's desperate raid had done what it had needed to do – given space for the main battleships to orientate themselves to the approaching enemy, to gauge their numbers and their positions, to formulate a defence.

Jubal strode back and forth among the bridge crews, issuing orders with every breath, tireless, imposing. Ilya admired him, just as all others did.

It would not be long now. Through the viewports she could already see the first of Shiban's outriders limping back from the initial raids, their flanks streaming plasma. Beyond that were the mammoth beasts of the void, the pale-prowed monsters of the XIV, the gaudy barges of the III.

She rubbed her eyes again, scouring away the ever-present urge to give up, to let it all go. Every time she stood still for a moment, the same thoughts raced to clog her mind.

This has been wasted. There is nothing here. He is not here. They have found us, and now it ends, far from Terra, alone.

She staggered over to a nest of sensor-lenses. The *Swordstorm* remained in close proximity to several heavy cruisers and three personnel transports – the manoeuvre to turn and bring its lance into optimal range was not trivial.

It was then that she saw the signals, hundreds of them, swarming out of a lone vessel running almost dark, its engine signature flaring off the scale.

'What is that?' she asked one of the sensorium menials, pulling him from his station and showing him the markers.

The man looked at them dully for a moment, blinking. Then he pulled himself together. 'The *Xo Gamail*,' he said. 'Out of position. Drifting. They have been hailing.'

Ilya turned away, strode over to a comm-station and took up the equipment. There were many shuttles out in the void, pulling ahead of a greater crowd of saviour pods. She isolated the ident of the lead craft and patched in a link. 'Declare yourself,' she ordered.

It took a moment for the link to punch through. When it did, the quality was grainy, almost inaudible.

'Open the hangars. Vessel abandoned due to engine failure. We are one hundred and thirty-two Legion blades, many more standard crew. Open the hangars.'

She recognised the voice instantly. She had been at the trials, and had never forgotten them. 'You have left it late,' she warned, pulling up a schematic to assess if a transfer were even possible. 'The shields are up.'

'We can serve. We will not be wasted. Please, open the hangars.'

She looked up, over to where Jubal was roaring out new orders. The commander was fully occupied now, consumed with the business of bringing the Legion's still formidable firepower into line. There was still much to accomplish, and in the greater scheme of the fighting even a hundred warriors was an acceptable loss to bear.

And yet the Khagan had not returned. They would not complete the manoeuvre and lock in final combat status – not while he remained on Dark Glass.

'Come alongside,' she said. 'Hangar Forty-Five. You have ten minutes. Caution – the target will be moving fast.'

There was a confident laugh, then the link cut.

Ilya removed the comm-shroud, stood up again and looked back towards Jubal.

He would not like it. He would not be easily swayed.

'But I did it before,' she said to herself, setting off to waylay him, to make the case. Perhaps that would always be her role in this damned Legion – to speak truth to power, to temper the foolishness of the brave. 'And I can do it again.'

THE KHAN REACHED the Stormbird hangar. One gunship had already taken off, and was holding position just outside the void-doors, ready to lead the escort. The others were all powered-up, their atmospheric engines whining within the station's restored gravity bubble.

Namahi went on ahead. The Khan cycled through the hundred comm-bursts his armour's systems were picking up, thrown out from the fleet and detailing all that was transpiring. The first shots had already been fired, and the engagement was racing towards finality.

He had to be there.

'Khagan, we are ready,' voxed Namahi from the Stormbird's cockpit.

The primarch moved up the embarkation ramp. Across the apron, other squads were returning, filing towards the waiting gunships. As the Khan ducked under the shadow of the Stormbird's inner bay, he noticed one more warrior stumbling across the hangar's desolate expanse.

'Wait,' he ordered.

Arvida looked wounded. The sorcerer limped his way to the primarch, his vox-grille emitting a hoarse scraping intake.

'Alone?' asked the Khan. 'Where is Yesugei?'

Arvida tried to collect himself. He looked half-dazed. 'He is not here yet?'

The Khan ushered him inside the gunship. The Stormseer would have to take the next one. 'No time remains. He will follow.'

They took up position within, the keshig lumbering after them, the ramps hauling closed and the Stormbird powering cumbersomely from the deck. Arvida collapsed against the interior of the inner hull, holding his head in his hands. The Khan remained on his feet, riding the tilt of the deck as the gunship rotated towards the exit.

Then they were out, boosting hard, angling steeply under Dark Glass' lowering mass. The escort gunship came with them, as did the interceptors, leaving the remaining three behind to lift the last of the boarding parties clear.

The Khan watched the void station recede. It would have been better to have explored it further. Whether or not Ilya's contact had ever held the promise of a path through the mazes of the warp, there was surely some secret buried in the station's reaches, one that linked back all the way to Terra.

Arvida coughed violently and pushed his head back. The Khan moved over to him. 'What happened to you?' he asked.

It took a while for the sorcerer to answer. When he did, it sounded like his throat was constricted. 'The warp,' he croaked. 'In that place.'

'Aye. We knew that. Can you resist? I will need you.'

Arvida snapped out a bitter laugh. 'Yes, I can resist. Just a little more. Then the end comes.' He stared up at the primarch. Arvida's helm-lenses looked odd, as if they were running with condensation on the inside. 'But I have seen it, my lord. I have seen what waits for mankind.'

The Khan stooped to Arvida's level. The Stormbird

was now speeding at full power, its void-thrusters roaring. 'What did you see?'

'Different defeats.' Arvida's gauntlets were twitching. 'Two sides of a card, each one blank.' His speech was slurred at the edges. 'They were all dead. Now they live. What does that mean? If I had stayed, would I be with them now?'

Dozens more comm-signals clamoured for attention across the Khan's helm-lenses. The *Swordstorm* was fast approaching.

'I do not understand you,' he said.

Arvida looked directly at him, seeming to shiver uncontrollably. 'I am already corrupted,' he said. 'But I am not alone – it comes for all of us. Even you. I saw it. I saw what we are building.' He hacked up more wet coughs, and the Khan saw thin lines of blood leak from his gorget seal. 'Do you hear me, Master of Chogoris? There is no victory. No victory.'

The Khan placed his heavy head on Arvida's shoulder. On another day, he might have slain a warrior for saying such words, but he had seen the sacrifices the sorcerer had made for a Legion that was not his own. The warp was thrumming from every surface around them, tainting all minds.

'I do not doubt your visions,' the Khan said, quietly.

The thrusters began to decrease in power, the slowdown before the passage through the crystal barrier. Arvida's shivers diminished.

'But what do they change?' the Khan asked. 'Shall we stare up at the shadows and let our blades fall from our hands?'

Arvida's tremors began to ebb. The further they went from the void station, the quicker the recovery.

'Know this, son of Magnus,' said the Khan. 'There is more under the arch of heaven than victory and defeat. We may fall back, but not forever. We may feint and we may weave, but not forever. We may yet be doomed to lose all we cherish, but we shall do so in the knowledge that we could have turned away, and did not.'

First vox contact with the *Swordstorm* came through. The docking cycle began.

'We remained true,' the Khan said. 'They can never have this, not if they burn all we ever built and scorn us through the dancing flames. You hear me? We remained true.'

Arvida made no response for a moment, then his head dropped. He seemed to shrink, as if his body inside his armour had somehow relaxed, pulled back into itself.

'The rift...' he began, his voice more like it had been, though thick with weariness.

'I know it – feel no shame.'

The Khan looked up, out through the narrow viewports. The *Swordstorm* was visible now, foremost among the other great line battleships, its proud lines as majestic as they had ever been. Just laying eyes on it brought a pang of joy to him, just as he felt when taking a fine weapon from the rack and balancing it in his grip.

'But recover yourself swiftly,' he said, rising to his feet. 'I want you with me. I want your witchery alongside my zadyin arga.'

He felt his hearts-beat pick up, preparing him, steeling him.

'My brother Mortarion is here,' the Khan said. 'And this time he does not come to convert us.'

✠ ✠ ✠

FOR A MOMENT, Yesugei had believed he was real –
a flesh-and-blood presence before them. It took a
few seconds to realise that Achelieux was a hololith,
projected up from the centre of the machine-chamber –
another sign, if one were needed, of how weakened
his mind was by the warp's poison.

The apparition stood before them, lifelike save for
a hint of translucency around the edges. The Novator was just as Arvida had described him – holding
a black staff with a white stone, his robes adorned
with sapphires. His face was almost without flaw, and
the colour of sun-dried earth. He was not looking at
them. He was looking, as hololiths always did, into
the middle-distance, his eyes out of true focus, and
with an intelligent smile on his attractive face.

'I can guess what you wish to learn,' the hololith said.
'What happened here, why you had to come to find out.
The answer is simple – weakness of will. You will know
that we expended much labour on selecting the crew for
this, knowing the risks. For the most part, that labour was
rewarded. I take some pride in that. Fifty-two years and no
disturbance, no hint of betrayal. Consider it – the Seethe
lies within sight of this place, open as a wound, and still
we endured. I hope, when all is taken into account, that
will be remembered. I do not see it as a failure... I see it
as resolve beyond all expectation.'

It was hard to know how long ago the projection
had been recorded. Veil had withdrawn to the far side
of the chamber, his attention fixed on the speaker.
Yesugei could not see his face well, but spied that his
eyes were wide with something like fascination.

'I am unsure what caused the change,' the Achelieux-
spectre continued. 'I must surmise the cause – the

Paternova, who has ever been against this policy. If I could have been here all the time, I might have prevented it, though we must have been infiltrated at last. If there is fault to be admitted, it lies with me. I acted too late. When it became clear the situation had gone beyond my power to contain, I enacted the protocol and flushed the station. I am alone now. They did not succeed in disrupting the programme, for it has now reached a stage where I can control the Gate without aid. A fortunate chance.' Achelieux paused, looking briefly troubled. *'Yet do not think me a monster. To open this place to the raw Seethe, to see those with whom I laboured for so long dragged into the immaterium, both friend and enemy – that was not an easy sight. There was no other way.'*

Yesugei began to piece the events together. The lack of bodies, the bloodstains – there had been some kind of rebellion on board, triggered up in the command levels. Somehow Achelieux had employed the proximity of the warp to end it, and somehow had preserved himself. The place had been scoured, stripped of all but the inert metal, its very structure made toxic.

'Nonetheless, we have done as you asked,' Achelieux said. *'Know this, it works. Trans-Geller harmonics are operative, the principles of stratum-breach are sound. There are matters that are less clear-cut, of course – the via sedis remains the province of mental acuity, of force of will. I am aware of your intentions for this place, and accept that only the nominated primarch has the strength to maintain an active link, but I am also aware of the war, and my observation of this leads me to believe that he is in no position to fulfil that role now.'*

Via sedis. The way of the Throne. What did that mean? Which primarch?

'So, being isolated here and with little hope of timely rescue, I take this thing upon myself. The rift grows, my dreams are bad, and so my time grows short. I will dare it, knowing the risks. I fear it, of course I do, but we must all dare that which we fear. You would agree, I think. I make this record in the hope that you will witness the results, and that despite the rebellion, your faith in the Gate has been amply rewarded, and that this place and all that was done here yet has the power to turn the tides'.

Achelieux smiled. It was a confident, pleasant smile. Yesugei found himself understanding how such a man could have had influence over others, and why Ilya had been quite so anxious to find him again.

'So I dare the infinite,' Achelieux said, making the sign of the aquila. *'Ave Imperator!'*

Then the hololith snapped out. The lumens faded, and the chamber returned to darkness.

For a few moments, no one spoke.

'Who was he speaking to?' asked Yesugei, vocalising his thoughts.

Veil shuffled over to the dormant hololith projector node. 'To the one who sent him.' His voice had changed. It had been variously wheedling, arrogant or fearful before – now it was calm. He reached into his suit, searching for something in the recesses. 'The Master of Mankind. Or had you not worked that out for yourself?'

Veil's manner had completely switched. As one, the legionaries around the chamber lowered their bolters. Yesugei fed power to his staff.

'Do not, please,' said Veil, bringing out two vortex charges, one in each hand. 'These are quite capable of destroying this chamber and everything in it. If I loose my grip, they will both go off.'

Yesugei reached out with his mind and met a wall of blank psychic force. That was interesting – he had not detected that before, and neither had Arvida.

'No, that will not help you either,' said Veil. 'The Paternova finds ways to ward his agents.'

'So I see.' Yesugei relaxed. 'Then this is feud between your Houses – we have no part in it.'

'No, you do not.' Veil backed away, moving clear of the nearest White Scars legionary, his hands held out clear of his body. The one encased with bandages was clearly strong enough to keep a grip on a charge. 'I told your general that there were different schools of thought. It was your misfortune to stumble into one such disagreement. You should have left me on Herevail.'

'Where you are sent, from Terra, to track Achelieux's progress,' said Yesugei. 'But you don't make it to Dark Glass. Did he suspect you?'

'He barely knew I existed.'

'So what happen here?'

'Betrayal.' Veil's voice was fervent – he really believed that. 'We were faithful. We were the guides. We built the Imperium around you all, and so might have been trusted a little more.'

Yesugei probed, gently, with his mind, searching for weakness. Veil had been given some kind of psychic aegis, possibly an implant he could activate at will. The charges were powerful, as he said – comfortably enough to turn the entire chamber to a soup of null particles, and even power armour would be little defence.

Veil's erratic demeanour, his alternate arrogance and timidity, had been his greatest weapon, one that should have been seen through earlier. Now things were delicate.

'I do not understand,' said Yesugei, speaking evenly, playing for time.

'How could you?' asked Veil. 'You have not been on Terra for a long time. There are secrets murmured in the Palace, and the Paternova has keen ears for them. Where *is* the Emperor, do you suppose? Why does He not travel to meet Horus in the void, to lay waste to his armies before they near His greatest fortress? Perhaps there is some task that keeps Him shackled to His walls of gold.'

Something was jamming Yesugei's comms, preventing him from sending a signal. That might have been the case for a long time – he had been sloppy. The psychic aegis around Veil was powerful, enough to damp down all but the bluntest attack, the violence of which would only trigger the charges.

'There are other paths,' said Veil, bitterly. 'Deeper paths. Certain among the xenos have known of them for aeons. They carved ways through the aether's foundations. Do you see what that means? *Under* the storms. No Astronomican, no warp drives, no creatures of living nightmares scrabbling at your portholes. There is a foul doctrine, a perverse doctrine, that claims this realm for ourselves, that would end the reign of the Houses and cast us out as mutants whose long age has passed. Machines have been created. The greatest of them, the *sedem auream*, is complete, and the universe screams against it. But there were others. There were prototypes.'

Yesugei could sense the fervour in the man's voice. He was ready to die. Keeping him talking was the only way, just until he could find some way to disarm him.

'Prototypes of what?' he asked.

'Gates. Gates into hell. You are standing on the threshold even now, and still you do not see it. Achelieux was never charting the warp – he was creating the means to bypass it. They built this place here, away from Terra's trillions of souls, to perfect their abomination while the Crusade marched across the void. If the war had not come it would no doubt be in use by now, but come it did, and that has forced his hand.'

'Achelieux said he dares the infinite. What did he mean?'

'That he is dead.'

'Then your task is over. You have done what you were ordered to.'

Veil smiled sadly. 'The Gate exists. His words remain.'

Yesugei prepared himself. Veil was protected, but the man was no psyker – he could not prevent the manipulation of matter. 'We are not your enemy.'

Veil's smile remained regretful.

'No,' he said. 'You are not.'

Yesugei moved first. His reactions were far quicker than a mortal's, and his staff blazed as power flooded through it. Twin bursts of matter-ripping energy thundered out from his clenched gauntlets, crashing into the two grenades in Veil's open palms.

One of the charges, the one held loosely in Veil's broken hand, was caught within an imploding sphere of fractured real space, cast out of the realm of physics and hurled into nothingness, all before Veil could so much as twitch in its direction. But striking truly at two targets within a fraction of a millisecond, even for one of Yesugei's gifts, in that place, with the malign effluent of the warp leaking out of every molecule of the station, was nigh impossible – Veil's other hand snatched back, evading the barrage for the split-mote of time needed for his thumb to slip from the microdetonator.

With a sickening snap of reality cracking apart, the charge went off.

TWENTY-ONE

THE ENDURANCE CRASHED through the aether-barrier. Its engines dragged it up towards the centre of the raging battlesphere, trailing enormous gouts of smog. Its ranks of broadside guns were slammed out, deck after deck, hauled by toiling crews of menials working chain-lifters and rail-shunts. White Scars war vessels hove into range instantly, raking its shields in close-range attack-runs, and the defensive gunnery teams were soon knocking them out of the void with smother-patterns of flak.

Mortarion stood on the bridge, his Deathshroud arranged about him, his crew working frantically to compensate for the difficult passage and to adjust to the hail of incoming fire. The flagship's entire structure shook as it thrust steeply upwards, absorbing the hits, powering its heavy weapons arrays for the first strike.

On the far side of the unfolding void battle, the *Proudheart* emerged from the cloud-banks, its hull alight with las-beams. It had broken through at higher speed, and was already rolling over to expose its cannon broadsides to the V Legion attackers racing into close quarters.

'Lord commander,' voxed Mortarion to Eidolon, watching as the III Legion formation ran the gauntlet of lance-strikes. 'You may wish to adjust your speed. You are pulling clear.'

There was a hesitation before the reply came back – a sign of irritation, perhaps. *'They are coming in fast, my lord,'* Eidolon said, evenly. *'We have the power to match them.'*

'Do as you must,' said Mortarion, watching as the *Endurance* sent the first coruscating lance-beam spitting out into the void, striking a V Legion destroyer at long range and crippling it. 'But not too far. Our advantage is our numbers – do not squander it.'

Another pause before the reply. *'As you advise.'*

The link cut out. Mortarion smiled to himself. It had been a command, not advice, but Eidolon was wise not to take it as such. They were a proud Legion, the Emperor's Children, even in their growing debasement, and that was as it should be. 'Maintain cruising speed,' he commanded Ulfar. 'If they truly wish to break their necks in some contest of velocity, let them.'

As he spoke, the Death Guard deployment was already recovering from the initial attacks, resuming its shape and bringing its more powerful guns to bear. The *Endurance* was joined by the other major battleships, the *Indomitable Will*, *Reaper's Scythe*, *Moritatis Oculix* and *Stalwart*. Accompanying them came a horde of support craft – frigates, destroyers, gunship-carriers and light cruisers. Some had taken a beating on emergence, but most had weathered the storm and were now shifting into defensive lattice-patterns, adopting the overlapping fire-lane doctrine that had guided the Legions for more than two centuries.

The Emperor's Children detachment, less numerous and more thinly spread, had suffered worse and continued to do so, taking on the White Scars on their own terms – with flamboyance, trusting to daring to bring their close-range guns to bear.

Watching that, Kalgaro grunted his displeasure. The Siegemaster was conservative in matters of void warfare, trusting heavy armament over mobility. 'They will race to their deaths.'

Mortarion nodded in agreement. 'Yet their vigour serves us well. Let them soak up the fury – we will reap the harvest.'

As if to underline to the point, the first of many White Scars frigates swam into the *Endurance*'s sights. It had just emerged victorious from a vicious fire-fight with a III Legion escort of a similar displacement, and was coming about to power alongside Eidolon's starboard flank.

'Now, demonstrate the virtue of patience,' Mortarion ordered, addressing Lagaahn, the gunnery master.

The order raced along the command-hierarchy, filtered down to the sweltering depths of the battleship's macrocannon decks. Amid these humid, cramped spaces, where cannons the size of Imperator Titans were hauled and serviced by teams over nine hundred strong, coordinates were deployed, crane-chains hauled tight, shells clanged into breeches and gunwale-plates slammed open.

'Fire,' commanded the primarch.

The *Endurance* complied, and its starboard flanks disappeared behind a wall of belched smoke. Shells shrieked in ramrod-straight lines, ploughing their way across the space separating the vessels before crashing hard into the oncoming frigate's angled prow.

The barrage shattered the ship's main void shield aegis and exposed its underbelly. More shells rammed home, one after the other, tearing up hull plates and driving deeper inside.

If they had been conventional armaments, the crippled ship might yet have survived, but these were phosphex shells, triggered on detonation to explode in clouds of metal-eating corrosion. Hundreds of the bombs exploded, flooding the frigate's lower decks with boiling green fogs that churned and hissed their way through solid adamantium. The crew, even those in protective armour, were eaten alive, their atmosphere-filters blown and their eye-masks fizzing. When the corrosion hit the main engine containment units, it took mere seconds to gnaw into the reactors, triggering the explosions that blew the frigate apart from the inside and scattered its still-burning parts across a swathe of space.

On the *Endurance*'s bridge, there was no cheering, no roars of aggression, just a near-silent murmur of satisfaction from Kalgaro. The first kill-rune of the encounter glowed into life on the main status lens.

Mortarion observed the wider theatre of slaying unfold. He watched the V Legion react, pulling back, forming up for the fighting retreat that would bring them into range of their own line battleships. He noted the dimensions of the greater sphere, and the location of the lesser sphere, and the positioning of the Khan's assets between them. Everything was assessed, ordered, gauged and accounted for.

The numbers were in his favour. There was no way out. The hunters had been trapped.

'Run them down,' he ordered, observing with approval the way his commanders brought their heavy battleships in train with the *Endurance*, opening up with their own salvoes of long-proscribed bio-weapons. 'Get me the coordinates of the flagship. That is the target now.'

THE SUZERAIN ACCELERATED hard, driving ahead of the III Legion warships around it. Cario watched them fall back, already diverted by the thousand tiny battles that made up a void war, their commanders fielding a flickering hellstorm of las-beams. He had no such concerns, for his quarry was singular. Every sensorium drone on the ship was now bent towards the same task, ignoring all other targets.

The void around them was already a mass of burning metal. Hemmed in by the aether-clouds, the carnage had been concentrated and brutal. Starships crashed into wheeling wreckage, smashing apart the burning shells and succumbing to the flames themselves. Torpedo volleys scythed through whole nebulae of exploding promethium, igniting as they flew and spraying debris over reeling squadrons of gunships and fighters. The greater ships swam through the midst of it all, lumbering and massive, their hulls already blackened from collisions and lance-hits.

Cario found the experience exhilarating. He relished the swerve of the *Suzerain* as it barrelled ahead, engines roaring. The brothers of his fraternity were already poised to take the boarding-tubes, waiting for the command. The gunnery serfs were primed to unleash the ship's arsenal at his order, though in truth Cario gave little thought to such weaponry, for its only function was to keep him alive long enough to get close.

I will take him with the sabre, he promised himself. *I will rip the metal mask from him and look into his eyes as the killing edge ends him. And before the end I will know his name.*

Above them, a large V Legion destroyer was tumbling towards nadir, its hull punctured with pinpoints of savage light. A slew of pursuing missile-boats followed it down, hammering it brutally and making its void shields shimmer. Below that was an arrowhead formation of gunships, spinning clear of a foundering Death Guard escort.

Harkian, busy overseeing the sensor-crew pits, nodded suddenly in recognition. 'There it is.' He looked up towards the throne. 'The *Kaljian*. We have it.'

'Show me.'

Real-viewers zoomed into a segment of the battle-sphere, cycling past a hundred other craft. The ship was close, heavily engaged at the heart of the fighting, marshalling wings of interceptors in its wake. It was being flown expertly, and had just despatched a vessel of its own size before powering into contact with another. Cario watched it come about, tilting severely, then thrusting at close to full power.

That was better than expert. That was beautiful.

'Lock in coordinates,' he ordered. 'Take us in.'

Even as the *Suzerain* responded, leaping like a hound from the slips, the proximity grid flashed red. Klaxons blared out, forcing Harkian to engage a last minute shift to zenith.

Cario rounded on the source – another III Legion warship, far bigger than the *Suzerain*, powering up underneath them on an intersecting course.

'Hail them!' Cario shouted. 'If they do not give way, loose guns on them.'

Harkian grinned. He was perfectly capable of doing that. In the event, though, the ship barely made any adjustment – just enough to slide into a parallel course, less than five hundred metres below the *Suzerain*.

'What ship is that?' demanded Cario, ready to make the order.

'*Prefector*,' said a voice over the comm-link from the other ship, which was identifying itself as the *Ravisher*. '*Did you not heed the tactical plan I sent? We are to be a unified spearhead, you and I.*'

Konenos. Eidolon's lap-dog. What was this madness?

'You have your battles, orchestrator,' Cario responded, keeping his voice cool. 'We have ours.'

Konenos laughed. '*My brother, this thing is about more than you.*'

The comm-link cut out. The *Ravisher* remained on a parallel trajectory, neither pulling ahead nor dropping back. Together, the two ships carved their way through a shoal of lesser craft, each maintaining the same blistering pace.

'What does he purpose?' asked Harkian, intrigued.

Cario snorted. 'Let him follow, if he needs to. We will outpace him to the prize.'

Far ahead, the cumulative punishment was beginning to tell on the White Scars' formations. They had done what they had come to do – hit the incomers hard on emergence – but now the weight of numbers was against them. They were turning, swivelling tightly on their axes and firing engines for the run home. The *Kaljian* would be no different, though its position left it near the rearguard now, a victim of its headlong race for glory.

'Keep fixed on it,' Cario ordered, watching the frigate loom larger on the real-viewers, already feeling a twitch of febrile excitement. 'No deviation. Konenos can do what he wishes, but that one is ours.'

A SMOOTH ORB of utter blackness rushed out from the epicentre of the vortex detonation, instantly devouring Veil and the closest legionaries. Yesugei, thrown back by the explosive matter-compression wave, hurled everything he had against the rapidly expanding warp bubble. Where his power met the racing event horizon, both energies shattered into flailing tongues of phosphorescent flame, and the fractured chamber blew apart around him.

The vortex effect had already cut through the conduits lining the walls, sending pure promethium gushing into the path of jetting plasma, and an inferno of liquid immolation joined the destructive crescendo, atomising the floor.

Yesugei plunged, crashing through dissolving decking, propelled through the chaos by chain-reaction detonations in the feeder lines around him. Thrown wildly from side to side, he experienced a blurred series of cartwheeling sensations – the receding warp bubble chewing through metalwork in an orgy of destruction, generating fresh bursts of fire as burning physical matter met the raw stuff of the empyrean.

Only the power still humming in his staff had saved him from the initial blast, warding against the full potential of the lone charge, preserving a kernel of psychic defiance amid the howling conflagration. Now, though, as he smashed through collapsing deck-plates, his armour driven in, torn free, his helm ricocheting, the psychic backlash became the greater threat.

He cried out, feeling his exposed flesh begin to bubble, before smashing into solid ground at last, his head cracked back, his staff cleaved in two. He sucked in a flame-hot breath, and coughed it back out, spraying blood up from his seared lungs.

Yesugei rolled over, dragging his tortured frame across a new deck, even as flaming debris from the chambers above rained down around him, thudding and slamming and sending cracks lancing across rockcrete.

He spat out more blood. His helm display splurged into a messy mosaic of bright reds. He crawled on his hands and knees, panting hard, needing to get clear of the rolling waves of sun-hot rubble. He had no idea where he was, no idea which direction was *up* or *down*, only that he had to somehow keep moving, keep breathing, keep his hearts beating. He could feel his genhanced systems trying to repair themselves, and knew then that he had been brutally hurt. The aether's stink pressed in all around him, weighing him down, sending spikes of savage agony lancing through his mind.

Somewhere far above him, explosions were still booming out – there must have been plenty to ignite in that chamber, full of volatile compounds, full of esoteric devices.

He collapsed, his arms skidding out from under him. For a moment, his shaky vision dropped to perfect black and a stifling numbness shot up his limbs. He picked himself up, crawling onwards, dragging himself through the wavering sheets of flame, roaring with defiance as the heat seared his body.

Agonisingly, grindingly, he pulled clear of it. The rain of wreckage fell away behind him and the ferocious heat ebbed. Darkness pooled once more amid the struts and deck-brace columns. He twisted his head and looked back the way he had come.

The fires still thundered, and molten metal cascaded down, framing the black skeleton of Dark Glass' battered underbelly. He tried to send a message, but his helm comm-system was smashed. Something was wrong with his respiratory unit, too. It was ferociously hot. It was freezing.

He crawled on, reaching a circular blast portal, already cracked open by the pressure of the destruction that had been unleashed. He got to his knees, clamping his hands on either slide-door, heaving them apart. It took him four attempts, and each one tore another muscle-bundle. A new light flooded across from the gap, this time composed of many colours. He heard a deep, deep roar from up ahead, like the tide coming in. Then he was through. For a moment, he could see nothing but a whirl of hazy, merged hues dancing in the air.

Slowly, the sensory overload slid away. He managed to regulate his breathing. He pulled himself into a seating position, his back against the inner ring of the blast portal.

He had emerged into the open base of a great shaft.

Above him, empty space soared, climbing back up, up and up into the heart of Dark Glass. Its iron walls shimmered with multicolour. The shaft continued, eventually disappearing into a crackling cloud of discharging energies on the edge of vision.

The decking ahead of him was punctured by pits arranged in a wide circle, and the dancing hues were cast up through their apertures. Without needing to look, Yesugei knew then where he was – directly over the abyss, open to the raw universe-bending corruption of the rift. He had fallen to the very bottom, the foundation of all that had been raised. Under that fragile floor was the great anchor, the metal stave that dropped down into the unfiltered warp, fuelling the abomination that Veil had tried to destroy.

He might yet succeed. Cracks had formed across the walls. Explosions continued, half audible over the roar of the aether, smashing their way through the innards of the station, burrowing like a cancer through the corpse of Achelieux's little empire.

Wincing from pain, Yesugei forced himself to his feet, hauling on the wall behind him to keep from falling. In the centre of the chamber's circular floor was a spire of iron, tangled with coolant ducts and draped with heavy cables like a spider's web. Plasma lightning snapped and slipped against it, licking across the gulf between the walls and racing up the thundering shaft where the warp light refracted.

For the first time, Yesugei saw the truth of it.

The whole place, the whole void station, was a single machine, colossal in scale and form, its mechanisms built into the walls, threaded throughout Dark Glass' entire substance. The place was suffused with the warp.

It channelled it, pulling the raw aether up and into itself, where it fed greedily. Down here, unlike anywhere else on the station, the mighty energy coils glowed, swollen with stored energy of tremendous potency. Here, the valves were active, the cables trembled and the heat exchangers vibrated.

Yesugei began to limp. He fell twice, having to catch himself as he staggered out into the open, heading towards the mountain of iron. He passed the apertures but did not peer over their edges, knowing the unfiltered warp would be visible down there, virulent, malignant.

The iron mountain was grotesque. It could have been xenos, or some nightmare fusion of xenos and human, a hybrid of Martian ambition and alien technotheurgy. Just to look on it made Yesugei nauseous – something about it was uniquely hateful.

At its base, flanked by six mottled granite pillars and crowned with a huge iron aquila, was a single command throne. Thick bundles of cabling threaded into it from all sides, feeding it with power as arteries fed a pulsating heart. The seat itself was greater than mortal dimensions. It had been made for one of the Legiones Astartes, or perhaps for one even greater in stature. Its surface was golden, burnished almost to the red of fire, and its twin arms terminated in the heads of two eagles, one sighted, one blind.

The seat was occupied. A wasted cadaver, open jaws thrown back in agony, sat in place, flaking hands clamped to the arms. Its robes had burned away, exposing charcoal-black flesh stretched tight over desiccated bones. The eyes were gone, seared away, all three of them. The sapphires over its brow had melted, the olive skin crisped to nothing.

Yesugei limped up to the throne's edge. Its power made the air shake.

So this was Achelieux. What had he tried to do?

Achelieux was never charting the warp – he was creating the means to bypass it.

Yesugei remembered the massive, static shock wave the fleet had passed through on the way in – the crystals in the void filled with light. Had the Novator activated his machine? What would that do?

Gates into hell. You are standing on the threshold even now, and still you do not see it.

The throne was the machine, the machine was the throne. It had never been made for mortals.

Only the nominated primarch has the strength to maintain an active link.

Then he understood. He knew what had to be done. Slowly, his bloody hands trembling, Yesugei reached out to pull Achelieux's withered remains from the throne.

TWENTY-TWO

THE KHAN SWEPT up from the docking bays towards the bridge. The corridors were clogged with menials running, many carrying heavy burdens. Warriors of the ordu guided them, driving them harder, pulling those who had fallen to their feet and hurling them back to work.

This was not the way he had ordered his Legion in the past, but he could already see the reason for it. Though free of the worst aether-sickness on the void station, the *Swordstorm* was buzzing with a barely suppressed fever, the kind of madness only borne from warp-exposure. The faces of the mortals were scored with it – a haunted look, etched with the deepest species-fear.

'How close are we to combat?' the Khan asked his escort, Qasahn, one of Namahi's warriors.

'It is already upon us, Khagan,' came the reply. 'Tach-seer falls back to the fleet, and the enemy comes for us in his wake.'

They entered the bridge antechambers, scaling the winding stairs. The air reverberated from the hard growl of plasma engines at full stretch, orientating the flagship and bringing it into optimal position.

When they reached the command bridge, Jubal was waiting.

'Welcome back, Khagan,' he said, bowing, then standing back from the throne.

The Khan made no movement towards it. 'Tell me.'

'We reaped a toll as they came through the barrier. We are now in defensive orientation, and all ships stand ready.'

The Khan studied the tactical displays, then looked up and out through the real-view portals. The White Scars fleet had adopted *khuree* formation – a loose sphere, with the line battleships at the centre surrounded by their flanking escorts. The deployment allowed development of flanks in any direction, responding instantly to the attack pattern of the enemy.

Shiban's ships were already visible to the naked eye, racing back before they could be overwhelmed. Behind them, as yet only a speckled line of silver against the void, came the pursuing vanguard, burning hard to get into contact, their lances flashing sporadically as they sought their range.

Jubal had pulled a long way clear of the crystal sphere, aiming to give the fleet as much room to manoeuvre as he could, and yet the basic situation was lost on no one – they were hemmed in, with nowhere to run to. The enemy stood between them and the Catullus Mandeville points, and any attempt to break back out of the aether barrier while under fire would be ruinous.

The Khan turned away from the vista. Hundreds of

crew worked at their stations, all overseen by Jubal's warriors. The open spaces before the command throne – wide plazas where normally the keshig would have assembled in defence of their lord – was instead occupied by warriors from many brotherhoods, as yet placed in no order, looking like they had only just arrived.

Ilya stood before them, and she was looking back at him strangely – defiant, and a little nervous.

'The sagyar mazan, Khagan,' she said. 'It was not fitting, for them to rot in the void when there was need for warriors here.'

The Khan ran his gaze across the assortment of warriors. They were equipped in wildly different ways. Some wore their old Legion armour, others had taken battleplate from those they had slain. They carried a motley assortment of weapons – bolters, power weapons, straight blades bearing the marks of other Legions. Those with no helm displayed their heritage proudly – the dark skin of the Chogorian, the more varied of the Terran, all marked with the pale scar on the left cheek.

They, too, were wary. He had passed judgement on them a long time ago. Some of their khans he had executed, others he had exiled and were now dead.

He walked up to them, and they waited in silence, none taking a backward step.

'This is a place of honour,' the Khan said. 'You have been given the chance to earn it again.'

Then he was looking at all of them, at Jubal, at Namahi, at Arvida. The Stormseers had assembled there, as had those of the keshig who were not still on Dark Glass.

'So the storm breaks, my brothers,' he said. 'We will meet it together.'

DOWN IN THE depths of the *Proudheart*, the growing sounds of battle made scarce impact on the humid silence. Von Kalda's daemonic nursery had been heavily warded, both from the physical and the metaphysical.

Containment vials, dozens of them, ran down along the inside of the summoning chamber's walls. Each was occupied with a writhing denizen of the warp, thrashing and kicking like a foetus in the womb. Daemon-smoke frosted thickly against the armour-glass now, solidifying, curdling before his eyes.

Von Kalda felt the lines of sweat drip from his forehead as he knelt. The rites had been as hard as anything he had ever known, tearing at his soul with every uttered word and drawn symbol. A hundred slaves had been butchered for every neverborn now shivering in the columns of glass and sorcery.

They whispered in broken half-sounds, coming close to full speech again, growing stronger as the flagship powered its way closer to the warp rift. The daemons could sense its proximity, and their bodily strength swelled as the stuff of reality thinned.

Von Kalda rose to his feet, allowing himself a moment for the dizziness to clear. He dropped his sickle to the floor, where it thudded wetly into the sea of viscera slopping across the stone.

Nearly there, said Manushya-Rakshsasi, as ever the foremost of those that he summoned. *I can feel the gate.*

'Not... yet,' panted Von Kalda, knowing that timing

was everything. They needed mortal souls, vectors for instantiation, and the rites had not been completed. 'Observe.'

He staggered over to a huge altar set into the chamber's walls, a fusion of bioforms and Unity-era technomancy. He placed his palm against a receiving plate, and columns burst into blood-red illumination.

Between them, five metres up into the cloudy smog of the birthing chamber, hololith images spun into existence. Translucent ship-outlines danced about an axis, swimming in and out of close-focus.

'Vessels,' Von Kalda announced. 'Objects of your instantiation.'

Three clusters of shipping could be made out – the main formation of White Scars battleships, the smaller raiding party the *Proudheart* was currently pursuing, and the greater mass of Death Guard and Emperor's Children signals. Von Kalda manipulated the scope of the hololith, zooming close to the rear of the retreating V Legion vanguard. Three ships came into sharp relief – the *Kaljian*, *Ravisher* and *Suzerain*.

Manushya-Rakshsasi studied the lithocast eagerly, its almond eyes narrowing to peer through the swirls within its cage. *Prey.*

'You desired a name. I have marked this soul for you.'

And he is already mighty.

The *Suzerain* was close to its quarry now, shadowed by the larger *Ravisher*. Von Kalda noted just how close Konenos was keeping, barely maintaining enough space between him and Cario's ship to keep the void shields from interacting. It was clear what was happening – the prefector had got close enough to launch boarding torpedoes, and was already raking the fleeing White Scars frigate. The hololith showed the impacts, trembling each time a projectile collided with the *Kaljian's* shielding.

'This will be his apotheosis,' said Von Kalda, beginning to smile. 'He does not yet see the full potential of the Legion, but you will instruct him well, I am sure.'

The *Suzerain* was closer now, pulling in hard on the stern of the slowing *Kaljian*. The chase was almost at its end.

'They have caught the savages,' breathed Von Kalda, sensing the moment come upon him. The embryonic presences thrashed in their containment shells now, readying for the hex to carry them out and into the true world of matter, and he turned to the daemon in triumph. 'Now watch the slaughter.'

You dismiss your enemies too soon.

Von Kalda looked back at the hololith, and saw the truth of it. The White Scars frigate had not slowed because it was damaged – it had slowed to discharge boarding torpedoes of its own. The crew of the *Kaljian* had expended every last morsel of power to gain a breach in the *Suzerain's* forward void shield array, then sent their warriors hurtling back through the void to take on their hunters.

Manushya-Rakshsasi seemed greatly amused by this. *That is good. That is brave.*

Von Kalda rushed back over to the pentagram where he had enacted the rituals, breaking the hololiths as he barged through them. 'This complicates things.'

Warp light began to spin and scamper up the walls, stirring the pools of blood and making them simmer. The embryos hissed, sensing the change in the air. Von Kalda unlocked the last of his runes of power, and the lines of blood across the glass cylinders seethed and spat, evaporating into nothingness, releasing the seals and cutting the shackles that separated the worlds.

'I will give you the names,' he said.

We have the names.

This time more than one voice answered him – a whole choir of them, crystallising out of the aether, their eyes glimmering with refracted other-light. Whipcords, barbed and bloody, scraped across the containment glass, and cloven hooves stamped down amid the dissipating smoke.

A crack sang out across the chamber, resounding from the low ceiling and making the blood-pools ripple. As one, the embryonic daemons launched themselves upwards, swimming like fish in their tanks, their long sinuous bodies snapping in sine waves.

'Not yet!' Von Kalda blurted, stepping clear of the pentagram's protection, trying to call them back. They did not have the soul-patterns, the true names of the sacrificial victims – all they had was the hololiths, the evidence of their addled, matter-blind senses.

But it was too late. Manushya-Rakshsasi was the first to break the fetters, its containment shell bursting into blinding light, making the armourglass flex and crack. The others followed, shrieking in delight, dragged into full corporeality by the agonies inflicted in their name.

Von Kalda ran up to the birthing columns, pressing himself against the shielding. Within them, the spaces were empty, with just curls of dirty smoke slowly falling back to the ground. He looked back, helplessly, to where the hololiths still played out the void-borne drama and tried to ascertain what the daemons had seen, and where they had gone.

Then his eyes alighted on the central warship, the one that had drifted into the heart of the lithocast's roving eye.

'Oh,' he breathed weakly, slumping back against the glass. 'Oh, no.'

THE RAVISHER ROARED up in the *Suzerain*'s wake, firing in support at the listing profile of the *Kaljian*. The void beyond was thick with the star-bursts of munitions and las-fire, crammed with the interweaving paths of hunter and hunted.

Konenos watched from the bridge as Cario's vessel maintained its harrowing assault, pumping volley after volley of ordnance into the *Kaljian*'s retreating stern.

'He really is angry,' Konenos observed, voice thick through the vox-augmitters in his helm.

'Remain in close contact?' Erato asked, tentatively. It was not quite suicidal to stay in such narrow proximity to the thundering starships, but there was little advantage to be gained either.

'Oh yes,' Konenos replied, taking up his power sword. The blade was already humming angrily, vibrating in his grip. 'When Von Kalda gives the command, I wish to be within sight of it. They will be ours to leash – greater weapons than we have ever known, and bound by our words of command.'

The *Ravisher* loosed a full barrage then, denting its onwards progress by only a fraction but nearly annihilating the *Kaljian*'s rearward shield overlays. Below Konenos, down in the terraces beneath his throne, a hundred of Eidolon's Kakophoni waited with barely contained impatience, their armour donned, their psychosonic organ guns whirring in pre-combat build-up. Once the frigate was breached and open, they would be swiftly into the hull, chasing down Cario's fanatics to witness the change overtake them.

'They have launched boarding torpedoes,' said Erato, as if surprised.

'Good,' replied Konenos, barely listening, thinking of the slaughter to come in the narrow corridors.

'No, not the *Suzerain*,' said Erato. 'Its prey.'

Konenos reached out for a tactical lens and hauled it closer. The *Kaljian* had indeed loosed its own brace of torpedoes, which were whistling through an incoming barrage of las-beams to slam into the prow of the *Suzerain*.

He was about to remark on the daring of that, but found that his voice had suddenly stopped working. He tried to speak again, to force out the words, and nothing came. Frustration rising, he turned back to the Kakophoni. All of them were silent too, struggling, reaching up for their vox-grilles and banging the mechanisms.

Erato stared back at them, unsure if a reply had been forthcoming. 'My lord?'

Something very strange was happening. The vox-scream organs in Konenos' throat contracted, sending out a spasm of noise that smashed every lens within ten metres of him. Mortal menials, even those desensitised to extremes, dropped to the floor, their sutured ears bleeding.

Konenos tried to cry out, but his body was no longer obeying his commands. The atmosphere on the bridge ramped up sharply, becoming humid and cloying.

Screams broke out, but they were not from mortal lips. Sensor stations blew and more of the crystal lenses shattered.

By then Erato was shouting something, calling for support, backing away from the Kakophoni. Konenos could barely see a thing, his vision polluted by a blur of raw violet that spilled into his eyes like dye. His hearts went into overdrive, thumping and racing as if they would break out of his straining ribcage.

He staggered backwards, feeling his armour-plates swell and crack. A voice, at first soft, but then rising rapidly in pitch, breathed softly inside his head.

I had you marked from the start, it hissed. *So many gifts, so much to play with.*

Konenos tried to roar out in defiance, to marshal something with which to counter the consciousness that now crowded out his own, bloating like a tumour within his psyche and driving all out save its own madness.

The Kakophoni were on their knees now, their breastplates bursting, sending ceramite chunks clattering across the deck. The *Ravisher*'s mortal crew had taken up weapons and were beginning to use them, but that only hastened the pace of transformation.

Konenos cried out in agony, but no sound emerged. The daemon-soul seared into life, shoving the last of the orchestrator's physical self into oblivion. His outer battleplate exploded outwards, revealing a new, sinuous under-body of violet flesh and black veins. His stature swelled to obscene proportions, until he towered over those around him. Arms, four of them, corded and bound with leather, unravelled in place of his own, and horns erupted, twisting, from the bones of his dissolving face. He took a first step, and instead of a heavy-tread boot, a cloven hoof cracked the decking.

He opened his lungs, and a withering hyper-scream radiated across the bridge, scything through the solid metal around them, powderising rockcrete columns and sending wide crevasses zigzagging across the tilting decks.

All the Kakophoni were the same – expanding, growing, bursting out like parasites from the flaccid bodies of their hosts. They strutted on reverse-jointed legs, crouching obscenely, their long tongues flickering around slender, tooth-filled mouths.

The creature that had once been Konenos, but was now Manushya-Rakshsasi, threw its arms back, shedding the final scraps of armour, and howled in triumph. A long sword curled into being, which it gripped fast. The rest of the daemon-army shrieked back in answer, as graceful, bewitching and lissom as they had once been ponderous. Their eyes flashed with distilled malice, while their voices were unbearable to behold – like the death-screams of entire worlds, rendered down to a single, terrible point of maddening intensity.

Erato backed away, training his bolter on his erstwhile master, firing with typical precision. The shells punched into Manushya-Rakshsasi's exposed flesh, driving in deep and fountaining black blood. The daemon cried out in ecstasy, its pleasure-cries making the lumens shatter and showering it with multi-faceted crystal. It lashed out with its claws, seizing Erato by the neck.

'Brave child,' said Manushya-Rakshsasi, and squeezed.

Erato's neck crushed, the daemon discarded the limp body with a wet thunk.

All across the bridge, daemon-progeny were now let loose. Some capered across the decks, moving faster than any mortal ever moved, their jaws already moist with the hot blood of those in their path. Others rose up like savage angels, their lithe outlines blazing with coronas of lilac, holding the ripped spines of the slain in their claws as trophies. There was no resisting them – their augmented cries shrove the very atoms around them, splitting flesh and withering matter. They fanned out, smashing their way through terraces and delving deep into the servitor-pits.

Manushya-Rakshsasi watched it all unfold, a benevolent smile on its warped, terrible face. Twin claws, borne by its secondary arms, rose high above its tapered skull. Somewhere deep inside it, the one called Azael Konenos was bellowing in mute agony, his soul slowly pulled apart.

'The portal opens,' Manushya-Rakshsasi said, delighting in the echoing sound of its own voice.

Real space itself was coming apart, and the mortals were too slow-sensed to see it. The boundaries that kept the two worlds divided had been eroded, then broken, now bent back on themselves. And in the heart of the tempest were the storm-mages, mortals who dared to summon the elements of the aether to themselves. They were the choicest meats, the sweetened morsels that made eternity bearable.

'Now deliver me the ship, so we may carry ourselves closer,' Manushya-Rakshsasi commanded, feeling its body swell further, grow further, taller and taller, until it dominated the bloody charnel house of the *Ravisher*'s bridge. *'Then we feast.'*

YESUGEI HALTED ONLY once before taking Achelieux's place. He could sense the phenomenal power in the soul-engine, spilling out into the world of the senses like radiation from a reactor. The harmonics shuddered through him, snagging at his very existence, heedless of his physical armour and barely hindered by his psychic mastery.

He was afraid. That ought to have been impossible, such emotions having been banished by his long years of gene conditioning and training – but this thing, this agony-causer, made him fearful. It took a long time before he could kick the last of Achelieux's blasted corpse free of the burnished gold and prepare himself for what had to come next.

All around him, warp light raced and shimmered, surging up the shaft and into nothingness. He could feel the dreadful weight of the anchor below, plunging into a wound in the living universe, and briefly wondered how such a thing could have been built at all. Had *He* been here? Had this been made by Him, during the long years of isolation, or during the war-torn confusion of the early Crusade?

But these thoughts were distraction, desperate attempts to put off what had to be done. Achelieux had tried to open the Gate, and failed. The Novator had been mighty in the lore of the warp, but not a psyker in the true sense. The enormous, static blast wave that still stretched out into space, the crystal sphere around the station, all of it must have been caused when Achelieux had attempted to command the power of the throne.

Only the nominated primarch has the strength to maintain an active link.

A primarch. One of the Eighteen, each with his role, each with his purpose. Which one, then? A psyker-lord, surely. Magnus, perhaps? Or Lorgar? Maybe the Angel, or the seer Kurze? Or had this been abandoned, an experiment intended to be forgotten and only uncovered when the lines of communication were broken? The questions remained, clustering fast, all unanswerable.

He was vacillating again. Whatever the truth, the throne's intended recipient would never sit in place now, and in that at least Achelieux had been right. To even contemplate taking on the machine, attempting to use it, that felt like pride, or madness, or despair.

And yet, what else remained? Yesugei could already sense the deaths in the void, hundreds of them, soon to be thousands. The Legion's strength was being bled from it, far from where it needed to be, spilled out in a conflict that would do nothing to hinder the Warmaster's advance.

Yesugei edged closer to the throne. He slowly turned, feeling its malign heat run up his spine. He placed his hands on the two arm-rests, curling his fingers over the eagle-heads, gripping tight.

Then he took his place.

Until that moment, there had been no true pain, just what mortals called *pain* – the fleeting bodily damage that could either be healed, endured, or which resulted in death. This was different. This was an all-consuming, all-embracing hell of sensation, ripping out his soul and tearing it from his body, scouring what remained and flaying the last dregs of self into a howling, screaming ghost of memory.

Yesugei's head snapped back, locked against the metal just as Achelieux's had been. He screamed, his lungs emptying, but the sound was drowned in his ears by the boom and rush of breaking thunder. His hands and feet clamped down tight, locked into place by the throne's god-humbling power. For a moment, perhaps a long time, he thought it would kill him instantly. The fury of the warp, sucked up by the machine, augmented, altered and bent by its arcane innards, was thrust out *through* him, hurled up the shaft and out into the colossal maze of vanes and energy coils above. He felt his body burning, consumed like fuel. He felt his mind being flensed open, his soul dissipated. Nothing, *nothing*, had ever compared to the horror – the hurricane of agony, the bellowing maelstrom of infinite, abominable power.

The throneroom around him disappeared, to be replaced by a boiling mass of broken colour.

He saw a vast, flat plane run away from him, erupting like water, bisected by lightning and tormented by eruptions from within. Then he was soaring far above it, disembodied, dissipated, a mere spectre against the face of eternity.

He saw lights within the Seethe, pinpoints of intensity amid a roiling mass of soul-fire, and saw that they were worlds, millions of them, flung across the immensity of creation. He saw glittering paths between those worlds, some massive and filled with brilliance, others faint smears that meandered into nothingness.

His mortal body was still screaming. His flesh was

still burning. His soul was being drained away, eaten up, dragged into oblivion by the hyperpower of the throne unlocked.

He rose higher, and, through the agony, perceived patterns in the chaos. There was movement amid the light-channels – the passage of many souls, burning through the immaterium. He saw great armies marching, ranked like the cavalries of old, vast formations that had swelled beyond anything seen at Ullanor. They were all heading in the same way – towards the greatest point of light, set in the far galactic west, where all the glittering conduits met.

Above that world shone a mighty beacon, piercing and vivid, though faltering as the tempest swarmed in on it. The armies drew closer with every pulse of the galaxy's heart, strangling it, riding the riptide of the warp towards the setting of the siege.

There was a second throne on that world, like the one he sat on, though far greater, immensely more powerful, older, fouler, set deeper into the fabric of both reality and unreality. That throne, *the* Throne, was thrust into the heart of the aether, its roots going down and down, branching into the foundations under the shimmering veil of light.

There are layers. There is stratum aetheris, the shallow ways. There is stratum profundis, the greater arteries, plunging deeper. There is stratum obscurus, the root of the terror.

How does this help you? No living man can navigate the deep ways. Even he could not.

Veil's words came back to him in fragments, like an old dream. He could no longer envisage the man's face. He could no longer envisage his own.

You can see the Cartomancer's light. You can follow it. Go deeper, and the aegis shatters. The lights go out. The Eye is blinded. The deeper in, the worse the poison.

He perceived the truth. Both thrones had been made for the same reason – to plumb the deeper ways, to free the species from the nightmare of the shallow warp, to bridge a link across the hidden paths, ones that only xenos had known, and which the Emperor had found some way to access. Dark Glass was the lesser node, the one where the technology had been tested, anchored in the furthest recesses of the void while the Great Crusade scoured its widening path ever further from the home world. In the chaos that had erupted since, the portal had been left behind, lost but not forgotten, neither by its creators nor its opponents in the labyrinthine halls of the Paternova.

The way had already been opened on Terra, uncontrolled and damaged. Yesugei could see it clearly, bleeding like a severed artery, its ragged edges swarming with the warp-made-flesh, yaksha in their millions. There ought to have been a soul on the Throne above it, guarding it, able to complete the link between worlds, but the seat was empty.

To reach out to Terra – that was what Achelieux had tried to do, to open a path through the stratum profundis. No storms could block those ways, for they ran beyond the known, into the deeps of oblivion where only the ghosts of slain xenos gods sullenly lingered.

Ilya had been right. There was a path, albeit an incomplete one.

With all that remained of his self, knowing the peril, knowing the pain, Yesugei reached out into the throne, delving into its unholy complexity. He saw the energy banks within it burning like starlit nebulae. He felt its cold, mechanical spirit, pitiless and enduring, and knew it could be mastered, if only for a moment.

His lips were gone, charred to ashes. His eyes were burned away, his fingers melted in their ceramite casing, but still the strength remained, just enough, just sufficient for what needed to be done.

Sending his impending word of command, the throne exploded into golden light. Terrible energies unshackled, and the chamber about him broke apart, thrust open by the release of the primeval forces within. Columns of warp fire surged up the empty station shaft, smashing and gnawing through the many decks above and shattering the curved spars of black iron.

Yesugei reached out. First, he touched three minds, three living souls. That was for courtesy.

Then, with the last word spoken from his physical mouth, he gave his final command.

'Open.'

TWENTY-THREE

ARVIDA STOOD WITH the Legion's Stormseers, readying them for the action to come. None of them doubted that the enemy would board if it could, and the taint of yaksha had already been sensed. There were nine shamans on the *Swordstorm* and a few others stationed on the capital ships, and all were preparing themselves for the trial ahead. The Chogorians slowly mouthed the ritual words of the plains, letting the elemental powers of weather-magic swell in their veins.

Arvida retained his own rites. He rose up through the Enumerations, heedless now of the danger to his body. If the Change were fated to take him, then there was little loss, for he had seen all the outcomes of the war, thrown before him like the battered cards of his old master's tarot. Jaghatai had been correct, after a fashion – all that remained was defiance, but what that choice would entail, beyond the faint hope of temporary survival, was still unclear to him.

Out in the void, weight of numbers was beginning to tell. The abyss was aflame, punctured by the dying, falling corpses of mighty warships. The *Swordstorm* would be under assault imminently, just as soon as the enemy's core battleships could fight their way into close quarters.

Arvida was high in the Enumerations when the mind-voice first stirred. It startled him, for in that state he should have been inviolable.

But then Targutai had always been more powerful than he let on.

+*They will need a guide, brother,*+ came a strained psychic voice, laced with agony but still recognisably his. +*The way will be dark, and only you have the Sight.*+

+Where are you?+ Arvida sent back, suddenly alarmed. In all that had happened, with all its speed and fury, he had not thought for a moment that Yesugei was in danger.

+*Navigators will be no use.*+

The pain was heartbreaking, tangible even in Arvida's mind.

+*You will need to control the sickness just a little longer, I think.*+

Then the voice was gone, snatched away as if seized by a clenched fist.

Arvida snapped out of his meditations. Far away, across the bridge, the mortal woman Ravallion was shrieking uncontrollably. A surge of fear welled up within him, as profound as it had been when he had seen Prospero darkened for the first time.

He reached out desperately, trying to find Yesugei, to make contact, to save whatever was left – there was always a way.

Then the viewports went white, blazing with cold fire.

ILYA STOOD AMONGST the sagyar mazan. They were being issued with storm shields and power weapons by *Swordstorm*'s armoury crew, accepting the equipment with a kind of calm reverence. She had never doubted her choice, but this satisfied her – the forsaken had returned to the Legion, wishing only to fight for it, and now the moment had come.

Torghun stood at their head. He had yet to don his helm and was staring out through the viewports at the void battle beyond. A kind of fierce yearning burned in his eyes – the desire to see that battle come to him, to give him the last fight he craved, one free of shame or uncertain loyalty.

She was about to speak to him. She was about to tell him not to blame Shiban, who had been wounded deeply and might recover, given time, just as he had done.

But she stopped before reaching him. She suddenly felt a pulse within her mind, deep in the core of her being. Yesugei was there, standing behind her. She whirled around, but saw nothing.

+*I would have sheltered you, if I could,*+ the voice said, and something within it gave away an almost unbearable agony, and it made her want to cry out loud. +*You above all, for you were our soul.*+

Panic gripped her. 'Where are you?' she cried.

+*Do not grieve. We were made to do this, szu. We were made to die.*+

Then the voice was gone. The withdrawal was like a savage kick to the body, hitting her hard and driving her back.

'Not you!' she screamed out, incoherently, twisting one way then the other, as if she could see him still, standing over her as he had done on Ullanor, invincible, smiling. 'Not you! *Anyone* but you!'

Torghun raced over to her, menials reached her and held her up, but the tears were already streaming down her face, hot and angry, and she lashed out with her fists as if at her enemies.

Then the viewports went white, blazing with cold fire.

THE KHAN STOOD alone as the battle closed in around them. Reports of ship losses ran down the interior of his helm, one after the other.

He had fought to prevent this for so long. He had kept his sons alive against the fury of massed enemies, preserving the chance to reach the Throneworld. Now the end had come, the passage remained closed, and the failure wore at him.

His brother was close now, rampaging through the burning ships to reach him. That, at least, was something to cling to. During all the years of evasions, he had nurtured the memory of the clash amid Magnus' broken pyramids, and had always known that it would return to be concluded. They were soul-enemies now, bound together by fate, and it was impossible that they should not have their duel resumed before the end.

Yesugei had foreseen it. He had told the Khan, long ago, of the dreams that had plagued him all the way from Chogoris to Prospero, of the great creature of darkness rising up to engulf them.

But as soon as Jaghatai thought of the Stormseer,

a chill ran through him. His mind switched from thoughts of the war. He turned from his throne towards the sensorium master.

The command – *locate Yesugei* – died on his lips. With a synchronicity that could not have been random, the Stormseer's mind-voice was suddenly there, though wracked by agony.

+*In the beginning, I was Shinaz,*+ Yesugei said, managing to convey some kind of broken humour amid the pain. +*Remember that? You named me.*+

'Do not do it,' the Khan murmured, his mind racing, guessing at last what had happened. The machinery, the under-Palace, the absence of his Father from the war – with sudden, terrible clarity, the pieces fell into order. 'This is my command. Do *not* do it.'

+*The deep ways are perilous, and yaksha will thrive in it. You are their protector.*+

The Khan was moving then, striding down from the command throne. The teleporters might be usable, even now. 'Targutai, this will end you. Do *not* do it. Return to the ship.'

+*Know that I would have followed you to the end, my lord. I would have stood beside you on Terra. When I am gone, do not let them forget. Do not let them become what is hateful.*+

'Come back...'

+*You are their protector.*+

Then he was gone, wrenched out of existence.

Jaghatai staggered, slipping to one knee. The world seemed to sway, knocked from its axis. He looked up, and the entire bridge was tilting, falling. Ilya was screaming, the Prosperine sorcerer was crying aloud, the warriors of the sagyar mazan were looking out to the void, ushering in the final battle. His Legion was dying, thrust at last into the forge-fire of war, out of space, out of time.

He was *gone*. Hasik, Qin Xa, now Yesugei, the only link to the world he had forged when all that had existed was the plains and the sky and the thousand kingdoms between them.

I still need *you*.

The Khan cast his head back, his imperious reserve broken open. He clenched his fists to the heavens, and howled out his rage and his grief, and for a sparse moment there were no more sounds, no more thoughts – only the black thunder of a primarch's mortal fury.

Then the viewports went white, blazing with cold fire.

DARK GLASS IMPLODED. The central reactor flared, sending a crimson jet thundering through the crackling upper chambers. Bursts of vivid witch-light pulsed down the warp anchor, spearing directly into the heart of the rift. When they impacted, the void itself ignited into brilliance.

A sweeping wave tore outwards from the throne, devouring all in its lightning-crowned path. The crystal sphere was shattered from the inside, exploding in a hail of glittering glass shards. Their pent-up energies were suddenly released, fuelling the inferno further, ripping physical space apart, pulverising its ancient harmonies.

A colossal *boom* echoed out across void that was no longer true vacuum, and the rush of a billion mortal shrieks surged into aural instantiation. Real space rippled and shredded, exposing the multi-hued madness that seethed beneath the weft of the galaxy.

The base of the void station remained – a sphere of ink-black iron around the throne, spinning wildly like a pulsar, surrounded by a racing tempest of fire and aether-light. Plumes of silver shot out from its poles, lacerating the shreds of reality, flaying matter from its anchor.

The shock wave smashed through the starships battling far above the void station, sweeping over them in a deluge of static. Lesser craft were tossed like boats in a hurricane, sent rotating wildly amid the roar of unlocked power. Even the greatest, the Gloriana-class beasts and the line battle-barges, were driven hard by the onslaught, their outer hulls scoured, their void shields harrowed.

Unhindered, the wave swept onwards, picking up speed as it hurtled clear of the epicentre, propelled by what sounded like the massed choirs of species-screams. In its wake came swirls and billows of red-tinged smoke, punctuated by the half-perceived outlines of eyes or teeth or ravening claws.

The remnants of Dark Glass disappeared, devoured by the maelstrom Yesugei had summoned. Real space was consumed around it, rendered down into the bottomless maw of the infinite. In its place was birthed a far greater warp rift, laced with golden fulguration, gaping obscenely. Arcs of aether-matter lashed and dragged across the face of it, and the fire at its edges thundered as if fed by oxygen rather than souls.

The diameter of the newborn rift was far greater than the diameter of Achelieux's first attempt. This was a funnel down into the warp that could encompass an

entire battlefleet. Its walls were like that of a whirlpool, racing and concentric, flickering with spears of
electric discharge. Its base remained far beyond view,
but the horrific un-light – all shades and none, extending far beyond mortal senses – welled up out of it,
cascading into the world of the living like bile hurled
up from some gorged galactic throat.

The remains of the physical universe around the
edge of the rift shuddered, flexed and shivered. Fresh
explosions kindled, green-edged and violet-hearted,
wedged between the furious battle of elemental forces.
Somewhere in all that maelstrom, Yesugei's will still
lingered, maintaining the last dregs of psychic command. As the remains of the throne were smashed and
pulled apart, scattered across the planes of madness
by the vengeful aether, that will diminished, thought
by thought, dream by dream.

Arvida recovered his senses first. Like most of the
bridge personnel, he had been hurled to the deck by the
impact of the shock wave, his mind filled with massed
psychic clamour. He clambered to his feet, looking up
at the screens filled with hissing white noise, the servitors hanging limp in their fused mind-impulse cages,
the cogitators sparking. Warning klaxons were blaring
across all levels, and the flagship was clearly drifting,
its grav-compensators working erratically.

The Khan alone had not been felled, and knelt invi-
olate upon the command dais, staring into the maw
of the rupture. There was a look of drawn horror on
his lean face.

Perhaps he could sense the truth of it. Arvida cer-
tainly could – he could sense the hole in reality
Yesugei had torn, and could feel the light and heat

of the mortal realm draining into it. The path ran
deep, plunging into the very flesh of the warp and
penetrating a web of conduits beyond. The complexity was dizzying, almost beyond the capacity of the
human mind to comprehend.

They will need a guide.

'Khagan!' he called out.

As if waking from a nightmare-plagued sleep, the
Khan stood, and turned towards him.

'This is it,' Arvida said, walking towards him. 'The
Path of Heaven. He has opened it. There will never
be another chance.'

The Khan was sluggish, his mind elsewhere. The rest
of the bridge crew recovered themselves, restoring systems that had been primed for imminent attack. Out
across the aether-wracked vacuum, the enemy were
similarly recovering.

'My lord, we must take it.' Arvida was conscious of
the danger. The Change still pawed at him, prowling around the edges of his self, watching for any
weakness. The portal was the warp in its rawest, deepest form. It would be murderous, but it had to be
attempted.

'You saw no victory,' said the Khan.

'I did not.'

The primarch stared at the recovering scanner
screens, at the enemy fleet that was bearing down on
them again, barely halted by the tumult across the
fabric of space. 'Then the choice remains.'

Ilya burst between them then. The trails of angry
tears were wet on her cheeks. 'There is *no* choice!' she
hissed, her eyes flashing with anger. '*He* did this. Honour him. *Take the path!*'

Still he hesitated. The battleships were turning back towards them. Lascannons had started up again, slicing across the warp-lit abyss. The *Endurance* had carved its way into range, immolating anything that dared to block its passage. It was on the edge of sight now, unmagnified, colossal, its coming marked by spoilation and heralded by despair. Only one ship could hope to stand against it.

If the Legion turned now, if the order were given, then the retreat would be a bloodbath. Something needed to hold the line.

'I have to face him,' the Khan said, quietly.

'You do not!' raged Ilya, her grief making her wild.

'Lord, if you fight him, the chance will be gone,' urged Arvida. 'There will be other days.'

'Not for Targutai!' roared the Khan, suddenly bursting into fury. 'Not for Xa! My warriors have died for me, this day, and every day since my whoreson brother ignited this treachery. I have watched them die, year by year, their strength taken from them. No further! I will slay him, if I do nothing else.'

Arvida waited for the tirade to subside. To withstand the rage of an Emperor's son, even one cast into doubt by grief, was no trivial feat, yet he never moved away.

'The way is clear,' he said. 'I can guide us, if you let me.' He paused, breathing hard, knowing the peril. The rift was already beginning to close, its edges falling away back into real space as Yesugei's soul was consumed. 'Our destiny is on Terra. *Your* destiny is on Terra.'

A tense silence fell across the bridge, broken only by the sounds of battle-preparation from the decks below. Ilya waited, desperate, her face white. Torghun and the other sagyar mazan waited, still armed, making no move. Arvida waited. The council of Stormseers waited, as did Jubal and the assembled keshig.

The primarch looked out into the heart of the warp rift. He looked out at the onrush of the enemy. His hand strayed to the hilt of his tulwar, and still he said nothing.

No one moved. The maelstrom churned, sucking matter into its ravening jaws. The Death Guard came into lance-range, and the first tracks of macrocannon blasts appeared on the augurs.

The Khan did not look at Arvida. He did not look at Ilya, nor at Namahi, nor at Jubal.

Eventually, he turned to Taban.

'Order all ships into the rift, full burn,' he said.

Then his gaze strayed to the real-view ports, to where Mortarion's flagship loomed ever larger, a silhouette of decay against the tempest of the warp.

'But not this one,' the Khan ordered. 'Set course. Intercept the *Endurance*.'

TWENTY-FOUR

THE BROTHERHOOD OF the Storm smashed their way into the *Suzerain*, riding hard in the wake of torpedo strikes that had punctured the enemy's void shields and left the way clear to break the hull. The tubes crunched in deep, launched true, driving far into the ship's carcass. Three hundred warriors burst clear of the capsules, shoving aside burning launch-hatches, reaching for weapons and racing to rendezvous with their battle-brothers.

Jochi led one flank, fighting his way up from the lower foredecks. Yiman led another, taking a party deep into the under-hull. Shiban led the central charge, gathering his warriors about him and forcing a passage along the main grav-train artery towards the bridge.

They went like white ghosts, cutting through the crew in a whirl of blades and bolt-shells, picking up momentum as they raced. The mutants and the fleshweaver-twisted swarmed into them, blocking the narrow ways with their brutalised bodies, but they were hacked down before they had even got their battle-cries out of their scarified throats.

Shiban pushed himself hardest. The enemy rose up, and he cast them down, never pausing, never hesitating. His guan dao flew about him, blurred with disruptor lightning, a satellite that whirled and danced. Every movement gave him pain, but it was a pure pain now. For the first time in a long time, he was on the offensive. There would be no feints or false moves – this was the end, the clash of those who had remained faithful with those who had sunk into perversion.

He was fast, then, as fast he had ever been. He drove his metal armour-shell beyond its limits, powering into combat as if this were the Last Day and no more battles remained to be fought.

The first Emperor's Children Space Marines loomed out of the hazy murk, lumbering into contact, firing as they came. Shiban swivelled, still running, letting the shells sweep past him, before slamming bodily into the first of his enemy.

'*Khagan!*' Shiban roared, smacking the hilt of his glaive into the warrior's chest and sending him staggering. He followed up, slashing left, then right, carving the legionary open. The glaive rotated, arcing point-down, and Shiban grabbed it two-handed. 'Faithless,' he hissed, punching it down, jabbing the disruptor-charged blade through the armour and straight into the deck beneath.

His enemy spasmed, blood gushing up the length of the stave, then went still. Then Shiban was on the move again, heading up the charge of his brothers, carving a path through the ranks of resistance. They swept into a wide hall, decked in gilt embossing and lapis lazuli. Bolter-fire rained down on them, blowing the marble decks into spiralling flecks. The White Scars leapt and swung, responding preternaturally fast, returning fire and sprinting to where their blades could meet those of the enemy's.

Shiban charged towards two more of them, each bearing the charnabal sabre. They moved just as he did – graceful, driven by exacting velocity. They were disciplined, fighting in tight order, but he was as wild as the storm. The guan dao swung fiercely, just on the edge of flying from his grasp before he reeled it back in. Its energy-seared edge cracked through ceramite, knocking a sabre away from its owner's grip. The second Palatine Blade thrust back, taking advantage of the opening, only to be blocked by a new blade – a tulwar, rammed between the artisan steel and Shiban's trailing arm.

Jochi, emerging from clouds of blown marble-dust, spat a hard laugh. 'They are too good for that,' he voxed. 'One at a time, my khan.'

Shiban laughed back – a deep laugh, the sound not marked by scorn. 'Together, then.'

He and Jochi fought side by side after that, step by step, smashing the Palatine Blades back in stages. The enemy fought well – ridiculously well, matching their every stroke with a frenzied set of counters and parries – but Shiban had the fire again, burning in spite of the deadening of his false muscles and steel sinews. 'Hai, Chogoris!' he roared, smacking the glaive in a wide arc, clattering the facing sabre out wide.

Jochi struck, thrusting his blade into the gap, ramming it up steep and catching the Palatine Blade in his exposed armpit. He shoved the tulwar further, and Shiban brought his guan dao back round, lashing it heavily, nearly taking the enemy's helm off, gashing deep into his neck and digging out the flesh. The Palatine Blade fell at last, limbs jerking, and Jochi finished him off.

Then they were running again, all of them, hundreds strong, swarming through the halls and storming the corridors. The fighting was close-hemmed, as brutal as it was artful. The Emperor's Children had the numbers, and this was their ship, and they fought with the vigour and arrogance of those with surety of the greater victory.

But the brotherhood had been held back for too long, condemned to a running war that always defeated them, set against numbers that were ever too large, too overwhelming, a swamp of corrupted humanity that just kept on coming. Now they were free again, drawn together, given licence to do what they had been bred for.

'Jaghatai!' bellowed Shiban, and his helm amplified the war-cry so it made the jewelled chandeliers above shake.

'*Khagan!*' came the response from the minghan kasurga, the Brotherhood of the Storm, just as it had rung out on Ullanor, and Chondax, and a hundred other worlds of the Legion's wide and savage ambit.

They were on the cusp. The *Suzerain*'s bridge drew closer, blocked only by the approach halls, each one crammed with retreating Emperor's Children forces, mustering for a decisive clash. The attackers broke into a silver-lined chamber, dome-roofed, mirror-walled. That place was wide enough to accommodate hundreds of defenders, and so they had clustered there, ranked against the wide stone stairways and arranged around the gilded feet of the enormous columns. The Palatine Blades made up the central bloc, formed into phalanxes, supported by teams of mortal troops bearing las-weapons. Their bolters thundered in unison, pulverising the walls behind the racing White Scars and sending the door lintels crashing down. The mirrors shattered and the silver-edges melted into bubbling streaks.

Shiban's forces stumbled under the massed assault, breastplates burst inwards, helms blown apart, but others raced up to take the places of the fallen, vaulting to gain fire angles, skidding across the ruins and firing back. They wove through the storm of shells, riding the hits and adding their own layers to the chorus of destruction.

'For the Khan!' Jochi cried, his voice cutting through the roar and rush of battle. 'For Tachseer!'

They forced their way up towards the stairway, driving onwards in a blurred mass of ivory and red. When they closed with the ranks of Palatine Blades, the boom of bolters was overlaid with the glittering clang of powerblades. Yiman's warriors broke right, hacking their way up the far flank of the chamber. Jochi remained with Shiban, and together they hammered a path up the centre, supported by heavy ranged fire from warriors who poured through the great doors at the rear.

It was Jochi who was the fastest, out-pacing even his master in fervour. He sprang up the lower stairs,

barging aside a looming Emperor's Children legionary
and sending him sprawling into the onrushing wave
of his battle-brothers.

That only exposed the next in line, a champion
with a lacquered violet-and-blue face mask wielding
a charnabal sabre one-handed. Jochi leapt to engage
him, recovering well from the initial impact and hauling his tulwar in a whistling arc.

But it was over contemptuously quickly. The prefector took one stroke to rip Jochi's blade from his
grip, and a second to swipe the edge across his gorget,
cutting through the cables and lacerating the throat
within. Jochi crumpled to his knees, gasping through
a mouthful of blood, before a final stroke sent him
crashing face-down on the stair.

Shiban reached him too late, lunging to prevent
the final sabre-blow. He slammed his glaive upwards,
catching the prefector on the parry and throwing him
backwards. The Palatine Blade withdrew, as did those
around him. White Scars pursued them up the stairs,
their fury honed to a white heat, surging over Jochi's
body and driving the III Legion fighters ever higher.

'I know you,' hissed Shiban, his glaive-blows heavier,
impelled now by black rage. He was back on the bulk
carrier's bridge then, fighting to hold ground before
the Stormbirds came.

'I have hunted you since Memnos,' came the reply,
giving away an almost childlike delight. 'What are you
named, steel-helm?'

Shiban pushed on, wielding the glaive like a warhammer, blunt and fast, his vision edged with the raw
crimson of battle-rage. 'You wish to know my name?'
he spat, lashing out wildly, catching his enemy as he

tried to match the pace. 'Tamu, of the plains.' The blades flew, flailing trails of plasma. 'Tachseer, of the Legion.' The speed ramped up, the impacts ramped up, the world dissolved into a haze around them. 'Shiban Khan, of the Brotherhood of the Storm.'

He jabbed upwards, viciously, smashing his enemy in the chest and unleashing a blaze of disruptor-release. The prefector was thrown back up the stairs, dragging a gouge through the stone. Shiban went after him, panting like a wolf, giving no respite.

'But you need not these names, oathbreaker,' he rasped, bloodily, hungrily. 'For you, I am only retribution.'

THE ENDURANCE SWAGGERED into the centre of the battle-plane, high above the imploding portal. Its heavy flanks still sparked from the aftermath of whatever forces had been detonated in the heart of the warp well. In its wake the Death Guard rallied, swiftly joined in support by their more febrile cousins. The twin fleets swivelled back into the attack, powering up to attack speed. The raging void, running like wildfire, was etched again with las-strikes, and the behemoths of the abyss turned their baleful weapons systems onto fresh targets.

The *Proudheart* tacked towards the zenith, loosing volley after volley, hammering the retreating V Legion lines with a studied accuracy. The Death Guard retained the centre ground, their warships forging a straight path and aligning lances towards the central defensive mass ahead.

The *Endurance* was the greatest of them, the most immense, the most lethal, the most secure. Its guns had already consigned a dozen enemy vessels to destruction, and more swam into its sights with every moment. Colossal lance-coils thrummed at a furious, superheated pitch; phosphex-feeders belched their boiling contents into iron-rimmed launchers; dispersal torpedoes were hauled into dispatch-tubes by a thousands-strong army of serfs, straining in the eternal heat, the eternal humidity, the endless filth and dark and toil.

From the bridge, Mortarion watched his enemies fall back, still fighting but no longer contesting void-volume. The rupture beyond them circled rapidly, ringed with an aegis of silver fire. Many were trying to turn as the ordnance of the twofold fleet's arsenal scythed into them, but not all. Soaring above the yawning chasm, a lone battleship rose to defy the slaughter. This one was as vast as the *Endurance* but far leaner – a thoroughbred, its jowls as spare and austere as a hunting dog. Its white prow was marked with the patina of war, but still bore the lightning strike in faded gold, and its lances glowed with the savage illumination of pre-ignition.

'My brother does not run,' said Mortarion, curling his fingers around the haft of Silence. 'Yes, that is as it should be.'

The Death Lord swept down from his throne, and the silent entourage came in his wake.

'Concentrate all fire on the flagship,' Mortarion ordered, heading towards the teleporters. 'Break it open. I care not for the rest of his rabble – deliver that one to me.'

Kalgaro relayed the command. Soon every Death Guard ship broke from its attack, pulling away and turning to intercept the oncoming *Swordstorm*. Torpedo tracks raked out, snaking from all quarters and zeroing in on the lone flagship. With no escorts to protect it, the *Swordstorm* took the hits, one after the other, smashing into every void shield zone and bathing the entire length of its hull in rippling explosions.

Still it came on. Its guns burned, hurling rounds into the flickering void. The rate of fire was tremendous – a cycle of devastation that smashed into the gathering packs of XIV Legion hunters, cracking prows and puncturing hull-spines.

It was burning towards its sister vessel. Eschewing all thoughts of sanctuary or preservation, the Gloriana-class monster was ploughing a fiery path straight at its tormentor. The shipmastery was impeccable – it rolled and dipped through the waves of plasma and burning promethium, shepherding its remaining strength even as the wounds came in – shuddering wounds, dragged up from the depths of the XIV's proscribed vaults of terror-weapons.

It should have been halted. By rights, even that mighty starship should not have made it into the *Endurance*'s ambit, but somehow, whether by guile, fortitude or merely through bloody-minded determination, the *Swordstorm* crashed its way through the combined assault of the system-murderers the *Indomitable Will* and the *Reaper's Scythe*. Flank gunnery blazing, it knocked both of them back in a welter of macrocannon hits, immolating shield plates and overloading thrusters.

The movement was neither mad nor suicidal – the concentration of fire on the *Swordstorm* had bought time for the bulk of the V Legion to escape to the warp rift's lip, pursued now only by Eidolon's forces. And yet it had not been bought easily. The flagship's hull was blackened and cobwebbed with cracks. Its void shields flickered, tearing away at the edges, and its over-laboured engines trailed long plumes of red-tinged smog into the vacuum.

Mortarion took his place on the teleporter pads. He could still view progress through the forward viewers, watching as his enemy's fortress burned. Until that moment, the *Endurance* itself had not fired, but then the primarch gave the gesture to Kalgaro, and the flagship's full, devastating power was finally unleashed.

Lance-strikes shot out, the beams as vivid as young suns, angled at the very centre of the *Swordstorm*'s superstructure. A rain of explosive projectiles – vortex charges, corrosion clusters, iron-eaters – peppered the void, cracking into the target in driving waves. In their wake came more beam weapons, mass-drivers, and everything that the armourers could deliver, all in a single, rolling, barrage of utter destruction.

The *Swordstorm* did not enter that arena without doling out pain of its own. It fired back, and the full complement of the flagship's arsenal remained fearsome. Its missiles speared out, shooting through the blooms of plasma and smacking into the circling hulls of its pursuers. Its lascannons flashed in a never-ending strobe-pattern, draining every generator on board to maintain a thicket of adamantium-melting intensity.

And yet, when the *Swordstorm* finally came through *Endurance*'s assault, it was already half broken, its void shield coverage fizzing into nothingness, its atmosphere venting. Like some mortally wounded aurox, it surged up from the mire of drifting smoke, still vast, still intact, but weakening rapidly.

'Enough.' Mortarion's command was a single word, barely whispered, but the barrage stilled. The Death Guard forces loomed close on all sides, barring any escape, but their guns fell silent. 'Clear the path.'

The *Endurance* launched the coup de grace – a lone lance-beam that leapt eagerly from the battleship's spinal macro-barrel, searing across the gulf between the two flagships before slamming into the *Swordstorm*'s burning bridge-spire. As its void shields exploded, the devastation briefly outshone the warp rift itself. The *Swordstorm* shuddered, rocking on its axis, halted in its onward charge. Secondary explosions daisy-chained down the length of the gunwales, blasting out hull-plating and sending fresh debris tumbling.

'Fix locus,' commanded Mortarion, his old hearts thudding hard, his grip on Silence tighter, the anticipation both toxic and sweet. 'And take us over.'

The Deathshroud assumed their places, twelve of them, their scythes glowing with pale disruptor fields. Many more Legion warriors took position in other transporter stations, their Cataphractii armour glinting dully under glaring lumens. All told, three hundred would make the first passage – the best of the Legion, a fitting bodyguard for the primarch – and more would follow on their heels.

Mortarion felt the sudden heat of the teleport-column cycling up to full power, then the surge of warp-rending metaphysics. The bridge before him disappeared, lost behind a blinding screen of white.

The heat turned to extreme cold, the fractured, brief

shriek of aether-passage, and then the world of the
senses came racing back.

His boots crunched into solid ground, and the curtains of silver ripped away.

The primarch tensed, gripping Silence two-handed
and whirling around, ready for the thunder of bolters. His Deathshroud fanned out, their helm-lenses
glowing a pale green, each one of them prepared to
weather the storm.

Nothing came back at them. The Swordstorm's bridge
was empty, its thrones deserted, its halls echoing. As
the last clangs of the teleport-beams died away, the
silence swelled up, spilling over the banks of flickering lumens and empty tactical lenses.

Mortarion moved warily, his skin taut with alertness.
'My brother!' he called out, peering into the shadows.

He reached the command throne. It too was empty.
Severed power cables sent flares of light tripping
through the dark, but no living thing rose to contest him.

The Deathshroud followed, making no noise but for
the low grind of their ancient armour and the tread
of their iron-rimmed boots. Mortarion turned back
from the throne, his fury now stoked beyond reason.

'He *runs* from me!' the primarch thundered, cracking the heel of his manreaper into the marble and
breaking it open. 'Find him! Get me after him – time
enough remains to locate his spoor.'

But no teleporter beam came burning into existence to carry him away. Across the empty servitor-pits,
cogitator screens suddenly shook into life. All across
the bridge, the Swordstorm's void shields snapped into
being again, furling back across cracked armourglass

real-viewers like thrown gauze, preventing any external locus from being imposed. From down below, the sound of engines kicking back into life made the decks tremble, and great lumen-banks blazed into brilliance once more.

The Deathshroud moved instantly, forming an unbroken ring around the primarch. The rest of the boarding squads swung their bolters in searching arcs, looking for the hidden enemy.

High up in the terraces overlooking the command throne, one hundred and thirty-two power weapons kindled, flooding the heights with a wave of neon-blue. One hundred and thirty-two storm shields slammed into place, and one hundred and thirty-two throats opened in battle-challenge.

'*Khagan!*' they roared, in perfect unison.

The sagyar mazan launched themselves over the edge, dropping down to the deck like falling angels. Bolter-fire roared out, flying across the gulf, punching into the metal columns and smashing through stone, and then they landed, blades whirling.

Mortarion strode out to meet them, detecting the telltale whine of engine overload building up below him. The bridge remained shielded, keeping him from teleporting away, and already the entire space was consumed with desperate fighting.

'Get these shields down,' he hissed over the comm to Kalgaro, drawing his Lantern sidearm and opening fire. 'Unleash every level of hell, but get them *down*.'

Then he swept into range, his scythe pulled in terrible arcs, cutting them down, but not fast enough, never fast enough.

The *Swordstorm* burned from within, its reactors

bulging, its lower decks already swimming with burning plasma. The great lightning sigil hanging over the command throne crashed to the deck, smashing across the polished marble.

Still the savages came on, fighting to reach the primarch, to drag him down and hold him up. The White Scars fought like the daemons themselves, shrugging off wounds that ought to have felled them, laughing with feral abandon as they surged up against the implacable Deathshroud.

At their head was a lone khan, wielding a Terran longblade two-handed. With him came the others, whooping the war-cries of their bestial home world.

They were hopelessly overmatched, but their charge never faltered. The Deathshroud sliced them apart, their scythes throwing blood across the deck, but they refused to fall back.

Mortarion himself came among the desperate attackers, sweeping three aside in a single blow and hurling their mangled corpses back into the pits. He blasted the chest of a fourth open, then strode towards the leader, the one who held them together. As he approached, the White Scars legionary dispatched his opponent and swung around to face the primarch.

'Hail, Lord of Death!' he cried, sounding almost ecstatic, angling his longsword to strike. 'Torghun Khan greets you!'

'Why do this?' asked Mortarion, holding Silence back, just for a moment. 'Why waste yourselves?'

But it was not waste, and he knew that. Every passing second brought the flagship's doom closer. Every passing second gave time for the rest of the fleet to slip away. The ire of the XIV had been concentrated on this point to the exclusion of all others, and even now the lances were firing again, striking the shields that trapped their master on the rapidly decaying void hulk.

'Why, my lord?' the khan laughed, poised for the coming strike. 'Atonement. At last.'

Mortarion readied his scythe. 'No such thing exists.'

THE KHAN WATCHED the *Swordstorm* die from the bridge of the *Lance of Heaven*. Every wound the flagship took was like a strike to his own body. The great hull was reeling again now, rocked by the flurry of beam-weapons aimed at the command bridge. They would break the last of the shields soon, retrieve their troops, resume the attack. The sagyar mazan would not last more than moments against his brother's dread entourage.

Shame gnawed at him. Once again, his sons had died in his place. Once again, the battle had been interrupted before the end, and this time it was him racing away from the epicentre, his fleet in retreat, the vengeful guns of the enemy trained on their over-burning thrusters.

Your destiny is on Terra.

They had all told him that – Yesugei, Ilya, the sorcerer. The Stormseer's dreams, surely, had been of the final battle on the fields before the Palace walls, and it would be *there*, if anywhere, that the culmination would come.

But the cost. The *cost*.

To race into battle, knowing that honourable death was the only result – that was easy. Any berserker could do it.

To leave, though, to run, to dare the passage of the unknown and let the taunt of *craven* ring in his ears – that nearly ripped his hearts in two.

Around him, the bridge of the new fleet flagship boiled with furious activity. All the legionaries and crew who could have been extracted had been, either by Stormbird or teleporter-beam. The Stormseers were out, as were the keshig and Jubal's command group. All the gunships had launched before the *Swordstorm*'s final attack run, taking with them every weapon their holds could carry.

Jubal was busy now, a furnace of energy, realigning the *Lance of Heaven*'s defensive grids and bellowing commands to pull the fleet back further. The Stormseers were immersed in their rites again, summoning up their elemental forces for the journey ahead. Arvida had taken the principal place among them, and none had gainsaid him, for with Yesugei gone there was none more powerful among their number, whether or not he was a true member of the ordu. The warriors of the keshig took up guard-places all across the bridge, and legionaries from the *Swordstorm* had been dispersed across every surviving capital ship of the fleet, bolstering the defences against madness and warp-fatigue.

Ilya limped up to him, her arms folded around her body as if in protection. Her eyes were rimmed red.

'You had to do it,' she said.

The words were no comfort, as much because they were true as anything else.

Out in the void, the battle raged as fiercely as ever. The bulk of the Death Guard fleet had been distracted by the *Swordstorm*'s sacrifice, but the Emperor's

Children had not been deflected, and stayed in tight pursuit.

'The rift!' cried Taban. 'The horizon clears!'

Its edge swept towards them, a river of fire that bucked like massed horse-heads on the charge. Space flexed and stretched, putting further stress on already damaged hull structures, and vast arcs of aether-lightning licked up against the raging thrusters.

For the first time, they could see over the shrinking lip of the rupture. Immense walls of raging static raced around and around, dizzying in both scale and speed. On the far side was a haze of gold and sapphire, a boiling mass like superheated promethium. In that terrible morass swam half-visible images of torture and insanity, breaking the surface for moments before sinking again in an endless ferment.

'Warp shutters!' ordered Jubal. 'Lock down for aether translation!'

Every White Scars ship was hurtling now, running ahead of the guns of the III Legion. Geller fields flickered into solidity, warp drives cranking into life, plasma drives still piling momentum onto the fleeing starships. The real-view ports locked closed.

'What is to stop them following us in?' murmured Taban, studying the fleet tactical readouts. The first of the big V Legion war vessels was already plummeting down the chasm, half in real space and half in the warp.

'The rift is closing,' said Jubal, indicating augur-sweeps showing the neck of the rupture collapsing in on itself.

'Not quickly enough,' said Jaghatai. Like Taban, he was looking hard at the tactical scanners. The vanguard

of Emperor's Children attack craft at least would make
the horizon before it finally fell into ruin.

Jubal nodded. 'They are not enough to prevent us,'
he said, cautiously.

The Khan narrowed his eyes, watching rune-patterns
creep across the glass. The malign nausea of the warp
grew stronger, calcifying in the air around them. It felt
as if every surface swam with static electricity, and it
would only get worse once they were inside the rupture. The enemy ships flew strangely, erratically, risking
foundering just to remain in contact.

'But what drives them now?' he asked. 'What do
they carry?'

THE RAVISHER VEERED hard to zenith, its thrusters
wildly overfiring, its enginarium overflowing and spilling raw coolant into the bilge-decks. It no longer fired
weapons, for its gunnery crews were all dead, torn
apart on the flail-hooks of the ship's new masters,
their souls sucked from their chests and consumed
in an orgy of psy-gluttony.

Every deck swam with blood. It gurgled down fuel
tubes and vaporised through the atmospheric cyclers.
The lumens had all blown or were oscillating wildly,
making the decks sway between pure darkness and
blinding over-illumination.

The children of Von Kalda's half-understood magicks loped through the corridors and the transit shafts,
hunting for more to kill. They had grown, all of them,
swelling obscenely fast. The smallest of them towered far above the measure of a legionary, crowned
with slung-back spikes and flailing long poison-barbed
tails. They went lasciviously, alluringly, slinking and

sliding through the wheeling lights, their whiteless eyes flashing like pearls.

Manushya-Rakshsasi squatted amid the ruins of the bridge, relishing the vibrations of the tortured ship. A long slick of gore ran down its chin, fresh from where it had gorged on the last legionary to resist.

It had grown far greater than the others. The blood, the warp, the deaths – all of it magnified and redounded upon its true nature – the persona it had enjoyed in the realm of dreams, unfolded and stretched and become true-flesh.

So many names it had employed over so many long centuries of consciousness. It had been there in the very beginning, created amid the beautiful decay of the first star-empire, rising to sentience as those city-worlds of abundance were consumed by the tumults of a god's birth. It had stalked across the riven planetscapes, dissolving them into pure sensation, drinking the spirits of the world-makers as they howled and wept. Manushya-Rakshsasi had taken the spell-casters of those worlds, the warlocks and the seers, and ground its teeth on their living souls, drinking in the essence of their power and of their knowledge. The daemon had grown strong then, just as its counterpart fragments of the Dark Prince had grown strong, as young as the blue stars in the abyss and as lethal as the greatest servants of older powers.

Thus Manushya-Rakshsasi was still young, as the galaxy reckoned age, and that made it vital, and cruel, and in rapture with all it surveyed. It stretched out, and its lissom flesh glistened in the flickering lumen-beams.

'*I am indeed beautiful,*' Manushya-Rakshsasi said,

and its choirs of lesser Intelligences chimed their agreement.

It rose up, unfurling its full majesty. A Keeper of Secrets, they called such creatures on mortal worlds.

And there were many secrets to keep – the last gasped memories of the elder species, laced with the brutal hidden desires of the younger, all destined for dissipation into the deeps of the empyrean, locked in a stasis of exquisite agony for all ages.

Manushya-Rakshsasi gazed out across the void, seeing through the blackening shell of the mortal vehicle as if it were translucent crystal. The world of the senses was thinning, melding into a mix of matter and mind. That made it stronger still, anchoring its wayward selfhood into the weave of temporal forces, bolstering muscles and steeling sinews.

Soon they would not need the void barges of the mortals at all. In moments, they would be free to break out, to glide through the seething tempest as they did in the crucible of their birth-states.

Manushya-Rakshsasi surveyed the carnage, scattered widely over the turning gyre of the warp bridge. It saw the starships like clots of blood in a vein, each one rich and glutinous and ripe for intoxication. One of them swelled more violently than any other, a great battleship filled with the singing souls of the aether-weavers, clustered around their prince, whose soul burned like the circles of pleasure themselves.

'That one,' Manushya-Rakshsasi intoned, sending the psychic command to its new-birthed legion, bidding them take flight. '*We take that one.*'

TWENTY-FIVE

THE STEEL-CLAD WARRIOR had grown stronger. Every blow was heavier, judged more precisely, driven with a purer anger.

It would not be enough, for Cario's art was of a different kind – the disinterested pursuit of martial perfection, immune to the vagaries of battle-lust. It was one of the great galactic ironies that the doctrine, once shared universally in his Legion, had been changed into the pursuit of unbridled excess. But then, the ruin of the Great Crusade was replete with ironies.

The two blades clashed again, sabre and glaive, one darting like a sliver of ice, the other whirling like a chain-flail loosed from its moorings. The tide of battle carried them both up the stairway, and he let it flow.

'We are hunting you now,' Cario said coolly. 'Your flagship burns.'

Shiban hammered another blow in – a furious

strike, pushed with venom. 'Better to burn than to break faith.'

'Faith.' Bolt-shells crashed into the archway above them, the passage to the high bridge. 'Ironic, that you celebrate it. It was to have been expunged.'

The White Scars powered up to the top of the stairway, to where the Palatine Blades' banners hung from golden rails. Across the reflective floor, hundreds of legionaries clashed, some at close quarters, some racing to secure vantages. Each side was totally committed now, fighting with every scrap of genhanced expertise. Gauntlets crunched into flesh, blades sliced through ceramite, shells cracked bloodily home.

'Not by us,' Shiban grunted, evading a crossways swipe that would have severed his helm-cabling.

'Ah yes. You were the exceptional Legion.' The gates loomed, burnished and many-columned. A giant aquila, unsullied, shone above them, its severe head gazing out over the carnage. Beyond the doors, the bridge itself could be glimpsed. 'Except for the other seventeen.'

Cario was still fighting within himself, driving the blade in glittering figures-of-eight, containing the rage set before him and letting it exhaust itself. Shiban showed no signs of tiring yet, though, and kept up the barrage, his brothers beside him forcing the defenders back into the shadow of the burnished eagle.

'Look what you have done to yourselves,' said the White Scars legionary, contemptuously. 'Look at the wounds you give yourselves.'

'This, from the Scars.' Cario felt the first stirring of his inner tempter then, and a spasm of alarm passed through him. *Too soon.* 'Besides, not all of us indulge.'

'Your master made his bargain.' The glaive thrust

deep, surrounded by a blinding halo of disruptor-light. Something had happened – the Scar was fighting beyond himself, more exuberantly than on Memnos. 'It will come for you too.'

The fighting spilled over into the bridge proper, and the barrage of bolter-fire cranked up further, exploding out against the armourglass real-viewers and the serried command columns. Cario retreated with his brothers, withdrawing in close-packed phalanxes towards the great throne at the head of the bridge.

'None are immune,' Cario said, his attention now wholly consumed on surviving the onslaught, for deep within him, a pair of eyes opened again. 'You are in sickness yourselves.'

'I have been.' Shiban slammed the glaive down, two-handed, making the sabre flex almost to breaking point. 'But now, here at the end, I remember how we were before.'

The combat, close and brutal, swarmed up on the throne dais, surging in a locked wave of ivory and purple. The White Scars just kept on coming, defying the hail of bolter-fire and the swordmasters ranged against them.

Cario felt the throne itself approach. As the bridge fell into the confusion of pitched battle, he was only dimly aware of the warp light raging across the void outside, and the tongues of flame licking out from the edge of the great vortex.

But he knew what it meant: they were going over the edge. They were racing towards it, unmanned, blind, with no hope of pulling out.

Deep within, the horned creature smiled, exposing its black teeth.

'*No...*' he said out loud.

Cario smashed out a brutal sideswipe, clattering the glaive aside, then swept back and angled down for the throat. Shiban parried, but only barely, and for the first time recoiled from the impact.

'Your effort is wasted,' Cario spat. 'Your gods are slain, your idols broken. This is now a world of greater powers.'

The sabre danced, faster and faster, unstoppable, driven with superlative control and unmatchable power. Shiban was beaten back, struggling to match the sudden acceleration of swordmastery.

'You fight for a cause already dead,' Cario told him, listening as his own voice became tight-edged, suffused with the echo of another's. 'I told you before – there is no courage in being blind.'

Shiban did not reply, his breathing coming in rasping gasps now. He hacked and flailed with the guan dao, but was now on the defensive.

'And for the strong, there will always be a path,' Cario hissed, driving his enemy back two paces and pursuing him remorselessly. 'We control the things we use. They are subjects. They are *slaves.*'

He thrust the charnabal sabre, catching the glaive in its centre and shattering the haft. With a snap of released energy, the weapon broke, each half spinning away in circles. Shiban toppled, his momentum carrying back down the dais steps. He sprawled onto his back, struggling to reach for another weapon.

Cario pounced, leaping into the air, holding his blade vertically, aiming it at his opponent's heart.

As he did so, the presence within reared up, roaring in pleasure, becoming fully visible in his mind's eye. Its flesh was luminous, its body as dry and glossy as a snake's, and it was laughing, just as those in the rupture were laughing.

Cario fell to earth, braced over the legionary, ready to drive his sword down to its target. As he did so, a massive explosion rocked the ship's deck, coming from the void beyond. The real-viewers flared into light, hot and dazzling.

For a split-second, Cario looked up.

The *Ravisher* had gone, blown apart in an orgy of overloaded drives. Its hollow carcass rolled away, tumbling towards the gaping maw of the warp rift, and from its fire-torn heart came the creatures that had consumed it – a legion of them, swarming out into the mixture of warp and real space, screaming with delight. They were headed by a vast horned daemon-beast bearing a longsword, rising like an angel of destruction over the flames and the blood-wells, impossibly huge, impossibly beautiful.

The creature within him responded. Cario felt his blood heating, his hearts racing. Sweat ran down his skin, fizzing as it boiled against his swelling carapace. His skin and the bone at his temples flexed. His greaves and vambraces began to bulge, to break out from the hardening of mortal muscle in warp-spun flesh.

And for the first time, he wanted it.

For the first time, he witnessed the empyrean's hosts unleashed, and knew that there was no escape, that all he had ever had was time, ticking slowly down, and that it was now ended.

Shiban drew a long dagger from his belt, clambering back to his feet. Cario could have lashed the blade out of the warrior's grasp. He could have plunged his sabre into the legionary's stomach and twisted his entrails clear. Instead, his own blade dropped, leaving the opening.

Shiban leapt up to take advantage, plunging the dagger deep into Cario's chest. The pain was intense, but not from the physical wound. The creature within him writhed, suddenly fearful, suddenly angry.

Cario fell to his knees, fighting hard to contain the forces unleashed. Shiban loomed over him, ready to strike again, but then hesitated, holding the blade up high.

By then Cario could hardly speak. His body would soon not be his own. The beast had uncurled, infecting his blood, taking over his limbs. The whispers were no longer whispers – they were commands.

Every soul he had ever ended, he had done so as the mortal warrior he had been from the start, bearing the colours of the Legion as they had been forged on Chemos. Throughout all – the great Turn, the slaughter of the Terra-cleavers, the march towards the Throne – he had been himself: Ravasch Cario, Palatine Blade, most perfect warrior of the most perfect Legion, devoted to nothing but the quest for exactitude.

He regretted nothing, no choices, no kills, for he had wished for all of it. But no longer. The fate of Konenos would not be his, and he would die as he had lived – the true and only Child of the Emperor.

'You are as doomed as I,' Cario told Shiban, grinning. 'But that, my brother, was well fought.'

Shiban rammed the dagger home, and with a flash of disruptor-fire it cut through Cario's armour and deep into his primary heart. The White Scars legionary took the hilt in both hands and dragged it laterally, ripping the prefector's chest apart and cleaving to his spine.

The horned creature roared, thrashing wildly to the surface. But it was too late – Cario's consciousness ebbed away as he fell back to the deck, his sabre clanging to the metal.

At the end, as the roar of battle faded away to a blur of echoes, and he saw the vengeful White Scars carry the fight that they would surely win now, nothing could quench his joy.

The beast howled, but it would be denied.

'Unsullied,' he gasped with his last breath, and knew no more.

THE LANCE OF HEAVEN thundered over the portal's edge, its entire structure shaking as the tremendous forces took hold. There was a kind of gravity in the vortex – a pull that ripped every starcraft in and yanked it deeper, sucking like quicksand. What remained of the V Legion fleet was hauled faster and faster, blurring from the speed, dragged far in excess of the power locked in their warp drives.

Walls of force roared past, flashing like heartbeats, accelerating with every second. The profiles of those on the bridge became smeared, the voices distorted. Behind them, far behind now, the portal collapsed shut, sending fresh buffets of force haring after them. Strangled curves of neon-white aetheric lightning pursued them, snapping at their heels, curling around the burning engines and reaching, futilely, to snare them in their desperate chase.

As the last of the warp shutters slammed down, the

Khan caught a final glimpse into the roiling madness ahead, and perceived a split-moment in the heart of the storm. Far ahead, too far to catch, the remnants of Dark Glass spun and disintegrated. He saw the last of the black iron casings fly free, burning into ash.

Beyond it was the stuff of the underverse, the warp space that Veil had spoken of – the stratum profundis, the Seethe, the Deep Warp.

Then that too was gone, locked away from mortal sight, cocooned behind lead and iron and ancient sigils carved by the technomancers of Terra.

We always knew, the Khan thought. *We always knew it needed symbols and arcana to control. How easy it was to forget, to pretend, and that was the first error.*

The first hull breach was signalled by a sudden slew to starboard – a kick far greater than warp turbulence would give.

Jaghatai glanced up at the tactical displays. His fleet stretched away ahead of him, in close formation, all travelling at the same insane speed. The chronos rattled around, the sensors cycled, the velocity meters fused and burst. On the flickering augur screens, he saw that III Legion ships had followed them in and had broken up on the cusp of the portal. Burning remnants flew along in the momentum-stream, clustering close to the *Lance of Heaven*'s plasma-trails.

Nine Stormseers remained on the bridge, plus the sorcerer Arvida, and they broke off from their warp-scrying rituals. Naranbaatar, the greatest in power after Yesugei, an age-steeped warrior in rune-carved armour bearing a staff of carved ebony, looked up at the bridge's lofty ceiling, his unhelmed face suddenly tense.

The noises followed, like steel spikes dragged over rusty iron, digging deep. Great rattling clangs resounded along the length of the domed structure.

The Khan knew those sounds. They had ever been in his dreams since the earliest memory, the distant whirls of ice and fire that had preceded his first true recollection on Chogoris.

They had tried to claw their way in then, too.

'Be still!' he cried, striding to the edge of the command dais. Every face on the bridge lifted to him – the menials working at the nav-stations, the officers in their white robes, the legionaries standing at every intersection and gantry-head, the seers with their bone-chains and horsehair staffs. 'We are now in the realm of the gods. This is their place, where they do not suffer the mortal to endure.'

The hull vibrated again, riven by heavy blows from the outside. There were no cracks in the adamantium, for the denizens of the empyrean fought not against the physical constraints of matter but the psychic barriers of tech-sorcery that sheathed it.

'They come now, hungry for more blood,' the Khan told them. 'But we have bled enough, and others have bled to bring us here, and they shall have *no more.*'

The first claw broke through, punching out of the inner roof, shimmering like a hololith. A pungent stink of maddening perfume bloomed across the entire bridge, followed by the distended shrieks of another world.

The Khan drew his tulwar. All across the bridge, every warrior took up a blade. The warp shutters rattled, the warp drives whined.

'They seek to bring us down, because we guide the

others!' the Khan cried, striding over to where Arvida stood. 'We must not fall!'

More claws burst through. The aether-screams reached fever-pitch. Barbed whips snaked out through living metal, curling like a sentient things, and the internal shielding layering the bridge vaults shattered, dissolving the last elements of the Geller field.

'So we stand here!' roared the Khan, defiant against the gathering swarm. 'We stand in this place! We are the Talskar, Sons of Chogoris, and this is the last test!'

They broke through then, screaming and yowling, the heralds of the greater horror – slim-limbed, hook-handed, horn-headed, cloven-hoofed, dropping like liquid from the inner hull.

'To the ends of time!' the Khan thundered, braced to meet them. *We defy the dark!*

Then every mortal voice rose up in acclamation and fury, undaunted by the legion of terror bursting through matter to claw at them, bearing every weapon they still possessed, and led into battle by their primarch as the fleet plunged deep into the forgotten ways of the aether.

Khagan!' they roared, drowning out the screams of the empyrean. *'Ordu gamana Jaghatai!'*

Then the gap closed, the daemons came among them, and battle was joined on the *Lance of Heaven* even as it raced through the deeps of the living warp.

TWENTY-SIX

ARVIDA NEVER SAW the daemons, though he sensed their presence. By the time the *Lance of Heaven* was invaded, his mind was bent on the warp. His mortal eyes were closed, his mortal body prone, his mind turned in on itself, and thence to the aether beyond.

He had expected the passage to trigger the flesh-change, to force the mutating horror to rise up and transform him for good, but the truth was the opposite. As soon as they entered the rift's mouth, the pressure at his temples dissipated, the roar in his ears guttered out and the pain in his joints eased. In took a moment for him to realise the truth – the place they had entered was *shielded* from the greater mass of the Seethe. Vast walls of psychic matter held the tides back, enclosing the entire fleet in a barrier of swimming sorcery. They were hurtling along titanic tunnels, bored down into the foundations of the aether, burrowing like the tracks of insects under the very feet of creation.

Freed from the need to fight the flesh-degradation, Arvida's mind roved ahead, outpacing the fastest of the ships as they raced. He saw branches upon branches, breaking into a web of staggering complexity. The more he roved, the more colossal it became, a galaxy-spanning network of channels and thoroughfares, each one linked and switch-backed and threaded under and tangled with a hundred others. No human mind could have conceived of such a thing, far less built it.

There was no Astronomican in that place, just an endless, dizzying labyrinth of tunnels winding through the dark, each suffused with sorcery greater and older than he had ever encountered, even on Prospero at the height of its glory.

He remembered Yesugei's final words.

They will need a guide.

The Navigators could not follow this path – they had been trained to perceive the Emperor's light amid the eddies of the true warp. Arvida exerted himself, projecting his mind's strength out ahead of the fleet. He scanned the web of passageways, divining which led most truly towards their goal, and lit the way himself, projecting a beacon that every psychically attuned individual could follow.

They responded. One by one, the ships of the fleet latched on to the signal. By then they were all travelling at speeds beyond thought, exceeding by orders of magnitude anything experienced by normal human starships, carried along by the elemental forces that raged and burned in the hidden ways.

Arvida traced the route ahead unconsciously at first, letting his future-sense guide them. The lattice spread out, vast and shimmering, a tangle of gold flung across the face of eternity. Against all reason, he found himself wishing he could linger – to study it, to trace its thousands of ways and discover all its secrets. Amid the blur of velocity, he caught sight of wonders buried yet deeper down – vast gulfs that plummeted into utter velvety darkness, mighty chambers that glimmered like starlit geodes, clusters of red-tinged clouds burning from within, great glittering stalagmites ringed around the ebon globes of chained suns.

They went in deeper. He felt the faint presence of minds pressing against his, as alien as any minds he had ever sensed. They were bitter, those minds, like long-deposed kings bereft of their armies, watching intruders rampage across lands they had once been able to defend. He felt mordant anger, but also empty impotence. They were ghosts, mere afterglows of elder powers, lingering like curls of smoke over embers.

He focused his powers. Freed of the terror of the flesh-change, he was empowered to move high in the Enumerations, practising the scrying-methods taught to him in Tizca. The visions came tumbling in on him, fast, on top of one another in a disordered jumble. He scryed a thousand worlds spinning in the void, all laid waste, or besieged, or burning in war. He saw the numberless tides of daemon-kind clustered at the threshold of reality, poised to leap beyond the gap, and saw with dreadful clarity what they would do once unleashed.

Then Arvida remembered what he had seen on Dark Glass.

He remembered that planet of sorcerers, and the dark tower, and the shuffling lines of robed magicians.

He remembered the fractured god, his lone eye all that remained true of the creature he had once been.

He could take them there, if the place were real. For a moment, his mind crept tentatively in that direction, seeking for a sign that the lattice extended that far.

They will need a guide.

Even there, amid the foundations of the infinite, there was temptation to resist.

He collected himself, gathering all his strength, moulding the fractured facets of a thousand potential futures into a single whole. The great maze had been constructed by minds for whom Terra was an unknown backwater, a mere mark on star charts. Even now there would be no straight ways, no easy paths back into the world of the living.

Arvida extended his future-sense, travelling further and further down the maze of possibility. As he homed in on the place where the vortex led, he saw for the first time the tumult arrayed about their destination. The link Yesugei had forged at Catullus had lacked an answering voice, and so every path to the heart of Terra was blocked, crammed with armies of the empyrean boiling up out of the profoundest pits of the abyss. The tunnels were aflame, blocking the light of the greater Throne, and some secret war raged unchecked amid the vaults of hell.

But he could take them *most* of the way.

There were portals of the labyrinth that flared out into real space before the margins of the Solar System, yet still ahead of the Warmaster's advance. They were distant still, but the incredible speeds only grew, accelerating the entire time, making the void ships stretch and shake. If he could maintain the beacon, if he could find the path, they would yet achieve it.

Dimly, he could sense the stink of daemon. In the world of the senses, they were fighting towards him, screaming to claw at his soul, but he could not let his concentration drop, could make no move to defend himself. For if he faltered, they all faltered.

The walls of sorcery rushed past, glowing, racing. He heard voices raised in anger and pain. He felt the hard deck beneath, and saw the empyrean soaring above, majestic and terrible.

Hold on, he breathed. *Just a little longer.*

Hold on.

THE DAEMONS BURST through the failing Geller field, jaws wide and claws outstretched, bringing with them the frenzied chorus of damned souls.

The Stormseers responded, hurling the tempest back at them. The first creatures of the aether were ripped asunder, their warp-wound flesh exploding in shivers of unleashed energy, but more came in their wake, shrieking and laughing.

Jaghatai took up position by Arvida, as did Jubal and the keshig, fortifying an island before the throne. Further out across the bridge's expanse, the warriors of the ordu opened fire, sending massed volleys of bolter-shells punching through the tides of daemonic flesh.

The creatures of the empyrean howled, dropping to the decks and scampering into range, eyes flashing. Dozens spilled into being, then hundreds, swarming through the metal of the hull, pushing up from the deck, plunging from the vaults. They strutted on switchbacked legs and snapped with crab-clawed arms, brandishing flails and scourges with dazzling finesse. Every move they made was sheathed in a shimmering curtain of false colour, a whirl of unlight that defied mortal eyes, and they grinned from split-flesh mouths.

Bolters hurt them, but only the weapons of eternity – blades, fists, spears – ended them. The White Scars met them in close combat, making use of all their speed, all their power. Tulwar met flail in a riot of thrusts and parries, and soon the upper levels of the bridge were locked in a crush of close-quarters struggle.

Daemons ripped into the chests of mortals, lifting them clear of the deck and hurling them down into the pits below. The sons of Jaghatai fought back with equal savagery, cutting the glimmering flesh from the neverborn as they capered and spun.

The Stormseers strode into the heart of the fighting, summoning more destruction, crying out Khorchin words of power. Lightning forked down, crackling with psychic force, and where it struck the daemons they burst into consuming flame. The stormwind accelerated, tearing across nav-stations and cogitator-banks, sweeping the damned and the cursed from their hoofs and sending them flailing.

But more kept coming, ever greater in stature, more steeped in malice. Remnants of the Kakophoni lingered on in their sinuous skins – flecks of purple armour, clinging like scales to the supple flesh of the neverborn. Those hybrids opened their throats, and ear-bursting sonic horror flooded the bridge-space, shattering eardrums and bursting eyeballs. They extended their twisted arms, fused with the residue of the old guns, and loosed tsunamis of raw noise that cut up decking and pulverised columns.

No mortal could stand against that. The ship's crew were slain in droves, their carapace armour and helms scant protection against the overwhelming force of the daemon host, but still they held their ground, buoyed by the presence of the legionaries among them.

The Legion's warriors, assembled from those taken from the *Swordstorm* and the *Lance of Heaven*'s own complement, tore back into the enemy, racing to hold the strategic points. They moved in a whirl of steel, driving their bodies as hard as they had ever been driven, striving to keep up with the preternatural movements of their foes. The hard light-bursts of the zadyin arga wreathed them, slewing from their bodies as they fought, blinding the horrors and making them scream. The least of the daemons was greater than any legionary, but the ordu fought together, parrying, slicing, rushing the creatures wherever they landed and striking them down.

As the armies clashed, their arena became deafening, a holocaust of unfettered noise and projected nightmares.

Jaghatai was at the thick of the combat, for the denizens of the empyrean latched on to Arvida, and knew that it was he who guided the entire fleet. Like hornets, they streaked towards the sorcerer, flooding the air with killer-harmonics from splayed-wide jaws, desperate to reach him with a barbed scourge or poisoned spear-tip.

The Stormseer Naranbaatar countered those attacks, generating a hemispheric kine-shield across the kneeling Arvida. Its shell blazed with a pure fire every time it was struck, showering cascades of refracted warp light with every impact.

Jubal led the keshig out into the heart of the assault, and the Terminator-armoured bodyguard cut their way through ranks of racing daemon-kind, wielding their heavy glaives two-handed. Despite their massive battleplate, they matched the warp spawn for speed, weathering the horrific barrage of sound and then striking out with neon-wreathed blades.

Every soul was engaged, every mind focused, every weapon-hand occupied, and still they came. The air became ferociously hot, shaking from the discharge of plasma-bolts and warp-magicks, and the blood boiled where it fell.

Right at the epicentre, Jaghatai wielded his blade, injecting every stroke with fearful poise. He lashed out, catching a screaming horror in the throat, severing its horned head from its ophidian neck, then swung around and thrust the blade-tip into the entrails of its swooping counterpart. He shivered the blade, and the daemon blew apart, its severed elements spiralling across the crammed press of fighting souls.

None could withstand the primarch. He towered above the neverborn, reaping a path through the horde, carving a way for his keshig to follow. Step by step, metre by ichor-stained metre, they drove the daemon vanguard back from Arvida. The storm-lightning snapped and lanced, skewering more even as they materialised, shredding their essence and sending it howling back into the Seethe.

'Hai Chogoris!' came the battle-roar, loosed from every legionary's throat across the bridge, and for a moment their fury outmatched the screams of the aether.

But then the ship buckled, falling sharply. Its last, faint residue of Geller coverage imploded, showering the bridge with a deluge of broken silver. A new and enormous shape coalesced before the command throne, twisting into solidity like smoke running in reverse, blooming into lurid purple smog and then filling out into a hulking spectre of humanity's darkest dreams.

No trace remained of Konenos' armour. Four pale arms thrust out from a writhing torso, two of them terminating in long crab-like claws, the other two in taloned, human-like hands. Its tapered skull, crowned with blood-red horns, was pierced and riven with ritual scars, animated by eyes with no whites. When its mouth gaped, a long violet tongue whipped out from between close-packed fangs. Its every move was achingly alluring, at once repellent and intoxicating, blurred with clouds of pungent incense.

The daemon was immense, crashing to the deck and making the stones crack under its hooves. Thrice the height of the primarch, it was an avatar of corruption hurled into the world of the senses. Storm-lightning snapped across it, burning away in ribbons of steam as it recoiled from the unholy flesh.

'Hail, son of Anathema,' it said, and its voice contained every foul and beautiful thing within it – the howl of an infant's terror, the cry of mortal ecstasy, the gasp of pain under the torturer's knife. 'You are far from home.'

The Khan looked up, taking in the full splendour and degradation, all encompassed in the pale flesh, the shimmer of gauze, the scent of desire and abhorrence.

'Bar my way, yaksha,' he said, keeping his sacred blade in guard, 'and I shall end you.'

The daemon laughed, and the sound was like glass being scraped across bone.

'Attempt it, and your flayed soul shall sweeten the passage of eternity.'

Then the daemon moved, sweeping its sword down. The Khan swung his blade to parry, and the clash rang out like mountain ice breaking. Then the primarch was moving again, spinning to intercept the scything claws. His tulwar shuddered on impact, shearing a slice of daemonic chitin from the inner curve, before he thrust upwards again to lash across the grasping talons.

Beyond the greater daemon, the battle raged unabated. Storm-magic rose up against warp-devilry in a welter of psychic detonations, punctuated by the physical combat of blade-thrust and bolter-volley. Jubal and his retinue took on the greatest of those who had followed Manushya-Rakshsasi, and the Terminator guard wrestled with psychosonic hybrids of talon and fused vox-augmitter. The Master of the Hunt roared out the name of his primarch with every one he cast back into the underverse. Namahi stayed at his side, swinging a guan dao in a glittering corona.

None matched the perfection of the Khan in combat. Set against the mightiest denizen of the aether, matched against the most powerful of all the gods' sendings to the mortal plane, the primarch rose to a level of controlled fury that passed into the sublime. His sword flew, whirling faster than the plains-wind across driven grass. Every daemonic attack was thrown back and matched with a counter of his own. The two

blades clashed, again and again, lost in a tornado of
strike and parry, thrust and evade.

Manushya-Rakshsasi screamed, drenching the Khan
in a molecule-shaking torrent of sound, but he powered through it. Its rune-burned longsword snarled
across his guard, its claws reached out, scraping across
his gold-and-pearl armour, and he cast them back.
All the while the tulwar hacked, cutting deep into
aether-knitted sinews, making the daemon roar.

'*You cared much for your storm-witch, I think,*' said
Manushya-Rakshsasi, pulling away from the Khan's
furious assault. '*Do you wish me to show you his
agony?*'

The primarch only pressed the attack further, driving
his limbs ever harder, wielding the blade so fast now
that it felt like reality would split around it. Flames
kindled about both combatants, bursting into life as
the weapons spun.

The Khan could sense its limitation now. It had
thrown everything at him, and still he lived. His warriors lived, and fought, and roared their defiance. The
creature fed on fear, but there was nothing to feed on
aboard the *Lance of Heaven*.

'*Soul-engines were not meant for your kind,*' taunted
Manushya-Rakshsasi, summoning a fresh charge that
nearly sent the Khan staggering. '*They are beyond you,
just as we are beyond you.*'

The Khan shoved his energy-flaming sword-tip clean
through Manushya-Rakshsasi's torso, ripping it out
the far side, before the daemon's claws raked down
across his breastplate, nearly tearing it from the flesh.
Blood now joined the circles of fire, mortal-red and
daemon-violet.

'You should never have dared this.'

The daemon screamed again, hurling the Khan back a pace and dissolving the ground beneath his feet. It followed up with a brutal lunge with a clenched claw, catching him under the chin and forcing him back further.

'This is our *realm.'*

The Khan struck back instantly, slamming the daemon's sword aside and going for the creature's midriff. The blade thrust true, ripping another wound in the creature's flank. Where the ichor shot through the blade's disruptor trails it ignited, dousing both of them in rippling blood-fire.

'They are all *our realms. You are a plague on them, a contagion to be excised.'*

The creature's talons raked around, and the Khan bludgeoned them away. He dragged his blade across the daemon's leading thigh, and muscle parted with a slick shiver. Then he swept back across the daemon's ribcage, slicing into the bone-claw.

'And excised you will be.'

Manushya-Rakshsasi kicked out with its hoof, cracking it into the Khan's side and shattering armour-plate. The primarch went skidding, hurled out of position. The daemon screamed its contempt again, and hammered the flaming sword down. The killing edge seared through the tortured air, fizzing with serpentine magicks.

The Khan angled his blade to parry, and the two swords crashed together. A massive clang resounded, there was a blaze of light, and the Khan's tulwar shattered. The daemon hurled a bone-claw around, crunching the primarch aside and sending him clattering into the empty command throne.

That exposed Arvida, still locked deep within his future-sense, unwitting, alone. The Khan sprang back to his feet and raced to close the gap. Manushya-Rakshsasi lurched towards the sorcerer, claws stretched, the lust of destruction in its narrowing eyes. The primarch, weaponless now, leapt for the daemon's throat.

Manushya-Rakshsasi reacted too late. The Khan grasped its neck, seizing the lilac flesh and using his momentum to drive the creature from Arvida. He pushed his gauntlets together, driving them deep into the creature's taut skin.

Caught by the ferocity of the lunge, Manushya-Rakshsasi was thrown off balance, crashing onto its back, and the Khan smashed down atop it, hands still clamped around its throat. The daemon arched its back, trying to throw the primarch, but the Khan, drawing on every sliver of genhanced strength, pushed down harder, snapping warp-spun bones and crushing multiple, twisted windpipes.

Manushya-Rakshsasi choked and lashed out harder. Its sword sliced across the Khan's back, severing armour-plates and lifting them loose. Its talons scraped across his side, puncturing muscle where his battleplate had been ripped clear. The vast creature twisted like a snake, trying to throw its tormentor off, but the Khan only pressed harder, driving his fingers into the daemon's throat and tearing up the sinews.

'There is *nowhere* left to hide,' the Khan hissed, throttling the dregs of life out of the flailing daemon. 'We know you now. We shall hunt you in every plane of reality. We shall cleanse the void, then we shall cleanse the warp.'

Manushya-Rakshsasi spat its defiance, but the spittle

was laced with ichor now, and its eyes had clouded.
A shudder rippled through its ravaged frame, and the
talons went limp.

'So look on me now, yaksha,' said the Khan, 'and
know your slayer.'

The daemon dragged up a final, strangled breath,
gazing up at Jaghatai with both loathing and horror.
Then the primarch released his grip and seized the daemon's own sword from its slackening grip. Taking its
flaming hilt in both hands, he twisted round, pulled
it back, then plunged it into Manushya-Rakshsasi's
chest. The daemon screamed, impaled on the burning blade. The Khan hauled the sword back out, then
thrust his gauntlet deep into the gaping wound.

'*For the Emperor!*' he cried, ripping the daemon's
heart from between its ribs and brandishing it high
above his head. Ichor as thick and dark as oil ran
down his arm, steaming as it came.

Across the bridge, the White Scars heard their master's cry of triumph, as did the daemons, and all saw
the Keeper of Secrets' still-thudding heart held aloft.
Every warrior rose up then, fighting still, their blades
plunging and their fists clenched hard.

'*For the Khan!*' they roared.

Then the primarch cast the daemonic heart aside
and took up the shards of his tulwar, still lashing with
power, and strode back into the fray. His keshig fell in
around him, laying waste to all that stood before them.
The Stormseers renewed their assault, tearing the elements asunder and hurling them into the oncoming
ranks of neverborn. Bolters roared, battle-cries were
unleashed, and the hordes of the underverse screamed
in hatred and desperation.

Amid it all, the sorcerer Arvida knelt, untouched, unharmed, driving them onwards.

Beyond the confines of the hull, the universe thundered past, ever faster, ever further.

'Fight on!' roared the Khan.

The daemons screamed. The White Scars met them, defiant and unbending.

'Fight on!'

TWENTY-SEVEN

A LAST GREAT crashing lance-impact told Mortarion everything he needed to know – the *Swordstorm's* shields had been broken, truly this time, and he was free to teleport clear.

He looked down at the slain around him, each one ended by the cut of scythes, and watched the blood-trails pool and drain across the floor of the deck. They had all raced onto his blade, eager to meet it, fighting as furiously and as well as any warriors of any Legion, but there had been something more with them – a kind of mania.

Their khan, Torghun, lay on the deck, his back broken. He had been hard to finish off – not as fast as his brothers, but tough to grind down. In the end, Silence had ripped the helm from his head, and Mortarion had seen his expression under it – bloodied, on the edge of death, yet his eyes were alive with joy.

Then he was gone, ended like so many thousand

others, cut apart, his spine trodden down into the metal.

'*My lord,*' came Kalgaro's voice over the comm. '*Loci established. I am bringing you to safety.*'

Mortarion nodded, numbly. The combat had been wearying – a procession of slaughter that was no consolation for missing the greater prize, and even in victory there was no small measure of humiliation.

Beams of aether-light slammed down, and once more the chill of the abyss shivered through him. The haze cleared, and he was back on the bridge of the *Endurance*, surrounded by the ice-rimed outlines of the Deathshroud.

Kalgaro stood to greet him. Beside the Siegemaster stood ranks of XIV Legion retainers, bridge crew and menials. Beyond those, isolated from the others, was a small retinue clad in gold and purple. At their head was the Lord Commander Primus, who bowed.

'My lord, forgive the liberty,' said Eidolon. 'But as you see, the battle is over. I wished to ensure that you were returned to us.'

Beyond him, through the bridge's real-viewers, Mortarion saw the void glowing red with burning ships. The *Swordstorm* itself was racked with explosions, its massive shell lit from within, its equilibrium gone. Slowly, it was tumbling away from the battle-plane, shedding the charred extremities of its ravaged hull, too far gone now to be salvaged.

On the far side of that holocaust, the last of the White Scars fleet was also gone, withdrawn across the edge of the rupture, leaving behind only their broken and smouldering wreckage. Any pursuit, from his own vessels or those of Eidolon's, was now impossible – the rift had closed.

'The Khan?' asked Mortarion grimly, more for the sake of completeness than anything. He already knew that Jaghatai was gone, swept out of reach just as the claws closed around his neck.

'Fled, my lord,' said Eidolon. 'Doubt not – this has been your victory. He runs from you, and the warp will not be kind.'

'Victory?' roared Mortarion, whirling to face the Lord Commander, spitting bile from his ancient rebreather. '*Victory?* One to record in the annals? Hells, mutant, if this is victory then you must enjoy pain even more than your reputation suggests.'

Out in the void, the battleships of the III and the XIV had slowed to full halt. The great guns were doused in steaming vats of coolant, and the overheated plasma drives were shut down before they could run away to ruin. The last flickers of the void battle played out on the margins – isolated pockets of V Legion resistance too slow to make the warp rift, hunted down for informants, even though the need for such had now largely gone.

Mortarion paced back towards the throne, his mind already working hard.

Another failure, another mark to set against his record. He would have to go back to Horus, to his brother primarchs, and the weight of his shame would lie just as heavy as it always had.

Kalgaro waited patiently, as ever, saying nothing before being addressed. His entourage remained at their stations, as dour and silent as ever. They were waiting, all of them, for the word of command. As he looked at their expectant faces, Mortarion felt a kind of loathing well up within him. He had killed, but it had not been enough. He had hunted, driving his sons hard across the void and away from the sites of glory, and it had not been enough.

Deep down, closeted away, chained up, the broken monster Grulgor lashed against his bonds. The grimoires remained in his chambers, unread, slowly rotting. The psykers that populated every ship in his fleet still lingered, exercising restraint for the moment, but the words of power were still on their lips.

He recalled Eidolon's earlier words. *You cannot defer the gods forever. You may build walls and you may issue laws, but you cannot put back what has been taken out.*

'Finish all tasks remaining,' Mortarion growled at length, lowering his lean body back into the throne. 'Do it swiftly. Then we make for the warp.'

He turned his gaze back to Lord Commander Eidolon.

'You found my brother well enough,' Mortarion said. 'Do the means still exist?'

Eidolon looked uncertain. 'I fear the Khan is beyond us now, lord.'

'Another, then. If I gave you the name, do the arts still answer?'

'It would depend on the name.'

'One I would bring to heel before we reach the Throneworld.'

Eidolon looked amused. 'You might be more precise.'

Mortarion thought of Grulgor then. He pictured him slurring his foul breath amid the bilge-rotten hold-space. On Molech, he had been the weapon that had levelled cities.

He was an abomination. There had to be better way.

'I will be at the Warmaster's side,' Mortarion said. 'We will take our place at the vanguard, and give the Legion the honour it deserves. But not without our full strength. Not without those who were there at the start.'

Mortarion looked down at Eidolon, at his finery and his debauchery, and his weakness and his strength, and felt sickened by it all.

'So take me to my First Captain,' he said. 'Bring me Calas Typhon.'

EPILOGUE

THE FIRST SIGNALS came in from long-range augurs on the outrider *Valja*, hunting off the Thalion Shoals. From there they were passed back to the primarch's battle-group, two warp-stages away on the edge of the Proxima Sol-Tertius subsector, less than two weeks out from Terra. At first the provenance was doubted, and so requests for confirmation were beamed straight back.

When the *Hrafnkel* itself detected fleet-mass warp-wakes, that settled the issue. The flagship was taken into full battle alert, as were its seventeen escorts, Administratum liaison craft and sundry auxilia transports.

For the Wolves, patrolling the very edges of Lord Dorn's watch, their wounds from Alaxxes healed and their warriors itching to take the fight back to the Warmaster on his own ground, the sensor-spread was what had been expected for months – the first signs of the enemy, bearing down on the Throneworld at last. The *Hrafnkel* issued requests to Terra for immediate aid, but did not wait for replies before breaking the veil.

Only when the VI Legion flotilla reached its forward coordinates and switched to finer-grained sensor sweeps did the identity of the incoming fleet become clearer. Thralls ran test after test, not believing what they saw, before the tidings were eventually deemed reliable enough to be given to the primarch. The evidence was shunted to the bridge stations, where the sensorium master, after checking again, finally signed them off and headed up, warily, to the command throne.

Leman Russ took the data-slate and studied it for a long time. Eventually, he lifted his frost-blue eyes from the runes.

'This cannot be true,' he said.

'We have checked, and checked again, lord.'

'But why now? Why is he here *now*?'

The sensorium master shook his head. 'I cannot tell you. The contacts are still three days away.'

Russ stood, and the true-wolves at his feet rose too, snarling and whickering. A look like breaking thunder crossed his flushed face, and his right hand reached for Mjalnar's hilt.

'Arm all ships,' he growled. 'Flay the engines, but get us to him ahead of any other. I will be the first one he sees.'

Already menials were running to comply, and the *Hrafnkel*'s vast bulk began to turn, angling for the boost of plasma drives.

'Jaghatai,' spat Russ, striding to the edge of the

throne dais. 'Damn you, you should *not* have come back.'

IT TOOK LESS than three days for the *Hrafnkel* to cover the distance, imperilling the engines of its escorts as the flotilla thundered through the void. By the time the flagship reached the coordinates, every gunwale was open and every Thunderhawk manned and primed for deployment. The main lances were keyed for immediate fire, and the entire battle-group assumed attack positions. As the first of the real-viewer data came in, orders cascaded down from the bridge, activating kill-markers for the waiting hunt-packs and identifying primary assault vectors.

But no counter-deployment came.

The V Legion, what remained of it, eventually limped into view, shields down, plasma drives operating on half-power. The vessels were no longer arrayed in white – the passage through the Deep Warp had blackened the ships' hulls, coating them in a thick layer of carbon. Russ had witnessed the White Scars assembled for war at the height of the Great Crusade, and the spread of warships had been twice this size, glittering in ivory, gold and red. What remained was battered, diminished, scraping along on burned-out engines.

The flagship was gone. At the forefront was a line battleship with the ident *Lance of Heaven*, its flanks bearing scars like claw-marks. The rest of the fleet came behind it, marker lights flickering intermittently, thrusters glowing dimly.

Both sides came to a halt, separated by less than a hundred kilometres of open space. VI Legion guns locked on to targets, fixing points of weakness, of which there were many. No White Scars guns fixed targets in return, and the ranks of ships hung in the void.

Silent. Broken.

Russ watched them carefully, scouring the forward vessels for signs of movement. They outnumbered his battle-group heavily, but looked in little condition to fight.

'Have they made contact?' he demanded.

Grimnr Blackblood, his huscarl, shook his head. 'Nothing yet.'

Russ pushed clear of the command throne. 'Train lances on the lead vessel, aimed at the bridge. Make ready to disable.'

As the thralls hastened to comply, a warning rune lit up on the consoles ahead. 'Lord, they are attempting to establish a teleport locus.'

'How many?'

'Just one.'

Russ snorted a raw laugh. 'He has gall, I'll give him that.' He drew his frostblade, and the naked metal gleamed coldly. 'Let him come.'

The *Hrafnkel*'s forward void shield coverage was lowered, just for a moment. A second later, a lone column of aether-light crackled down from the bridge's vaults, hitting the deck a few metres ahead of Russ' position. The blaze flared, guttered, then cleared, revealing a tall, lean figure standing at the heart of it.

The Khan bore no weapon. His armour was gored deeply, blackened like his ships. His helm was gone, revealing a blood-streaked face, his long hair dishevelled. Initially, it looked as if he had trouble standing, but he steadied himself, pushing his shoulders back, meeting Russ' gaze.

Seeing him again, all Russ felt was fury. He poised to launch forwards, to wheel Mjalnar around his shoulders, ready to plunge it into the chest of the one who had left him to die in the void. The frostblade felt light in his hands, apt for murder.

Yet he did not move. The Khan did not move.

They faced one another, Wolf King and Warhawk, separated by silence.

'Do you know, my brother, how many of my sons died at Alaxxes?' Russ growled eventually, forcing the words through clenched teeth.

When the reply came, the Khan's voice was as it ever had been – resonant, heavily accented, measured. 'We had to be sure,' he said.

'*Sure.*' Russ closed the gap between them, keeping his blade unsheathed. The Khan was almost a head taller, yet leaner, and carrying deep wounds. At the edges of the throne-dais, a hundred bolters remained trained on the White Scars' master, but neither primarch paid them any heed. 'And did you find that surety? Do you still name me the Butcher of Prospero?'

The Khan's gaze never wavered. 'I saw your work, and I travelled beyond it. Yes, I found surety, but if you are looking for blood-debt, then I have none to give you, for we have paid our own price.'

Russ came right up to him then, their faces now a hand's breadth apart. 'I often thought of what I would do, what I would say, were we to meet again,' he snarled. 'Many name you as a traitor in the Palace, Jaghatai, you know this? I could kill you here, where you stand, and few would mourn. That would be my blood-debt satisfied, and I could stand before the ghosts of the slain and tell them I avenged them.'

'I bring no weapon, brother,' the Khan said, coolly. 'Strike me if you wish, but know that I come through the fires of hell to bring my sons to Terra. No one, not you, not Horus, not even our Father, will prevent me from bringing them to where they were destined to be.'

There was the old arrogance again, bleeding so casually out of his brother's words. For a moment it merely stoked Russ' long-nurtured anger, goading him to finally swing the blade, to enact the retribution he had imagined many times before.

But then the absurdity of it pricked at him. A cold smile crept across his blunt, scarred lips. The smile broadened, and he began to chuckle, first a low, snagging growl, then a full laugh. Russ threw his head back, and roared his mirth.

'You always were a pompous bastard,' he said. 'You come to my halls as a beggar and speak as if you owned them. Who else would dare it?'

The laughter subsided. Finally, he sheathed his blade. All across the bridge, bolters were lowered.

'It would make me feel better to give you a fresh scar to remember me by,' Russ said. 'You might learn from it. But you look half dead already, and I have no wish to blunt my sword-edge on your scrawny neck.'

The Khan shot him a wintry smile. 'Save it for those who come at my heels.'

Russ' face became serious. 'It will not be long. Malcador will welcome your blades, if you can make your peace with him. There are never enough loyal legionaries for his liking.'

'You will come back with me, then.'

'No. Not yet.' Russ shook his head. 'It is best we remain apart, I think. I am still angry with you, brother, and may remember it again. In any case, I am caged here, and there are battles waiting in the void. Horus' forces are gathering for their final attack – there are reports of Traitor movement from across the segmentum, even as far as Yarant.'

The Khan nodded. 'Then I will wait for you at the Palace. I told you I wished to fight beside you again, just as we were meant to.'

'Be assured,' said Russ. 'The day will come.'

IN THE LOWER reaches of the *Lance of Heaven*, the Stormseers kept vigil.

Arvida's body lay in the centre of an etched circle, surrounded by braziers. The sorcerer had been placed on his back, still in full armour, for those who had borne him down from the bridge had been unable to remove it.

Incense curled up over his prone outline, dark in the gloom of the coals. Powder-trails had been thrown across the ceramite, earth-brown and russet-red, tracing out sacred shapes to ward against the dark.

In the final moments of the warp passage, with the Legion's crashing return into real space, the sorcerer had collapsed. As the last echoes of the empyrean still rang from the high vaults, the Stormseers moved to revive him, only to recoil when his body began to rebel. Fluids, black and lurid pink, had forced themselves between the gaps in his battleplate and run across the XV Legion sigils he still wore. His limbs had spasmed, and a throttled gurgle had spilled from his vox-grille.

Naranbaatar had overseen his removal then, and they had carried him swiftly down to the chambers of the

zadyin arga, where wards were drawn across his shuddering body and ancient words of yaksha-banishment
spoken over him.

Slowly, the bodily changes stilled. Arvida never
regained consciousness, though, and was tended
through the long hours by those he had guided
through the aether's depths.

When the Wolves came, a guard was placed on the
chambers, and by order of the Khagan, none of them
ever got close to the last son of Magnus. When the
packs left again for their ships, the vigil was resumed.
The chants persisted, over and over, through the nominal night and day, accompanied at all times by the
twist of smoke and the aroma of sacred oils.

Now, as preparations for the final stage to Terra
neared completion, Naranbaatar resumed the watch
again, relieving his brother zadyin arga, Oskh. The
two of them stood over the body, scanning for any
sign of change.

'We cannot halt it,' admitted Naranbaatar at last.

Oskh nodded. 'Then it will return soon?'

'It already has.' The Stormseer reached into a brass
bowl, pulled out blessed dust from the plains of Chogoris, and scattered it across Arvida's breastplate. The
ceramite curves were over-swollen, as if a mass of flesh
pressed up underneath them, striving to break free.

'How long did he suffer from this?' asked Oskh.

Naranbaatar smiled. 'If he had wanted to keep it
from us, perhaps he could have done so forever,' he
said. 'I only wonder that Yesugei did not see it.'

'But what is to be done? Can he be taken back to
Terra?'

'What else is there?'

'Yet... he is Fifteenth Legion. If it is found–'

Oskh was interrupted by a soft pulse from the door-lock, cycling through a ciphered entry-code. Both Stormseers turned swiftly, moving to interpose themselves between the body and the portal.

'Who comes?' demanded Naranbaatar.

The doors slid open, revealing a man, a mortal, in a close-fitting bodyglove and thick damask cloak. He was not of the Legion and had a dark-skinned, Terran face.

Naranbaatar opened his fist, and incipient flickers of psychic force rippled over the ceramite gauntlet. 'Declare yourself,' he warned.

The man lifted his arms slowly, showing he was unarmed.

'This is the one?' he asked. 'The Prosperine sorcerer?'

'I said, declare yourself.'

'Khalid Hassan,' said the man, peering past them at Arvida's body. 'Chosen of Malcador. I came out with the Wolves, for we had received auguries. Does he live?'

Naranbaatar kept the gauntlet raised. 'He is one of ours. If even the Sigillite wishes him harm–'

'Harm?' asked Hassan. '*Harm?* No, my lords, you misunderstand this. He is sick – we know it. You cannot cure it. My master can help, though, and he wishes very much to. I do not think you know just what you have here. Believe me, we would not permit you to let him die.'

'How did you get on the ship?' asked Oskh.

'That is my business. I would have done it openly, but you will appreciate the difficulties. If Lord Russ were to discover what you are keeping here...'

'He will never do so.'

'No, quite.' Hassan lowered his arms. 'Listen, you need do nothing now. There are more travelling with me, and they can help. It can all be done quietly, even if the Wolves circle you all the way to Terra. You will be taken to the Palace. The Sigillite will be waiting. He will speak to the Khan, all will be made clear then, but for now, just for now, do not obstruct this. Allow help to be given.' Hassan placed his hands together. 'There is no deception. We all wish for the same thing.'

Naranbaatar hesitated. The man before him was unshielded – his mind was open. Finally, he lowered his gauntlet.

'His sickness is advanced. You say you can help?'

'If you let us, but time is short.'

'But what interest is this to you?' interjected Oskh, his voice full of suspicion.

'Because we have been waiting for him,' said Hassan, looking past them at the unconscious Arvida, his expression close to reverence. 'And now, at last, he is here.'

THE SUZERAIN HAD come through with the others. Now back in real space, it hung at the rear of the V Legion formation, out of place among the scarred ivory hull-flanks, a last fragment of Eidolon's old battle-group.

With the warp-passage achieved and the encounter with the forces of Terra negotiated, Shiban had given over command of the ship to Yiman and withdrawn to the Palatine Blade's old chambers. Once the death-rituals of the brotherhood's slain had been completed, Jochi's armour was sent there too. His pauldron, bearing the mark of the minghan kasurga, had been placed under the soft light of taper candles, and Shiban contemplated it for many hours.

The losses had been heavy, stripping the heart out of his brotherhood. Few now remained who had fought with him on Chondax, fewer still with whom he could share any recollection of the past beyond that.

He let his head lower, feeling the pistons stretch in his nape. The Shackles had been badly damaged by the prefector towards the end, and there would be no opportunity to attend to the mechanisms for some time. Not while the needs of the battered fleet and surviving crew were so pressing.

That was no hardship, though. The pain was a pure one, and he found he was able to meditate through it now.

Perhaps I was always able to, he thought. *Perhaps I did not try hard enough.*

A chime sounded from the far side of the door.

'Come,' he said.

Ilya Ravallion entered, and Shiban greeted her, rising, with a bow.

'Szu,' he said. 'They did not tell me you had made transit.'

Ilya looked over at Jochi's artefacts. 'Kal damarg is complete?' she asked.

'For now.'

Ilya moved closer, taking a seat on a leather-cushioned bench opposite the armour fragments. She looked almost ghostly in the low light, translucent with age and care, and her weight made no impression on the upholstery.

'They kept their quarters more richly than us,' said

Shiban, rising and moving over to a mahogany stand, upon which crystal goblets and vials of wine had been placed.

Ilya gazed around at the dead prefector's finery, and her lips curled with distaste. 'They are the most hateful of all, do you not think?'

'I will not argue. But how have you fared? How is the new flagship?'

Ilya tried to give him a smile, but it was a weak attempt. 'Yesugei spoke to me, from the void station. Did you know that? I do not know why he did, but now I cannot forget it. He seemed to wish me to keep living. For myself, I cannot say that I much agree.'

'These are not words I am used to hearing from you.'

'No, no doubt, but I am weary to my bones, and my soul is sickening. Perhaps I shall recover. Maybe there is medicine on Terra for what ails us all.'

'Maybe.' Shiban reached out for a goblet, poured some wine, and offered it to her.

'Is it safe?' she asked, doubtfully.

'It will make your head foul,' Shiban said. 'Nothing worse.'

Ilya took it and drank deeply. Her hands shook. 'I shall miss him, Shiban,' she said, suddenly, her voice catching.

'I shall too.'

'He was fond of you. You know this?'

Shiban smiled. 'He was fond of everyone.'

But that was not true. Targutai Yesugei had been the one to take him from the plains, who had shepherded him through his Ascension, and who had proudly watched his rise through the ranks with those calm, golden eyes.

'You were right,' Shiban said. 'Is that any comfort? You were right about Torghun. They tell me he was on the *Swordstorm* at the end. They tell me you had something to do with that.'

'A habit I learned on Prospero.'

'It grieves me that he stood alone.'

Ilya shook her head. 'Do not grieve. I saw him before we were pulled out. He was already laughing.'

Shiban bowed his head. 'That is good to know.'

Ilya's trembling got worse then, and she drained the last of the wine. 'And what, then, for us now?' She put the goblet down and reached out for Shiban's hand, an instinctive motion, almost childlike, clasping her fingers over his gauntlet and gripping it. 'I *envy* them both,' she said. 'That is shameful, is it not? But it is true.'

Shiban reacted awkwardly, unsure how to respond to the sudden gesture of mortal need. Eventually, he brought his other hand across and placed it over hers, moving the armour as gently as he was able.

'We survived,' he said. 'There may yet be victory.'

'Can you see it?' she asked, looking up at him, a kind of desperation in her frail face. 'Tell me truly – can you see it?'

He could not lie to her. He could not lie to himself.

'After all this, we remain ourselves,' he said to her. 'Yesugei would have called that victory.'

Ilya smiled at last, though tears still clung to the edge of her eyes.

'Yes,' she said, keeping her hand locked in his. 'He would.'

THE STARS WERE strung out in a long swathe, the glittering band of the galaxy arcing across the high viewport.

From the vantage, high up in the *Lance of Heaven*'s observation tower, battered ships could be seen sliding silently across the wide vista. Some were V Legion outriders, all bearing the scars of their aether passage. Others were Space Wolves ships, in better condition, maintaining a discreet distance.

'Do you think they will suffer us to make the final stage unwatched?' asked the Khan, standing before the high window.

Jubal, standing next to the primarch, shrugged. 'I would say not. Did the Wolf King not tell you his intentions?'

'I did not ask. I was pleased enough to get off the ship without having to fight.'

Jubal chuckled. 'But he will go out to face the Warmaster, sooner or later.'

The Khan nodded. 'So it seems.'

'Such a waste. He could come back with us, bolster the defences.'

'Yes, but who can persuade the Lord of Fenris? His mind is made up.' The Khan sighed. 'It changes nothing for us. We will fulfil the oath.'

Jubal looked up at him. 'There has not been the time to ask you, Khagan. You were on that place – Dark Glass. What was it?'

The Khan thought on that. Maybe only Yesugei really understood, and yet the machinery Jaghatai had witnessed in the lower shafts had told him much. It had surely all been part of the same project, the one that had taken his Father away from the Crusade, and that in time would have made the entire panoply of empire – the Navigators, the Legions, the warp engines of the Mechanicum, even the primarchs themselves – obsolete. No wonder it had been kept secret, a secrecy that had contributed so much to the years of suspicion and mistrust.

There had been betrayal before Horus, that much was clear. Perhaps the fruits of that were only now becoming evident.

'It was a failure,' the Khan said. 'A dead end. We are left with what we see – our wars, our blades, our mutants. Our daemons.'

Jubal turned back to the starscape, a dry humour on his features. 'Nonetheless, a failure that opened the Path of Heaven.'

'Speak of it no longer,' said the Khan, tiring of the memory. 'It was a tomb to many who should have lived to see the Palace.'

He fixed his eyes on the void, on the glittering belt of stars ahead. Somewhere among them, perhaps even visible now, was the Throneworld, within reach again after so many years of toil.

'There will be trials ahead,' he said. 'We have not witnessed the greatest of them yet, and only postponed the reckoning with my brothers. But for now, for a short while, I will not think on that. We must heal, mend our wounds, be ready to take up the blade once more.'

Jaghatai let a smile crease across his hawkish profile.

'We kept the faith, Jubal,' he said. 'We fought, we overcame, and now, at last, we are going home.'

ABOUT THE AUTHOR

Chris Wraight is the author of the Horus
Heresy novels *Scars* and *The Path of Heaven*,
the Primarchs novel *Leman Russ: The Great
Wolf*, the novella *Brotherhood of the Storm*
and the audio drama *The Sigillite*. For
Warhammer 40,000 he has written *Vaults
of Terra: The Carrion Throne*, the Space
Wolves novels *Blood of Asaheim* and
Stormcaller, and the short story collection
Wolves of Fenris, as well as the Space
Marine Battles novels *Wrath of Iron* and
War of the Fang. Additionally, he has
many Warhammer novels to his name,
including the Time of Legends novel *Master
of Dragons*, which forms part of the War
of Vengeance series. Chris lives and works
near Bristol, in south-west England.